THE ROUGH RIDER

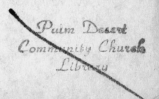

BOOKS BY GILBERT MORRIS

THE HOUSE OF WINSLOW SERIES

The Honorable Imposter
The Captive Bride
The Indentured Heart
The Gentle Rebel
The Saintly Buccaneer
The Holy Warrior
The Reluctant Bridegroom
The Last Confederate
The Dixie Widow
The Wounded Yankee
The Union Belle
The Final Adversary
The Crossed Sabres
The Valiant Gunman
The Gallant Outlaw
The Jeweled Spur
The Yukon Queen
The Rough Rider

The Iron Lady
The Silver Star
The Shadow Portrait
The White Hunter
The Flying Cavalier
The Glorious Prodigal
The Amazon Quest
The Golden Angel
The Heavenly Fugitive
The Fiery Ring
The Pilgrim Song
The Beloved Enemy
The Shining Badge
The Royal Handmaid
The Silent Harp
The Virtuous Woman
The Gypsy Moon
The Unlikely Allies

CHENEY DUVALL, M.D.[1]

1. *The Stars for a Light*
2. *Shadow of the Mountains*
3. *A City Not Forsaken*
4. *Toward the Sunrising*
5. *Secret Place of Thunder*
6. *In the Twilight, in the Evening*
7. *Island of the Innocent*
8. *Driven With the Wind*

CHENEY AND SHILOH: THE INHERITANCE[1]

1. *Where Two Seas Met*
2. *The Moon by Night*
3. *There Is a Season*

THE SPIRIT OF APPALACHIA[2]

1. *Over the Misty Mountains*
2. *Beyond the Quiet Hills*
3. *Among the King's Soldiers*
4. *Beneath the Mockingbird's Wings*
5. *Around the River's Bend*

LIONS OF JUDAH

1. *Heart of a Lion*
2. *No Woman So Fair*
3. *The Gate of Heaven*
4. *Till Shiloh Comes*
5. *By Way of the Wilderness*

[1]with Lynn Morris   [2]with Aaron McCarver

GILBERT MORRIS

the ROUGH RIDER

BETHANYHOUSE
Minneapolis, Minnesota

The Rough Rider
Copyright © 1994
Gilbert Morris
2005 edition

Cover illustration by Dan Thornberg
Cover design by Josh Madison

Published by Bethany House Publishers
11400 Hampshire Avenue South
Bloomington, Minnesota 55438

Bethany House Publishers is a division of
Baker Publishing Group, Grand Rapids, Michigan.

Printed in the United States of America

Library of Congress Cataloging-in-Publication Data

Morris, Gilbert.
    The rough rider / by Gilbert Morris. — 2005 ed.
        p.   cm. — (The House of Winslow)
    Summary: "Aaron Winslow, The Rough Rider, is determined to protect his
younger brother in the fight against the Spanish in Cuba"—Provided by
publisher.
    ISBN 0-7642-2962-1 (pbk.)
    1. Winslow family (Fictitious characters)—Fiction. 2. Spanish-American
War, 1898—Fiction. 3. Americans—Cuba—Fiction. 4. Brothers—Fiction.
5. Cuba—Fiction. I. Title. II. Series: Morris, Gilbert. House of Winslow.
    PS3563.O8742R68   2005
    813'.54—dc22

                                                                      2005020475

To my pastor—Artie Grimes,

Some pastors have wit. Others have wisdom. And some have a genuine love of their flock. A few have the gift of bringing the Scripture to life—and you encounter a few rare shepherds who have evangelism in their bones.

Artie Grimes is a man in whom all these qualities are combined—and I am grateful for his leadership and his friendship. And I must add that his companion, Cathy, has made him what he is today. I hope she's satisfied!

GILBERT MORRIS spent ten years as a pastor before becoming Professor of English at Ouachita Baptist University in Arkansas and earning a Ph.D. at the University of Arkansas. A prolific writer, he has had over 25 scholarly articles and 200 poems published in various periodicals, and over the past years has had more than 180 novels published. His family includes three grown children. He and his wife live in Gulf Shores, Alabama.

CONTENTS

PART THREE
SAN JUAN HILL

PART FOUR
A TIME TO EMBRACE

THE HOUSE OF WINSLOW

★ ★ ★ ★

THE HOUSE OF WINSLOW

★ ★ ★ ★

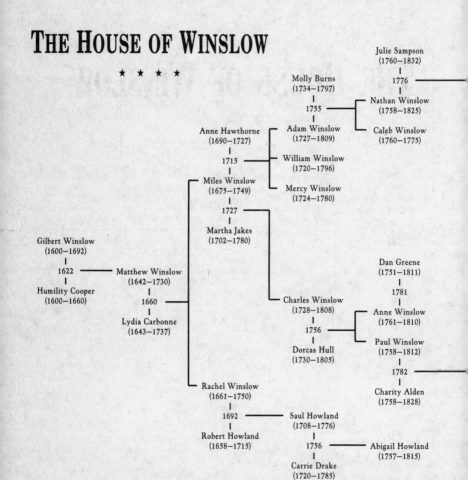

Julie Sampson
(1760—1832)
|
1776 ————
|
Nathan Winslow
(1758—1825)

Molly Burns
(1734—1797)
|
1755 ———— Caleb Winslow
| (1760—1775)
Adam Winslow
(1727—1809)

Anne Hawthorne
(1690—1727)
|
1715 ————
|
Miles Winslow
(1675—1749)

William Winslow
(1720—1796)

Mercy Winslow
(1724—1780)

|
1727
|
Martha Jakes
(1702—1780)

Gilbert Winslow
(1600—1692)
|
1622 ———— Matthew Winslow
| (1642—1730)
Humility Cooper |
(1600—1660)   1660 ————
|
Lydia Carbonne
(1643—1737)

Dan Greene
(1751—1811)
|
1781
|
Charles Winslow   Anne Winslow
(1728—1808)   (1761—1810)
|
1756 ————
| Paul Winslow
Dorcas Hull   (1758—1812)
(1730—1805) |
                     1782 ————
                     |
                     Charity Alden
                     (1758—1828)

Rachel Winslow
(1661—1750)
|
1692 ———— Saul Howland
| (1708—1776)
Robert Howland
(1658—1715)
|
1756 ———— Abigail Howland
| (1757—1815)
Carrie Drake
(1720—1785)

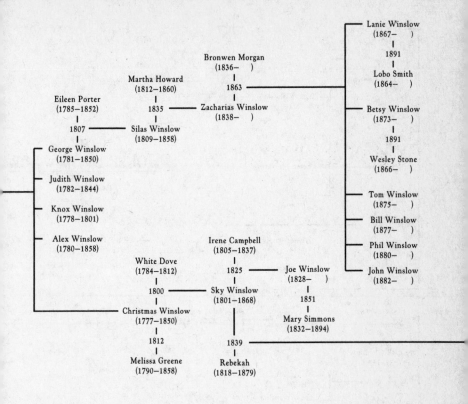

Lanie Winslow
(1867–   )

1891

Lobo Smith
(1864–   )

Bronwen Morgan
(1836–   )

1863

Betsy Winslow
(1873–   )

Martha Howard
(1812–1860)

Zacharias Winslow
(1838–   )

1891

Wesley Stone
(1866–   )

Eileen Porter
(1785–1852)

1835

Tom Winslow
(1875–   )

1807

Silas Winslow
(1809–1858)

Bill Winslow
(1877–   )

George Winslow
(1781–1850)

Phil Winslow
(1880–   )

Judith Winslow
(1782–1844)

Irene Campbell
(1805–1837)

John Winslow
(1882–   )

Knox Winslow
(1778–1801)

1825

Joe Winslow
(1828–   )

Alex Winslow
(1780–1858)

White Dove
(1784–1812)

Sky Winslow
(1801–1868)

1851

1800

Mary Simmons
(1832–1894)

Christmas Winslow
(1777–1850)

1839

1812

Rebekah
(1818–1879)

Melissa Greene
(1790–1858)

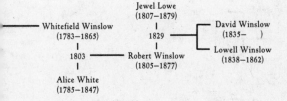

Jewel Lowe
(1807–1879)

David Winslow
(1835–   )

Whitefield Winslow
(1783–1865)

1829

Lowell Winslow
(1838–1862)

1803

Robert Winslow
(1805–1877)

Alice White
(1785–1847)

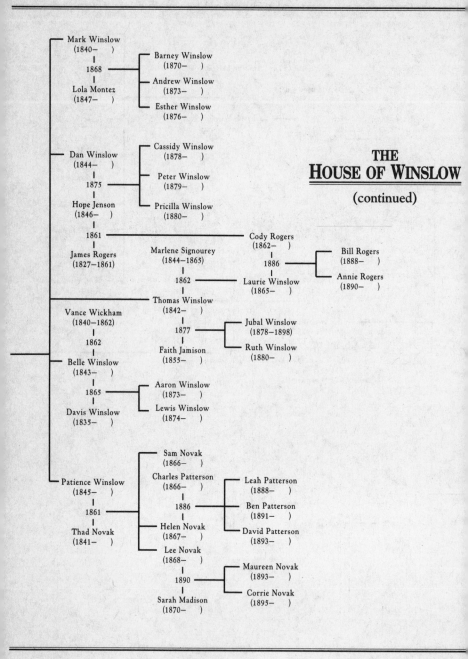

THE
HOUSE OF WINSLOW

(continued)

Mark Winslow
(1840–)
|
1868
|
Lola Montez
(1847–)

Barney Winslow
(1870–)

Andrew Winslow
(1873–)

Esther Winslow
(1876–)

Dan Winslow
(1844–)
|
1875
|
Hope Jenson
(1846–)

Cassidy Winslow
(1878–)

Peter Winslow
(1879–)

Pricilla Winslow
(1880–)

1861
|
James Rogers
(1827–1861)

Cody Rogers
(1862–)

Marlene Signourey
(1844–1865)
|
1862

1886
|
Laurie Winslow
(1865–)

Bill Rogers
(1888–)

Annie Rogers
(1890–)

Thomas Winslow
(1842–)
|
1877
|
Faith Jamison
(1855–)

Jubal Winslow
(1878–1898)

Ruth Winslow
(1880–)

Vance Wickham
(1840–1862)
|
1862
|
Belle Winslow
(1843–)
|
1865
|
Davis Winslow
(1835–)

Aaron Winslow
(1873–)

Lewis Winslow
(1874–)

Patience Winslow
(1845–)
|
1861
|
Thad Novak
(1841–)

Sam Novak
(1866–)

Charles Patterson
(1866–)
|
1886
|
Helen Novak
(1867–)

Leah Patterson
(1888–)

Ben Patterson
(1891–)

David Patterson
(1893–)

Lee Novak
(1868–)
|
1890
|
Sarah Madison
(1870–)

Maureen Novak
(1893–)

Corrie Novak
(1895–)

PART ONE

SHADOW OF WAR

★ ★ ★ ★

CHAPTER ONE

ANGEL WITH AN ACCENT

★ ★ ★ ★

As Dr. David Burns walked briskly down the hall of Baxter Hospital, he glanced casually out of a window—and halted abruptly to stare at the scene that was unfolding outside.

Two young boys had captured a rat—a large, black, evil creature. Somehow, they had managed to place a string around its neck. The one lad held the rat, while the other held the collar of a small terrier that was lunging and barking furiously at the crouching vermin. The noise soon drew a small crowd of raggedly dressed children who had gathered to watch the cruel spectacle. As the crowd grew in numbers, Burns thought sadly how tragic it was that children who should be in school or on farms found pleasure in the inhuman scene that was about to take place. "Poor tykes," he muttered to himself. "Not much future for them, I'm afraid."

He quickly turned from the window as a cry went up from the waifs, indicating that the battle was on. Moving down the hall, he stopped beside one aged patient struggling along the corridor on crutches. "Are ye all right, auntie?" he asked. His voice rang with a thick Scottish burr, and the old woman looked up at him quickly at the pleasant sound of it. She was frail and her hands trembled on the crutches, but she managed a smile.

"Yes, Dr. Burns. I'm fine today."

"That's guid," Burns smiled and patted her skeletal-like shoulder. "Be sure ye take the medicine, mind ye."

Burns stood there chatting amiably with the elderly woman for a few moments. Early in his practice, he'd discovered that a kind word from a doctor or nurse often did more good than some medicine.

The physician was not an impressive-looking young man. He stood no more than five feet nine inches tall, but there was a military straightness to his posture. He had a Highlander's look about him with bright blue eyes, brown hair, and a carefully trimmed mustache. His face was thin—not handsome at all—but there was a cheerful gleam in his steady eyes that was attractive enough. He moved quickly and precisely, with no loss of movement, as he continued his walk down the long hall. He had a purposefulness about him—most likely bred by his barren boyhood in Scotland. He was no stranger to hunger and poverty, much like that which many of the poor urchins who roamed the streets of New York City experienced. Poverty in a small Scottish village was not greatly different from that found in a tenement district. It left its scars on the soul as well as its marks on the body.

But Dr. David Burns had survived his difficult childhood and fought his way through the rigid educational system. It had been an arduous struggle, but after years of dedicated study, he finally achieved the status of M.D. Shortly after graduation, he said his goodbyes to his family and immigrated to America to build a new life. He counted himself fortunate to have been accepted on the staff at Baxter Hospital.

Turning down another corridor, Burns glanced up and saw the head nurse of the ward, Agnes Smith, engaged in some sort of argument with a young girl. Nurse Smith was a large woman of fifty, with iron gray hair tied in a bun, and a large, broad face. She was as tough as an army sergeant and ran her phalanx of nurses and cleaning women—and indeed even the doctors!—as if she were a general. It was not strange that behind her back she was often referred to as "General" Smith.

"I tell you that there's no way we can send a doctor to your house. Now, off with you, girl. I'm a busy woman!"

Dr. Burns was well aware that part of the peripheral duties of Nurse Smith was to ward off the incessant demands placed on the staff at Baxter. Every day a constant stream of men, women, and young people appeared at the door seeking medical help. And it was Smith's job to weed out those who could be helped and shuffle off those who could not. Burns did not envy the big woman her job, for he was a kindhearted individual who found it difficult to say no to anyone in need of medical help. He paused for one moment, intending to go on, and then halted, turning as he caught a glimpse of the young supplicant. Perhaps it was the plaintive quality of her voice that caught at him. In any case, he stopped long enough to take in the bedraggled figure.

"Please, ma'am—my ma, she's bad taken. I'm afraid she's gonna die!"

The speaker was young, no more than fifteen, Burns judged. She was a small girl, dressed in a tattered dark gray dress that had been soaked by the dismal, icy rain that had been falling intermittently throughout the day. Her shoes were large, cumbersome affairs of shabby black leather, laced up over the ankles— obviously not made to grace the feet of a genteel young lady. Glancing back up, he took in the light honey-colored hair that framed her oval face, visible under the shawl she wore. Despite her bedraggled appearance, he was surprised to note that the girl was very pretty. Her large dark blue eyes held a gaze of youthful innocence. Long lashes gathered together by the rain made them more pronounced. There was a beauty in the sweep of youthful cheeks and the curve of full lips. She looked like a delicate rose, he thought suddenly, growing in the midst of a forsaken garden of vile weeds. He had often seen pretty girls like this and knew to his regret the fate of most of them in the Fourth District of Manhattan in the year of 1896. Driven by despair and need, many of them ended up trapped in the brothels and dance halls that filled the rundown parts of the city.

"What's the trouble, Nurse Smith?"

Agnes Smith turned quickly, her lips drawn tight together. She was a homely woman, with almost a mannish look, which hid a heart that was not as adamant as many thought. "This girl says her mother's sick. I've told her that she'll have to get her to the hospital to be seen."

"Oh, ma'am, I can't do that!" the girl exclaimed. "She can't get out of bed." The voice was troubled, but clear and pleasant enough—though made desperate by the anxiety reflected in the dark blue eyes. She turned to Burns quickly, recognizing his authority. "Doctor, I'm afraid for my ma! Can't you come and help her?"

Burns was almost trembling with fatigue. Under normal circumstances, he was strong and active, but he had just put in three grueling days of sixteen-hour shifts. The staff was already stretched beyond its limits, and young Burns was a conscientious physician. From the very first day of his arrival at Baxter, Burns had given himself to trying to meet the never-ending stream of people needing help. It wasn't long before one of the older doctors had snorted at him, "You'll calm down once you've been in the business awhile. You can't get emotionally involved with all these people. Just take it easy and do the best you can."

A square three-story red-brick building, Baxter Hospital appeared to rise like a mushroom among the shabby tenements of Five Points. Its blank facade looked out on the streets milling with ill-clad immigrants whose faces were drained white by the incessant warfare against starvation, illness, and poverty. No ornament or decoration graced the front of the building. It sat there almost glumly, glowering over the ramshackle tenements that sprouted around it. Bringing cheer and jolly times was not the function of the institution, and now Burns wished heartily that a touch of grace had been given to the edifice in its bleak setting.

The eyes of the young physician took in the bedraggled young girl before him as he hesitated. He thought of his tidy room and longed to go get a quick meal, wash, and fall into bed for a night of long sleep. But something about the plaintive quality of the girl's voice and the slight tremble he noticed in her lips made him pause. Pushing his shoulders back, he cleared his throat, then glanced almost guiltily at Smith. "I suppose I could go and have a look."

Nurse Smith sniffed and shook her head vigorously. "You'd best go home and get some sleep. You can't go trotting around all over town. Besides, it's not safe, Dr. Burns."

"Oh, I expect the guid Lord will watch over us," Burns said with a smile. He reached out and gently patted the shoulder of the head nurse. He was fond of her and not afraid to show it. Smith, at first, had been taken aback by this unaccustomed show of warmth, but she had soon come to enjoy it. She took a proprietary attitude toward the young Scottish physician and the tightness of her lips relaxed. "You're going to kill yourself," she complained. "Well, go on, then—but be sure to eat a good meal and come in late tomorrow."

"I may do that, nurse." Burns turned to the girl and said, "Let me get my coat and we'll go have a look."

"Oh, thank you, Doctor," said the young girl, her large eyes wide with appreciation.

Burns moved to the room set apart for the few conveniences provided for the doctors, sat down, and made his final notes for the day. When he finished, he rose and put on the heavy brown overcoat and a rounded bowler, which he set squarely on his head. Stepping back into the hall, Burns closed the door behind him, then turned and said, "Now, what's your name, girl?"

"Gail—Gail Summers."

"Well, Gail Summers, let's be on our way. How far do ye live from here?"

"On Water Street. It ain't too far," the girl said quickly, as if in apology. She wore a thin black coat that she pulled together, as it had long since lost its buttons somewhere.

"We'd better take a cab since it's raining." As they stepped outside, Burns noticed the girl was trembling with cold. A harsh February wind whistled and howled through the streets. Glancing down the street, he saw a cab, then lifted his fingers and uttered a piercing whistle.

The girl was startled at the shrill sound and turned to stare at him with alarm. "It's all right," Burns smiled. "I didn't mean to frighten you." When the carriage pulled up, Burns opened the door and nodded to her. "In ye go." He reached out and took the girl's arm, helping her get inside, noticing that she was almost as tall as he. When he sat down across from her, he asked, "What's the address?"

"I don't know the number, but it's right down the street from the mission across from Sixth Avenue."

"Go to Sixth Avenue on Water Street," Burns called out. The coach lurched forward as the horses moved against their harness.

"How long has your mother been sick?" Burns asked. He sat there listening as the young girl spoke of her mother's illness. Her face was drawn with fatigue, Burns noticed, and underneath her eyes were faint shadows—the marks of one who had worked too long and too hard for her age. She had a gauntness about her, too. She was older, he decided, than he had thought at first, somewhere between that age where girlhood ends and the age where womanhood begins. Looking down, he saw her hands held open on her lap. They were reddened with the cold, but when he saw the palms, he leaned forward.

"What's wrong with your hands?"

"Oh—nothing, sir!"

"Let me see." In puzzlement, Burns reached forward, picked up one of the girl's hands, and though she resisted, he gently spread it open. The hand was firm and strong, but the palm was red and swollen, laced with fine lines that seemed to be infected. "What have ye done to yer hands, girl?" he asked in concern.

"Nothing, Doctor. It's just—" Gail Summers was not accustomed to speaking with fine gentlemen, and the fact that he was holding her hand made it even more difficult for her to talk. She looked shyly into his warm bright blue eyes, swallowed hard, then whispered, "It's just from the work."

"The work? What work is that?" he asked, his voice thick with his native burr.

"I work at the rope factory. It's handling the fiber that does it. I don't mind it no more," she said.

Burns knew that the city of New York ran partially, at least, on child labor. Youngsters of no more than six or seven had been discovered working long hours in many of the city's factories. And now as he looked at the reddened palm of the girl in front of him, an intense anger rose in him. He had a temper, this young Scotsman, that he normally kept under firm control. But when he saw wanton abuse like this, he became deeply troubled. He shook his head, touching the scars, and said, "Ye should wear gloves, lass. I'll see that ye get some ointment to put on them. That will help them heal."

"Thank you, Doctor." Gail sat back against the seat, clasping her hands together to keep the palms hidden. She had never ridden in a carriage before, and the very act of coming to the hospital seeking help for her mother had been a test of her courage. She had watched her mother get sicker with each passing day. The women of the neighborhood had offered to help, but none of their remedies had been effective. Finally, in desperation, Gail had informed her mother, "I'm going to get you a doctor, Ma." Now as she rode along through the streets, she felt both elated and frightened. Clearing her throat, she said, "Doctor. . . ?"

"Yes. What is it, Gail?"

"I . . . I ain't got no money to pay you with."

Burns smiled at the girl. "I didn't expect ye had," he said. "We won't worry about that." He saw the tenseness of the girl's body relax somewhat, and smiled. "Tell me a little about yourself. Do ye have a large family?" As the carriage moved along, he discovered that the girl had one brother named Jeb, apparently named after a Civil War general. She also had two stepbrothers and one stepsister. Burns was very quick-witted, and as the girl spoke haltingly with bad grammar, he understood that she loved her mother and brother more than anything else. He also discovered from the manner in which she spoke of her stepfather, Harry Lawson, that the girl was deathly afraid of him.

As the carriage turned and made its way through the fast-falling darkness, Burns glanced out at Water Street. This infamous avenue traced its way along the East River on the southern bank of Manhattan Island, and was perhaps the most notorious of any part of the great city.

Burns, who practically possessed a photographic memory, recalled a recent article he'd read concerning the vice and crime plaguing New York. An entire paragraph now leaped into the young physician's mind as the carriage rattled over the roughness of the streets. "If you put all the grog shops, all the houses of ill-fame, and all the billiard saloons into one continuous street, it would reach from City Hall to White Plains, a town twenty miles north, in Westchester County. Every night there would be a murder every half a mile, a robbery every one hundred sixty-five yards, six outcasts at every door, and at frequent intervals men dividing loot, eight preachers trying to convert the criminals, and thirty newspapermen to report on it all."

"That's it—that's our place," Gail blurted out suddenly.

"Here we are, driver," Burns called out. When the carriage pulled up to the curb, he stepped out, followed by the girl. He paid the cab driver, then turned, saying, "Now, let's see aboot your mother."

The sidewalks, even at this hour, were busy with men and women talking, shouting; and a vile, rank odor hung in the air. A few street vendors moved toward them selling bandannas, tin cups, peaches, and damaged eggs. The garbage-strewn street was full of noisy children who had gathered to watch, squeezing through the crowded streets like slippery eels. For some, as Burns well knew, the street was their only home—the gang that thrived on petty thievery and pick-pocketing.

"This way, Doctor."

Burns followed the girl inside a narrow doorway and up three rickety flights of wooden stairs that vibrated under his feet. His nose wrinkled at the pungent smells of cooked cabbage, sweat, dirty clothes, and sewage as they made their way upward. There was little light, and the darkness was falling quickly outside. When they reached the third flight, the girl led him down the narrow hallway. Stopping at a door, she opened it and turned to him, her face gleaming palely in the murky light admitted by the single window at the end of the hall. "Come in, please."

Burns entered and suddenly felt rather crowded by the smallness of the place. The room evidently served as kitchen, dining room, and living room for the entire family. There was a large iron stove off to the side, serving both for heat and cooking. On the other side of the room, Burns saw four young people staring at him.

"This is my brother, Jeb," Gail said quickly. Jeb was a small, thin boy of ten, with the same light hair and blue eyes as his sister. He was sitting on the floor reading a tattered book, but when he looked up and saw the doctor, he scrambled to his feet.

"Are you going to make my ma well?" he whispered.

"I'm going to try, son," Burns said in a kindly fashion. The other young people he saw were of a different heritage, having black hair and black eyes. *Must be the stepbrothers and stepsister*, he thought. But he had no time to consider them, for a large, hulking man had emerged through the door leading from the living area.

"Wot's this?" he rumbled. His black hair hung down in his face, and he had a pair of oddly colored eyes, hazel as it were. His manner and large size made him look threatening, but Burns was not a man easily intimidated.

"This is Mr. Lawson?" he asked. "I'm Dr. Burns. Your daughter here tells me your wife is very ill."

"I ain't sent for no doctor." Harry Lawson stood there, a hulking man, blunt featured and loose-lipped. He was weaving from side to side, obviously half-drunk. "Ain't no money for doctors. Be on your way!"

Burns sensed the tension in the girl, who had gone to stand beside her brother. He faced the big man firmly, saying, "No charge. Let's see what we can do for her."

Harry Lawson stood glowering at him, and Burns could tell the man was about to order him out of the house. But when Gail whispered, "It won't cost anything. Let him see her, please," he hesitated, then shrugged.

"You won't get no money for this," he snapped, then lurched across the room, leaving and slamming the door behind him.

Burns at once moved into the sickroom, where he found a thin woman lying in bed covered by tattered quilts. She stared up at him with feverish eyes, set in a pale and gaunt face. He saw the resemblance to the daughter at once. "I'm Dr. Burns," he said.

Gail slipped by the doctor and leaned over the frail figure, saying, "Ma, I brought the doctor."

Martha Summers Lawson turned a pair of faded blue eyes on the doctor, and when she spoke, her voice was barely a whisper. "You shouldn't have done that. We can't pay."

"Now don't ye be worrying about that," Burns said cheerfully. He came over to the bed and sat down in the chair next to it and began to examine the woman. He saw at once that she was very ill indeed. He also saw that Martha Summers, though now thin and frail from her illness, had once been a very attractive woman. But hard work and the cruel poverty that left none untouched in Five Points had managed to drain most of that former beauty from her. Her hair was still the same honey blond as that of her daughter, and there were traces of beauty in the defined bones of her gaunt face. Burns worked quickly, then straightened up and said, "Well, ye're going to be all right, Mrs. Lawson. Ye'll just need some guid nursing."

The woman reached out and took Gail's hand, smiling faintly.

"Gail is better than any nurse you've got in your hospital, Dr. Burns," she said quietly.

"I'll wager she is that." Burns nodded and then said, "Ye'll be needing some medicine." Sensing the tension his words brought, he said at once, "I'll take care of that. No charge. Would ye be able to go get it with me, Gail?"

"Oh yes, Doctor," she said, her large blue eyes elated at the doctor's word.

"Fine." Burns gave a few more instructions to the sick woman, then closed his bag and left the room.

Gail turned back to the bed and said, "I'll be right back, Ma. I'm going with the doctor to get some medicine."

"Can I go with you, Gail?" the younger boy asked at once.

"Can Jeb come with us?" Gail asked the doctor when she stepped back into the other room.

"Of course. Bring him along. But it's cold and damp outside."

"I've got me a good coat," Jeb said. He rose and put on a coat that was designed for a full-size man. His hands were swallowed by the long sleeves, and the coat itself hung down below his knees. Gail went over and buttoned it, then pulled a black cap over his head.

As they made their way down the stairs, Jeb tripped over the long coat. He would have gone sprawling down, but the doctor was quick to reach out and grab him. Burns was touched by the warm grin of thanks the boy beamed back at him.

When the three finally reached the street again, Burns asked, "Would there be a place to buy medicine close by, Gail?"

"Yes, sir. Down on Seventh Street. I'll show you."

The wind whistled down the street, numbing Burns's face. He noticed that the other two seemed inured to the biting cold. A taste of snow hung in the air, and the dull smoke rising from the tenements almost shut out the sky completely. They passed several saloons along the way, and the rank odor of alcohol and cigarette smoke wafted out of the dark interiors. The men's voices that carried through the constantly swinging doors were loud and raucous, and more than once, the physician felt the eyes of hulking men fall upon him. But he gave no sign that he was aware of the dangers that lurked all along Water Street.

"Here it is, sir." Gail opened the door, and Burns and the boy entered.

When a man wearing a short white jacket approached, Burns said briskly, "I'm Dr. Burns from Baxter. I need a bit of medicine." He gave his order to the man, and when it was filled, Burns reached inside his coat and pulled out his money and paid for it. Turning, he handed the small package to Gail and carefully explained when to give the medicine, then said, "Be sure and take good care of your mother."

"Yes, I *will*, Dr. Burns—and thank you!"

Burns put his hand on the boy's head and said, "And you take care of your sister, Jeb. All right?"

"Sure," Jeb said sturdily.

Burns stepped outside and watched as the young people made their way quickly back down the street. "Let me hear how she is doing in a few days," he called out.

Gail's voice came to him over the whistling wind. "Yes, sir. I will."

*   *   *   *

Chief Nurse Agnes Smith stared across the small table at the young physician, slipping her shoes off her aching feet. The small room was filled with the aromatic smell of tea. David Burns had formed a habit of taking a break with the chief nurse just before leaving in the afternoon. Now, Smith wiggled her toes and sighed. "It's been a busy day. If I had to see one more patient, I think I'd scream."

"You're a guid nurse, Agnes," Burns said. "I never saw better."

The face of the nurse flushed with pleasure. Unaccustomed to compliments, she took a quick swallow of tea to hide her embarrassment. She glanced across at the young doctor, searching for the telltale signs of fatigue. His constant encouragement and kind words had endeared him to her. In fact, he'd become almost like a son to her. Looking over the cup of tea she held, she muttered, "Well, I don't think much of doctors as a breed—but I'll have to say that you've come a long way since you came to Baxter."

Burns smiled at her words and leaned back, enjoying the small respite at the end of a tiring day. The two sat talking quietly, and finally Agnes shook her head dolefully. "Mattie quit this afternoon. Left me without anybody to do the cleaning."

"There's plenty looking for work," Burns said. "She wasn't too guid, anyway."

"No, she wasn't. We've got to find somebody more dependable."

Burns nodded in agreement, then took the last swallow of tea. Rising to his feet, he rubbed the back of his neck and said, "I'll see ye in the morning, Agnes. I need some rest." He left the room and, pulling on his coat, made his way to the front entrance. He was settling his bowler firmly when he heard a voice calling his name.

"Dr. Burns. . . ?"

Turning, Burns was taken off guard at the sight of Gail Summers and her brother, Jeb. He had wondered about the sick woman since his visit, and had thought once or twice about going back, but the constant demands at the hospital had made that all but impossible.

"Well, now, this is fine," he said, going over to them with a smile. He put his hand on Jeb's shoulder and looked down at the young boy. "And how is it with yer guid mother?" he asked in a kindly fashion.

"She's doing good, Doctor," Jeb said stoutly. He looked up with a smile on his thin lips. "That sure was good medicine you gave her."

"She's much better now, Dr. Burns," Gail broke in. There was a breathless quality about her, and her eyes seemed brighter than when she first appeared at the hospital door. She struggled with the words and then stuck out her hand, which held a small package in it. "I've brought you this."

"For me? Why, you shouldn't have done that!" Burns tore off the brown wrapping paper and found a fine white linen handkerchief folded neatly inside. He was touched by the gift, surmising that the girl had sacrificed to get it for him. He had learned, however, to never refuse a gift. He looked at her now with a broad smile and said, "Why, this is just what I needed! How did you know that?" He fingered the handkerchief and said, "Fine quality, too. Thank you so much."

The girl's face lit up with pleasure at his ready acceptance of the small gift. "I hope you like it," she said shyly.

"Well, I certainly do!" Pulling the handkerchief out, he held it up and looked at it, then he glanced at the pair and said, "Where are you going? You didn't make this trip just to bring this package to me, did you?"

"No, we're on our way to the mission."

"The mission?"

"Yes. The Water Street Mission. We go there every time we can."

"Why don't you come with us, Dr. Burns?" said Jeb. "You'd like Awful."

The boy's words caused Burns to blink. "I'd like awful what?" he asked.

Jeb laughed at the doctor's question. "You'd like Awful Gardner. That's the minister's name, except he ain't really a preacher."

Gail added eagerly, "Awful Gardner runs the mission. That's not really his name, but that's what everybody calls him. He was such a bad man and grew up with the name. He went to Sing Sing . . . the prison, you know."

"Did he really? And now he's running a mission?" Burns was a devout Christian himself and had read about the mission work going on in the Water Street area. He thought for a moment, then said, "I think I read something in the paper about that mission." He hesitated, then looked down at the two pale faces waiting for his answer. Suddenly, an idea came to him. "Tell ye what, I might go with ye myself. I haven't heard any good preaching in quite a while."

"Oh, that would be wonderful!" Gail beamed.

"Come along. We'll have to get a bite to eat first. I haven't had anything since lunch." He did not miss the light that came into the boy's face and the girl's embarrassment at his invitation.

He led them out the door and down the steps to the street. After a few minutes, they reached a restaurant not too far from the hospital. It was a favorite spot, where the doctor often stopped after his long days at the hospital. He found the food well prepared, but he also enjoyed the warmth of the place. They found a table, and when the waiter came, Burns said, "Well, now, we might as well eat hearty. I always like to have a full stomach when I hear a guid sermon. What if I order for all of us?"

"Oh yes," Gail whispered quickly. The two young people sat

there until the meal was brought—hot soup, mutton, and potatoes. David Burns did not miss how they wolfed it down. Memories of similar looks from a village high in the mountains of Scotland flashed in his mind. *Half starved,* he thought to himself. *Too bad!—Too bad!*

Just when Gail and Jeb had finished their portions of mutton, the waiter reappeared carrying plates with generous slices of apple pie that Burns had ordered. He couldn't help smiling at the look of surprise that filled their eyes.

Finally, the meal finished, they left and walked along the street until they turned down Water Street. Before long, they came to a simple frame building with white boards in the front, and Gail said, "This is it. Come on. . . ."

Jeb took the doctor's hand and said, "I'll get us a seat down front."

As they stepped inside, Burns's eyes swept the interior of the simple room. It was large and rectangular with rough benches, and at the front stood a small, single table with a pitcher of water on it. A tall, middle-aged man with black hair and a thin face approached them at once. "Well, now, you've brought a visitor, have you, Gail and Jeb?"

"Yes, sir. This is Dr. Burns," Gail said quickly. "He's the one that made my ma well."

"No, I didna do it. The guid Lord made your mother well." Burns smiled and took the outstretched hand of Awful Gardner and instantly liked what he saw. Gardner was a thin-faced individual with a rich Irish accent and an honest, able look about him. "I've come down to hear the Gospel. I've been to several churches in the city, but they're a little thin on substance."

Gardner grinned broadly. "Well, sir, you'll hear nothing here but the blood of Jesus for sinners! That's all we are, sir, just lost sinners. The service is about ready to start. Won't you take a seat?"

Jeb grabbed Burns's arm and half dragged him to the front of the room. As Burns sat with the two young people, he looked around, noting that the entire congregation was altogether of the rougher sort. Men and a few women, all of them shabbily dressed, filled the benches.

Awful took his place at the front and welcomed those who had gathered, then went right into the service. It was a spirited meeting, at least from Awful Gardner's standpoint. He stood up and began to sing, and Burns was able to join in. Some of the songs were the same ones Burns had learned as a boy in his native Scotland. The service was going smoothly enough until a huge man with a red shirt on the bench across from Burns began to shout. They'd just started singing "Rock of Ages," when the man, obviously drunk, began to sing the words of an obscene saloon song.

At once, Awful Gardner put down his hymnbook, walked over to the man, and said firmly, "You must leave or I'll put you out, Jackson."

"What's the matter with you?" Jackson shouted. "Get out of here or I'll smash your face."

Awful Gardner reached out and caught Jackson by the collar. The drunk reached back and locked his hands around the back of the bench. "Go ahead, old feller," he grinned.

Gardner got a tighter grip on Jackson's shirt and surged backward. By this time, everyone else had jumped off the bench. Jackson was lifted to his feet and the bench with him. The congregation continued to sing "Rock of Ages," but all eyes were on the fight. Gardner dragged Jackson and the bench into the aisle. The bench hit the ceiling and Jackson's grip was broken. The drunk tried to put up a fight, but Awful Gardner grabbed him around the neck and hauled him down the aisle. Wildly, the man grabbed at whatever he could—benches, even heads of those foolish enough to stay in the way. There was a final lunge near the door. They both slammed into it, and as it swung open, Gardner gave the man a hard push out into the street, then slammed the door. His face was somewhat flushed, but despite the interruption he seemed unperturbed. Walking back up the aisle, he picked up his hymnbook and joined the others, singing, "Rock of Ages, cleft for me, let me hide myself in thee."

After the song service Gardner gave a simple but clear sermon. When it was over Burns came forward to shake his hand. "That was a guid sermon, sir. I'll be looking forward to hearing more of the same. Sorry you had a bit of trouble there with that fellow drinking."

"Don't mind the poor fellow, Doctor. He's been taking a little too much, but the Lord Jesus will win out."

"I'd like to hear a wee bit more about yer work here. Maybe I can help in some way."

"Would you, now! Well, that'd be right fine," Gardner said enthusiastically. "Come along. You can meet some of my helpers. Here, Miss Simms, you just take charge of these two young ones while I show the doctor around. . . ."

It was an interesting half hour for Burns. He had done mission work in Scotland and felt a warm surge of approval for Awful Gardner, who had chosen to hold up the banner of the cross in the worst part of New York City.

Gardner finally began to talk about the people. "They're the roughs of the city, but I was one of them. Just a drunk I was, chiefest of sinners! I even did time in Sing Sing."

Burns listened attentively, then said, "I feel sorry for the children of the area. You have to get their parents saved before they can have a decent chance at life."

"That's right," Gardner nodded, then he grew solemn. "That young girl and her brother—the Summers children—they've got a hard way to go." Awful Gardner shook his head sadly. "Did Gail tell you about losing her job?"

"Why, no. She didn't say a word."

"Ah, that's the way of it. She keeps her troubles to herself." Gardner shook his head regretfully. "She's worried about it, though. That brute of a stepfather of hers, Harry Lawson, he'll beat her. He's done it before."

Burns became profoundly disturbed at Gardner's words about Harry Lawson. He ran his hand into his pocket, took two or three quick steps toward the window, stared out into the darkness, then turned back. "Is there nothing to be done? She's a fine girl."

"Well, I'll ask about. There's not much work in the winter though. Even some of the factories have closed down." He shook his head dolefully. "If she doesn't find work, I don't know what'll become of them. Her father drinks up all that he makes, and the meager earnings Gail brings home puts food on the table."

"What about the other children? Don't they help?"

"Wild as bucks. All three of them. Too much like their father, I'm afraid," Awful growled. "I never have said it, but Mrs. Lawson and her two youngsters would be better off by themselves."

Burns suddenly snapped his fingers. "Wait a minute! I know

of a job that might do. Not much, but—"

Eagerly, Awful said, "It don't have to be much. What is it, Doctor?"

"Well, someone just left the hospital, and we do need a girl to help out."

Gardner listened carefully as the doctor explained about the need for someone to help out with the cleaning. "It's just the thing for her!" Gardner exclaimed. "That way, you can kind of keep an eye out for her. I don't like the children—especially the young girls—to have to roam these streets. Do you think she can have the job?"

"I think I can talk the head nurse into it. Let's ask Gail if she wants it."

At once, Awful called out, "Gail, come over here, please." And when the girl came, he said, "You know, we've been praying about a job," Awful said. "And—well, I think we might just have an angel here to answer those prayers."

"An angel?"

Gail looked doubtfully at the doctor, and Awful grinned broadly at the girl's confusion. "Well, sort of an angel. I've never heard an angel with a Scottish accent, but it may be that God sent the good doctor our way. Tell her what you just told me, Doctor."

"It's just that I heard the head nurse say that they're going to have to hire someone to do cleaning at the hospital. It doesn't pay much, but if you want it, I think I can get the job for you."

Gail's face lighted up. She reached out as if to touch Dr. Burns, then drew her hand back quickly. "Oh, Doctor, that would be so good!"

"Well, that'll be the way of it, then. I'll hurry back to the hospital and tell Nurse Smith that I've found her a new helper. It's hard work," he warned. "And not a lot of money."

The girl looked at him with glowing eyes. Her face was thinned down by poverty and hardship—yet somehow there was an almost ethereal beauty in her at that moment that Dr. Burns found intriguing.

"I ain't never gonna be able to thank you enough, Doctor!" she whispered. Then tears filled her eyes, and she quickly turned and walked away. When she found Jeb, she put her arm around him. "An angel has found me a job, Jeb," she murmured. She whispered some of the details and looked over to where the doctor was talking with Awful Gardner. "He's an angel with an accent." Her eyes were almost worshipful as she watched Dr. Burns. "Ain't he wonderful!"

"He don't look like no angel to me. He don't have no circle around his head, and he ain't got no white robe on. He just don't look like an angel's supposed to look." Nevertheless, when he saw the look on his sister's face, he smiled and said, "But I guess he's okay. In a pinch, I guess any kind of angel will do. . . !"

CHAPTER TWO

AN OPEN DOOR

★　★　★　★

The winter of 1897 had been particularly hard on the tenement dwellers of Lower Manhattan. Snow had fallen out of the sky as if dumped from celestial wheelbarrows, clogging the streets. The omnipresent clothes of tenement dwellers that hung out over the balconies and on the rooftops were frozen stiff, and the shrill, keening winds whistled down the canyons of poverty, turning lips blue and freezing hands into raw, red knuckles. The poor had done what they always did during inclement weather—survive as best they could—while the rich ordered servants to throw more wood in the fireplace, or simply chose to travel to exotic places that offered a warmer climate. Those of Five Points had no such options.

This year, to everyone's surprise, an early spring had loosened winter's icy grip on the city. And it was on one of those warmer days that Awful Gardner was walking along the roof of the rescue mission. Standing near the edge, he took a deep breath and looked out over the city with satisfaction. "Faith, it's good to feel the warm winds again! Maybe my old bones can thaw out a little now."

A cool March wind blew slightly, but as Gardner walked along, examining the city that stretched out beyond him, he had a feeling that better things were coming.

He had come often to the roof of the mission to do his thinking and praying. This particular morning he carried a small cage built of sticks, which he now set down gently on the roof. The occupants of the cage—two sparrows that he had found freezing in the snow and had nursed back to health—began chirping in the warm spring sunshine. At the sound of their chirping, Awful smiled and stopped to whistle to them. They'd come to recognize him, or so he thought. When he opened the door, one bird hopped out onto his hand, peering upward with a bright, beady eye until Gardner produced a large mealworm that he had in his other hand. The small bird took it eagerly, ate it, and then emitted a long series of cheerful-sounding chirps. Gardner held his hand high, and the bird looked around, as if confused at this offer of freedom. Giving a slight cry, the sparrow spread his wings, which beat furiously, then rose into the air, circled around, but finally returned to where Awful stood. As the bird moved back toward the cage and hopped inside, Gardner muttered with astonishment, "Just like too many folks I know—can't wait to get back into their prison." He laughed, left the door open, and freed the other bird. Awful stood there smiling as he watched the sparrow wing high above the city.

"Now that's the way," he nodded with satisfaction, watching the small bird disappear into the falling darkness. "Find your own way. God never intended for birds to be caged." He gave one look at the first bird, then laughed and said, "You'll have to go, old boy—now find your way." Reaching inside, he grasped the bird, pulled it free of the cage, and tossed it high into the air. For a time it circled, peeping in a piteous tone, then rose and disappeared around the corner of a neighboring building.

Gardner went back to the narrow stairwell and descended past the top floor that contained his small quarters and those of some of the workers, and then down to the second that had been converted into a large area filled with cots for vagrants and derelicts. Half of this space was devoted to a kitchen and dining room where meals could be prepared and dispensed to those in dire need.

As he descended to the first floor of the mission, he heard the tinkling of the tinny piano that had been donated by a saloon. Pausing at the foot of the stairs, Awful cocked his head and listened to the pleasant music. The strains of "Rock of Ages" came to him, and a smile turned the corners of his lips upward. "The boy's doing so well," he muttered to himself. "It's a shame he can't have proper lessons." He listened while the next song floated through the air. "There is a fountain filled with blood. . . ." he sang along softly. When the music finally ceased, Awful turned and headed into the main part of the building, where he spotted Jeb Summers sitting on a stool at the old, beaten piano. Standing over him was Tony Gibbons, listening and beating time against his thigh with one hand.

"Now that's fine, young man," Tony said, nodding approvingly. He was a short, pale-faced man with the red-veined face of a chronic drinker. Despite his obvious poverty, there was an air of dignity about him, and he attempted to keep some semblance of respectability in his worn clothes. His suit had been made for a larger man and hung loosely upon his thin frame. His tie, though worn and frayed, was neatly knotted and hung over a white shirt that was missing most of the buttons. His shoes had seen their day of wear, but they were polished, and his hair was neatly combed. Tony had been one of those derelicts who had been hauled bodily into the mission—dead drunk and in desperate need. He had stayed at the mission for a week, been soundly converted, and now had reached the point where he could work some. He was a quiet man, and when he had discovered that Jeb Summers longed to play the piano, he surprised everyone with his knowledge of music. He had proven to be a good teacher for the boy.

Leaning over the boy now, Tony said quietly, "Your fingering was good on that one, Jeb. But let me show you what to do with your left hand." Jeb hopped off the stool as Tony sat down to demonstrate. The man's stubby fingers flew over the ivory keys. The piano was tinny and chronically out of tune—yet Tony's power and skill coaxed an amazing sound from the ancient instrument.

Jeb Summers was small for his eleven years, yet there was an eagerness in his eyes as he looked up at the small man. "Gosh, Tony, I don't think I'll ever learn to play like that!"

" 'Course you will, Jeb," Tony encouraged him. He smiled at the boy, and memories seemed to come back to him. *Must've been a million years ago when I was his age*, he thought, watching the boy's eager face. *I wish I could go back and get some of the years that I threw away. Oh, well, it's too late for that. But if I can help this one, maybe it'll make up for a little of what I've done to myself.* He allowed none of the regret to show in his face, but smiled at the lad. "Now—I found this for you." He reached over to the table and picked up a book. "About time you learned a little bit more about reading music," he said. "This playing by ear is well enough, but a good musician's got to be able to read the notes."

Jeb took the music book, looked at it, and with one finger began to call out the various notes. Tony chuckled and said with a smile, "Why, there, you see—you're well on your way! Now—you try to find these on the piano. See—this is E."

Gardner stood watching the pair fondly. After a few minutes, he moved across the room and said, "Well, we may have a whole orchestra on our hands the first thing you know."

"Gee, Mr. Gardner, Tony's teaching me everything!" Jeb was so excited that his pale face seemed to glow. He ran through a few notes for Gardner and said, "Look—that's what it says right there on that page!"

"That's fine, Jeb! You do what Tony says and you'll be playing at a fancy concert hall before you know it." Then he added, "It's getting pretty late for you, isn't it, Jeb?"

Jeb looked up and a startled look suddenly crossed his thin face. "Oh no!" he said, "it's dark already. Pa'll thrash me for sure!" He scrambled off the stool, grabbed the book, and ran for the door. He disappeared, slamming the door as he always did.

"Does the boy have any talent, Tony?" Gardner asked.

Gibbons sighed deeply, sat at the piano, and ran his fingers over the worn keys, then shook his head. "It's like finding a fresh, bright flower in a garbage dump, Awful. If he had any chance at all, he could become a fine musician. But he tells me that his stepfather is against anything to do with music. All he wants is for Jeb to work, so he can drink up what the boy brings home."

"Well, we'll just have to see if we can get that stepfather of his converted, then. He's a rough one, Harry Lawson is. The last time I tried to talk to him, he got angry and threatened to punch my lights out if I ever mentioned God to him again." His eyes moved to the door and he said, "I'm afraid young Jeb there won't get much of a greeting from Harry Lawson." Gardner shook his head at the thought of what awaited the young boy at home.

★ ★ ★ ★

Jeb ran down the streets dodging traffic. More than once a curse was hurled at him as he narrowly avoided collisions with the men who moved in and out of the saloons and billiard halls lining Water Street. Any other boy of his age thrown into such a setting from a gentler world would have been sorely frightened, but Water Street was the only world that Jeb Summers knew. He passed by gamblers, pimps, prostitutes, drunks—paying them no heed at all, for his mind was racing to devise a way to avoid a thrashing when he got home.

When he reached the tenement, Jeb stopped to catch his breath, then warily climbed the three flights of stairs. As always, the familiar smell of cooked cabbage and sour clothing lingered in the air, and his stomach growled. When he reached the third floor, he stopped abruptly and wished suddenly that he didn't have to go in. "If I had anywhere else to go," he whispered, "I'd go there. I hate this place!" Yet deep inside, he knew his lot in life ended here, with little hope for change, so he walked to the door, hesitated, then slowly opened it and stepped inside.

"Well, look what the cat drug in!" Bart Lawson, a younger version of Harry, was the oldest of the three children that Harry Lawson had brought into his marriage with Martha Summers. He smirked over at his father and said, "Look at him, Pa! Ain't he something now?"

Harry Lawson had both elbows on the table. He held a fork in one hand, as if it were a shovel, and stopped scooping the beans into his mouth long enough to grunt, "Where you been, boy?"

Before Jeb could answer, Martha pulled his chair out, saying, "Sit down, Jeb, and eat your food before it gets cold."

Riley, the second boy, brushed the black hair out of his dark eyes. He was eating as steadily as the others and said with his mouth full, "I ain't heard you answer Pa yet. Where ya been?"

Jeb had learned to lie when necessary. It was one of those habits needed for survival on Water Street, along with fighting. "I went to see if I could work some for Mr. Henley down at the grocery store."

"You did, eh?" Harry said. He chomped his beans, swallowed, then loosed a tremendous belch. "What'd he say?"

Quickly, Jeb improvised a story. "He said the boy he's got now may be leaving and I could have his job when he left."

"See you take it then, ya hear me, boy?"

"Yes, Pa, I will," Jeb said, taking his seat quickly so as not to anger the man.

There was little talk round the table. Harry Lawson was often drunk when he got home, and everyone knew the smallest thing could set him off. Silence was a common part of most meals, lest someone get a cruel thrashing for crossing him. The food, which consisted of one large bowl of beans, the remnants of a roast, and two loaves of hard brown bread, soon disappeared almost magically down the throats of the Lawson family.

Hurriedly, Martha scooped the last of the beans out of the bowl and put them on Jeb's plate. Then she took a piece of roast from her own and added it, along with a crusty piece of bread. She spread a minuscule amount of butter across the hard bread and said, "Eat now, Jeb." Her face was worn, and she looked at her husband from time to time with a nervous and frightened expression. The life had been bled out of this woman. She had known better days once, but Harry Lawson was a hard man, one who was enough to drain the life and joy from any woman.

Spoons broke the silence as they scraped on the plates. Harry looked up from his empty plate and said, "Give me some of that coffee, woman."

"All right, Harry." Carefully, Martha measured a cup full of steaming coffee into a chipped cup and set it before Harry.

"Where's the sugar?"

"We . . . we're all out of sugar."

Lawson cursed vilely. It was typical of him to choose a minor thing like this to loose the violence within him. No one escaped his anger—he cursed the government, the ward, the state, the President, the police; then he started on the preachers and do-gooders of the country. The others all sat quietly, while Bart and Riley grinned at each other as they listened to the vulgar tirade that flowed from their father's thick lips.

Pearl, Harry's daughter, sat to one side, thoroughly enjoying the scene. She had her mother's dark hair and prominent eyes. She was nothing like her stepsister, Gail. Pearl was lazy and hated work. She preferred to be out and around, and already at her youthful age, she was being drawn to men with less than honorable intentions. "Give it to 'em, Pa," she encouraged her father. "They ain't no good—none of 'em."

Right then the door opened and Gail walked in. Pearl grinned and said, "Well, it's her majesty back again!"

Gail Summers had grown accustomed to Pearl's sarcasm. All three of Harry's children from his first marriage constantly called her "your majesty" for her honest attempts to keep herself clean and decent. They saw this as "airs" and lost no opportunity to ridicule her for it.

"Well," Bart grinned, "it's the princess." He reached over, picked up the bowl, looked into it, then glanced up with his piggish eyes glinting. "Too bad, your majesty, you missed out on the meal. You'll have to go to the Waldorf Astoria and eat with the other swells."

Gail said, "It doesn't matter. I'm not hungry."

"Here, have some bread," said Martha. "I think there's a few beans left in the pot on the stove." She scurried around and managed to find a small plate and place it with its meager contents before Gail, who sat down and began to eat in silence.

"Why are ya late? You and your brother there can start gettin' to meals on time!"

Jeb glanced up, anger flashing from his eyes. Harry Lawson did not appear for half the meals, but usually was down drinking in some tavern. But Jeb knew better than to reply and ducked his head again.

Gail said merely, "I'm sorry to be late."

"Well, this is payday, ain't it?" Lawson grunted.

"Yes." Without argument, Gail reached into her pocket, pulled out a handful of coins, and handed them to Lawson. He put them in his palm, raking them over with his grubby fingers, then scowled, "Where's the rest of it?"

"I . . . I kept out a little to get some groceries."

At Gail's words, Lawson brought his fist down on the table. Then he rose, walked around the table, and, grasping Gail by the neck, lifted her to her feet. She was helpless against his brute strength and bit her lips to keep her cry back.

Martha stepped forward, whispering, "Please, Harry—!"

"Shut your mouth or I'll give you what for," Lawson raged furiously, shoving his frail wife back. He turned Gail's face around and said, "Come on, give me the rest of it, I says!"

Gail reached back into her pocket, pulled out a few more coins, and handed them over.

"Now—let's have no more of your thieving ways!" he shouted, pushing Gail away. The frightened girl staggered, and when she caught her balance, she started to move away toward the bedroom.

Lawson moved back to his chair and sat down in front of his coffee, jingling the coins in his hand for a moment, then shoving them into his pocket.

"Going out to have a bit of a drink, are ya, Pa?" Bart grinned from across the table.

"Never you mind," Lawson scowled. "Keep your mouth shut or I'll give ya the back of my hand."

Bart flinched, for he knew well the weight of that large hand. Realizing it was best to turn the attention from himself, he said, "I know where Jeb's been going and what's making him late every day!"

Lawson glared at him. "What are you talking about?"

Bart pointed at Jeb, who had fixed a cold stare on him. "He's been going down to that mission place, playing that piano."

"How do ya know that?" grumbled Lawson.

"Cause I heard him telling Gail, that's why," Bart said, sneering at Jeb.

"Is that right, boy?" demanded Lawson.

Jeb, plainly caught in the lie, suddenly turned pale. He had felt the weight of the thick belt around Harry Lawson's middle too often, but now there was no way out from another savage beating. "I ... I just stopped for a minute," he stammered, his whole body shaking in fear.

As he drank his coffee, a somber silence settled on the small room. Everyone there knew that Lawson himself was one of the vilest liars in New York City. They also knew that he needed little provocation to mete out punishment with his belt. And now, with the hard look on his face, they all knew what was coming.

Jeb sat there trembling as his stepfather got up and slowly removed his thick belt from his bulging middle. He doubled it, making a swishing movement, and said, "Now yer goin' to git it! Bend over that chair."

"Please, Harry, don't be hard on the boy. He's doing no harm," pleaded Martha.

"Doin' no harm! He could be out working instead of wasting his time at that mission place! And for that piano playing, I'll have none of it! No son of mine's going to be playing no pianer. Now bend over that chair, boy!"

Jeb's mouth was twitching, but he obeyed. He bent over the chair, gritted his teeth, and shut his eyes. When the first blow struck him, he could not help but cry out.

"Shut yer mouth," Harry said. "Learn to take yer medicine without squalling like a baby." He raised the belt, then brought it down sharply again and again.

Just then Gail suddenly appeared at the door and raised her hand to her mouth in horror at the beating her brother was enduring. She saw his white face and the tears making tracks down his cheeks. His whole body was shaking from the blows. She had witnessed this before, but this time an anger rose within her heart. Without thinking, she ran forward and stepped between her brother and the raised belt, grabbing Harry Lawson's arms. "That's enough, Pa! You'll kill him!"

If the moon had fallen from the sky, Harry Lawson could not have been more shocked. He lowered his arm and stared blankly at the girl, who looked up at him in defiance, holding on with her hands to his thick wrists. "Wot's this?" he gasped. "You dare tell me what to do? I'll give you more of the same!"

He raised the belt, and Gail only had time to raise her arm before it struck her. A searing pain like fire ran through her arm, leaving a large red welt. Without hesitating he unleashed his anger on her. She raised her hands over her head and crouched down against the wall. Harry stood there shouting curses, then raised the thick belt, and like angry rain, let blow after blow fall down on her trembling body.

By now Martha was beside herself, crying and screaming, but he shoved her away, while the other three simply watched. They all disliked their stepbrother and stepsister, but they knew that in a feral mood like this, their father could turn his vicious anger on them just as quickly.

Finally, it was over. His face a gray restraint, but with a macabre pleasure in his eyes, Harry put on his belt. Then he reached down and grabbed the girl, saying, "You'll learn what a father's authority is!" He half dragged her across the room and growled, "Git yer coat!"

Gail, her body crying out with pain, moved toward the bedroom, picked up her coat and put it on.

"What . . . are you going . . . to do, Harry?" Martha pleaded, her sobs choking her words.

"I'm going to teach this little daughter of mine what it's like to pay a little respect to her father," Lawson growled. Grasping Gail by the arm, he shoved her toward the door and said, "Come on, say goodbye. You won't be coming around here for a spell."

"What do you mean, Harry?" said Martha. "You can't throw her out—she's too young and she doesn't have anywhere to go!"

"She can come back when she's ready to act like a decent girl."

"She can't be decent on the streets, you know that," Martha whispered. "You know what'll become of her."

"That's her lookout. She should've thought of that before she went and challenged me. Come on, girl!"

Gail was numb as the massive hand tightened on her arm. She said not a word, but cast a look back and saw her mother's stricken face and Jeb staring at her with fearful eyes. Then the door slammed. She had to run to keep up with Harry Lawson as he dragged her down the flight of steps. When they reached the street, he shoved her so that she staggered away.

"You don't like the way I do things—let's see the way you take care of yerself. You stay gone until ya can come back and act like a dutiful daughter. Now—get out of my sight!"

Gail watched Harry Lawson turn and walk down the street. She knew he was headed for a saloon, where he would drink up all she had earned. A darkness seemed to close in on her, and she looked up and tried to pray. She'd never felt so alone and abandoned. A terrifying fear that she had never experienced gripped her, making her shiver all the more at what had just happened. Slowly, she turned and moved down Water Street, the shadows closing in about her.

* * * *

"I tell you, Doctor, it's a hard thing—a hard thing, indeed!"

David Burns had dropped by the mission, as had become his custom over the past year from time to time, and had found Awful Gardner in a low state. Normally, Gardner moved through every day spreading his cheer and faith to those less fortunate. Today, however, he seemed strangely depressed. The tall man had been sitting in one of the rough pews staring at the whitewashed wall behind the simple pulpit. When the doctor entered, Awful rose to meet him, then slumped back down, making his doleful statement.

"What's the trouble, Awful? Are you having financial problems?"

"Oh, dear boy, we always have those." Gardner waved the suggestion away. "But the good Lord will supply all of our needs as the good Book says. No, we can handle that with the good Lord's help. The problem is with people, as always." He suddenly turned and cocked his head to one side. "This will be a disappointment to you, too—it's young Gail Summers."

"Gail?" At once, Dr. Burns grew alert. "Why, she was doing well the last time I talked to her." Burns had taken a personal interest in the girl's situation and made it a point to keep informed, more or less, about the Lawson family. He had contributed a little money to buy clothing for Gail and her brother, Jeb. Nothing new, knowing their stepfather would have resented that, but at least something warm to get them through the hard winter. "What's wrong with Gail? Is she sick?"

"No, it's worse than that!" said Awful, rubbing his chin in thought.

"Worse than being sick?"

"Yes ... you get over being sick, don't you, Doctor? You know," he said, "sometimes I think your profession is the most hopeless. The death rate's still one hundred percent, ain't it now, Doctor?"

But Burns was not about to get sidetracked by Gardner right now, and he pressed him further. "What's wrong with Gail?" He'd become interested in the young girl from the first day she appeared at the hospital. He knew that she had it within her to make something of her life, and he hated to hear of her difficulty. A thought clouded his thoughts, and he said, "Trouble at home?"

"Too right!" Gardner said. "It's that stepfather of hers."

"What's he done now? Drunk again?"

"Oh, he's more or less drunk all the time, but he thrashed Gail and threw her out of the house."

"What!" said Burns, clenching his fists at his sides.

"That's right. She tried to stop him from whipping her brother, and he turned on her, then threw her out on the street. He's a brute—that's what he is!" said Gardner, shaking his head.

"Tell me about it." Burns listened as Gardner gave him the details. The more he heard, a burning anger began to rise within him. "I'd like to take a cricket bat and teach that Harry Lawson a few manners!"

"Ah, well now—that wouldn't do no good, would it, Dr. Burns? It's only the Gospel that changes a man from an animal. I know that well myself. I was no better than Harry Lawson most of my life."

"I can't believe that!" said the doctor, amazed at Awful's words.

"It's true enough," Gardner said, shrugging his shoulders. "I was no more than a brute myself—a thief, a liar, a reprobate— anything you can mention. But when the Lord Jesus came into my life, all that was changed. That's what the Gospel is all about— change, isn't it, Doctor?"

Burns stood to his feet and took two or three paces. He clasped his hands behind him, holding them tightly as was his habit when he was deep in thought. As usual, he was physically exhausted. He was a dedicated professional and gave his very best to his patients. Long after the other staff doctors at the hospital would finish their rounds and head home, Burns would remain in the wards, checking in one more time on patients and giving another encouraging word.

As he stood there, he thought about Awful and the work at the mission. He was convinced that such dedication and selfless giving was what the city of New York needed to help heal the lives of those beset with such dismal poverty and hopelessness. The derelicts who roamed the streets of the Lower East Side could be saved no other way. But Gail—what was to be done about her?

He turned and clapped his hands together in an impulsive gesture. "Something's got to be done!" he said, shaking his head. "She can't roam the streets. You know what could happen to her."

"Oh, don't you worry, Doctor, we'll keep her here. We have a young woman who lives here full time and helps with the cooking. Gail can stay here for a time, anyway."

Burns felt relieved at Gardner's offer and said, "Well, that's good. I hate to think of her being out on the streets all alone."

"Yes, but I'm worried about the boy, too—and so is Gail. She doesn't sleep well for worrying about what's to become of the lad. Nothing we can do about that, though. We can't take in everybody that's having problems, although I wish we could."

The two men talked for a time, wrestling with the problem, and finally, a glimmer of an idea came to Burns. He stroked his trim mustache, letting the idea filter through his mind. He was a man who could move quickly, but there was a thoroughness in him, too, that made him analyze every side of a proposition before taking any action. Finally, he lifted his head and said slowly, "You know, Awful, I think there might be one way out of this, but it might be a bit difficult."

Awful glanced at his friend quickly. "What is it, Doctor?"

"I've been watching Gail at her job now for quite some time. At first I wasn't sure that it would work out since she was only seventeen. But she's done amazingly well. Why, even Nurse Smith—who doesn't toss around compliments, I can tell you— says Gail's the best worker in the whole hospital." He stroked his jaw slowly and thoughtfully and said, "I've been thinking lately what a marvelous nurse or assistant she might make."

"But don't that take a lot of education?"

"Well, yes—it does take some special training. Especially to become a regular nurse. But the hospital's started a new program where we take in young women and train them for nine months. It's not the full training of a nurse, but they can do most of the things that a regular nurse can."

"And you're thinking," Awful said, "that this might work out for Gail? You think she could do it?"

"Oh, she could do it all right, but it's a little expensive, I'm afraid!"

Awful made a face and said, "This is one of those times that I wish I had money. How much would it cost?"

Burns explained the program, mentioning the cost, and said ruefully, "I don't have it myself, or I would be glad to pay for it. It was expensive paying for medical school and leaving Scotland. And I'm just getting established here."

"Well, dear boy," Awful said quickly, "we'll just pray and see if something can't be done! The good Lord is just as concerned for Gail as we are."

"Perhaps it's better not to say anything to Gail. If it doesn't work out, then she won't be disappointed."

"Right you are, dear boy." Awful rose and bid the doctor good-bye.

For the rest of the morning, Awful walked around visiting the widows in the neighborhood and doing what he could for them, but he couldn't stop thinking about Gail Summers' plight.

Finally, he returned and helped one of the workers prepare the lunch for the men who had come to stay at the mission. The young lady he worked with had become a favorite of his.

"Well, this is a good lunch you fixed, Deborah. I don't see how you can do it on the scant funds we allow."

Deborah Laurent had never mentioned her age, but Awful thought she must not be more than eighteen or nineteen. She had appeared out of nowhere one evening and sat through a service. Afterward, she had come and offered to work as an unpaid volunteer. Awful, always in need of such help, gladly accepted, and in a few weeks had found her to be the best help that had come forth. She had finally moved into the mission, occupying a very small room, and worked long and grueling hours doing whatever needed to be done. She was of average height and had an oval face, which was pretty, although not overly beautiful. Her crowning glory was her rich brown hair, which shone with auburn tints when the morning sun touched it. She had steady brown eyes and full lips that seemed to hint at something that Awful couldn't seem to figure out. Though he wondered about her past, everything about Deborah was committed to unselfish devotion to those in need.

"I think we'll have a few more today, Reverend." She always referred to Awful as Reverend, even though he insisted that she shouldn't. It seemed to give her pleasure to honor the man. There was a quietness about this girl. She was lively enough when speaking to the men and women whom they took in off the streets, and was always cheerful with them and full of encouragement. Yet, for some reason, there was a mysterious wall around her. She never spoke about her past, and Awful was careful not to ask her about it. As they began to pull the meal together, Awful mentioned to her about Gail and what Dr. Burns had said.

Deborah listened carefully, asked a few questions, then nodded. She agreed that it would be a wonderful opportunity for Gail. Deborah had been sharing a room with Gail for a time and had gotten to know the young woman quite well. Deborah knew that Gail really didn't have anything to go back to at home. From their little talks, and the bits of information Gail confided in her from Jeb, the situation at home had only worsened. Gail had at least brought in some extra money, but now with her gone, Harry Lawson's anger seemed to fall on everyone of late, including his own children. He no longer had Gail's money to spend on drink and, therefore, came down hard on the others to find work.

"The doctor said there would be a room provided for her at the hospital, if she wanted it, so she could be close to her work. Sort of a dormitory for the young women in the program, I take it." He shook his head and said, "I don't see how it'll happen, though, unless the good Lord sends the cash!"

"It's only a matter of money, then?" asked Deborah as she sliced a loaf of bread.

"Only that, but you know how money is—the world runs on it."

Deborah Laurent moved to the blackened stove and began to spoon the greens out of the huge pot into a bowl. She was as careful and methodical at this as she was at all things, and nothing showed on her face. Finally, when the chore was finished, she turned to Awful and said, with a slight smile, "I think something might be done."

*   *   *   *

Dr. Burns had just finished his examination of one of his patients and was about to go to another ward when Agnes Smith interrupted his rounds. "There's a young woman who wants to see you, Doctor. I don't know what she's after. She won't say."

"Well, what's her name?"

"Deborah Laurent," she said, "or some funny name like that. She's waiting in your office. Be careful of her—these young women—they're all out after a husband."

Burns laughed. He could not resist reaching over and giving the large woman a hug. He knew it confused her and yet delighted her all the same, though she never stopped fussing about it. "You think every woman in New York is out to marry me. I wish I were half the man you think I am, Agnes."

"That's all very well, but you mind what I say. Now, stop mauling me," she said, but did not pull away. When the young doctor left and walked down the corridor toward his office, her eyes followed him fondly.

When Burns opened the door to his office, he found the young woman standing there. She was wearing an inexpensive dress, and yet he sensed an inner strength about the girl, a serenity that impressed him. Her dress had been out of fashion for several years, but it was clean and neat. "I'm Dr. Burns," he said. "What can I do for you?"

"My name is Deborah Laurent, Dr. Burns."

"Ah, yes, Mr. Gardner's told me about you. You're doing a fine job at the mission," he said.

"Reverend Gardner's very kind."

"Won't you sit down?" said Burns, motioning her toward one of the chairs.

"Thank you." Deborah took a seat, then in a very straightforward manner said, "I've come to talk to you about Gail Summers and about—other things."

"Oh, you know Gail, of course."

"Yes, she's been staying with me in my room since she came to the mission. She's a precious girl, and I can't see any future for her if she goes back home."

"No, it's a terrible situation, and she's worried about her brother, too."

"Yes, I know. We're praying about that. In the meantime, I wanted to talk to you about this program for nursing assistants. I don't quite understand it. What would it mean exactly?"

Burns blinked his eyes with surprise at the girl's interest. Walking behind his desk he took a seat and began to explain the program. When he'd finished, he shrugged and said, "It's not the best thing in the world, but doctors need help. It takes a long time to train a nurse, but this short-term program would adequately prepare a woman to do most things. Then, later on, they can go on and continue their education and become full-fledged nurses."

"And you think Gail would be able to do this?"

"Oh, I'm sure she could—it's just a matter of finances."

Deborah Laurent was silent for a moment. There was an unusual quietness about this woman. She was not beautiful, yet there was a winsomeness about her. She had a trim figure, Burns noticed, and was not like some of the women that sometimes drifted into the Water Street Mission. Somehow, there was a reticence in her that he felt was habitual. She was evidently a young woman who thought deeply and slowly, and he waited until she spoke.

"I would like to pay Gail's expenses for this program—and I would like to join it myself, if that is possible, Dr. Burns."

"Why . . . of course," Burns stammered. He was taken aback at the ease with which Miss Laurent had made the generous offer. "I'm sure the hospital would be most fortunate to receive both of you into the program. Are you certain this is what you want to do?" He wanted to inquire about her finances, but something about the young woman's bearing made him know instinctively that to question her on this point would not be right.

"Yes, I'm sure. And I would request that you promise not to reveal to Gail the source of this gift, please."

"Of course, Miss Laurent," said Burns, amazed at this young woman sitting across from him.

"When will the program begin?"

"Why, it can begin at once. The new classes started a week ago, but I'm sure you and Gail could catch up easily."

"Would you like to tell Gail about this or should I do it?"

"Well, as a matter of fact, I'd like to talk to her myself. If you could wait for a few moments, I think I could arrange to go with you."

It took a little doing, mostly explaining to Nurse Smith that he was not running away with the young woman. "We'll get two assistant nurses out of this. Don't worry, Agnes—you know Gail, and this one seems to be even more mature."

Dr. Burns hailed a cabbie, and after helping Deborah Laurent up, the two of them made their way to the Water Street Mission. Awful Gardner was standing in front of the mission when the driver of the cab reined the horses to a stop. He had a twinkle in his eyes when he saw who the occupants were that stepped down. Dr. Burns and Deborah greeted him and quickly told him that Gail was going to be able to join her in the nurses' program at Baxter.

"Well, the good Lord has answered our prayers, then," smiled Gardner as he sent them off to the backyard where they found Gail washing clothes. She turned to them and her eyes widened with surprise.

"We have good news for you, Gail!" Burns turned to Deborah and said, "You have a real friend here in Miss Laurent."

"What is it?" Gail asked quickly.

"We've been looking at a program at the hospital—the assistant nurse program—are you familiar with it?"

Gail had heard of it, but had not felt the slightest chance of taking part. She knew it was expensive and far beyond her hopes, so it never entered her head. "I don't have any money!" she protested. "I can't do it!"

"That's all taken care of. The two of you will be going into it together."

"Won't that be fun?" Deborah said to Gail. She went over to the younger girl and put her arm around her. "We'll be working together and living together in the dormitory at the hospital. Will you do it?"

Gail looked at the young woman steadily and could not speak. Her eyes suddenly filled with tears, and all she could do was nod silently.

Burns saw the girl's emotion and said gruffly, "Well, well, I'll be your boss now, so you must expect hard treatment. I'm a hard man to get along with. Everybody says that."

Deborah Laurent turned and a small smile touched her lips. "I can see you're an ogre, Dr. Burns. But we'll try to put up with it—won't we, Gail?"

Gail brushed the tears from her eyes. Her lips trembled, but then she smiled and whispered, "Yes, we'll put up with you, Dr. Burns." She hesitated, then offered him a beautiful smile. "I don't think that will be too hard!"

CHAPTER THREE

A CHRISTMAS TO REMEMBER

★ ★ ★ ★

Several dozen people had gathered in the small reception room of Baxter Hospital. The room was gaily decorated with boughs of evergreens festooned around the walls, and shiny crimson holly berries caught the reflection from the lights. At one end of the room a small tree sparkled with colorful decorations, and at its feet were several ornately wrapped packages. The Christmas season had invaded all of New York—even the rather grim and gloomy halls of Baxter Hospital.

Dr. Alex Templeton, the administrator of the hospital, looked around with satisfaction. He was standing at a table laden with several varieties of refreshments, including punch, chocolate, lemonade, cakes, and cookies to start off the holiday season. Turning to the young man beside him, Dr. Templeton said, "Well, Burns, we'll celebrate the end of your second year at Baxter. It was about Christmastime that you came, if I remember correctly."

Burns smiled and sipped hot chocolate from the mug in his hand. "Yes, sir, it's been a very good time for me. I've learned a great deal."

"Decidedly so—and I must congratulate you. Your service here has been exceptional. I hope you'll stay with us for a long time."

"I have no other plans, Dr. Templeton."

Templeton nodded with satisfaction. He was a tall, distinguished-looking man with a full Van Dyke beard and gray hair. He wore a well-cut single-breasted suit with matching waistcoat and trousers. His immaculate white shirt had a winged collar and his cravat was neatly tied. "Now, then," he said, "I suppose we'll have to honor these dedicated young ladies."

"Yes, sir," Burns nodded. "I think they deserve it. They've all done a fine job."

"Exactly so." Templeton sat down, and his voice, a piercing tenor, rose above the hubbub of conversation. "Ladies and gentlemen," he cried, "may I have your attention, please!" He waited for it to quiet down and then smiled. He was a man who loved his theater, having told more than one that he would have done well had he not chosen to pursue medicine. "We're here tonight to celebrate the Christmas season, of course, and as head of Baxter Hospital and on behalf of the Board of Trustees, I wish you all a most happy holiday season, a Merry Christmas and a Happy New Year to come!" He waited for the returning answer and then said, "If you young ladies will come forward—it will be my distinguished privilege to present you with your certificates."

At once, the crowd began shifting itself and nine women, ranging all the way from Gail—who was the youngest at eighteen, to Mary Huggins, who was the oldest at thirty-two—came to stand in an irregular line before the administrator. Dr. Templeton beamed at them and launched into his speech. With an excited and captive audience, he could no more give a short speech than he could leap over Baxter Hospital, for he was a man who loved the sound of his own voice. Gail, standing next to Deborah, covered her smile and leaned to one side, nudging Deborah, so that the two of them laughed inwardly at the loquacious physician as his words rolled on and on in a sort of linguistic Niagara. Finally, however, it came to an end.

"And so, it is my privilege to confer upon you these certificates which state that you have satisfied all the necessary requirements and hereby have been certified by Baxter Hospital and the Board of Trustees to serve as assistants to nurses and physicians. Your training has been hard and arduous, but you have been faithful to carry out your duties. So, as I call out your name, please step forward. Helen Abraham . . . Susan Blakely . . . Miriam Helfinger . . ."

Gail was the last to be called, and as she stepped forward she felt a thrill of accomplishment beat in her heart, for she had thrown herself into the course with all her strength. She had been accustomed to hard work, but the past nine months had been especially difficult. Unknown to her employer, she had done extra work to make a little money. This small amount had gone to her mother, who had secretly managed to pay for a few luxuries for herself and especially for Gail's brother, Jeb. As Gail reached out and took the certificate with her left hand and shook the firm hand of Dr. Templeton, a sense of triumph swelled through her. At last, she had done something right!

Dr. Templeton beamed at the young ladies, saying, "Now, let's have a hearty round of applause for these fine additions to the medical profession!"

The room broke out in applause, and Dr. Burns quickly stepped forward to congratulate Gail. He took her hand in both of his and gently squeezed it. His long, Scottish face was beaming with unchecked pleasure as he said, "Congratulations, Gail! I'm so proud of you, I could burst!"

"I couldn't have done it if it weren't for you," she whispered.

"Oh, that's nonsense—you did it all yourself! Come, let's go congratulate Deborah and the others."

There was a flurry of talk as the ladies were congratulated by the visitors, who were mostly relatives and the staff. Agnes Smith came to tower over Deborah, saying rather sternly, "Well, you did make it after all!"

Deborah was amused by the large woman. "Yes, Mrs. Smith—I did!"

"Now see to it that you don't forget what you were taught." Agnes was actually pleased about the two girls—who had been her pets—although she'd never shown the slightest favoritism. She glanced over at Dr. Burns, who was grinning broadly. "I suppose you take all the credit for their success. Men usually do things like that."

"Why certainly, Agnes." Burns winked at the two girls, his face averted from the large woman. "We men are a terrible lot, but I must say that I'm very proud of our young ladies."

At that moment, Dr. Templeton came forward and joined their little circle. "I'm glad to find you together, Miss Summers and Miss Laurent. I have a surprise for you both." He put his hands behind his back, swayed forward, rolling on his toes and back on his heels, and turned his head to one side. It was an affectation that he often used when pontificating, and Burns knew that something was about to be announced in his usual grandiose manner. Looking at the four of them, he nodded to Agnes Smith and said, "Mrs. Smith already knows the secret that neither you two ladies, nor you, Dr. Burns, know yet."

"What is it?" Burns asked curiously.

"I have decided—and Mrs. Smith concurs with my decision—to offer these two ladies permanent positions with Baxter Hospital."

Gail was astonished, her hand going quickly to her mouth. She blinked her eyes twice, then cried, "Oh, that's wonderful, Dr. Templeton! I'm so grateful to you. I'll do the very best I can!"

Deborah, at once, nodded. She was much quieter, but there was a smile on her lips. "Yes, it is an honor, Doctor. We will both try to hold the standards high."

As soon as Dr. Templeton was satisfied with the outcome of his news, he turned and left. Dr. Burns turned to the three and said, "Well, it's time for a celebration—all on me! Come on, Agnes, I'm buying lunch."

Agnes was surprised at the invitation, for she did not receive many, and nodded in agreement at once.

Gail and Deborah hurried to get their coats, and the four of them left the hospital. Dr. Burns led them down the street to a respectable restaurant, the Deluxe, where he sometimes ate. He ushered his three guests inside, and when the head waiter came over, he requested a good table, saying loudly, "We have two new medical assistants here who deserve the very best!"

"Oh, Doctor, you shouldn't say that," Gail whispered as he led her to the table.

"Nonsense!" he said airily, waving his hand around. "I believe in tooting the horn when it's deserved." He seated the three women personally, then took a seat. When the waiter came, the doctor asked, "What's the specialty of the hoose? Never mind, we'll have it! Bring four orders of it."

Gail sat there thoroughly enjoying the time. She had eaten out on occasion at a couple of inexpensive restaurants, but the Deluxe was fancier than anything she'd ever seen.

The decor of the restaurant was done in rich wood that was cast in a golden tone from the lights that burned about the dining room. Each table was covered with a crisp white tablecloth and more silverware than Gail had ever seen. She felt honored to have been invited to such an establishment, and even more so with friends who had stood by her and helped her turn her situation around for the better. She smiled to herself at her good fortune, and looked up to see the waiter returning with their meal. The specialty turned out to be steak, baked potatoes, and vegetables.

Burns talked rapidly and Deborah smiled warmly at him, saying, "I didn't know you were such a host, Dr. Burns. You've been hiding your true talents."

"Well, this is a celebration and a victory," he smiled. "I propose a toast to Miss Deborah Laurent and Miss Gail Summers—the latest and brightest lights in the medical field."

"Hear! Hear!" Agnes said unexpectedly, adding her own words. "If all of my girls were as dedicated as these two, I wouldn't have all of my gray hairs."

As they enjoyed their meal, Dr. Burns happened to mention the gold strike in the Klondike, which was appearing in the headlines of every newspaper across the country. It caught the interest of Deborah at once, who always seemed to be knowledgeable of everything that was happening. She was an avid reader of newspapers and magazines. She spoke up and said, "I think the whole country's gone mad, or so it seems, over gold. I recently read that the streetcars in Seattle had to stop running because of the thousands of gold seekers who've come there filling the streets."

"That's right—I read the article. Men are acting like fools! Some of them have sold their businesses and bought passage to Alaska, leaving everything they had behind."

"Strange, isn't it—the power that gold holds over people! It makes men do crazy things—women too, I suppose."

"Well, I don't know," Gail said slowly. She was looking very pretty, having saved up as much money as she could to buy a new dress for the special day that ended her term. She'd actually managed to buy a dress that had been damaged, which she had mended with the help of her mother, but it looked splendid on her. It had a white collar and puffed sleeves with blue lace. The dress, itself, was a pale blue that fell to the floor. The hem was also laced with blue ribbon. Her hair was pressed flat to her head and she wore a hat, the first she had ever owned.

She toyed with her glass and said, "I can understand a little, I think. Life gets so boring and hard for some people. You can understand why they run off to look for gold."

Dr. Burns stared at her thoughtfully. He knew more now about her difficult childhood and nodded slowly. "I believe you're right," he said. "Only it's not just poor people, but wealthy men selling everything and going." He shook his head. "Money and gold are just a disease. Most of them will come back broke."

"Or get eaten by a polar bear! They ought to just stay home and work."

The doctor laughed and said, "Well, I guess I'm ready for dessert." He signaled for the waiter, who brought out four plates of apple pie, each with a large dollop of ice cream on top. Agnes tried to protest, saying she was satisfied, but when the others told her to help them spend the good doctor's money, she chuckled and joined them heartily.

"I've been reading a lot about what is happening in Cuba," Deborah said. "It looks like there could be serious trouble down there."

"I don't know much about that," Burns said. "What's happening?"

"Oh, the Spaniards have been persecuting the Cuban people. They sent out a general, named Weyler—Butcher Weyler—and he slaughtered the poor Cubans by the thousands. It's awful! Look at this!" She fumbled through her reticule and pulled out a picture.

The three leaned forward to look at it and passed it around. It was a line drawing of a beautiful young girl standing naked and helpless as rugged Spanish soldiers pawed through her clothing.

"Why—this is awful!" Gail cried. She handed the picture back to Deborah.

Deborah shrugged and replaced the picture. "Well, it's just some artist's concept, and it's from Mr. Hearst's paper. He always makes the worst of everything."

"Now, no more talk of wars and gold in the Klondike! Let's have another toast for our newest additions."

They held up their glasses once more and Dr. Burns said solemnly, "To the courage of those who follow their stars and become what God has intended them to become." The seriousness of his face and the solemn timbre of his voice affected all three women.

"You really believe that, don't you, Dr. Burns?" Deborah said quietly. There was a strange look on her face and she was tremendously sober. "I hope you always do!" She sipped her water after making this dramatic statement and then rose, saying, "Dr. Burns, this was most kind of you. Thank you, but I must go, if you'll excuse me." She hesitated, then said, "I'm leaving town for a few days and I need to get packed."

Agnes rose as well and said, "I'll go with you, Deborah. I have things to do."

Burns stood to his feet and helped the two women put on their coats. When they had left, he sat down again, a thoughtful look on his face. "Gail, where is Deborah going?" he asked.

"I don't know. She hasn't said a word about it until now."

"That's strange—you two live together. It seems like she would've mentioned it."

"She's a very private person," Gail said slowly. "She's very kind, but I don't really know her. There's something in her heart that she doesn't share with anyone."

They sat and visited for a while, then he said, "You're troubled, aren't you, Gail?"

Startled, she lifted her head. She had become very good at hiding her feelings, almost a necessity in her home. Now she was surprised at how easily the young physician had seen beneath the facade she had put on for the celebration. "It's nothing," she said briefly.

"Come now—tell me. It's not like you to be downhearted."

Gail bit her lip, then took a deep breath. "It's Jeb—I'm worried about him." She twisted her hands in a nervous gesture and hesitated, then she began to speak rapidly. In effect, she informed Burns that Jeb was running with a rough crowd. He was staying out all night, and her mother had said there had been reports that he was involved in criminal activities. "He's only twelve, Dr.

Burns. He's going to end up in reform school, if something isn't done!"

The doctor reached across the table and took Gail's hand. She looked at him in surprise, but he held her hand firmly, noticing how strong and warm it was. He looked at her and said thoughtfully, "I'm sorry about Jeb. He's a fine boy. Is there any chance of getting him away from the house? I'm afraid it is your stepfather and his children that are responsible."

Gail was surprised. "You've seen that? I didn't know that you had noticed." She was very much aware of his strong hand on hers and felt awkward about it, but finally he released it and she sat back, saying, "There's no place for him. They wouldn't let me take him, so God will just have to step in."

David Burns looked at her and nodded. "Then that's just what will happen. We'll pray for God to step in."

★   ★   ★   ★

"Look—my first salary!"

Dr. Burns smiled at Gail, who was standing before him holding up the bank notes. Her eyes were sparkling like jewels and her whole face was alight with a childlike pleasure. He thought again of how pretty she had grown. The good food, rest, and peace of the hospital had transformed her from an awkward adolescent into a mature young woman. "What're you going to do with all that money?" he asked, smiling at her fondly.

"I'm going shopping! I'm going to spend every penny of it on presents for my family."

"Better save some for a rainy day."

"No—I've lived in rainy days all my life. Now it's time to be foolish."

"I guess it's not so very foolish," Burns said slowly. "I wish I could do the same for my family back in Scotland—maybe next year I can."

Gail was suddenly aware that she knew little about David Burns and realized that a tinge of sadness marked his words. "Oh, I'm sorry," she said. "I know you must be lonesome. You don't have any family at all in this country?"

"Not a soul. I suppose I'll go to the mission for their service."

"Come with me," Gail said impulsively, "and you can carry my packages for me!" She held up the money and said, "With all this money I ought to be able to buy a lot of presents."

"Not as many as you think," the doctor said. "Prices are just terrible these days, but I'd be glad to go with you."

The two of them left the hospital and caught a cab. Leaving the East Side, they made their way to Fifth Avenue where the streets were packed with holiday shoppers. They passed a Salvation Army band and stopped to listen as the trumpets blared out the sound of "Onward Christian Soldiers" and "Are You Washed in the Blood?"—another favorite. The weather was cold and the exercise had brightened their cheeks. A Salvation Army major stepped forward with a Bible and began to preach a sermon, and when he was through, Gail reached in her reticule and pulled out her small earnings. Extracting a bill, she stepped forward and dropped it into the kettle that was used as a collection plate. "Why, thank you, miss, and may God bless you and restore you a hundredfold," the officer said, smiling at her broadly.

"That was nice of you. I never think of things like that, but it's something I might've expected from you, Gail," Dr. Burns said warmly.

Gail ignored his comment and said, "Come on—let's start spending this money. It's burning a hole in my purse!"

Two hours later the doctor groaned, "Are you going to look in every store on Fifth Avenue?" His voice was plaintive as he shifted the packages that he was carrying in both arms. Observing Gail in store after store, he'd discovered that growing up on the Lower East Side had taught one to be a bargainer. Some of the clerks in the Fifth Avenue stores were somewhat taken aback when the young woman with the dark blue eyes had bargained with them so relentlessly. More often than not, she had gotten them to lower their price, and now she turned to him and laughed. She had a delightful laugh, although he had not heard it too often. "You volunteered for this, Doctor! Now, take your medicine. That's what you say to all your patients, isn't it?"

"I don't treat my patients as badly as you're treating me!" Actually, Burns was having a marvelous time. He had even joined in and insisted on buying some gifts of his own. "Since I don't have a family here, maybe you'll let me give some to yours," he said.

Gail looked into her purse and said, "Well, that's about the lot. I've saved enough for cab fare. I'm going to take these tonight."

"No—the cab is on me. Are you going to wrap the presents?"

"Oh, I hadn't thought of that!"

"We can go by the hospital. There's still some wrappings there, I think."

Returning to the hospital, they found wrappings and spent an hour in the front parlor wrapping the gifts. Agnes had come along and even come up with some brightly colored ribbons to add. As soon as they were finished, Dr. Burns and Gail left the hospital and hailed a cab. As they made their way to the tenement where the Lawson family lived, the two chatted and laughed over small things.

"I can't ever remember feeling so happy!" Gail said. "I've never had anything to give to somebody before."

"That's not true! You've been giving to people all your life, especially to Jeb and your mother."

"Yes, but this is different," she said. She grew silent for a moment and tapped her chin thoughtfully with her forefinger. As the carriage left the more affluent part of the city and they were once more submerged into the world of Water Street, it sobered her. "There are so many who will get nothing this season," she said quietly. "I'm so glad that God has made it possible for me to do something for my family this year."

The doctor said merely, "It really is more blessed to give, isn't it? The Bible's right about that."

After they arrived at the tenement and Burns paid the cab driver, they mounted the stairs. When they arrived at the door to the Lawsons' rooms, Gail hesitated. "I'm a little bit afraid," she whispered. "You know how Pa is—he might be abusive."

"I don't think he'll abuse Santa Claus, and that's what you are. Go ahead, knock!"

Encouraged, Gail knocked on the door, and when it opened, she said, "Merry Christmas, Ma! I've come to play Santa Claus."

Martha Lawson, as usual, looked tired, but her faded eyes brightened when she saw her daughter. "Why . . . why, Gail—what's all this?"

Gail shoved her way past her mother and saw that the evening meal had already taken place. Her stepfather was seated in a rocking chair by the window and was staring out. When he turned to look at her, she was a little shocked at his appearance. He looked ill and his clothes hung loosely on his body. She had not seen him in over a month, but said only, "Hello, Pa! You remember Dr. Burns? We came by—he's been helping me shop."

Burns said, "Sorry to barge in like this, Mr. Lawson, but this daughter of yours insisted on playing Santa Claus tonight. I was enlisted to do the donkey work."

Harry Lawson stared at them. His blunt features were whittled down by sickness. He got up slowly and carefully and said, "Well—come in, I guess."

"Isn't Jeb here?" Gail asked, disappointed at not seeing her brother.

"Yeah, I'm here!" Jeb came sailing out of the bedroom. He had grown over the past year and was at least six inches taller. At twelve, he was still thin and lanky and shooting up like a weed. "What're you doing here, sis?"

She went over and wrapped her arms around him and said, "I'm here to play Santa Claus. It's not Christmas yet, but I couldn't wait! How are all of you?" She looked over to where Bart, Riley, and Pearl were sitting on the couch looking a little sheepish at her appearance. They mumbled their greetings, and Gail felt the tension in the room. Quickly she said, "Well, here's something all of you can enjoy! Let's have it, Doctor!"

Burns set his bundle down awkwardly, reached into the sack, and brought out a smaller package. "The prize bird!" he said proudly, holding up a huge plucked chicken. "Already smoked and the fattest hen we could find!" He put it on the table and added to it a cake and several other good things to eat.

Martha reached out and touched the huge chicken with a trembling finger. "I haven't seen a bird like this in a long time," she whispered quietly. "It'll be so good!"

"Well, that takes care of Christmas dinner. Now, here's what I brought you, Ma." Gail brought out a package that contained a warm black coat, a pair of real gloves, and a new hat. "This will keep you warm!" She looked at her mother, who was holding the garments almost reverently, stroking the fine wool.

Gail patted her and said, "Now, Pa, this is for you!" She handed him a package, and when Lawson sat there staring at it helplessly, she said, "Go on—open it! It won't bite you."

Lawson stared at her with a strange look in his red-veined eyes, then fumbled at the paper, opened it, and held up a pair of fine leather gloves with wool lining inside.

"I know how you hate for your hands to be cold, Pa. These ought to last you a long time," Gail said.

Harry Lawson had not said thank you often in his life. Now he sat there staring at the gloves as if they had suddenly appeared magically. He could not seem to speak, and it was only when Pearl said, "Go on, Pa—try them on," that he awkwardly tugged them onto his large hands. He sat there looking at them, and finally he lifted his eyes and whispered, "Thank you, daughter. It was a kind thought."

It was Jeb's turn then, and to his delight, he got not only a fine new pair of boots just his size but also a bone-handled pocketknife that he had wanted for years. He stood holding them, and then gave his sister a broad smile that made it all worthwhile. "Thank you, Gail," he said. "I ain't ever gonna forget this Christmas."

Gail passed out the remaining gifts to Bart, Riley, and Pearl, who sheepishly received them, mumbling their thank-you's.

Finally, when all the gifts had been opened, Martha said, "I wish we had something to give you, Gail, but we don't."

"Oh, that's all right, Ma. Next year things will be better, you'll see!" A spasm of coughing came from her stepfather and she said, "Pa, are you not feeling well?"

"He had a spell three weeks ago," Martha said quickly.

"What was it?" Burns inquired, at once aware of the pale face of the big man. He walked over and said, "I've got some free medical advice leftover from last year. I wouldn't mind looking you over while I'm here."

"Please do, Doctor!" Martha said. "He ain't been right since then. Go on into the bedroom, Harry. Let the doctor examine you."

Harry got to his feet and mumbled, "I guess it wouldn't hurt since you're already here." He moved slowly and carefully into the bedroom, and Gail noticed that he was rubbing his chest strangely.

While the two were in the bedroom, Gail told the family about her certificate for completing the medical assistant program. "Now I'll be able to make some money and help you more," she said. She talked with all of them for a while and turned to her brother and said, "I haven't seen you at the mission lately, Jeb. Everyone's missed you!"

Jeb dropped his head, bit his lip, and handled the bone knife lovingly. "Well, I just ain't had time, sis," he said. He was aware of her gaze, and when he lifted his eyes, she couldn't help noticing the guilt on his face. "Don't worry about me. I'll be back."

Gail saw at once that the openness that she'd always appreciated in Jeb was gone. She glanced at her mother, who shook her head warningly, and said no more about it.

Inside the small bedroom, Burns gave Harry Lawson a quick examination, asking questions rapidly. "What was the sickness like, Mr. Lawson?" he asked as he listened to the man's heart.

"It was like getting stabbed in the chest, it was!" Lawson said. "Caught me off guard—I was just walking down the street, doing nothing, and all of a sudden it hit me. I had to go sit down—couldn't draw me breath." He reached over and picked up his left wrist and said, "And I can't use my left wrist so good anymore. I ain't been able to work since."

"I see. Have you had any pain since then?"

"Once or twice, but not like that first one, though." Harry Lawson was a man who had never known anything but excellent health. He'd never had a sick day in his life, so the last three weeks had been terrible for him. He said now, as he stared at the doctor with fear in his eyes, "What do you think it is, Doctor? Do you have any medicine that'll help me?"

Burns shook his head and continued the examination, listening as well as he could to the heart. He asked several more questions, and finally he took a deep breath and said, "Impossible to say really. Hopefully it is nothing, but it is possible that you've had a stroke or a mild heart attack."

"I ain't never had no heart trouble!" Lawson protested.

"Well, it sounds very much like you've had something like that. If I were you I'd get plenty of rest—and drinking isn't the best thing in the world for a bad heart. I'll get some medicine for you and send it back with Gail. You need to come to the hospital so I can examine you better."

"I ain't got no money."

"Not necessary—you just come in and ask for me." Burns had felt nothing but contempt for Harry Lawson, but now he saw the fear that was gripping the big man. He put his hand on the sick man's shoulder and said, "We'll hope it's nothing, Mr. Lawson." He hesitated, then said, "But I always pray for my patients when they've had trouble. Would you mind if I pray for you now?"

The old Harry Lawson would've shaken the hand off, and cursed him out the door and all the way down the stairs to the street. Instead, he bowed his head. The fear had risen in him—a black, sickening fear that took his breath—and he'd realized he was not ready for death. He knew no life but the hard one he had. Silently he nodded, and as the doctor prayed, Lawson remained totally still. When the prayer was over, he mumbled, "Thank you, Doc," and moved out of the room.

The visit did not last long after that. Gail went around and kissed them all goodbye, and Harry did not know what to do with his hands when she put her arms around him. He'd never understood her, and now for one moment as she held to him, he leaned forward and whispered for her ears only, "Sorry—like!" It was the best he could do and Gail took his meaning, for she knew his ways, and she patted his arm, saying, "I'll be praying for you, Pa—God can do miracles."

When the two were outside the house, she asked, "What's wrong with him?"

"He's had a stroke or heart attack."

Gail looked at him quickly and asked, "Will he live?"

"Hard to say. Some people who take care of themselves live a long time, but sometimes they have another attack. There's no way to tell. It's in God's hands, Gail. I'll do what I can for him, though. I promise!"

Gail said, "I feel so bad. He's had such a hard life and brought so much misery on himself. Now he's facing the end of it and doesn't know God."

"It might be well if we asked Awful and the others at the mission to pray for him. He needs it," Burns said grimly.

They reached the mission in time for the annual Christmas dinner, and as they entered, Awful met them, saying, "You're just in time! I want you to meet Katy and Barney—Barney Winslow and Katy Sullivan. They're two of the group of us that are going to Africa."

This had come as quite a shock to the community, for Awful Gardner and a small group from the mission had volunteered to leave America and go to the darkest wilds of Africa as missionaries. Now as Burns shook the hand of the tall man beside him, he said, "I congratulate you—Barney, is it?"

"You might have heard of him," Awful said. "He was once known as Bat Winslow when he was fighting in the ring. But now he's fighting for Jesus. Ain't that right, Bat?"

Barney Winslow was a tall, fine-looking man in his late twenties. "God's coming up mighty short of preachers to send me." He reached over and touched the shoulder of the young woman standing beside him. "Katy, here, has to do most of our preaching."

"Come on in and meet the rest of our group," Awful said. Grabbing Burns by the arm, Awful led them inside the room, which was already packed with people celebrating what Christmas truly meant to them. Gail and Dr. Burns met the other volunteers—including Barney's brother, Andrew—then they participated in over two hours of celebration. Hymns were sung, testimonies were given, shouts of praise were heard, and then a meal was shared at which each missionary was asked to stand and give his or her testimony.

Finally, Dr. Burns and Gail left and took a cab back to the hospital. It was late when they arrived, and they both shivered from the biting cold in the air, hinting of snow lying somewhere over the skyline. "It's so quiet," Gail whispered when they stopped outside the hospital entrance. The streets were deserted, and she stood there looking up at the moon, which was casting its silver beams down over the city. Suddenly she said, "I wish I were going to Africa or somewhere like that."

Burns looked at her in astonishment. "That's an odd thing to say. You might get eaten by a lion."

"Oh, don't be silly! I never heard of a missionary being eaten by a lion."

"Well, there's snakes and lots of bugs. You'd better stay right here. There are a lot of sick folks to take care of."

They stood there talking softly, then she turned to him as a few cabs passed by carrying their passengers and said, "I'm so excited! It's been the most exciting day in my whole life."

The young doctor was suddenly aware of how lovely she really was. The moonlight softly silhouetted her face, making her eyes look like dark pools. She was a tall girl—practically as tall as he. Suddenly, he had an impulse and said huskily, "Merry Christmas!" He leaned forward, gently took her by the shoulders, and pulled her toward him. His lips touched hers and he felt a shock run through him at the softness of them. He held her for a brief moment, savoring the touch of her youthful body as he held her, and for that time, he seemed to know little else except the feel of this young woman.

Gail had been pursued ever since her adolescent days. She had often had to fight off men and boys, and had even been kissed once or twice. But it had never felt like this! This was different— gentle and from an honest man she didn't fear. Those other times had been rough. Suddenly, she kissed him back for a moment, enjoying the touch of his caress. Then she stepped back and said quietly, "I don't usually let a thing like this happen."

"I meant nothing wrong by it," Burns said quickly. "I'm sorry. It's just that—you're such a fine girl and I admire you so much."

She reached out and touched his cheek. "I know. I'm glad you feel that way," she said. "And I've admired you since the first time I saw you. Remember the first time I came in all ragged?"

"Yes, but you don't look much like that young girl now, Gail Summers! I know God's going to do great things with you."

She turned, saying, "Good-night . . . David Burns."

The doctor felt something strangely stir inside him as he smiled and watched her climb the stairs to the entrance of Baxter Hospital and slip through the front doors.

Gail went at once to her room. She undressed quickly and slipped into bed. Deborah was gone and the room was quiet. She looked out the window at the moon and trailing clouds and for a long time lay there and thought about David's kiss. *He's so sweet*, she thought, *such a fine man*. Then she thought about Jeb and her thoughts grew darker. "Oh, God," she whispered, "you've just got to help him—you've just got to. . . !"

CHAPTER FOUR

LEWIS FALLS IN LOVE

★ ★ ★ ★

"Well, there it is! What do you think, Lewis?"

"Think? Why, I think it's one of the prettiest places I've seen, Uncle Mark. Did you build it yourself?"

Mark Winslow flashed a quick grin at his nephew. "No, of course not!" He looked over the large red-brick house with white columns rising in front and shrugged. "I've been too busy running a railroad to do anything like that. Lola liked it, so we decided to move out of the city. I couldn't stand living in that hubbub. Never go into the city anymore except for business reasons—" He paused suddenly and nodded. "Look—there's Esther!" He shook his head almost angrily. "Riding that fool bicycle again! She's going to break her neck one of these days."

Lewis looked across the expansive yard that the carriage had pulled into and saw a young woman wheeling madly at full speed on the oystershell driveway that swept into a graceful circle in front of the house. "She certainly knows how to ride that thing, doesn't she?" he exclaimed with admiration. "How about you, Uncle Mark? Have you joined the bicycling craze?"

"Not while I'm in my right mind," Mark Winslow growled. "I think the blasted things ought to be against the law!"

"Daddy—!"

The young woman brought her bicycle to a stop in front of the horses, causing them to rear, and Mark Winslow shouted, "Esther, get out of the way!" Grabbing the reins tight, he got the team quieted, but even before he did, the young woman came to stand beside him.

"Hello, Father," she said. "Hello, Lewis! It's great to see you again!"

Lewis grinned, and Mark turned to him, saying, "You'll have to forgive her, Lewis, she's not grown up yet."

"I'm twenty-one years old," Esther pouted, her full lips reddened by the cold February wind. Her cheeks were rosy also, and her black hair hung rich and full down to her shoulders. Her brown eyes took in her cousin and she reached past her father, putting out her hand. "Well, Lewis, welcome to New York."

Lewis, somewhat overwhelmed by his beautiful, exuberant cousin, nodded. "Why . . . thank you, Esther, it's good to be here."

"Will you please get that pile of junk out of my way so I can get by!" Mark grumbled.

"Oh, I'll do it, sir!" Lewis leaped out of the carriage and ran at once to pick up the bicycle. He'd seen several of them, but never up close.

"Have you ever ridden one of these?" Esther asked him as he moved it out of the driveway.

"No, never have."

"Try it—it's an experience of a lifetime!"

Lewis looked down at the fragile-looking machine and recklessly grinned. "All right—how do you do it?"

"Just bring your leg over it, grab the handlebars, put your feet on the pedals—and away you go!"

Lewis awkwardly threw his leg over the bicycle, took a firm hold on the handlebars, and put his right foot on the pedal. He shoved himself off with his left foot and fumbled frantically for the other pedal. He rode across the yard, aware that Esther was calling to him, "Hold it! Watch out! Don't run into a tree!"

Lewis quickly discovered that riding a bicycle proved more challenging than he had anticipated. It required three things—holding on to steer, pedaling, and keeping his balance. He was so preoccupied with trying to coordinate all three that he forgot to watch where he was going. Suddenly he heard Mark cry out, "Look out—!" Lewis looked up just in time to see a steel fence looming in front of him. He cried out, "Whoa!" and instantly ran the bicycle with a clash and clatter into the fence. He went flying over the handlebars and struck his head on one of the uprights. Flashing lights danced before his eyes as he fell heavily to the ground. Sprawled out on the lawn, he had never before felt so humiliated.

"Oh, did you hurt yourself?" Esther was at his side at once, pulling him to a sitting position. She reached up and said, "You cut your forehead—you're bleeding!" She quickly pulled out a lace handkerchief and began to dab at it.

By that time, Mark was calling, "Bring him into the house before you kill him! Blasted fool machines are going to be the death of people yet!"

Lewis slowly stood to his feet and found himself looking at Esther, who seemed to be torn between tears and laughter. "I'm all right," he said with a grin. "Good thing that fence was there or I might've run right into the Atlantic Ocean! How do you stop these things?"

"Well, not like that! I'm so sorry, Lewis. Come on—let's go inside and take care of that cut."

Lewis rather enjoyed the girl fluttering over him. He'd heard that Esther Winslow had grown into an attractive woman since he last saw her, though she was spoiled to the core. And now, he was pleased to find that she was filled with fun as well.

When they reached the front door they were met by Esther's mother, Lola, who began to scold the girl at once. "I'm going to take a carriage whip to you, Esther!" Lola was a beautiful woman of fifty with hair as black as her daughter's. There were traces of the earlier beauty that Lewis had heard of when she used to deal blackjack in a saloon in a town in the early years of railroading. She put out her hand and welcomed Lewis, saying, "Come in before this daughter of mine kills you! Come along and I'll put some antiseptic on that cut."

"It's really nothing, Aunt Lola!"

"It needs to be attended to. Now, come along." She led the young man to a room off the kitchen where she found a brown bottle filled with some antiseptic. Taking a small cloth, she swabbed it on his forehead liberally and smiled when he blinked at the burning sensation caused by the amber medicine. "That hurts worse than the fall, I bet! Well, welcome to New York, Lewis. I wish you could have brought your parents with you. They've promised to come, but they keep putting us off."

Just then Mark entered the room. "Stop fussing over him, dear, and bring him into the parlor as soon as you're finished."

When Lola had finished dressing his cut, she led Lewis into a sitting room, which was rather informally furnished. Two large windows at the end of the room were festooned with dark blue draperies, and a chandelier and two brass lamps on the wall reflected in the pier glass, which also mirrored an etagere.

"Sit down there, Lewis!" Mark motioned, throwing himself onto a settee covered with a light yellow material. "Supper ought to be ready soon."

"Tell us about your trip," Lola said, taking a seat by her husband.

For a while, Lewis spoke of his journey from Richmond. He was an athletically built young man, an inch short of six feet. He had light brown hair and dark brown eyes that lit up his squarish face. His mouth was wide and mobile and he smiled often, exposing a perfect set of teeth. Finally he said, "It was kind of you to ask me here for a visit, Uncle Mark and Aunt Lola." He hesitated for a moment, then shrugged. "I feel like a bum really. I'm too old for school and don't have a profession yet."

"How old are you, Lewis—twenty-three, aren't you?" Mark said, grinning lazily. His dark hair graying at the temples gave him a distinguished look. "When I was twenty-three," he remarked, "I was studying for the gallows. Any ideas at this time?"

"Not an idea in my head!" Lewis smiled suddenly and said, "I was hoping you might put me on in a position at the railroad—something that pays a lot of money and doesn't require any work."

"I've got the only one of those," Mark grinned. "Don't worry about it—I think we can find you a place."

A tall woman wearing a gray dress covered by a white apron stepped inside the sitting room. "Dinner's ready, if you please."

"Be right there, Miriam," Lola said.

They rose and Mark ushered Lewis into the dining room. It was an ample room tastefully decorated with oil paintings in gold-leaf frames on one wall; the other contained a bank of windows that admitted the sunlight during the day. There was a white cloth on the table, and the china and highly polished silverware glistened under the lights.

"Sit down and we'll treat you to some good cooking!" Mark said.

Lewis took his seat to the left of his uncle, across from Esther, and watched as Miriam set out the meal. It consisted of pheasant, which he had never tasted before. It had been expertly prepared by a cook somewhere in the recesses of the kitchen. He found it juicy and finely flavored, and the vegetables were seasoned to his liking. Lewis enjoyed the meal and the casual conversation with his aunt and uncle. As his parents had told him, he found them to be the perfect host and hostess. After exchanging family news and a few interesting tales from Mark about his railroad career, the conversation came around to Lewis's brother, Aaron, who was in the Klondike.

Mark said, "Your cousin Cass was here recently. When Aaron heard about his going to the gold mines, nothing could stop him."

"I know—I wanted to go with him, but Dad said that one of us out on a wild adventure was enough. I was pretty sore about not getting to go, but I guess he knew best."

"I just hope they get home in one piece," Mark shrugged. "That's dangerous country up there!"

"Well, I'm going to take you to something tomorrow that's better than any old gold rush!" Esther smiled at Lewis as he looked at her, raising his eyebrows in surprise. "We're going to a ball at the Astors' with the Four Hundred."

"The four hundred what?" Lewis asked.

Esther laughed aloud, and Mark and Lola smiled at each other. "Why, Mrs. Astor's Four Hundred," said Esther.

"Who's Mrs. Astor?"

"She's the head of society in New York!" Esther said in surprise. "Surely you've heard of her!"

She spoke of the wife of millionaire John Jacob Astor, who ruled New York society. Her private ballroom could only fit four hundred people, so her invitation list was comprised of the top of New York's upper society.

Lewis found this amusing and said, "How do you get into the Four Hundred?"

"You get rich!" Mark replied cynically. "You'll see tomorrow." He toyed with his fork for a moment, then tossed it on the table. "A bunch of foolishness. They should be made to go to work instead of throwing money away like it was water."

"Don't fuss, dear," Lola said. "It'll be interesting for Lewis."

"Well, I'm not rich," Lewis said, "but I'd like to go and take a look at those who are."

★ ★ ★ ★

The next night, Lewis was amazed at the size of the mansion as the cab pulled up in front of the sweeping staircase leading to the entrance.

As they all stepped out, Mark turned to Esther and Lewis and said, "You two go ahead. We'll be right along."

Esther could hardly contain herself, for she couldn't wait to show her cousin the eccentric life of New York's high society. Grabbing his arm, she said, "Come on, Lewis, this is going to be a night to remember. Not everyone has the privilege of dancing with the elite."

As soon as they reached the door, Esther presented their invitation to the head usher, who escorted them to the ballroom. When they walked in, Lewis stopped in surprise at the scene before him. Never before had he seen such an ostentatious display of wealth. Massive crystal chandeliers showered their light on the hundreds of elegantly fashioned guests swirling about the ballroom. Glittering jewels winked from the hands and necks of every woman in the room, and the ladies in their luxuriant silk gowns seemed to be competing with one another for attention. The men escorted the women with finesse, decked out in black tails with richly patterned cummerbunds to add just a dash of color. Lewis was awestruck as he watched the dancers dip and glide to the strains of a Tchaikovsky waltz. As he surveyed the sumptuous scene, he spotted a table off to one side running the entire length of the ballroom, piled high with fruit sculptures and French cuisine, and dripping with fragrant flower bouquets and garlands.

"Come along—I'll introduce you to some of the young women." Esther pulled him along, adding, "I'll tell you which ones you should dance with."

After an hour of following Esther, Lewis found his head whirling. He danced with a dozen young women until all of them seemed to look alike. Finally, he protested to Esther, "Are all these girls rich?"

"Every one of them! Follow me, I want you to meet Alice Cates."

"Who's she?"

"She's a young woman who delights in devouring young men!" said Esther as she pulled him across the ballroom.

Lewis grinned at her. "Sounds like a black widow spider. Don't they eat their mates?"

"Alice doesn't marry them. She simply meets a handsome man and sucks him dry, then tosses him aside." She led him to a young woman surrounded by a group of men. Simply shoving her way through, Esther said, "I have someone I want you to meet, Alice. This is my cousin Lewis Winslow."

"I'm happy to meet you, sir." The young woman who turned from her suitors was beautiful in a rather strange way. She had blond hair and blue eyes, but there was an aggressiveness about her that was lacking in most genteel women. She put out her gloved hand, which was adorned with an enormous ruby ring, and held on to Lewis's hand a moment longer than necessary. "I didn't know you had any handsome cousins like this, Esther," she said with a smile. "Where are you from?"

"Virginia."

"I love Southern gentlemen! Come along now and dance with me!"

Lewis took her hand and led her onto the floor, and soon discovered that she was not an easy woman to dance with. He laughed, saying, "I guess we should take a vote on who's going to lead—you or me."

Alice laughed and squeezed his arm. "I know—I'm awful, aren't I? But I surrender. You Southern gentlemen certainly know how to charm a young woman. I'll have to be on my best behavior with you."

The dance lasted long enough for Lewis to become attracted to Alice Cates. As soon as the music ended, a young man came to claim her. She shook her head and said, "No—not now, Roger, later."

"Sort of hard on Roger," Lewis smiled. "He looks like he'd enjoy taking a gun to me."

"Oh, Roger wouldn't do a thing like that—he's too tame. What about you? Are you tame, Lewis?"

"I suppose I am. You don't like tame men?"

"We'll see," Alice said, with a promise in her eyes.

After one more dance, Alice excused herself and made her way back to her circle of friends. Lewis watched as she took the arm of one of her admirers and teased him with her eyes.

Later in the evening when he spoke to his Aunt Lola, Lewis mentioned how attractive the girl was. "Yes, she is—and very rich! Her father owns a string of factories," said Lola, sipping punch from a crystal glass.

"She wouldn't be interested in a poor young man, I don't suppose."

Lola looked over to where Alice Cates was moving around the ballroom with a heavy middle-aged man. "Nobody knows what Alice will do! She does what she pleases mostly."

Lewis danced with Alice twice more that night. On the last dance, she turned her eyes on him in a strange way. Finally, she said, "Come to my house tomorrow. I want to talk to you some more." It was like a command, but Lewis found himself enjoying the way this beautiful girl acted toward him.

Later that night when Lewis and Esther were on their way home, Esther said suddenly, "If I were you, I wouldn't go to visit Alice."

Lewis stared at her in surprise. "Why, you don't believe that about her devouring young men, I hope!"

Esther shook her head and her lips tightened. "There's something about her that draws men to her. I'd hate to see you be one of those who gets hurt."

Lewis laughed. "I'm not likely to get hurt. She wouldn't be interested in a man like me. I've no money and no prospects that would interest her. Don't worry—I won't be seeing her more than once anyway."

★　★　★　★

After spending the next afternoon with Alice, Lewis Winslow, to his surprise, found himself plunged into a whirlwind of activities in the following days. For some reason that even he couldn't understand, Alice Cates had chosen him to be her escort, and night after night he entered into the social whirl of New York City. The vitality of the nineties was reflected in the vigorous vaudeville that filled the stages, the blatant burlesque, and the heart-rending melodramas . . . and Alice loved it all!

The two attended *Dangers of a Great City* and *The Girl I Left Behind Me* on Broadway, and laughed themselves silly at Weber and Fields' music hall routine. They also were thrilled by Buffalo Bill Cody's appearance on the stage. Cody was accompanied by Wild Bill Hickok, and after the play, Alice Cates led Lewis back to meet the famous scout and gunman.

Lewis told Alice about his cousin Laurie and her husband, Cody, who had traveled for a time with Bill Cody's show as star performers.

After they left the theater, Lewis said doubtfully, "I think they're more actors than Wild West heroes."

"I know, but it was so exhilarating!" Alice said, hanging on to his arm as she led him to a restaurant.

★   ★   ★   ★

Two weeks after Lewis's first meeting with Alice, his social whirlwind was interrupted by a social gathering of a different sort. His aunt took him to a meeting at the Water Street Mission. After having seen some of the finest homes and restaurants as Alice's escort, Lewis was shocked at the bare appearance of the hall they now sat in. As he listened to the service, he was rather dumbfounded by what he saw. This was not a conventional church, nor a conventional revival with fiery exhortations or loud declarations of fate. Awful Gardner, the preacher, had placed a large sign over the front of the auditorium that read, "Speakers are limited to one minute."

Lola leaned over and whispered to Lewis, "There were some long-winded testimonies at first, but Brother Gardner put a quick stop to that." After the service, Lola led Lewis to the front of the hall to meet Awful Gardner, who grinned broadly and shook his hand firmly.

"Let me show you around," he said. "Or better still, let this young lady show you what we do here." He turned and put his hand on a young lady's arm who was standing close by. "Allow me to introduce Miss Deborah Laurent. Miss Laurent—this is a visitor to our grand city, Mr. Lewis Winslow."

Lewis exchanged polite greetings with the young woman, and then she showed him around the simple facility. Lewis was curious and possessed a keen sense of perception. Most of the women, as well as the men at the mission, showed signs of a rough up-bringing. But there was a delicacy and grace to Deborah Laurent that did not quite fit the setting. Tentatively he asked, "Are you from New York, Miss Laurent?"

"No, I'm not," she said simply.

Expecting her to go on, Lewis felt awkward when she said no more. Her answer seemed to shut a door in his face. He tried again, saying, "Have you been with the Water Street Mission for a long time?"

"A little over a year now." Again, there was a calm smile on the girl's face, but it was very plain that she didn't want to discuss anything concerning herself. "What about you, Mr. Winslow?"

"Oh, please—call me Lewis," he said. "Actually I don't know what I'm doing here—in New York, I mean." He explained how he'd come to visit his uncle and aunt and was looking for a profession. As they stood talking, Lewis noted that she was a sensitive young woman who could listen well, though she did not speak much herself.

She showed him the few rooms they used to help those who came in off the street. One was a small dining room sparsely furnished with some rough benches and a few tables donated by a merchant. The kitchen in the back was tiny, with a Windsor stove to prepare the meals. She explained that the upper floors had a few rooms where Awful Gardner and some of the volunteers stayed, and some for those who had made a commitment of faith in Jesus and wanted help to change their lives.

Lewis was impressed at the dedication he sensed in Deborah Laurent and thanked her for showing him around. Right then his aunt approached and said it was time to go.

Later, in the carriage on the way home, he mentioned the girl to his aunt.

"Yes, she seems to come from different stock, doesn't she! She and the other young lady, Gail Summers, have just finished medical training at Baxter Hospital." Lola gave him a sideways look. He was wearing a new suit that Mark had insisted on buying for him as a birthday present. It was made of gray wool, and the tailor they'd gone to had made it to fit him excellently. Lewis was not as striking in appearance as some of the other Winslow men, but he had a vitality and earnestness about him. "Are you interested in Miss Laurent?" she asked.

"Oh no," Lewis denied quickly. "I was just curious about her. She seems of finer upbringing than most people we saw there."

Lewis visited the mission twice more the following week on the nights he was not out with Alice Cates attending another party. One night early in the service, at Awful's insistence, Lewis gave his own testimony. He always enjoyed speaking of his relationship with the Lord.

After his brief talk, Deborah Laurent came up to him, smiled, and said, "That was a fine testimony."

"Well," Lewis flushed, "it wasn't much—not after some of the dramatic conversions I've heard about happening around here. Some of these men and women have gone through some hard times." His words seemed to make an impression on Deborah. She lowered her eyes suddenly and, it seemed, was struck silent. Lewis wondered if he had offended her, but he was not sure how. Deborah's silence puzzled him.

Finally, she lifted her eyes and said, "I think it's wonderful—someone saved when they're very young." Again, she hesitated, and there was a vulnerability in her soft lips as she whispered, "It would save so much grief and heartache."

Lewis waited for her to continue, but she did not. Instead, she told him how much Awful had done to help so many people. Then someone came looking for her and she excused herself. Later he asked Gail directly about the young woman, but Gail merely said, "She's a very private person, Lewis. I suspect she's suffered some type of tragedy, but she's got it all locked up inside her. That's too bad—we ought not to hide those things, but she won't speak of it even to me."

★ ★ ★ ★

During Lewis's visit to New York, he heard much about the trouble that was stirring in Cuba. At many of the social galas he had attended with Alice, it seemed to be the foremost topic of discussion among many of the prominent businessmen. According to what the papers said, the Cuban Revolution had been a thoroughly unpleasant affair—ruthless, in fact, with men and women killed indiscriminately. As the reports came back, many in the States were horrified at the stories of searches, tortures, and executions.

Thirty-two-year-old William Randolph Hearst was using his *New York Journal* as a powerful weapon to stir up feeling against the war. His competitor, Joseph Pulitzer, had entered into a newspaper war, and the two incited not only the people of the United States, but Congress and President McKinley as well.

With the heightened interest in what was occurring in Cuba, the battleship *Maine*, the newest commissioned warship in the American Navy, was ordered to make a courtesy call in the Port of Havana. Actually, the voyage was the first step in international activities for the United States of America. The *Maine* arrived in the harbor on January 25, 1898, and set anchor. On the night of February 15, at 9:40 P.M., a tremendous explosion rocked the harbor. The blast ripped into the hull of the USS *Maine*, and of the three hundred fifty officers and men aboard, two hundred sixty of them perished in the explosion. The proud vessel was demolished completely, sinking into the harbor, leaving only the tip of the twisted wreckage as a memorial of the disaster. An American court of inquiry was immediately convened, but their findings were inconclusive. It could not be decided if a mine had sunk the *Maine*, or if an internal explosion had ripped the hull apart.

But no such doubts troubled the press, and bold headlines appeared in the *Journal*: "The Warship *Maine* Split In Two By An Enemy's Secret Infernal Machine." Soon the words, "Remember the *Maine* . . ." were heard chanted in front of government offices all over the country. Antagonistic feelings toward Spain reached a boiling point, and the nation surged toward war. No one seemed able to stop it.

★　★　★　★

"If I were a man, I'd go at once." Alice Cates had gathered a doting audience of young men and women from the upper ranks of New York around her at an afternoon party. Alice was not particularly known for her political opinions, but since the sinking of the *Maine*, she had agitated loudly—vehemently and constantly—for the country to avenge the "foul and unnatural deed" as she deemed it.

One of the young men, a tall, languid fellow named Derek Hansen, said, "Why, Alice, we're not even sure the *Maine* was destroyed by a mine!"

"*I'm* certain—and so is everyone with any sense, Derek!" she said, casting a glance around the room that would tolerate no challenge. Once her mind was made up, there was no more chance of turning her than one could turn a powerful locomotive. At every gathering now, she continued to harangue those who were not ready to jump into a full-scale war.

She looked beautiful, Lewis had to admit, as she stood there surrounded by her admirers. She had on a pale green dress with an emerald necklace and a tiara of flashing diamonds crowning her blond hair. He himself had been caught up by her rhetoric and now said, "I think Alice is right. We can't let this incident go by. If Spain pushes us around, what's to stop any foreign power from doing it?"

Alice beamed at him and came and took his arm. "That's exactly right! Lewis has the spirit of a true American!" She looked scornfully around at the other young men, saying, "I'm ashamed of all of you. If I were a man, I'd do something right away!"

"Do what?" Derek protested. "Even President McKinley is telling us to go at this with caution. He's not rushing into war."

"He will, though," Lewis said quickly. He'd been studying the headlines carefully and talking to his Uncle Mark, who knew a great deal about foreign policy. "You wait—we'll be at war with Spain in thirty days."

Alice hugged him, and he felt a surge of attraction at her closeness. Knowing she wanted to hear it, he said recklessly, "And I'll be the first one to sign up!"

Alice stepped back, pleased at his words, then took up Lewis's announcement at once. She spoke of it as a foregone deed as she turned to those around her, saying, "When Lewis's unit arrives in Cuba he'll be a real hero!"

When word of Lewis's intention to enlist reached Mark Winslow, he was very disturbed. That night in the parlor Mark said to Lola, "That girl's getting Lewis all stirred up. He's liable to go out and do something foolish!"

"He's not the only one," Lola said. "The whole country's ready to go to war against Spain." She shook her head sadly. "I never saw anything like it. They talk about it as if they were going on a picnic, and it's not going to pass either. Did you see the paper this morning?"

"No," said Mark as he stood up and began to pace around the room.

"Teddy Roosevelt, Secretary of the Navy, has volunteered himself as a commander and offered to raise a company of cavalry to fight in the war. Even Buffalo Bill Cody has done the same thing. He says he'll raise a bunch of cowboys and they'll finish the Spaniards off in a month. It's like a fever, Mark—I don't understand it!"

Mark shook his head. "I've been talking to a group of the young men in the office and they're all talking like this." He hesitated, then said, "Some of them talk about the Civil War. It was long before their time, and in a way, I think they've romanticized it and now want their own war—to put on a uniform and march out with flags waving and bugles blowing . . ." He shook his head in disgust. "It just wasn't like that, Lola. War's a nasty, dirty business! There's no glory in it—men dying, and women, too. Families are torn apart by it all."

"Mark," she said, "we'll have to write Davis and Belle. I'm sure they don't have any idea of all that's going on with Lewis."

"I think that's a good idea. It'd break their hearts if anything ever happened to Lewis. They've placed all their confidence in him. Aaron just doesn't seem to be going the way of the Lord, although I'm praying for him." The two talked for a while, both of them burdened by the pressures that lay over the country underneath the shrill cries of "Remember the *Maine*!"

★　★　★　★

Gail stopped by the apartment with a small parcel of food for her mother and to look for Jeb. When she went in, she found her mother sitting at the table. "Hello, Mother. Where's Jeb?"

"He's not here," she said. Her brow was furrowed and her lips were drawn tightly together. "I'm worried about him, Gail. He's starting to run with a rough crowd. They're older boys and they use him, I'm afraid."

"Why does he do it, Mother?"

"He's flattered, of course, to be taken in as young as he is. I want you to talk to him, Gail."

"He used to listen to me," Gail said sadly, "but not now. How's Pa?"

"He's gotten better and gone back to work some. He's quieter now, though." She did not say so, but the sickness of Harry Lawson had made her life immensely better. Lawson still tipped the bottle from time to time, but nothing like the old days, and he had practically stopped abusing her. She came over and put her arm around Gail, saying, "I'm really worried about Jeb. I wish he could go somewhere else. The streets are no place for a boy."

Gail tried to comfort her mother, but there was little she could say, for she too was worried about her brother. She left the house, promising to come back when Jeb was home, and went at once to the mission. When she entered, the service had already started, and she was not surprised to see Lewis Winslow sitting on one of the rough benches near the front. She was a little startled to see that he had brought a young woman with him, dressed in fine clothing and wearing expensive jewelry. Taking her usual place, Gail did not look at the pair again. But after the service, Lewis brought the woman over to Gail, saying, "Miss Alice Cates, I'd like you to meet Miss Gail Summers."

Gail smiled at her and said, "We're glad to have you visit the mission, Miss Cates. Did you enjoy the service?"

Alice Cates had practically forced Lewis to bring her to the mission service. She'd heard of the Water Street Mission and how it was flowering in the roughest section of New York. Always interested in anything new and exciting, the girl had wanted to experience it at least once. But after hearing Awful Gardner's message on everyone's need for a Savior, and feeling out of place with those around her, she had been appalled by the whole thing. Now there was a curl to her lips as she said, "Very nice, I'm sure." She looked around at the ill-clad group of men and the few women who appeared rough and bedraggled. She turned to Lewis and, with disdain edging her voice, said, "I think it's time to go, Lewis."

"Of course, Alice." Lewis turned to Gail and said, "I'll see you later."

As soon as the pair left, Gail walked over to where Deborah was speaking with one of the women who'd come in. When Deborah had finished encouraging the woman, Gail asked, "Did you meet Lewis's lady friend?"

Deborah's eyes narrowed. "Yes—I talked with them for a while."

"What did you think of her?"

Deborah's shoulders stiffened, and Gail sensed almost a hardness in her friend—something she had never seen before.

"I didn't like her," Deborah said abruptly.

"You didn't?" Gail was surprised. In all the time they had been together, she had never heard Deborah speak an unkind word about anyone. "What's wrong with her?"

"She's playing at God," Deborah said sharply. "She didn't come down here looking for the Lord—she came down here to flaunt her station in life and gape at us as if we were a bunch of animals." She turned angrily and walked away.

Gail mentioned the incident to Awful Gardner, who said thoughtfully, "I saw the same thing. Deborah's a good-hearted girl, but something about that high-society woman Lewis brought in here raised her back up. I don't know what it was—it was a puzzle to me, too."

*　*　*　*

On the way home, Lewis asked, "How did you like the service, Alice?" He had been extremely nervous about taking her there. Somehow, he knew he'd made a mistake and felt ashamed by it, but he wanted to know how she felt.

"Oh, it was amusing," she said. "Such efforts for those kind of people need to be done, I suppose. But I'm surprised that you'd spend your time there. I'll introduce you to the bishop tomorrow.

If you're interested in this sort of thing, you can do it on a much larger scale."

Lewis felt her rebuff and said stiffly, "You needn't do that, Alice. I think it's a good work and I'm content to be where I am."

At once, Alice turned to him, pulled him forward and kissed him. "I'm sorry," she whispered. "I just seem to have to boss men. You'll have to take a stick to me."

Lewis was taken aback by her sudden gesture. He'd kissed her before, but he sensed something in this kiss that caused him to be a bit slow in answering. He started to pull her toward him, but she resisted him, saying, "Oh no—we can't let this get to be a habit." She laughed and said, "Wait till you get your uniform. Won't you be handsome!" She studied him with a self-satisfied smile, then whispered with promise in her voice, "I could never resist a man in a uniform!"

CHAPTER FIVE

"You May Fire When Ready, Gridley!"

★　★　★　★

A large wave that comes crashing in on the sandy beaches of a country originates miles away—sometimes days earlier. Beginning as an almost inconsequential swelling of a small volume of water, it travels under the surface for miles, causing only a mound on the expanse of the huge ocean. As it approaches the shore, it gains volume and speed until finally it breaks, raising an enormous white-capped, rolling expanse that crashes onto the shoreline with a roar.

Theodore Roosevelt's career might well be said to have begun in such a fashion. The sinking of the battleship *Maine* was the tiny, almost unnoticed beginning in the life of the man who would be known to the world over as Teddy Roosevelt.

Roosevelt was a brisk young man with conspicuous eyeglasses. His mouth was packed with large white teeth, which he loved to bare when he grinned. He often uttered the word, "Bully!" to express his admiration for almost anything, from beef steak to a triumph in the State Department. He'd arrived in Washington in April as the new Assistant Secretary of the Navy. He was, however, no stranger to that city, for he'd served there as a civil service commissioner for five years.

Theodore Roosevelt was not ignorant of naval affairs. When he was a stripling of twenty-two, he'd written a book entitled *The Naval War of 1812*, a work recognized by military historians as the definitive record of that struggle. Roosevelt's thorough understanding of the importance of maritime sovereignty had turned him into a longtime public advocate for a larger and more modern fleet.

Roosevelt's carefully tailored suit, his precise enunciation, and his upper-class accent that had echoes of Harvard misled many of his observers. A huge bully wearing two guns had made that sort of mistake in a Dakota saloon once. Roosevelt had taken away the man's guns, knocked him senseless, and then dumped him in a shed until he woke up and found his way out of town.

Those who were acquainted with the thirty-year-old aristocrat knew him to be a man of action, as well as a man of words. He was a fearless advocate of the strenuous life and proved it by his vigorous activities—hunting big game in Africa, turning himself into a cowboy by sheer determination, boxing, and other difficult pursuits that he felt made a man what he should be.

The state of the Assistant Secretary's mind about war had been greatly influenced by a book written by Alfred Thayer Mayhan, a naval officer and historian. Roosevelt had devoured Mayhan's *The Influence of Sea Power Upon History*, declaring it to be "a bully good book"! Basically, Mayhan had advocated that America could depend on one thing to preserve its sovereignty—sea power. The annals of history had already proved this true with European nations such as England and Spain. In 1884, as a result of this rising awareness, the Naval War College had been established at Newport, Rhode Island. Mayhan had been appointed as president of the newly formed college. Mayhan, a son of a West Point professor, began to develop his thesis on sea power there, and his maritime acumen influenced Roosevelt tremendously in the years that followed.

As the Assistant Secretary of the Navy, Roosevelt delivered a speech to the student body and faculty at the Naval War College. It was, however, a speech intended for public consumption and was a plea for the country to build and maintain a bigger and better navy. Roosevelt took as his theme George Washington's rule, "To be prepared for war is the most effectual means to promote peace." The tone of the speech, so characteristic of Roosevelt, was so militant-minded that it startled the professional officers in the audience.

> All the great masterful races have been fighting races; and the minute that a race loses the hard-fighting virtues, then it has lost its right to stand as the equal of the best.
>
> No triumph of peace is quite so great as the supreme triumphs of war. It may be that at some time in the dim future of the race the need for war will vanish, but that time is yet ages distant. Diplomacy is utterly useless when there is no force behind it; the diplomat is the servant, not the master of the soldier.
>
> There are higher things in this life than the soft and easy enjoyment of material comfort. It is through strife, or the readiness for strife, that a nation wins greatness. We ask for a great navy partly because we feel that no national life is worth having if the nation is not willing, when the need shall arise, to stake everything on the supreme arbitrament of war, and to pour out its blood, its treasure, and its tears like water, rather than submit to the loss of honor.

In Teddy Roosevelt's mind, as he struggled over the crisis of the Spanish War, he was extremely concerned about the position of Commander of the Asiatic Squadron, which was soon to be vacant. He well knew that the new commander would control to a great extent the events of the war that was sure to come. Roosevelt had his own candidate for that command—George Dewey, a fifty-nine-year-old Civil War veteran.

Roosevelt demonstrated his political prowess by adroitly manipulating the War Department until Dewey was appointed to the position. "Now," Roosevelt exclaimed, "we've put this thing in the hands of a self-starter. He'll know how to handle those Spanish fellows!"

After the explosion that destroyed the *Maine*, a furor swept through most of the Western countries. Germany sent armed naval forces into Manila, for Kaiser Wilhelm II was anxious to become involved in the fray. With the rising tide of antagonism, the Spanish Court began to seriously strengthen its military buildup. The court met for long hours, trying to ascertain what had happened in the Port of Havana, but they couldn't come to any real conclusions. Eyewitnesses recalled two explosions—a sharp, gun-like report, followed a second or two later by a more massive and prolonged blast. However, after much discussion, there was never any conclusive evidence that the Spanish or anyone else had deliberately blown up the *Maine*.

That Spain was innocent apparently never once occurred to Teddy Roosevelt. He plunged ahead with his characteristic energy, and on February 25, the small wave that had begun years ago when as a boy he had become interested in politics and warfare finally crested and thrust Roosevelt into his career. The scene was set that would propel him into the developing political conflict. The Secretary of the Navy had left his Assistant Secretary in charge, and Roosevelt immediately began issuing a steady stream of orders. He sent guns from the Washington Navy Yard to New York, where they were used to arm merchant ships as auxiliary cruisers. Cables went out to American squadron commanders around the world ordering them to stock their ships with coal and make preparations to sail at once. But his most audacious action involved the Asiatic Squadron.

It was evident that this fleet anchored in Hong Kong was in the most advantageous position to attack Manila. Hong Kong lay only some six hundred miles from the Philippines, while most of the squadron remained at Nagasaki, twelve hundred miles from the Spanish-controlled islands. Teddy Roosevelt was a bold man. In the absence of the Secretary, he seized upon the opportunity to cable Dewey: "Order the squadron to Hong Kong. Keep full of coal. In the event of declaration of war with Spain, your duty will be to see that the Spanish squadron does not leave the Asiatic Coast. Then offensive operation in Philippine Islands. Keep *Olympia* until further orders. Roosevelt."

It was sheer audacity. Those who later wrote the biographies of Teddy Roosevelt pinpointed it as one of the most propitious acts of his fiery political career. The next day, a stunned Secretary of the Navy, John Davis Long, wrote in his diary that the Assistant Secretary had come very near to causing more of an explosion than what had happened to the *Maine*. "The very devil seemed to possess him yesterday afternoon!"

But the orders to Commodore Dewey were not revoked, and

the first phase of the Spanish-American War plans had now been set in motion. The navy was armed and ready to move at a moment's notice.

★ ★ ★ ★

Lewis pulled up in front of the Mark Winslow home and stepped out of the carriage. Sam, the lanky handyman who worked for Mark and Lola, came to take the lines. "I'll put them up, Mr. Lewis," he said amiably. "Mr. Mark and Miss Lola have been waiting for you."

"There was a lot of traffic," Lewis said, handing the lines to the man. "We'll be going back after lunch, Sam. You might give the team a good feed."

"Yes, sir, I'll take care of it."

Lewis went over and helped Alice out of the carriage. Taking his hand, she stepped to the ground, looking at the low-lying house. "What a pretty place! Not as big as I'd expected."

"It's very comfortable, though not like your home. Uncle Mark and Aunt Lola aren't much on big places." He spoke offhandedly of the colossal manor where Alice Cates lived with her family. Lewis found it impressive, but was never very comfortable there, despite his many visits. He liked Mr. Cates well enough, a mild-mannered man, who gave no indication of the wealth he had accumulated—but he had felt the resistance of Mrs. Cates from the first day they met. He knew instinctively that the woman had high ambitions for Alice—primarily a rich husband. And the coolness and distance he had sensed at that meeting had not changed in the following weeks.

"Look—they're waiting for us." He led Alice up the steps, where they were greeted by Mark and Lola.

"Come in," Mark said heartily. "You're just in time for lunch. How are you, Alice? You're looking beautiful, as usual."

Alice smiled at Mark and put out her hand. She was fascinated by Mark Winslow. "I declare, Mrs. Winslow, you must have had a time being married to a good-looking man like this!"

Lola said, "Don't encourage him! He's vain enough as it is." She smiled at the girl, shook her hand, and said, "Come inside—lunch is on the table. Why are you so late?"

"Oh, Alice wanted to show me Madison Square Garden." He grinned at Lola and winked. "There's a statue of a young lady in that place wearing no more than a few leaves. I think it's indecent."

Alice laughed. "I noticed you looked at it long enough to take notes. Are you planning on writing a letter of protest to the papers?"

The four of them entered the dining room and sat down to the luncheon. Mark bowed his head and asked the blessing. As soon as he had finished, Alice began speaking of the war.

"Isn't it just terribly exciting? The war, I mean!"

"A little bit depressing, if you ask me," Mark shrugged. He picked up a fork and nibbled at the salad on his plate, chewing thoughtfully. "It's going to be a tough go of it, I think."

"Oh, Mr. Winslow, you can't mean that!" Alice said, her eyes sparkling. "We've got to teach those Spaniards a lesson!"

Lewis ate slowly as he listened to Alice go on about the war. He knew she was impulsive about her ideas, but he was drawn to her, just the same. She was wearing a beautifully designed gown. The dress had a bodice cut in the Eton shape, with a skirt that fit closely over her hips and fell in folds to the ground. The jacket was fit to her figure with a high satin collar and wide satin revers. The small bonnet she was wearing was one of the new styles, topped with small ostrich feathers. *Probably cost more than Dad makes in a month!* Lewis thought as he surveyed her outfit.

Lola was listening carefully as Alice began to speak of the importance of the war to free the Cubans. She was aware that Alice Cates was one of the most eligible young women in New York, and she could not understand what had sparked Alice's sudden interest in Lewis. They had only met a few weeks before. At one time, after Lewis had brought Alice for dinner, Lola had said to Mark, "He's just a poor young man with no prominent family, so I can't understand why she's after him."

"Don't you?" Mark had replied. "I think she's using all her charm to turn Lewis into her pet volunteer." When Lola had expressed surprise, he'd gone on to explain. "She wants a soldier going to the front—one she can call all her own. The bugles are going to start blowing and the flags will be waving. Sooner or later there's going to be an army leaving. I think she's been reading some silly novels about what war is like."

Now as Lola listened to Alice, so enthralled with the adventure of war, Lola became convinced that Mark was right. *Lewis needs to be careful*, she thought. *He's idealistic enough, and with this girl fanning the flames, there's no telling what he might do!*

The afternoon was pleasant enough, except for the fact that Lola now clearly saw how infatuated Lewis was with the girl. After the couple left, headed back for a ride across the Brooklyn Bridge upon Alice's insistence, Mark and Lola walked slowly along the border of the flower garden, speaking of the issue.

"I'm worried about Lewis," Lola said. "He's old enough to know better, but he's acting like a foolish teenager."

"I think he's been pretty well protected from life. Davis and Belle live in an academic atmosphere, and they've raised their boys that way."

"But Aaron's broken out of it—running off to the Klondike."

"I think he's a different sort of fellow. Aaron's always been rash and headstrong." Mark put his arm around her and whispered, "Like all of us Winslow men—just like I was when I stole you away."

Lola was pleased with his foolishness. It was something that she'd had to cultivate, for when they were first married he had been far too serious. She reached up, pulled his head down, and kissed him, saying, "You are a handsome thing—just like that silly girl said! I thought so the first time I saw you."

"No, you didn't. I was locked up in that dirty Mexican jail. You've just romanticized that time—it was pretty rough."

Lola thought back to the time when they had escaped from Texas—she from an abusive brother-in-law and Mark from an unjust jail sentence. They had gone through a great deal of hard times during the building of the Union Pacific Railroad. Now she reached over, took his hand, and said, "I know it was hard, but look what it did for us. It made us one more than anything else. Hard times do that, Mark." She hesitated for some time, turning it over and over in her mind, then said, "I think this is Lewis's first time out on his own, so to speak. He's never seen a young woman as enticing as Alice. She's spoiled, aggressive, and not like the college girls he's used to."

"She's bound and determined to get this war going—and to

influence as many men to get involved as she can." Mark's lean face grew solemn. He thought of his sister Belle, and said at once, "I've got to talk to Belle. I don't think she and Davis have any idea of Lewis's foolish notions. I doubt if Lewis has said anything about this war to them. I'll try to talk to him, too."

"That'll be good, dear," Lola said quietly, but something inside her told her it would do little good to talk to their young nephew. She had a feeling Lewis could be very headstrong if pushed on the issue. "He's in love, or thinks he is," she said quietly. "And when a young man's in love for the first time, words won't do much to change him."

"But the war would," Mark said grimly. "It could get him killed—and that's why we have to try to protect him."

★   ★   ★   ★

If the war had simmered down, or the threat of it, things might have been different. There was always the possibility that diplomacy might prevail and that the Spanish Court might bend itself to meet the American demands, but certain events at home and abroad changed all of that.

On April 19, after a week of intense debate, the House and Senate passed a joint resolution: ". . . for the recognition of independence for the people of Cuba, demanding that the government of Spain relinquish its authority and government on the island of Cuba and Cuban waters and directing that the President of the United States use the land and naval forces of the United States to carry these resolutions into effect."

When the resolution was passed, all that remained was for President McKinley to sign it. After that, a state of war between the United States and Spain would be in effect. He did so and the wheels of war began to roll more rapidly.

The North Atlantic Squadron, under command of Admiral Simpson, formed off Key West and headed for Havana. At about three o'clock one afternoon, the dark medieval towers of Morro Castle loomed ahead. The blockade of Havana was in place—and the Spanish-American War had begun.

★   ★   ★   ★

Commodore Dewey's squadron swung at its moorings on gentle waves in Mirs Bay, a small inlet on the Chinese coast. The fleet was small, consisting of only seven warships, and some military strategists wondered if a force that small could accomplish anything. Dewey wrote in his diary early in the morning: "The prevailing impression is that our squadron is going to certain destruction. In the Hong Kong club, it was not possible to get bets, even with heavy odds, that our expedition would be a success. One of the British officers said at our sailing, 'A fine set of fellows, but unhappily, we shall never see them again.'"

Dewey knew there were some forty naval Spanish vessels in and around Manila. The coastal defenses that were in place seemed formidable. And the Island of Corregidor stood as a fortified sentry guarding the broad entrance to Manila Bay. There were reports that batteries of five- and six-inch guns had been installed there, commanding the entire entrance to the bay. Rumor had it that the bay was full of submerged mines waiting for an incursion of any kind. All in all, the entire invasion seemed a dangerous and foolish undertaking. But as the Asiatic Squadron steamed out into the South China Sea, there were no doubts in the heart or mind of Commodore Dewey. He was a leathery character, exactly the right kind of man to lead a naval squadron against such odds.

The American fleet slipped through the waters under the cover of darkness off the coast of Luzon. Dewey saw at once, however, that the Spanish Fleet was fully armed and waiting for them. "Now we have them," he said. "We shall enter Manila Bay and you will follow the movement of the Flag Ship which will lead."

Lieutenant William Winder, Dewey's nephew, spoke with the commodore after the meeting. "Sir, let me lead my ship through the channel. If she goes down, you'll be safe. It's the one chance I have to become famous."

Dewey smiled and shook his head. "No, Billy, I've waited for sixty years for this opportunity, and as much as I like you, mines or no mines, I'm leading the squadron in myself."

Dewey led the *Olympia* inside Manila Bay. A battery on shore opened up, and artillery rounds whistled around the heads of the sailors on deck. The guns of the fleet returned the fire and the Asiatic Squadron moved ahead. When dawn broke on the horizon, Dewey looked through his binoculars and saw the cluster of black hulls and lofty spars. It was almost five o'clock and daylight was slowly spreading across the bay. "Take her along the fire line, Mr. Catkins. Be careful not to run her aground." The squadron continued to advance, its guns silent. At 5:40 A.M., the *Olympia* had approached within two and a half miles of the enemy vessels. Dewey turned to the warship commander and gave the order that would put his name in every American history book: "You may fire when you are ready, Gridley!"

The American squadron steamed past the Spanish line, half hidden by the clouds of gunfire belching from its own guns. Thick clouds of smoke rolled up from burning ships and the losses were terrible. The Spanish gunners, ill-trained and low on ammunition, could barely return a spasmodic fire. Dewey led the fleet carefully and courageously through the blockades. Finally the enemy batteries could not answer the fire any longer. The Battle of Manila Bay was won and America had a new hero—Commodore George Dewey.

★ ★ ★ ★

The American newspapers blazoned the victory at Manila, and at every street corner newsies stood with their bundle of papers and shouted, "Victory Complete! Glorious, the *Maine* Is Avenged!" The country went wild as the news spread. Roosevelt's final act of insubordination was to release Dewey's telegram to the newspapers. Roosevelt had just been commissioned a Lieutenant Colonel in the U.S.'s first volunteer cavalry, an outfit that was soon to be known as the Rough Riders.

While the country sang the praises of Commodore Dewey, young men from all over the country began clamoring for a place in the army that began to take shape.

Lewis Winslow was one of these enthusiastic young men. At the urging of Alice Cates, he went to find a recruiting office. When he signed his name, he felt a sense of pride well up inside him. He felt himself the most fortunate of young men to be able to risk his life in a glorious adventure. He was an idealistic individual, and though he knew that Alice Cates was instrumental in his enlistment, he was no less convinced that it was his duty as an

American to lay his life on the line for his country. He could do no less, for his father had put his life on the line for the North so many years ago during a long and bloody war. He did not think of being killed or disabled—instead his mind was full of the glorious adventure that lay ahead of him.

When he walked out of the recruiting office, he hailed a cab and headed for Alice's home. Not long after, he pulled up in front of the large estate. Expecting to see the butler when the door opened, he was surprised to see Alice's mother standing there. She was polite at his request to see Alice, but her whole demeanor made Lewis feel that once again he did not meet her "standards" for her daughter.

Alice was coming down the large double stairs that led to the second floor. He looked up and, with pride in his voice, said, "I've enlisted, Alice. I'm going to Cuba."

Running the rest of the way down the stairs, she threw her arms around him and kissed him.

CHAPTER SIX

A Surprising Invitation

★   ★   ★   ★

Carried away by a wave of euphoria such as he'd never known, Lewis Winslow started each new day with a sense of excitement. He spent every evening with Alice Cates, who was thrilled to escort her "soldier" from one mansion to another. The thought had occurred to him once that with every new introduction, she was only presenting him as some sort of exhibition. She often introduced him as "My brave soldier!" It troubled him somewhat, but her flashing eyes and colored cheeks and obvious pride in his new profession-in-arms quickly dismissed any doubts or misgivings he had.

On one of the few nights he was not with Alice, he had accepted a dinner invitation from Esther. After the meal, his uncle Mark sat him down in the library and, for over an hour, tried to reason with Lewis about his sudden decision to join the army. Lewis respected Mark Winslow greatly, but his uncle's logic had little effect on the excitement that had built up in him over the last few weeks.

"Don't you see, Uncle Mark—I've *got* to go!" Lewis exclaimed fervently. "You've read the stories of how the poor Cubans have been hunted down like animals. The Spanish are tyrants and the oppression has got to be stopped!"

Mark Winslow patiently tried to explain that much of the furor raised by the persecution of Cuban peasants had been the result of zealous front-page articles written in the papers of Joseph Pulitzer and William Randolph Hearst. Despite his efforts, however, Mark could not dissuade his stubborn nephew. When Lewis left, Mark turned and stared out the window, worried at what was to become of his nephew. Would Lewis perish in a foolish war in Cuba? Hearing a soft step at the door of the library, he turned and saw Lola standing there. "It's hopeless, Lola. I've done everything I can, but he won't change his mind. I'm wiring Davis and Belle tonight. Maybe they can do something with him!" He spoke pessimistically, however, for Lewis was now twenty-four years old and able to make his own decisions.

★　★　★　★

One bright, sunny day, Lewis made one of his regular visits to the Water Street Mission. He was to meet Alice later for his first trip to Coney Island. While chatting with Gail and Deborah about it, he said, "Why don't the two of you come with us? Have you ever been to Coney Island?"

"No," said Deborah, "but we've heard a lot about it."

He spoke of the newest amusement park, which had once been a very posh resort where millionaires anchored their luxurious yachts. It had soon become a popular park, and now it was crowded with bathing houses, dance halls, shooting galleries, freak shows, and eating establishments. Special trolleys brought holiday throngs, and crowds from every walk of life filled the place.

"I don't think so, Lewis," Deborah said quietly. A smile touched her lips and she added, "You wouldn't have two respectable nurses like us go bathing, I hope!"

Lewis was caught off guard, as he often was, by Deborah's unexpectedly bright sense of humor. It lay beneath her quietness and jumped out at him from time to time. Now he laughed aloud and shrugged his trim shoulders. "That might make quite a headline, mighten it!"

"I don't think Baxter Hospital would care to see two of its female employees portrayed in Mr. Hearst's newspaper."

"Oh, I've seen a few of those bathing costumes, at least some of the Gibson girls paintings. It looks like they have at least ten yards of cloth covering them—more than some women wear to a dance," Lewis argued. "Come on, we can just walk around and see the sights!"

Deborah hesitated, for she was tempted. A time away from the demands of her job at the hospital and the volunteer work at the mission would be a nice change. She had grown very fond of Lewis, though she'd never mentioned her feelings to anyone. But good sense prevailed. She knew Alice would resent any encroachment at what she envisioned as her own private property.

"Thanks for the invitation, though. I hope you have a good time. "

"I can't go either, Lewis," said Gail. "I need to go home."

Something about her wan expression drew Lewis's attention at once. "Trouble at home, Gail?"

"Oh, there's always trouble, I suppose."

Seeing that Gail was upset, Deborah drew Lewis's attention back to herself, saying, "When will you be leaving with your unit, Lewis?"

"I'm not sure—any day, I suppose. It's really quite a mixed-up affair. The country wasn't really ready for a war, and now the War Department is scrambling around trying to organize. I'm ready now—I'd like to go today!"

Though Lewis appeared confident about the whole thing, Deborah sensed a subtle anxiety for some reason and asked quietly, "Aren't you afraid, Lewis?"

"Afraid?" he said, looking at her somewhat surprised.

"Yes, in a war men get killed and wounded."

"Why . . . yes, I suppose I might be a little afraid when the bullets start flying, but it's something that has to be done, Deborah. I hope you can see that!"

As a matter of fact, Deborah was not at all sure of the war fever that was sweeping the country. Nevertheless, she had a steady way about her that enabled her to envision the results. Such enthusiastic, idealistic young men, such as the one that stood before her, might be lying in a shallow grave, or blinded, or missing legs or arms. She sensed, however, that to speak of such things to Lewis was a waste of time. "I'll be praying for you," she said.

Gail had turned away to speak to someone else, so Lewis was

alone with Deborah. He had learned to admire Deborah Laurent, yet he knew there was a wall there that he was never able to penetrate. She was always kind and cheerful, yet something lay behind her dark brown eyes that he could not understand. She was, strangely enough, warm and outgoing at times, while at other times, she seemed almost unapproachable. "What will you do?" he asked abruptly.

"Do? What do you mean?"

"Will you stay on at the hospital?"

"I suppose so—and do my work here at the mission. Now that Rev. Gardner and the others are gone to Africa, the rest of us have to take up the slack."

"You never go out, do you—I mean with young men?" Lewis asked the question abruptly, for he had wondered about such things. Neither Gail nor Deborah seemed to have any inclination toward romance, and now he studied Deborah as she flushed slightly at his question. He could not understand her embarrassment, for it was a normal thing to ask. Both young women were attractive, yet neither of them seemed to be interested in what he assumed most girls spent their time thinking about.

"I have a job to do," Deborah said quietly. She lifted her eyes to him, and for a moment Lewis saw a slight break in her demeanor. She seemed vulnerable and open, and he thought she was going to speak about something personal. Her lips parted slightly and suddenly he was aware that, while she was not beautiful, there was a definite attractiveness in her trim figure and smooth cheeks and features. But she said only, "I suppose that might come some day. Have a good day at Coney Island!"

Lewis left, puzzled by the young woman. *I can't figure out what goes on with that woman*, he thought to himself. *She doesn't act like any young woman I've ever known*. But he was on his way to an afternoon of fun with Alice, so he put the thoughts out of his mind.

★ ★ ★ ★

Later that afternoon, after a long day, when the two girls went back to the room they shared at the hospital, Gail asked, "What do you make of Lewis?"

"Make of him? What do you mean, Gail?"

"I mean, his sudden decision to enlist in the army."

"I think he's caught up in the same fever that has this whole country dancing."

"Why? Does it trouble you?"

"I'd hate to see him come to harm. I've thought so much about all the young men going off to war. It's exciting, I suppose, with the drums beating, the flag flying . . ." She hesitated, then added, "And young women inciting men to join up."

Deborah didn't mention Alice Cates, but Gail knew at once the girl was on her mind. Gail began dressing carefully, putting on her best dress—her pearl gray affair with maroon ribbons on the collar and sleeves. She took more pains than usual, and finally she turned to find Deborah watching her. "Dr. Burns has invited me to dine with him tonight."

Deborah had watched the growing attraction that David Burns had for Gail Summers, though she had not commented on it. Being a very sharp observer of human nature, she had wondered what would happen if a romance sprang up between the two. Now she smiled briefly and said, "You look very pretty. I'm sure he'll be impressed. He always has favored you."

Gail flushed and pouted, saying, "No, that's not so—he's just kind." She settled a small hat on her honey-colored hair, studied her reflection in the small mirror, then smiled. "I'll see you later, Deborah."

When she left their room, she was met almost at once by Dr. Burns, who had just gotten off duty. He smiled when he saw her and said, "That's a pretty dress."

"You say that every time you see it," Gail laughed, her eyes sparkling. "That's very economical." She joined him as they walked down the corridor, adding, "Your wife will never have to buy a new dress—you'll always think the one she has on is new."

Burns shook his head. "I doubt that! Although it would be a Scotsman's dream, wouldn't it!"

Gail smiled at the slight lilt of his Scottish brogue that still colored his words. When they reached the front doors of the hospital, Burns stopped to give the night nurse some instructions, and then they stepped outside. As they turned and walked down the street, she asked, "Are Scotsmen really as stingy as all the stories about them?"

"Every bit," Burns assured her solemnly.

Gail teased him, knowing it was not so. He was not a rich young man, but she already knew that he was generous almost to a fault. It was common knowledge around the hospital halls that some of the most needy patients who couldn't afford some medicine were recipients of the doctor's generosity. She mentioned this now, saying, "Sometimes I think you're more generous because of all the stories. You think you have to disprove that Scots are stingy!"

"Wait till you see the stingy dinner I'm going to buy you tonight," he teased, "then you'll sing a different tune, I'll bound you!"

He took her to a restaurant a few blocks away, and as they entered she said, "This isn't an inexpensive place, Doctor!"

"I may make you wash dishes to pay for your meal," he said with a smile. He was wearing a lightweight gray suit with a spotless white shirt and a narrow lace tie that she'd never seen before. His hair was neatly trimmed, as always, and under his mustache his lips curved in a smile. He turned to the waiter, who seated them at a table near the window. Looking up at the waiter, he said, "Just bring us two pieces of dry bread and two glasses of water."

Gail looked up quickly at the waiter's face and burst into giggles when she saw the disgusted expression. "I'll have to have more than that, Dr. Burns. My work at the hospital of late has given me a hearty appetite."

Burns smiled at her. "I thought you might! Let's see what they have." He made a production out of ordering the special of the day—roast duckling bigarade with chestnut dressing and curried fruit—which turned out to be very good indeed.

Although most people wouldn't have noticed, Gail could sense a certain tension in the young physician. She'd studied this young man for months now and realized long ago that when he was nervous or uncomfortable, he had a habit of stroking his mustache with his forefinger. When he had done that several times during the meal, she thought to herself, *Something's bothering him—trouble of some sort*. She knew so little about his private life, except that he had no family here, that she couldn't imagine what it could be.

When they had finished their meal, Burns ordered ice cream with creme de menthe sauce along with steaming black coffee. As they sat there sipping it, Burns turned to her and said abruptly, "Gail, I want to ask you something."

The use of her first name took her by surprise. Although he'd called her that when they first met, he'd kept to a more formal Miss Summers when they were on duty. Now, however, she saw his blue eyes were troubled somehow. "What is it, Dr. Burns?"

He shrugged his shoulders impatiently. "Well, for one thing, you can call me David when we're not on duty."

"Well, all right . . . David," Gail smiled encouragingly. She saw that he was trying hard to find the words to say something to her, and impulsively she reached over and put her hand on his. She'd never done such a thing before and it startled him. "What is it?" she said. "You seem bothered by something."

The warmth of her hand seemed to encourage the young physician. He suddenly seized her hand, held it for a moment, and then looked down at it. Turning it over, he examined the palm. "I remember the first time I saw this hand all scarred from working at the rope factory," he murmured. "I was very angry when I saw that!"

"I remember that too," Gail said quietly. "I was very frightened—I had never been in a carriage and had never spoken to a gentleman. You were so kind to me that day. I've never forgotten it."

"Haven't you now?" he said, looking up and smiling at her.

"No, of course not." Gail drew her hand back and flushed slightly. "We mustn't be holding hands in public like this, even if I do use your first name."

"I don't suppose the world would stop if someone saw us holding hands," Burns said almost belligerently.

"No, but I might be dismissed," Gail retorted. "What's bothering you, David?" The look on his face made her feel he was going to open up to her, but he changed the subject.

"Young Lewis Winslow's bound and determined to go fight in the war. What do you think of that?"

Sensing he wasn't ready to divulge what was troubling him,

Gail did not press him. "Well, he's young and impressionable. I pray that he'll be safe. Why? Are you troubled about it, David?"

Burns did not answer. He stroked his mustache twice, then lowered his head and clasped his hands. For a moment, he did not speak or look up. Finally he did, and she saw that he was tremendously serious. "I've been asked to serve as a physician with the army on the expedition to Cuba."

Surprise shot through Gail and she stared at him in shock. "Why, you wouldn't do that, would you—leave the hospital, I mean?"

"Yes, I've decided to go." He was watching her carefully, and his face worked unexpectedly. "You may think I'm a fool. Some do, including the chief medical officer of the hospital."

"How did the army happen to come to you?"

"I can't say. I'll be a strange creature indeed with no military training at all, but I think it's typical of the way this army's being thrown together. They need doctors, and so they find a poor young physician that has no family. I think Dr. Stokes brought me to their attention. Anyway, I've decided to go."

"Will you be in the army?"

"Well, technically. I'll wear a uniform and have a rank—but only so long as the war lasts."

Dismay ran through Gail Summers. She had not realized until this moment how much she depended on the steadiness that this young man had brought to her life. If it hadn't been for him, and the program at the hospital, she might still be on the streets. "Why, David, I don't know what to say. I'll be lost without you at the hospital!"

David hesitated, then seemed to seek to find the exact words. "I want to ask you to go with me, Gail," he said hesitatingly.

Gail was even more shocked at his request. "Go with you? Why, what do you mean, David?"

"I've been empowered to take two assistants with me. I'd like for you to be one of them and Deborah to be the other."

"Why, you could get full-fledged nurses to go that are better trained than we are."

"That may be, but that's not what I want." He touched his mustache nervously, then seemed to gain some confidence. "I've prayed about it, and as close as I can discern the will of the guid

Lord, I believe He wants you two to accompany me. I don't know why."

Gail was speechless. If he'd asked her to accompany him to the Himalayas, she could not have been more shocked. She sat there quietly, a tumble of thoughts racing through her head, and then she finally said, "This is too much for me to take in. Have you spoken to Deborah yet?"

"No, not yet—I wanted to ask you first." He leaned back in his chair and shook his head dolefully. "I know it's a wild and crazy thing to ask of a young woman. It'll be hard and dirty—and dangerous."

Gail sat there trying to put her thoughts together. Finally, she shook her head, saying quietly, "I'll have to pray about it, David. How long would we be gone?"

"That I don't know for sure," he said. "Until the war is over, I suppose. There's no way of knowing when that will be."

"It'll be hard for me to leave Jeb. He's having trouble as it is."

"I knew that would be your first thought, and I have no answer for you." As he saw the struggle going on inside her, he realized it was futile to argue and said, "If you will pray about it, I would be obliged to you. I don't think there's much time. This army's going to be leaving soon, and we need to give notice at the hospital as soon as possible."

Suddenly, in the midst of her thoughts, Gail became conscious of a strange sense of the presence of the Lord. It had happened a few other times in services when she was praying. At those special times, she had felt God draw very close to her. Now in the crowded restaurant with the clatter of dishes and the hum of voices, it happened again. She sat very still and concentrated on what was happening. After a few moments, she looked at David with surprise on her face. "The strangest thing just happened," she whispered. "It was as though God were speaking to me just as He sometimes does."

"And what did He say, Gail?"

Gail Summers distrusted sudden visions and instant decisions. She had known too many people who said confidently, "The Lord told me. . . ." Some of them, she had been aware, had been following their own inclinations. Being a conservative young woman, she hesitated for a moment. But finally she looked into his eyes and said quietly, "I seem to feel that God is telling me to go with you. But I'll have to wait. It's not something I can decide right now."

Hope leaped into the eyes of the young physician, and he straightened his shoulders. "I'll not rush you," he said. "But I'll pray with you. I wouldn't want you to go if God said no. But if He does say yes, somehow I feel there is a work to be done among the young men who'll be dying out there. Who knows—maybe there's one young man that'll need the Gospel from Miss Gail Summers."

Gail had not thought of that possibility. She tried to imagine what it would be like to be in the middle of a war. It was impossible to know, and finally she said, "I'll pray about it, David."

It was two days later that Dr. Burns looked up from bending over a patient in a bed and found Gail standing on the other side of it, her eyes bright as diamonds. He knew instantly what she had come to say. Leaving the patient, he took her arm and they moved outside into the hall. "What is it, Gail?" he asked.

Gail's lips trembled and tears came into her eyes. "I'll go with you. The Lord has told me that there is work for me to do. Deborah's going too."

"God be thanked!" David breathed. He wanted to reach out and take the young woman in his arms, but instead he put his hands behind his back and squeezed them together. He took a deep breath and a smile came to his lips. "Now," he said warmly, "we'll see what the guid Lord will do with us in Cuba!"

PART TWO

WHEN KINGS GO FORTH

★ ★ ★ ★

CHAPTER SEVEN

A PAINFUL VISIT

★ ★ ★ ★

After the numbing cold he had suffered in the Klondike, Aaron Winslow felt strange descending into the spring weather of San Francisco. As soon as the grubby freighter *Meteor* anchored and lowered the plank onto the busy wharf, he disembarked, carrying a single suitcase. Almost instantly Aaron discovered that gold madness was still infectious in the States. As soon as he got into a cab, the driver began talking about the strike in the Yukon. When Aaron inadvertently mentioned that he'd just come from the Klondike, the driver, a round-faced man with a bristly mustache and moon eyes, stopped the team abruptly and began firing questions at him.

Aaron answered the inquiries briefly, then growing irritated, he snapped, "Take me to the station. I've got to catch a train out of here." From the scowl on the man's face, he knew the driver was insulted, but Aaron didn't care. He sat back moodily, not even looking out the window at the city he'd heard so much about. Ordinarily, Aaron Winslow would have been eagerly taking in the sights, but a weariness lay along his nerves, and the long white silences of the Yukon had changed him.

The bustling activity of the wharves and the crowded streets made him want to leave as soon as possible. After what seemed like a very long ride, he climbed out of the cab, paid the driver the exact amount of the fare, and moved with the flow of the crowd that was streaming into the busy railroad terminal.

"Ticket for one to Independence," he said through the tiny window.

"I can ticket you through, but you'll have to change trains," the agent nodded. He was a tall, dignified-looking man with meek blue eyes and an inoffensive air. When Aaron nodded, the agent worked with a set of tickets, punching them and fastening them together. Handing them over, he said, "That'll be $46.93."

As Aaron paid the fare, he was conscious of the thinness of the small packet of bills that he stuck back into his pocket. "What time does the train leave?" he asked.

"Two seventeen," said the man, motioning for the next person to step up to the window.

Aaron shoved the tickets into his shirt pocket and turned and walked away. He made his way through the crowd of waiting passengers and walked outside to the small cafe next door to the station and entered. It was almost vacant, and when he sat down at the table, the proprietor, a tall man with bleak gray eyes, sauntered over. "What'll you have?" he asked. "We ain't got dinner ready yet."

"Anything—you got sandwiches?" Aaron ordered a beef sandwich, and then sat there drinking a cup of coffee the man had set before him.

As he waited for his food, a woman at a table a short ways away looked across at him. Finishing her meal, she put a coin on the counter, rose, and walked by. She walked more slowly as she passed Winslow, who lifted his eyes and met her smile with a blank look of indifference. Giving a sniff, the woman clutched her reticule more tightly and swept out of the restaurant.

Aaron stared at his hands. They were rough and calloused from his time in the Klondike. He thought of Cass and Serena and wondered if they'd struck it rich yet. Then the bitter memory of Jubal's death clouded his thoughts, turning his smooth face rugged, and he swept his hand across his face in an impatient gesture. The meal came soon and he ate it without enjoyment. For over an hour he sat there drinking cup after cup of steaming hot black coffee.

Finally, he walked back to the station and waited until the boarding call for his train was announced. Moving quickly, as though anxious to shake the city from his mind, Aaron boarded the car, which was one of the new sleeping cars. It was only half-filled, so he chose a seat by a window. Soon a hoarse scream from the engine split the afternoon air. The train jerked, gathered speed, then moved out of the station through the outskirts of the city and finally into the open country. As San Francisco faded from sight, Aaron Winslow expelled a deep breath and leaned back in his seat, staring out at the landscape as it rolled by. Shrouded in a dark moodiness, his hooded gray eyes did not see the trees or the horizon as it moved quickly by. *I've got to stop thinking about it*, he thought desperately. *Jubal's dead, and there's nothing I can do to bring him back.*

He thought how different his trip to the Klondike had been . . . less than a year ago. Aaron had made the train ride from the East in what was called a "zulu" car. They were rough, unadorned cars for passengers, filled mostly by immigrants heading west to start a new life. At times he and Jubal had felt strangely out of place. Though they were clicking across the tracks headed west, English was not the prevailing sound in the zulu cars. They heard so many different languages, they thought they were abroad in some foreign country. The journey to the West Coast had been long and arduous. Aaron and Jubal had lived on groceries sold from car to car by raucous vendors. Often they had been sidetracked for scheduled trains and delayed by sudden washouts. It wasn't long before both men had grown weary from all the delays. There had been hasty stops at station lunch counters, which usually lasted ten minutes. The food was often poor and the prices were outrageous.

But now on the trip back east, Aaron found himself traveling in luxury. He took his meals in an ornate dining car. He had little money left, but he ordered the best on the menu—oysters, lobster, and fine wine—at a table covered with a white tablecloth and attended by a black steward who grinned at him with flashing white teeth when he brought the food. Setting the large china plate filled with lobster in front of Aaron, the steward grabbed the folded napkin on the table and snapped it open for him. A bit surprised at the motion, Aaron mumbled his thanks and started to eat.

At night he slept comfortably in a bed transformed out of one of the seats. The car was carpeted and the chair-beds were made of plush cushions, unlike anything he'd seen before.

If Aaron had been his usual, cheerful self, it would have been an exciting time for him. Yet he couldn't shake his somber mood and spent hour after hour staring out as the scenery changed. He rode the Central Pacific through the Sierra Nevada Mountains, arriving at the Great Salt Lakes, where he changed to the Union Pacific. As the train chugged by Fort Sanders, spewing a pillar of smoke, he thought, *Uncle Mark probably helped tame this town when he was helping build the railroad.* Just past Fort Sanders, he disembarked and waited for ten hours to mount a car attached to a coal burner with "Kansas Pacific Railroad" painted across the side. This train carried him through Denver, then wheeled east and out across the open plains. On the second day, the engineer came through the car calling out, "Independence! All out for Independence!"

Aaron quickly grabbed his bag and was the first in the aisle to get out of the car. As soon as he stepped onto the platform, he looked around, then asked the conductor, who was helping a woman off the train, "How do you get to Jefferson Barracks?"

"I don't know—ask the stationmaster."

Aaron made his way across the broad, open platform and moved through the people to the outside, where three buggies were drawn up waiting. "I need a ride to Jefferson Barracks."

A small man in the first carriage straightened up and said, "I can take you there for a dollar fifty."

Aaron threw his bag into the back, climbed up into the seat and nodded. The cab driver pulled his hat down over his face and picked up the lines. With a flick of the wrists he called out, "Right! Hup, Babe—Horace!"

The team stepped out and twenty minutes later they had cleared the outer city. The intense April sunshine beat down on the barren landscape, which already seemed to be baked as if in preparation for the hot, dry summer. The cab driver sat silently, and Aaron was grateful, for his head was full of thoughts after the long trip. Finally, the driver pointed with his buggy whip and said, "There's Jefferson, right over there!"

"Do you know where the adjutant's office is?" asked Aaron.

"Sure do!" The driver wheeled the buggy down the center of a parade ground and pulled the horses to a stop.

Aaron handed him two dollars, saying, "Thanks for the ride." Then grabbing his bag, he stepped down. The driver nodded, then clicked to the horses and the team moved off, the wheels raising a cloud of fine dust.

Aaron turned and saw a sign that read "Adjutant" over a narrow door near the end of a row of buildings. He entered and found a corporal with his arm in a sling sitting at a small desk and staring moodily down at a stack of papers.

"Help you, sir?" asked the officer in a bored tone.

"I'm looking for Colonel Winslow."

"Well, he's already gone home." It was late in the afternoon and the sun had begun to drop below the horizon.

"Where will I find that?" Aaron asked mildly when the corporal seemed to have ended the conversation. The man was busy shuffling through his papers when Aaron said, "My name is Winslow. I need to see the colonel." At once, the corporal looked up and blinked—the name of Winslow stirred him, and he sat up straighter and put a more amiable look on his face.

"Why, yes, sir—come along and I'll show you." Rising with alacrity, the officer led Aaron out the front door and pointed down the parade ground. "Go down till you come to the end of this street, turn right and just keep going. It's a big white house with pillars, sitting on the left under some cottonwood trees. You can't miss it."

"Thanks, Corporal!"

For a moment Aaron considered calling the cab driver back, but the buggy was already disappearing down the road in a cloud of dust. He shrugged and was glad for the chance to stretch his legs. The slow trip on board ship and the long train ride had been galling to him. Moving swiftly down the dusty avenue, Aaron turned a corner and soon was standing before a white-framed house shaded by six tall cottonwood trees. A white picket fence circled the house, and a tall, skinny private was listlessly pulling weeds in a small garden.

Aaron strolled past the soldier and walked up the front steps. Reaching the top, he thought, *I'd rather do anything than knock on this door!* He stood there immobile, shocked at how difficult the simple task of meeting Jubal's parents was turning out to be. He'd traveled thousands of miles—but now he wanted nothing so much as to turn and flee. He gritted his teeth and, with a forced effort, pulled his shoulders back and knocked firmly on the door.

After a moment's pause, it opened and a woman stood there. "Aaron!" Faith Winslow's eyes opened wide with shock, then she shoved the door open. Before Aaron could move, his aunt threw her arms around him. He held her awkwardly, his face frozen in an expressionless mask. She looked up, and seeing the shadow in his eyes, her lips turned gentle. "Come inside," she said quietly. As he stepped inside and put his suitcase down, Faith called, "Tom! Tom! Aaron's here!"

Almost instantly, Colonel Tom Winslow stepped out of the door down the hall. He was wearing an old uniform blouse and suspenders that revealed his lanky form—still youthful for his years. He came at once with his hand outstretched and a genuine smile on his face. "Welcome, Aaron! Come in—come in! It's good to see you."

Aaron cringed inside as the two drew him into the kitchen. "You must be hungry!" Faith said. "Did you just get in on the train?"

"Yes." Aaron found he could say no more than that one brief word. His uncle and aunt were as cheerful as he remembered them at the family reunion. For years he'd admired his uncle Thomas, a career officer in the United States Army. Tom Winslow had served with Custer's Seventh, being one of the few to escape annihilation at Little Bighorn. Since then, his career had been distinguished a number of times for his bravery and meritorious service. In fact, he was one of the finest line officers in the United States Army, as Aaron understood it.

As Faith busily set about heating a meal, Tom spoke of their daughter Laurie and her husband Cody Rogers. He explained that they used to perform with Buffalo Bill's Wild West Show, but were now ranching near his parents, Dan and Hope Winslow. Tom leaned forward, clasping his strong hands before him, and told Aaron that their youngest daughter was not home. "Ruth's gone out to a revival meeting in Independence. She'll be back late, I expect." Tom stared at the young man and asked, "Was it a hard trip back?"

Aaron shook his head. "No . . . not hard." He struggled to find something to say, but his throat seemed constricted. All he could think of was that Tom and Faith Winslow had lost their only son to the dangers of the Klondike. The clawing guilt that had plagued him since the avalanche came back to him as he thought of how he might have dissuaded Jubal Winslow from making the trip. The young man had been as excited as he had been, but as Aaron sat there thinking back, an overwhelming sense of grief and bitterness gripped him. *I should've said no. He'd still be alive if I had.*

Right then, Faith came and set a plate heaped with hot beef, warmed-up beans, fried potatoes, and corn bread on the table, saying, "Here . . . I'm sure you're hungry—with the trip and all."

Aaron was glad for the distraction, for he did not want to talk. He picked up his fork and tried to eat, but the food seemed to stick in his throat. Finally, he laid his fork down and said hoarsely, "I'm . . . I'm sorry about Jubal." The words had to be forced from taut lips that grew white when he pressed them together. It was not what he really wanted to say. Everything inside him wanted to cry out with bitterness that it was unfair, and that he should've known better than to take the boy. He could not meet their eyes, but sat there staring bitterly at the floor with grief-stricken eyes.

Quickly, Tom Winslow glanced over at Faith. They both grasped at once the terrible guilt that weighed down the man before them. In a voice that was strangely gentle, Tom said, "You must not blame yourself, Aaron. Jubal went of his own free will with our blessing. We all knew that it was a dangerous undertaking. We knew the risks that he might face."

Faith was standing at the stove getting more coffee. She put it down and came back to stand behind Aaron. "You've got to forgive yourself." Her voice was gentle, and yet her hand on his shoulder seemed to burn into Aaron.

Aaron said bitterly, "If I'd made him stay here, he'd be alive!"

"You don't know that—he might have been killed in a runaway wagon or gotten cholera. You've got no cause to blame yourself, Aaron," Tom said. The loss of his only son had been a pain worse than anything he'd ever known. He was, however, a man of strong Christian faith, and he and Faith through much prayer had come to grips with their terrible loss. Now Tom saw that Aaron did not have the same resources to handle such a tragedy. "Do you want to tell us about it?" he asked quietly.

Aaron hesitated, then blurted out, "Yes!" He felt relieved that he finally had a chance to unburden himself, to get it all out. He sat back in his chair and began to speak, slowly and with awkward pauses. "He was always cheerful," he said slowly. "I never heard him complain about anything. It was terrible trudging up those mud-covered passes, and the cold was the devil. The rest of us griped all the time, but Jubal never did. . . ."

Faith and Tom sat there taking in his words, and when Aaron

spoke of how Jubal's Christian faith had never wavered, how he'd witnessed of Christ to everyone he encountered, they smiled at each other. Faith lifted the corner of the apron she was wearing and wiped the tears from her eyes, but they were not tears of bitterness. They were ones of a mother who was proud of the life of her son.

Finally, Aaron halted. "He was the finest Christian I ever knew," he said hoarsely. "I'd give anything to bring him back. . . !"

Tom could tell that Aaron was stretched almost past the limit. "We'll talk about it more. Come on—I'll show you your room." Aaron followed his uncle to his room, and while he unpacked, Tom returned to the kitchen. "That young man is in bad shape, Faith. He's carrying a heavy burden. Grief can kill a man—maybe not as quick as a bullet, but just as painfully."

"He doesn't know the Lord, Tom," Faith said quietly. "He doesn't have a means of dealing with all this."

"I know," said Tom.

The two sat in silence at the table thinking of their son. They'd dreamed of a full life for him, as all parents do, and now he was gone. Finally it was Tom who said, "We'll have to do what we can to help bring Aaron out of this. He can't go on hating himself like this. Did you see his eyes? I've never seen such bitterness!"

Faith reached across to Tom. He took her hands and squeezed them. "We'll have to turn it over to God. Maybe Ruth can help. She's good at talking with people who are hurting."

Aaron was still up when Ruth came back. He was sitting on the front porch talking idly with Tom. It was after ten o'clock, and he had managed to gain some control of his nerves. When he heard the sound of a carriage, he stood as it stopped in front of the house. Out of the darkness a soft voice spoke, then a young woman came up the walkway.

"Look, Ruth—Aaron's here! All the way back from the Klondike!"

Ruth Winslow halted abruptly. The light from the oil-burning lamp filtered through the window and revealed a tall girl with light-colored eyes. Seeing her cousin on the porch, Ruth came to him at once. A smile curled her lips upward as she grabbed his hands and said, "I'm so glad to see you, Aaron! I want to hear all about Jubal."

"Not tonight!" Faith said quickly, knowing that Aaron could not face any more talk about his cousin. "You can hear all that tomorrow. Now, tell us all about the meeting."

Aaron stood for a while, listening to the three talk about the revival meeting Ruth had attended in Independence. He was glad his aunt Faith had averted any more talk about Jubal, for he knew he could not bear to speak of it right then. It had been hard enough to face Jubal's parents, but to talk about it again with Ruth would be too much. *I won't stay long*, he thought to himself. *This is no good—my being here—but I had to come.*

★   ★   ★   ★

All the next day, Aaron forced himself to be cheerful around his relatives—but it proved extremely difficult. He kept seeing the face of Jubal in the features of his parents, and he could not put it aside. Finally, he said at supper, "I've got to get back and see my folks."

"Stay a few days, Aaron," Faith urged. "We'd love to have you." She saw, however, that he'd already made up his mind and she nodded. "I know that Davis and Belle are anxious to see you. They wrote us and mentioned how much they've missed you." She went to him and put her hand on his shoulder. "Aaron, your uncle and I are so glad you came. It has helped us a great deal to hear about Jubal."

Later that night after Tom and Faith had gone to bed, Ruth came to Aaron as he sat on the front porch staring blankly out into the night. She was one of those women who, despite her cheerful ebullience, was able to listen well. After a long time, he found himself speaking about Jubal without being aware of it. He told of the time that Jubal had stood up and preached a sermon. "He was a good preacher," Aaron said softly, thinking of the time he had gone and heard Jubal preach in a feed store that had been converted into a church. "He preached on Jonah. I remember he said, 'A greater than Jonah is here.' It was a sermon on the resurrection of Jesus, and he made it all so . . . so *real*! Since the day I heard him, I haven't been able to get away from that sermon, Ruth." He turned and stared at the girl, whose face was silhouetted by the silvery light of the moon. "What Jubal said kept coming back to me. 'If you could find the tomb of Buddha, you'd find a body in it. And if you could find the grave of Confucius, that man would be there, but the tomb of Jesus Christ is *empty*!' " Aaron leaned forward and put his chin in his hands, thinking of that time. He said no more, but Ruth somehow sensed that her brother's stirring sermon had tremendously impacted this tall cousin of hers, who sat beside her staring out into the darkness of the night.

She wanted to urge Aaron to accept that Gospel, but somehow she felt the Spirit of God restraining her from saying anything. *He's not ready yet*, something seemed to say to her. *You must pray that he will be made ready.*

The silence dragged on until finally Aaron spoke with a distinct strain in his voice. "There's something I haven't told you."

"What's that, Aaron?" Ruth asked quietly, leaning forward to see his face. She saw that his lips were pulled tightly together, and even as she watched, he reached up and passed his hand over his face in an involuntary, almost helpless gesture. It was a strange sort of movement, yet enough to reveal the frustration and bitterness she had sensed in him from the moment she'd seen him.

"I . . . I told you and your folks how Jubal had died—that he was buried in snow from an avalanche and that we couldn't get him out in time."

"Yes, you've told us about that," said Ruth, waiting for him to go on.

"What I . . . what I *didn't* tell you was that when the snow came down at us, it came so fast I couldn't move. We were all out on a ledge and I . . . I just *stood* there! I froze and couldn't move. It was Jubal who grabbed me and shoved me back, away from the outer edge. I fell back and looked up just in time to see Jubal thrown over the edge by the avalanche." Aaron's voice had grown unsteady. He grasped his hands together tightly and his voice was a rasp. "If he hadn't done that, Ruth—he could've saved himself!" He struggled for a moment, then turned to look at her, his grief making his eyes bright in the pale moonlight. "He gave his life for mine—that's what I'm trying to tell you. And it's not right—Jubal's the one who should have lived, not me."

Ruth Winslow reached over and gently pulled Aaron's hands away from his face. She saw how tortured he was by the memory of her brother's death. She understood his pain and loss, for she and Jubal had been close—closer than most brothers and sisters. Her life had been tied to his, and when the news reached them that he was dead, it was as if the sun had been stricken from the sky.

Leaning forward, holding his hands tightly, she said, "Aaron, you must stop blaming yourself!"

"How can I help it?" His voice was bitter and the twisted features of Aaron Winslow's face revealed the heavy guilt he was suffering.

"It will destroy you if you don't put it aside," Ruth said.

"Put it aside?" Aaron snapped. "How can I do that? It's like I killed him!"

"No—that's not true!" Ruth shook his hands gently. "Listen to me, Aaron, please!" She waited until he calmed down, then said, "Jubal is with God now. His time on earth had meaning. Why, he was the one who led me to Jesus Christ, and he gave his life to save yours. That's more than some men do in a whole lifetime."

"Then why did God let him die?"

"We can never know things like that, but let me tell you this—" Ruth took a deep breath and continued, "His life will have whatever meaning you give it, Aaron." She saw his head jerk up at her words. He turned to stare at her, and then, she said even more slowly, "If your life is wasted, then so is his death. But if you do something great, it will be Jubal's work in a way, because he made it possible for you to do it."

Far away a dog howled stridently, then barked in a staccato fashion. Aaron sat there silently trying to make sense of Ruth's words. Finally he rose and said, "He was a fine man. I'd give anything, even my own life, to bring him back, but I can't do it!" Quickly he turned and went into the house.

The next day, Aaron left, and it was Ruth who followed him out to the carriage. The last thing she said to him, lifting her face to his, was in a whisper, "Remember, only you can make Jubal's life have meaning!"

Aaron stared at her, nodded, then solemnly climbed into the carriage and rode to the station. As the train carried him farther east, clattering over the rails, he thought about Tom Winslow and Faith and Ruth. *They've got a faith most don't have—and my folks have it too.* Most of all, he thought about what Ruth had said about Jubal. He could make little of it, for the bitterness within him still burned his spirit. Strangely enough, as the train wound its way toward the East, he felt better. Facing Jubal's family had been one of the hardest things he'd ever had to do in his life, but that was over. Now as the wheels clicked out a steady cadence, Aaron Winslow took a deep breath and looked out the window, wondering what the future held for him.

CHAPTER EIGHT

AARON MAKES A PROMISE

★　★　★　★

"Who could that be at this hour!" Davis Winslow rubbed his eyes and sat up abruptly in the large poster bed at the sound of pounding on the front door.

Across from him, Belle stirred and sat up as well. As Davis fumbled about, throwing his feet out of the bed and feeling for his slippers, she said, "I can't imagine! I hope nothing's wrong at the college!"

Pulling on his robe, Davis groped his way out of the bedroom, pausing to pull a cord that dangled in the center of the hallway. The new electric lights that had been recently installed in the college president's home flicked on. And as always, he was a little shocked by the bright light that instantly illuminated the hall. He was a very conservative man, this Davis Winslow, and he was fond of saying, "I've seen a lot of changes in my lifetime, and I've been against most every one of them!" However, he was grateful for this new wonder, if for no other reason than the lights saved his eyes for his long hours of reading every night.

Reaching the front door, he pulled it open and stood there, staring blankly at the tall figure in front of him. "Aaron! What in the world—"

"The bad penny's come home again, Dad!" Aaron smiled. He allowed his father to pull him through the door, and then he set his suitcase down. "I should have taken a hotel room, I guess, rather than wake you up in the middle of the night. It's after two o'clock."

"Aaron!" Belle entered the foyer and moved across the floor quickly, tying the belt to her robe. She threw her arms around Aaron's neck, and he bent over and kissed her noisily on the cheek. They clung to each other for a moment, for they'd always had a warm relationship. Belle often said, "You get all that devilment in you from me, Aaron! I was just like you when I was your age!" Stepping back, she reached up and laid her hand on his stubbled cheek. "Why didn't you wire us and tell us you were coming?"

Aaron stretched his shoulders wearily. "You never know when these blasted trains will get in!" He grinned at his father, adding, "Why don't you do something about that? This one was two hours late!"

"Come on in, son," Davis said, grabbing Aaron by the arm. They led him into the kitchen, and Belle stirred up the fire and began to heat the coffee. For half an hour they pumped him with questions faster than he could answer, until finally he threw up his hands. "Not so fast—you don't have to know everything at once, do you?"

But Belle and Davis were anxious to hear all about their son's travels. Belle poured the coffee, scalding hot as Davis liked it, and the three sat down. The two older people listened eagerly as Aaron told them of his time in the Klondike.

As president of a college, Davis had learned how to read young men. Listening to Aaron's story, he saw that something was troubling this son of his. Finally, as Aaron finished, Davis understood what was burdening his son. "You're hurting over Jubal's death, aren't you, son?"

Aaron shot a startled glance at his father. "You always could read my mind, Dad," he muttered. Leaning forward, he put his chin on his hand—looking suddenly very young. "Who wouldn't be?" he said quietly. "It was my fault he died. If he hadn't rushed to shove me out of the way, I think he would have made it."

"He was a fine young man," Belle whispered. She reached over and took Aaron's hand in hers and held it. "We'll never forget him, and I'm forever grateful to him."

There was a stubborn set in Aaron's face, she saw, and he said, "It's not fair! He had his whole life before him and now he's gone."

Belle shot a quick glance at her husband, then said, "How are his folks taking it?"

"Better than I am!"

"Tom and Faith have always been strong people in the Lord," Davis remarked. Realizing that it would do little good to talk at the moment, Davis skillfully led the questioning to other things about Aaron's trip.

Belle listened quietly, and then finally said, "We've got to get this young man to bed. We've got lots of time to talk later."

"That suits me," Aaron said, glad to end the talk about Jubal's death. He stood up, picked up his suitcase, and headed up the stairs toward his room. "I'm hungry for some of your good pancakes, Mother," he called out. "I've missed those more than anything else!"

Belle called back, "You'll have them for breakfast—all you can eat!"

As his footsteps faded down the upstairs hallway, Belle turned and said, "He's not doing well, Davis. He's hurting terribly over Jubal's death."

A troubled light flickered over Davis's eyes, and he ran his hand through his thick hair and shook his head. "You can't blame him for that, dear. I saw it happen a number of times in the war. It seemed like that was one of the worst things—when a man saved someone else, the fellow who lived sometimes never got over it. Thank God that Jubal was a Christian and is with the Lord now!"

"Yes," Belle said thoughtfully. She looked up the long stairway that led to the second floor and could hear Aaron shutting the door to his room. "He's got a streak of something in him that I've never seen before. I'm worried about him, Davis. We'll have to talk more tomorrow."

* * * *

The next day after a sumptuous breakfast of pancakes with rich syrup, Aaron and Davis sat talking. After the maid had cleared the table, they all moved into the drawing room. Aaron sat in a chair across from a cream-colored divan where his parents sat and said, "I feel out of place. At my age a man should have a vocation, a calling, and I don't have the vaguest idea of what to do, and I know you're disappointed about it."

"That's not true," Davis said instantly. "Lots of men don't find themselves until they're much older than you are." He stared at his son's face, then said, "Would you like to go back to college? We'll see to it if you would."

"I'm a little bit old to be a schoolboy," Aaron said, shifting his weight on the chair uncomfortably. "I'd hoped to strike it rich in the Klondike," he grinned sardonically. "Then I could just be a rich bum! I suppose that's all I'm suited for." He thought for a moment, then said, "I'd sure like to see Cass and Serena make a big strike, but I guess that's a long shot."

Belle bit her lip nervously and said, "Aaron, your father and I are worried about Lewis."

"Lewis? What about him? He's in New York with Uncle Mark, isn't he?"

"Yes," Davis answered slowly. "He went there hoping Mark could find him a job in the railroad. He really doesn't know what he wants to do either."

Aaron laughed shortly. "How does it feel to have two worthless sons that can't make up their own minds? You must be real proud of that."

There was a sharpness in his voice that neither of his parents had ever heard. They both realized instantly that the experience in the Klondike had done something to Aaron that was not good. There was a caustic quality about him that had not been there before he left.

Davis said quietly, "You'll have children of your own one day, Aaron. You'll learn that they might not always do what you'd like for them to—but they're still yours. I'm proud of you and Lewis. You're just slow in finding your way, but so was I. I thought I wanted to go to Europe and be a writer until the Lord—and your mother—came along." He smiled at Belle warmly. "I've never been sorry for it. It's not a very exciting life being president of a college, but I like to think I'm doing some good."

"Well, I don't know what good I could do. Maybe I ought to go to New York and see Uncle Mark. There's some excitement in railroading, you know!" His eyes lit up as he thought about the travels he'd had. "I wouldn't mind being an engineer or a brakeman, or just working on the train."

"Mark would be happy to help you, if that's what you want," Belle said quickly. She hesitated, then said, "I wish you would go to New York—for another reason."

"Another reason?"

"I wish you'd go talk to Lewis. He's in trouble, I think."

Instantly, Aaron was alert. "You mean, trouble with the law?"

"Oh no, nothing like that!" Davis said, holding up his hand in protest. "It's this war. Mark and Lola wrote us and said he's bound and determined to get involved with it, and we're afraid he'll get himself killed."

Aaron listened to what his father had to say about the sinking of the *Maine*, then shook his head. "We heard about it in the Klondike. Is the country as wild over this Spanish thing as we read about in the papers?"

"Yes. Everybody wants to go as a soldier—all the young men, anyway," Davis said. "Many of them see it as a great adventure for them, and you know Lewis—he's an incurable romantic. He sees himself as leading a charge and saving the Cubans from the oppressive tyranny of the Spaniards."

"He's always been that way," Aaron observed. "But he outgrew most of his strange notions without getting shot at." As he thought about what his parents had said, he noticed they were watching him, waiting. Surprised, he said, "You don't think I could really change his mind, do you? You've both tried!"

"I don't know whether you could or not," said his mother, "but I wish you'd go and talk with him. He needs someone right now. It'd be a good chance for you to talk to Mark, too."

Aaron sat very still, thinking hard. Finally he nodded, "Why, of course I'll go—and I think I'd better leave right away. From what I read in the papers, the army's getting pulled together right now. And I heard that Teddy Roosevelt is getting a volunteer cavalry group ready to go."

"That's the one Lewis is trying to get into, but it's hard," said Davis.

"But if he doesn't get into that, he'll volunteer for something else. New York's putting together a volunteer regiment," Belle said quickly.

Aaron made up his mind instantly. "Well, I don't know if I can do any good, but I'll go have a try. I wonder when the next train leaves?"

"There's one at three fifteen this afternoon," Davis said. "I hear the whistle every day from my office at the college." He was troubled about this older son of his and said plaintively, "Do your best, Aaron. You two have always been close, so maybe he'll listen to you."

"No reason why he should," Aaron said, shrugging his shoulders. "I haven't been exactly the best example in the world for Lewis—but I'll do the best I can."

That afternoon when the train pulled out, Belle and Davis stood on the platform watching. They waved at Aaron as he leaned out the window with a smile on his face. As they turned to leave, Davis said, "You know, Belle, I think I'm more worried about Aaron than I am about Lewis."

"I know. He's changed, hasn't he?"

"He could turn bad and go sour. I've seen it happen to men who can't find their way."

"I think Jubal's death has affected him even worse than he lets on. He feels awfully guilty, and when anyone does that, it can eat away at them."

The two continued walking slowly away from the tracks. The engine gave a shrill blast that seemed somehow to have a warning note in it. And as they left the station, neither of them could find the words to say what was in their hearts about these two young men who were their sons.

CHAPTER NINE

A STUBBORN YOUNG MAN

★   ★   ★   ★

The first week in May was waning as Aaron stepped off the train at Grand Central Station. He was stunned by the grandeur and immensity of the place and paused for a moment to gaze across the rows and rows of tracks. They were filled, it seemed, with huge chuffing behemoths—steel locomotives that belched great billowing gusts of steam—that threatened to engulf the throngs of passengers. As crowded as the station was, it took some time to buy a ticket for the smaller commuter train that made its way to his uncle's home. It was late afternoon and the shadows were long when he stepped off the train at the small station. A short, stubby Irishman standing beside the entrance to the station called out cheerfully, "Cab, sir?"

"I'm looking for my uncle's home—his name's Mark Winslow."

"Ah, yes, I know the place. Can I help you, sir, with your bag?"

Twenty minutes later, Aaron was walking up the tree-lined entrance to the Winslow residence. When he reached the door, it opened and his aunt Lola came out smiling. "I saw you coming, Aaron!" She reached up and gave him a quick embrace. "Lewis isn't here, but he'll be back shortly. Please come inside."

Aaron followed her inside to the large entryway. She called to a servant to carry his bag upstairs, then turned to take his arm.

"Come out to the arbor—it's cooler there." She led the way down a path to a grape arbor. A soft breeze fluttered the green leaves overhead, masking the brilliant sun. The two sat down at a white table, and Lola poured two glasses of lemonade from a crystal pitcher that a servant had brought out on a silver tray.

"Now, tell me about your travels," said Lola as she sipped the cold lemonade.

Aaron leaned back and spoke briefly of some of his experiences in the Klondike. "Uncle Mark's not here?" he asked finally.

"He'll be here tomorrow. He had to take the train to Chicago a few days ago on business." Lola leaned forward and studied Aaron's face. *Such a handsome young man,* she thought, *but there's something troubling him.* Aloud she said, "I suppose Davis and Belle are worried about Lewis. Your uncle and I wired them with our concerns."

"Yes, that's really why I came, Aunt Lola. What's going on with him?"

"It's this war," Lola said. "He's caught up in it like everybody else."

"It sounds like a pretty serious thing. From what I've read and heard on the trip up here, those Cubans need rescuing, don't they?"

Lola shook her head. "Don't you go believing all that foolishness. It's a newspaper war mostly. Mark's looked into it very thoroughly. Have you ever heard of William Randolph Hearst?"

"Why, just that he's some kind of newspaperman."

"Well, I'm afraid he's at the bottom of most of it. His father was called Wasteful Willie Hearst and was an enormously wealthy man—made a fortune in the newspaper business in California. Hearst came to New York and bought the *Journal*. He's determined to accomplish the same thing his father did in San Francisco, and he's been looking for some sort of 'cause' ever since." Lola leaned back and shook her head distastefully. "This situation in Cuba has given him a golden opportunity. It's got villains, gore, gunrunners, adventure—everything he needs for a headline story to stir up people."

"I don't see how one man can do so much—or one newspaper," said Aaron.

"Oh, they keep up a steady front-page sensation about the so-called atrocity in Cuba. Look at this!" She picked up a paper from the table and placed her finger on a sentence. "Look—it explains how the Spanish troops have 'resumed the inhuman practice of beating Cuban prisoners to death and even drowning them and feeding prisoners to sharks!' That sort of story's been going on every day, and it's got the whole country worked up to a fever pitch ready for war."

"And Lewis is ready to join up?"

"Ready? He's already gone ahead and signed the papers! He's waiting for a place with Roosevelt's Rough Riders, as they call them. He's dying to get in!" Lola snorted and shook her head. "I admire Mr. Roosevelt as a politician, but he's no soldier."

Aaron leaned back and sipped the lemonade. He listened to the pleasant hum of bees as they buzzed around the clover that bordered the grape arbor. He thought of the contrast this warm comfortable setting was to the frozen, icy waste of the Klondike. For a moment he wondered what Cass and Serena were doing at this time. Finally, he said slowly, "I'll talk to him, Aunt Lola. I don't know how much good it will do, though."

"It's not just the war," Lola said abruptly. "There's a girl involved."

"A girl?"

"Yes, her name is Alice Cates. She's a wealthy, young socialite—a beautiful girl, but I never have seen a more selfish one. Lewis has lost his senses and gone crazy over her."

"What does she have to do with his going to war?"

"Her latest fad was the bicycle, but now it's all the excitement surrounding the war. She's always caught up with a cause or some celebrity or other. When the strongman Sandow came to New York, she got into a physical culture kick. Everybody had to lift barbells and things like that to look like Sandow."

"Doesn't sound like she'd be too attractive to me," Aaron observed.

"She is, though—a beautiful girl! Lewis can't see straight when he's around her. She's taken him as her escort to dozens of social galas. He's quite caught up in it all. Esther can tell you about it— she goes everywhere with them. She'll be in later this afternoon." Lola bit her lip, then shook her head with a discouraging motion.

"I don't want to be negative, but Lewis is a very stubborn young man."

As she smiled suddenly, Aaron saw some of the youthful attractiveness that she'd had as a young woman, and he wondered what she must have looked like then.

"All Winslow men are stubborn, and I expect that you're no exception! But we'll do the best we can. God can help us."

At the mention of God, Aaron ducked his head, and Lola saw that he had thrown up a wall. Quickly she said, "Come along and I'll show you to your room. Lewis and Esther will be home soon."

Aaron followed her back to the house and upstairs, where she left him inside a large room. He stripped off his coat and shoes, then lay down on the bed, tired after his long journey. He had just dozed off to sleep, when he woke with a start, hearing voices outside in the hall. Suddenly, the door burst open and Lewis came barreling in, his face alight at the sight of his brother. "Aaron! Why didn't you tell me you were coming!" He threw his coat on a chair, and then tackled Aaron, throwing his arm around him as Aaron struggled to get out of bed. The two fell backward and the bed collapsed with a crash.

"You crazy fool! Get off me!" Aaron cried out.

But Lewis hung on to him, ruffled his brother's hair, then moved back, saying, "Gosh, I'm glad to see you! Tell me about the Klondike! What about Cass?"

Aaron struggled to his feet, then looked ruefully at the bed. "First, let's put the bed back together, then we can talk."

As the two reassembled the fractured bed, Aaron related some of his trip to the Klondike to his brother. They had just set it back together and put the mattress on when he turned and shook his head. "I didn't get rich." He hesitated, then said grimly, "And Jubal was killed. I wish I'd never heard of the place."

Lewis, who was a sensitive young man, could sense his brother's heavy burden. Putting his hand on Aaron's shoulder, he said, "I know—but we'll talk about it later. Come downstairs and see Esther."

"Just a minute! Before we go down—Mom and Dad are worried about you signing up with the army. They both think you're making a mistake."

"Oh, Aaron, they just don't understand! They're stuck away

in a little college town in an ivory tower. They have no idea of the oppression the Cubans are suffering from the Spanish. We've got to fight for the freedom of those people."

"From what I hear, it's more of a newspaper fight than anything else."

Lewis's face reddened and his lips met in a stubborn line. Shaking his head obstinately, he said, "No—that's not right! That's what some people are saying about it, but if it were our people being butchered by a military dictator, they'd feel differently. And they'd do something!"

"Sit down and let's talk about it, Lewis," Aaron said.

"I'll hear you out, Aaron. I at least owe you that as my brother," said Lewis.

The two sat down, and for the next half hour, Aaron tried everything he knew to convince Lewis to change his mind. He quickly saw, however, that it was like arguing with a stone wall. Lewis's mind was made up, and nothing he could say was going to change it. Finally, he said diplomatically, "Well, let's go talk to Esther. We can talk more about this later."

"It's good to see you, Aaron, but I've got my mind set on this."

The two went downstairs and Aaron renewed his acquaintance with his cousin Esther, a young woman whose beauty he admired. She threw her arms around him and smiled, saying, "Aaron! I'm so glad you've come! Now you can tell everyone about the Yukon—gold, sled dogs, and everything. . . !"

★ ★ ★ ★

The following day, Aaron accompanied Lewis and Esther to a party at the Cates' estate. Actually, after hearing a little from Esther the night before, Aaron was anxious to go meet the young woman who seemed to wield so much power over Lewis.

As the carriage pulled up to the house, Aaron looked around and remarked, "Some shack!" The Cates' mansion was an enormous Georgian house built of red brick, with a sweeping driveway that led to a set of pillars standing like two sentries at the front entrance. When they reached the large front door and knocked, they were met by a tall butler dressed in a dark suit, who smiled at once, saying, "Mr. Winslow—Miss Cates said to bring you to her as soon as you arrived."

"Where is she, Jordan?" Lewis asked eagerly.

"The guests are meeting in the small ballroom on the east side. Do you know where it is, or should I take you?"

"I know the way," Lewis said. "Come along!" He led Aaron and Esther down a series of halls and then through a double door. Inside, at least thirty people were gathered in the large room, and the sound of animated conversation bubbled through the air. It was growing dark, but two large chandeliers glittered overhead, throwing their golden light across the polished hard-pine floor. At once, a young woman dressed in a cream-colored gown with an emerald necklace adorning her neck separated herself from a group and came forward, saying, "Lewis, where have you been? You're late!"

"I'm sorry," Lewis said, taking the young woman's hands. "I had to wait on this brother of mine—he's always late. Let me introduce—my brother, Aaron Winslow. This is Alice Cates, Aaron."

Alice put her hand out, and when Aaron took it, she said, "I've heard so much about you! Come, sit down—we want to hear all about your adventure in the Yukon. Everybody's talking about it!"

"I'm afraid I'm not one of the winners, Miss Cates," Aaron shrugged. "For every ten people who went looking for gold, nine of them came back discouraged and, in fact, empty-handed. I'm one of the quitters."

"Oh, I can't believe that!" Alice said, raising her eyebrows in an arched look. "Come now—there are some gentlemen who were just talking about this." She led them to a small cluster of men who were standing around a table savoring some hors d'oeuvres a servant had just brought in. One of them turned at once. He had a long face, matched with an equally long nose and a pair of pale blue eyes.

"Mr. Hearst, you were talking about the Klondike, and this is Mr. Aaron Winslow—he's just returned from there! Aaron, this is Mr. William Randolph Hearst, the newspaper publisher."

Aaron shook the hand of the newspaper tycoon and found it strong and firm.

"I'm glad to meet you, Winslow," Hearst said. "You say you've just come back from the Yukon?"

"I've still got some of the mud on my feet, Mr. Hearst. But I'm no expert—I got stopped at the Chilkoot Pass."

"I'd like to hear all about it," Hearst said. As the others listened, he began to draw Aaron out, and the young man soon found that Hearst had an analytical mind. He was a natural-born conversationalist, always interested in hearing about people's lives. Hearst probed Aaron's experience and had the newpaperman's gift for picking out the dramatic details. The whole time, Alice clung to Lewis's arm, listening intently to Aaron's description of the hardships he faced in the far north.

After a while, Aaron grew restless from all the questions. "Really, Mr. Hearst, I'm not the man to tell you about all of this. Surely there are others with more experience, and more success."

"No, no, my young man. Americans want to know what's going on. You may not have made it to the gold fields, but just the struggle to get there—they're interested in that and in the people who are making this great venture!" Hearst stood there silently for a moment, then said, "Would it be possible for you to write down some of your experiences? I think there'd be some interesting points that could make for a feature story."

"Why, I'm no writer!" scoffed Aaron.

"Of course you're a writer," Lewis said, nudging him suddenly. "Remember how you were always writing something in college. It would be a good chance for you to get your experiences before the public."

Of all the things Aaron did *not* want, getting his experience "before the public" was one of them. The death of Jubal still burned in Aaron like an open and painful wound. He wanted to put all that behind him and get on with his life. Suddenly, now he was being asked to lay it bare before the public. Not knowing why, he shrugged, and said, "I'll do the best I can, Mr. Hearst."

"Fine—Fine!" Mr. Hearst beamed. "Why don't you bring it by my office tomorrow. If you come early enough, we can print it in the next day's *Journal*."

The rest of the party was an eye-opening experience for Aaron. He'd never been around extremely wealthy people before, and some of the men there, along with Hearst, were among the top magnates in the country, wielding considerable political and financial power.

Aaron, however, was more interested in Alice Cates than in

railroad tycoons and political buffoons. He did not have to maneuver her into a corner to talk, for he had not been there any longer than half an hour when she sought him out, leaving Lewis talking with a group of friends.

"I want to know all about you, and especially about Lewis. I'm sure you have some stories you could tell." She led him by the arm to a quiet alcove, and when anyone approached them, she waved them off with an autocratic gesture. Aaron readily spoke of Lewis and of himself in earlier days. After a few minutes, he finally understood why she was so interested. When she began to speak of the war, her eyes grew brighter. Grabbing his arm, she said, "Isn't it noble for Lewis to join the forces to go to free the Cubans?"

At first Aaron felt strangely tempted to tell her what he actually thought, but instead he said rather diplomatically, "Lewis is a very idealistic man. I'm not too surprised at his decision."

His lack of enthusiasm at what she believed to be an honorable cause prompted Alice to look at him in dismay. "Don't you feel the same way, Aaron?"

"I really don't know what I feel. I've been out of the country while this whole thing was brewing. I haven't had much time to think about it."

Alice beamed one of her coquettish smiles at him and said, "Oh, when you hear more about it you'll change your mind. My father's a friend of Mr. Roosevelt. I'm quite positive I'm going to be able to get Lewis into the Rough Riders." She hesitated, then said, "I think he might make a place for two, if I ask him."

Aaron smiled. She was a bold young woman, and he could tell she was accustomed to getting her own way. He shook his head and said, "Well—give me a few days to think about that."

Right then, a tall, dark admirer of Alice's walked up and insisted on whisking her away for a dance. Aaron stood and watched as the two walked back to the ballroom floor.

The party went on until nearly midnight, when Esther finally convinced Lewis it was time to go. Aaron and Esther walked to the carriage that had been brought around, and waited a few minutes as Lewis lingered in an arbor to say goodbye to Alice.

As the three made their way home, Lewis turned to his brother and asked eagerly, "Well, what did you think of Alice?"

"She's a beautiful young woman."

"Oh, I know that—I mean, what do think about her as a person?"

"Never seen a stronger one," Aaron said truthfully. He tried somehow to think of a way to warn Lewis against the girl, but he was aware that his brother would not welcome any criticism of Alice Cates. Tentatively, he said, "It was an interesting time. I heard so many new ideas and insights tonight, I'll have to think about it." He paused a moment, and then said, "I have to write that piece for Hearst, too."

"Maybe he'll give you a job as a reporter and send you back to the Klondike or something," Esther said.

"He might make me a reporter, but I'm not going back to the Yukon," Aaron said flatly. His statement brought a somber silence into the carriage.

"Well, we can talk about it tomorrow," said Lewis as they rode on.

★ ★ ★ ★

For the next two days, Aaron stayed as close to Lewis as he could. If he thought, however, to have any influence on the young man, he was sorely mistaken, for Lewis was adamant in his decision. Aaron discussed the matter with Mark, who returned from Chicago the following day. "He's just like a runaway train on a downhill track, Uncle Mark," Aaron complained. He shook his head, a despondent expression in his eyes. "He's bound and determined to get his head blown off, and he doesn't have the vaguest idea of what war is all about!"

Mark looked at his nephew and said, "I'm afraid you're right, Aaron! I'm sorry to hear it, but it's the same everywhere. Young men are trying to get in and can't." His eyes grew thoughtful and he said, "I wish we could have had some of these fellows when we were trying to hold the fort back in the Civil War. We finally wound up using sixteen- and seventeen-year-olds, and even men in their sixties. Now here are all these young fellows, by the thousands, trying to join up and get into a fight they don't even understand."

"Well, I'll keep trying," Aaron said. "I took the story in to

Hearst about the Yukon," he said suddenly. "I felt like a fool walking into that big office of his! I'm no newspaperman. Hearst glanced over it and seemed to like it, though."

"Don't give up on Lewis. Maybe you'll be able to pound some sense into his head."

"No, I won't give up. I'm going to some mission on Water Street with him tonight. I promised him that."

"It's an interesting place. You know that Barney and Andy are on their way to Africa now. They were pretty instrumental in starting and keeping the mission going before they left." He spoke of his two sons with pride, thinking of them as they headed to the dark continent. "Now, there's an adventure for you!" he said. "Going to Africa! That's better than any war in Cuba, I say."

"I'll agree with that, Uncle Mark. Still, I've got to do something quick."

"It's happening very rapidly," Mark said, nodding. "I wouldn't be surprised if they moved within a month and set sail for Cuba with a fleet."

That night, Aaron accompanied Lewis to the Water Street Mission. He was reluctant to go in and take a seat, for he was still bitter and did not want to hear anything about God. He was, however, interested in talking more with young Dr. David Burns, whom he had met briefly before the service. He'd been informed by Lewis that Burns was to accompany the troops to Cuba. As soon as the service was finished, Aaron walked up to the doctor and said, "I understand that you are going to Cuba as a surgeon with the army?"

"Yes, that's true, Mr. Winslow."

"You believe in the cause, then, I take it?"

Burns gave him a friendly smile. "I believe there'll be a lot of sick and wounded men, many of whom will probably die. Whatever the cause is—they'll need medical attention."

Aaron took a liking to the young doctor at once. There was an honesty in his forthright reply, and Aaron felt inclined to say, "I'm worried about my brother. He's dying to go, and I'm determined to keep him out of it."

"I doubt if ye can do that," Burns shrugged. "He's on fire about the thing." He would have said more, but he turned and said, "Ah, let me introduce ye to my two assistants." He led Aaron over to where two young women were standing and talking. "Mr. Aaron Winslow, this is Miss Gail Summers and Miss Deborah Laurent." There was a proud look in his eyes as he said, "These two women are also going to accompany me and be my nurses in the field."

Aaron was surprised to hear that two attractive young ladies had volunteered for such a cause. Soon he found himself talking alone to Gail Summers while the doctor took Deborah Laurent off to help collect the songbooks. "I'm surprised, Miss Summers," Aaron said. "I didn't know women like you were caught up in the Cuban issue."

Gail studied the tall young man. She'd heard much about him from Lewis and saw that he was better looking and larger than Lewis. His reply somehow troubled her and she said simply, "I'm going because God has told me to!"

Aaron blinked in surprise at her answer. It would have sounded pious from the lips of most people, but this young woman had a steadiness in her gaze that he found hard to meet. "I'm . . . I'm sure that's true," he said. He hesitated for a moment and said, "I had a friend that you remind me of." He was thinking about Jubal and how he had the same kind of steady faith in God, and the thought was painful to him.

Gail saw something dark flicker in his eyes and said, "Is there something wrong? What about your friend?"

"He's dead," said Aaron flatly.

Gail was slightly rebuffed by the harsh reply. She could sense that this was a part of Aaron Winslow's life that he had shut, and would not allow anyone to approach. "I'm sorry," she said quietly and turned and moved away.

Later that night on the way home, Aaron said, "Gail Summers is an attractive woman and pretty blunt too, I might add."

"Blunt?" Lewis raised his eyebrows in puzzlement. "Gail's very gentle, I think. Oh, you mean about her testimony. Yes, she came up the hard way. If you'd grown up in poverty in an overcrowded tenement with an abusive stepfather like she did, you'd probably feel the same way. When you get to know her, you'll think better of her."

"That's not likely. She's going to Cuba," Aaron said.

Lewis looked at Aaron in surprise, and started to say something but stopped.

It was a subject that had pushed the two brothers further apart—the matter of Cuba and Lewis's enlisting. They said little the rest of the way home, and later that night, Aaron sat down to write a long letter to his parents. He confessed his failure to change Lewis's mind and finally wrote, "And so my trip's been unsuccessful. Lewis is resolute in his decision to go to Cuba. If I could, I'd knock him in the head, kidnap him, and drag him home. But aside from keeping him locked up, there is no way of preventing him from becoming involved in this war. I'm sorry that I couldn't do better."

He put his pen down, stared at the words he'd written, and for a long time sat there thinking hard. Somehow he felt that failing with Lewis was the same as failing Jubal. The image of Jubal's face floated before him, and he shut his eyes and leaned forward, putting his forehead in his hands. He ran his hands through his hair almost in desperation. *He could get killed in this fool war—just like Jubal got killed in that avalanche.* The thought of losing his brother was almost more than he could bear. Finally, he straightened up and walked over and opened the window. He stared outside where the moonlight was casting silvery beams down on the trees that lined the spacious yard. From outside, the smell of mellow earth and flowers pressing through to spread their fragrance in the air came to him.

"I've got to do *something*," he said aloud, frustrated at the sense of helplessness he felt. "I've just got to do *something*!"

CHAPTER TEN

OUT OF THE NIGHT

★ ★ ★ ★

The following afternoon, Aaron made his way to the Bowery. He took some time to walk around the streets of Lower Manhattan. He'd been told that Broadway, which was the home of the fashionable elegant during the day, was haunted at night by prostitutes, con men, and assorted criminals. He wandered around Fifth Avenue, noting that the older houses had been torn down and replaced by Italian-style mansions, French chateaux, and gothic castles. He found something repelling about the street that was now lined with ornate mansions and gaming establishments catering to the wealthy.

When he arrived at Baxter Hospital, he couldn't help noticing that it had not been set among the opulent dwellings of the affluent. He wondered why the powers that be had even condescended to grant the poor and unfortunate of the city such a benefit. It was a rather plain building sitting squarely in the center of the notorious slums of Five Points.

He had heard that certain organizations had stirred an interest among the wealthy to fund such a place. Perhaps it had been built more out of a need to appear in the social spotlight of the city than a heartfelt gesture to help the poor and destitute of Five Points. Looking up at its plain facade, he climbed the stairs and entered the square three-story red-brick building, seeking Gail Summers.

The nurse at the entrance was helpful, and he found Gail without any difficulty.

She was busy helping an elderly patient back into bed when he walked up behind her and said, "I hate to bother people who actually have something to do." He grinned rather crookedly when she turned. "Can you take time out for a cup of tea or whatever it is you drink?"

Gail was surprised to see Aaron at the hospital. She was wearing her white hospital uniform and looked rather pretty. "I'm sorry, Mr. Winslow, but I don't have time for tea. I must finish up here, and then I have an errand to run. I hardly even have time to change clothes first."

Quickly Aaron responded, "Would it be all right if I went with you? And I'm Aaron, by the way, not Mr. Winslow."

Gail hesitated at his kind offer. "It would be helpful," she admitted. "I have to pick up a load of food that's been donated to the mission. I could actually use some help loading it."

"Well, then, I'm your man! You go ahead and change. I'll wait right here for you."

Gail left hurriedly for her small room. Almost as soon as she disappeared, Dr. Burns came striding down the hall. "Ah, guid afternoon to you, Mr. Winslow! Not sick I hope!" A bit of humor glinted in the eye of the young physician. "You look well and healthy to me!"

"Healthy as a horse, Dr. Burns!" Aaron said cheerfully. "I've agreed to go with Nurse Summers on an errand to pick up some food and take it to the mission."

"Ah, yes, some of the merchants in the neighborhood heard about our work and are very generous to the Water Street Mission. I wish I could go myself, but I've a full schedule today." Dr. Burns examined Aaron carefully and said, "You and your brother don't resemble each other too much."

"No, we don't—and we're even more different than we look," said Aaron amiably.

"Oh, how's that?" asked the doctor.

"Why, Lewis is a romantic, as you can guess from his charging off to join this war—" Aaron broke off suddenly, adding, "But then you're going also, so maybe you're a romantic as well."

"I've never been called that," Dr. Burns protested, a slight

smile curling his lips. "What about yourself? You have no romance in your soul, Mr. Winslow?"

"Not a speck! I'm a hard-nosed realist." Aaron nodded firmly.
The corners of his mouth turned upward as he grinned and
shrugged his broad shoulders. "A lot of romantic fools went for
the adventure of the gold rush in the Klondike—I just went along
to get rich. But I didn't, of course. That's what usually happens
with romantic ventures."

The two men chatted pleasantly for a while. Aaron liked the
young doctor very much. He found the Scotsman intelligent,
witty, and knowledgeable on a number of subjects. For one fairly
new to the city, he seemed to be quite informed on many of the
pressing needs of the people. From his views, and his involve-
ment at the mission, Aaron could tell Dr. Burns was a man of action—one who threw his energy into trying to make a change.

When Gail reappeared from her room, fastening a hat on her
head, she said, "Oh, Dr. Burns—Aaron's going to help me take the
groceries to the mission! Will we see you at the meeting tonight?"

"Very likely, Gail! I have a few more patients to check on, but
I plan to be there."

Gail led Aaron out of the hospital and down the steps to the
street. "I have the use of a wagon, but I don't know how to drive
one."

"Well, I do!" Aaron said cheerfully. "I'm no expert horseman,
but I guess I can handle a team as well as most men."

"Oh, that's a relief!" Gail said. "I thought I was going to have
to hire a man to drive me. Come along!"

She led him down a side street toward a livery stable, where
a hostler hitched a team of two large geldings to a wagon.

Aaron took her hand and helped her up on the front seat.
Climbing up beside her, he took the reins, and soon they were
driving along the busy streets of Lower Manhattan. They made
three stops at grocery stores, and at each place, Aaron helped load
the wagon with crates of food donated by merchants who had
taken an interest in the work at the mission. He listened as Gail
praised each one of the businessmen effusively and told them God
would not forget their kindness. When they had made their last
stop, he said, "It's decent of the men to do that."

"Oh yes—I think most people want to help," said Gail, looking back and smiling at the loaded wagon.

Aaron said nothing and sat on the wagon seat, holding the lines in his hands. "I'm glad you think that," he finally said quietly. "I hope you always do."

Gail turned to him quickly and could not miss the skeptical look on Aaron's face. She did not argue, for she had been quick enough to see that he was a man who had put up a shield between himself and the world.

They arrived at the mission and were met by the new director—a tall man named Robert Johnson. He was thrilled about the food that had been donated and insisted, "Now, you just go inside while I have some of the fellows help unload all of it. Your brother's inside, Miss Summers, playing the piano. I guess you can hear him."

Gail's face lit up at once, and Aaron was surprised at how pretty it made her look. "Your brother plays the piano?" he asked.

"He . . . he'd like to, but there's never been any money for him to take real lessons."

Aaron helped Gail down from the wagon. When they stepped inside, the notes of the out-of-tune, tinny piano filled the building. He smiled at the young boy who was sitting on a box in front of a battered upright piano and putting his heart and soul into his playing.

"He's really enjoying that, isn't he?" Aaron whispered to Gail.

Gail turned to him and nodded, her eyes bright, yet she shook her head in despair. "He could be a fine musician, if he just had a little help! I'm trying to find him a good teacher to give him lessons, but they're so expensive."

"I had lessons when I was about his age," Aaron remarked. He shook his head in mock despair. "It drove me crazy. Every time my mother told me it was time to practice, I was ready to run away from home. I hated every minute of it, but I can see that your brother loves it. He's got a real gift for it."

As Gail approached, she said, "That's very good, Jeb! A new tune?"

Jeb was so caught up in the music that he was startled at the sound of her voice right behind him. He turned around, his eyes blinking. "Aw, sis, you scared me! I didn't know anybody was here."

"Mr. Winslow and I came by to bring some food that's been donated." She went over, laid a hand on his shoulder, and said, "I didn't know that tune. What was it?"

"Aw, just one I made up myself." His eyes went to Aaron, and he studied the tall man carefully, more in the fashion of an adult than a young man.

"This is Mr. Aaron Winslow. Do you remember Barney?"

"Oh, sure! Are you his brother?"

"No, just a cousin, I'm afraid. How are you, Jeb?" Aaron put out his hand, and the small boy stared at it for a moment, as if it were a menacing object. Then he reached out and timidly shook it. "I wish I could play like that, Jeb!" Aaron remarked. "But you have to have talent, and I don't have any—for music."

"Mr. Winslow's been in the Yukon, though. He can tell you a few interesting stories about the gold strikes up there, Jeb."

Instantly, Jeb turned and said, "Gosh, is that right? Did you find a lot of gold? Is it true like the papers said? Are there big nuggets of gold just lying in the streams for the taking? Are you rich?"

"Jeb!" Gail flushed and laughed, almost nervously. "You shouldn't ask anyone if they're rich!"

"Why, it ain't nothing to be ashamed of, is it?" said Jeb, staring at the man innocently.

Aaron laughed at the boy's candor. "Some people act like it is, but I'd like to try it, wouldn't you?"

"Sure would!" said Jeb.

"What would you buy?"

"A big piano and somebody to teach me to play!"

Aaron nodded. "Well, that's a noble ambition. And it's not out of reach."

Jeb's face darkened. "Yeah, it is," he muttered. "It costs too much money."

Gail said quickly, "Let's go to the kitchen. Maybe we can have a glass of milk while they're unloading the wagon."

Aaron followed Gail to the kitchen, where she was greeted with enthusiasm by her former co-workers. She poured them each a glass of milk from the ice box, and then they went to sit at one of the wooden tables with the men who came to the mission. Aaron sipped the cold milk, then held it up and looked at it. "This is good milk," he said. "I've always loved milk, but I never seemed to get enough of it when I was a boy."

"Me too." She drank thirstily, then said, "I always thought heaven would be to have a cow and have all the fresh milk I wanted."

Aaron sat there chatting with the girl for a while, then finally asked, "You'll be leaving soon, I suppose. Are you ready for the war?"

"I'm a little bit nervous now that it's all settled. But I don't know when we'll be leaving yet." She glanced over in the direction of the tinny piano music and said in a low voice, "It's mostly Jeb that I'm worried about. I hate to go off and leave him. Things are still not going well for him at home."

"Well, I don't think this war will last long. You'll probably be back in a month or so." He set the empty glass down on the table, twirled it with his fingers, and sat there silently for a moment. Finally, he looked up and studied the girl. "What about Lewis—" he said. "Have you asked him about going into the army?"

Gail stared at him in surprise. "Why, that's all he can talk about these days!" She smiled quickly, saying, "He's the most excited one of the bunch." Noting the tension in the tall man's face, she said, "You're against his going, aren't you, Aaron?"

"Yes I am, and so are my parents. In fact, they sent me here to try to talk him out of it, but I'm not having any luck. Lewis is stubborn and won't listen to any sound advice."

"I don't think anyone could talk him out of it," Gail answered simply. "He's made up his mind. He's going, and that's all there is to it."

"I expect you're right, but I at least had to try for my parents' sake."

The two sat there talking for some time, and when they got up to leave, they found Reverend Johnson, the director, waiting for them near the entrance. "I left two big boxes of groceries in the wagon, Gail. Take them home to your folks."

Gail's cheeks flushed and she dropped her eyes at his kindness. "Thank you very much. I'm sure they could use it."

"Maybe I'd better get Jeb to go on home now. It's going to be dark pretty soon. It's getting late already."

Jeb started to protest, but Aaron said, "How'd you like to drive, Jeb?"

The boy stared up at him, his eyes big with doubt. "You don't mean it!"

"Sure I do! Come on—you sit here. I'll sit in the middle and your sister can sit over here."

Gail objected, saying, "Really, Aaron, I don't think he's ever driven before!"

"Well, it's time he began, then. Come on, Jeb! Hop up."

Jeb scrambled onto the seat, and Aaron sat down beside him, while Gail settled herself firmly on the far side. "Here—here's the way you hold the lines. Got 'em? Fine! Now then, we're ready!"

"But—what do I do?" asked Jeb, unsure about what to do next.

"Say, 'Giddyup!' and slap the lines on their rears."

Jeb looked at the large horses doubtfully. Then he lifted the lines, slapped the horses, and said, "Giddyup!" in a timid voice. At once the horses pulled against their harness and began to move forward. Jeb was startled and asked, "What do I do next, Mr. Winslow?"

"Well, you pull that left line to get us out on our side of the street and away from the curb. If you want to go right, pull the right line—if you want to go left, pull the left one. If you want to stop, pull both of them and say, 'Whoa!' "

It was a delightful time for Jeb Summers. Most of his young life had been spent learning to fend for himself on the street or trying to avoid a thrashing from his angry stepfather. Aaron Winslow's interest in the boy had surprised him at first.

As they rode along, Aaron smiled to himself at the boy's obvious pleasure at having a chance to drive the wagon. When Gail looked over at him, Aaron winked and saw her smile at seeing her brother enjoying himself. Fortunately, there was very little traffic on the street, and unknown to the boy, Aaron was poised, ready to grab the lines in case of any sign of trouble. By the time they pulled up in front of the tenement where he lived, Jeb was feeling quite pleased with himself.

"Gosh, Mr. Winslow, I bet I could drive a stagecoach!"

"I bet you could, Jeb," Aaron said smiling. He had found it refreshing to be with the boy and said, "Now, pull over there and say, 'Whoa,' and we'll get these groceries inside."

Jeb pulled on the lines, and after a few tries, he managed to get the wagon pulled approximately in the right position. Aaron said, "Now, wrap those lines around that wagon seat—right there." He showed the boy how to do it, then jumped down. "You're a certified driver now, Jeb! It was fun, wasn't it?"

"Sure was!"

Jeb leaped to the ground and Aaron reached up, and to Gail's surprise, he held out his hand. A flush crept up her neck, but she took his hand and let him help her to the ground. She turned to Jeb, whose eyes were still beaming, as he was excited over his newly acquired skill. "That was nice of you—"

"Well, lookee here at what we got—!"

Gail turned at once to see two large, burly men come rolling down the sidewalk. Both of them were obviously half drunk, which made them seem more dangerous. One of them, a lanky, hulking man wearing a pair of yellow suspenders, grinned loosely, showing a slug of tobacco tucked down around yellow teeth. "We've got gentry down here, Jiggs!" he sneered, then spit an amber stream on the sidewalk.

"Right you are, Bill!" Jiggs was short, but tremendously wide, and so corpulent that his neck seemed to be swallowed up by his muscular shoulders. He was wearing a ragged-looking pair of pants, held up by what appeared to be a length of braided cord. His chest swelled out against his black-and-white checkered shirt. "They look to me like they'd want to make a contribution to the cause!"

Aaron's nerves, at once, grew tense. He knew trouble when he saw it and quickly glanced around. There were no police down in this section of the city, and he thought grimly, *Those two probably noticed that!*

"Let the lady and the boy go on in and I'll talk to you two fellows."

But the shorter of the two suddenly reached out and caught Gail by the arm. "Naw, they ain't in no hurry. You just fork over a little coin—enough for me and my partner here to have an evening's fun."

"Let the lady go!" Aaron said, bristling. He was studying the taller man, who was grinning widely. There was a vacant looseness in his catfish-shaped mouth, but his arms were long and he had knotty-looking fists.

Aaron reached forward and chopped down on the forearm of the man called Jiggs. "I said, let the lady go! Gail, get on in—"

He had no chance to finish, for with a roar of anger, the man named Jiggs threw a roundhouse right that caught Aaron unaware. It struck him in the chest with such force that it drove him backward. He felt a deadly cold from the force of the blow.

"Get 'em, Bill!" Harry cried.

"I'll kick his teeth out," the stocky man laughed. He stepped forward, drew his foot back, and when he sent it forward, Aaron managed to roll over, taking the force of it on his shoulder instead of in the kidney or face. It numbed his whole side and he rolled quickly, kicking like a cat until he sprang to his feet.

Jiggs let out another roar of anger and ran straight at him, lowering his head. Aaron simply reached out and grabbed him by his massive neck, then whirled around. Like a whiplash, he sent the man sprawling through the air. Jiggs hit the ground with a muffled thud, rolled, and came up more dangerous than ever. The fall didn't even seem to hurt him.

"Look out!" Aaron had turned his back on the taller man, and suddenly the sound of Jeb's voice warned him. He whirled to see Jeb fastened like a leech onto the taller man. He had stopped, and was cursing and trying to shake himself free of the boy. Instantly, Aaron shot as hard a blow as he'd ever thrown in his life straight into the nose of the tall, gangly fellow. He felt the nose break, and a wild scream came from Bill as he fell backward. Gail reached over and dragged Jeb away. Aaron stood there watching Bill, when from behind he heard the feet of the muscular Jiggs. Whirling, he waited and put his left hand up, paring a powerful, sweeping left. Stepping inside, he deliberately threw a hard punch and struck low in Jiggs' stomach. When the man doubled over, Aaron raised his arm and brought his forearm down like a club on the man's thick neck. Jiggs dropped to his hands and knees, but he was not out—he was shaking his head.

"Take the boy upstairs, Gail!" Aaron ordered.

Gail, wasting no time, pulled Jeb away from the fight. He did not want to go, and loudly protested as she pulled him inside where the two waited.

Aaron put his fingers in his mouth and let out a piercing whistle. "I hope that'll bring the law," he said, breathing a little harder than usual as he looked at the two men sprawled out on the ground. Harry was holding his broken nose, moaning, and Jiggs was still on his knees shaking his head. "But if you don't get out of here right now, I'll break your necks!"

Both men crawled to their feet. They stood there staring at Winslow, and for one instant, Jiggs seemed inclined to continue the fray, but when Aaron stepped forward and drew his fist back, Jiggs threw his arms up. "All right—all right!" he said. "We're going. Come on, Bill."

Aaron watched as the two men limped away down the dark street. *I'll have to be careful later. They might be waiting for me*, he thought as they disappeared into the shadows.

He moved to the doorway of the tenement and instantly Jeb came flying out. "Gosh, Mr. Winslow! I never seen nothing like it—you whipped 'em both and they was both bigger than you!"

Aaron felt pleased at the boy's adulation. "Well, they weren't exactly in good shape. Here, let me get the groceries—those ruffians might come back."

★ ★ ★ ★

The two spent a brief time visiting with Gail's folks. Aaron felt sympathy for the girl when he saw the squalor she had grown up in. Her stepfather was withdrawn, and her mother was too beaten down by such a hard life to do more than smile. He was amazed at how Gail had overcome such a background, but said nothing. They took the wagon back to the livery stable, but before they left, Aaron promised to take Jeb horseback riding the next morning. He had no idea where a stable or riding path was, but the boy had appealed to him, and he could not turn down the earnest look in Jeb's eyes.

Now as they came to the hospital, they walked slowly. It was not late, but the city was strangely quiet. "It looks like the hospital's put itself to bed," Aaron remarked, "I'd miss the birds chirping and the dogs howling if I lived here."

"Do you live on a farm?"

"More or less—it's a small town right in the middle of some of the nicest country you ever saw."

They'd reached the side door of the hospital and Gail turned.

"That must be nice," she said. She paused and leaned back, suddenly looking up at him. "Thank you so much for helping me, especially for what you did with those men."

"I'm glad I was there," Aaron said. He stood looking down at her. She was a tall girl, taller than most, and had entered young womanhood with an attractiveness that was pleasing. Her face was lifted up just enough so that he could see her eyes shining in the soft moonlight. If she'd been any other girl, he might have tried to kiss her. But somehow that didn't seem appropriate. Instead, he smiled and said, "I'll be going to take Jeb horseback riding tomorrow morning. Would you like to go?"

"No," she said quickly. "But it's good of you to take Jeb." She hesitated. "He hasn't had much of a time—Jeb hasn't. It's been hard for him and I'm worried about him. Bart and Riley won't have anything to do with him. And he's starting to run with the wrong crowd."

"He's a good boy, I can see that."

"Yes, he is, but you have no idea how hard it is out on the streets, Aaron. Every day's a battle to stay alive—just to keep from getting hurt."

Aaron nodded. "It's been hard on you too, Gail. But things will be better now. You're a nurse's assistant and you can do something for your family." She smiled at him again. This time there was a contentment in her expression. He sensed a calmness there, too, and a serenity that he found appealing.

"Yes," she said, as if something troubled her. She took a deep breath, then said, "Good-night, and thank you for everything."

As he turned and moved away, he thought, *I wonder what's troubling her?* He had no answer and walked slowly down the street until he found a carriage. He'd been moved by the girl's innocence. It was obvious that her convictions and simple faith had kept her even in her terrible circumstances. Many girls her same age had long since thrown their lives away in the brothels and bars that filled the darkened streets of Five Points. "I don't think I could have been that strong," he said aloud as the carriage jolted along. Then he let his thoughts run back to the boy. *Maybe I can do something to help him,* he thought as he rode down the dark street. The thought pleased him, and he realized that he needed to do things like that—perhaps as much as the boy needed it.

CHAPTER ELEVEN

A VOLUNTEER FOR TEDDY

★ ★ ★ ★

William Randolph Hearst was considered by some to be the most powerful man in America. He did not wield his power through political office. Rather, it was through the prolific pages of his widely circulated newspaper that he swayed not only the millions who read it throughout America, but also the politicians that both feared and envied the publisher.

Aaron's first visit a few weeks back had been merely to drop off the article Hearst had asked him to write about the Yukon. The note he held in his hand was a request for a more formal meeting, requesting that he spend an hour with the newspaper tycoon.

Aaron had been surprised when he received another invitation to visit Hearst's office. It had come through his uncle Mark, who had said that morning at breakfast, with his eyebrows raised in surprise, "Well, you're moving in fast circles, Aaron."

"What does that mean, Uncle Mark?"

"This note came yesterday from William Randolph Hearst. He wants to see you in his office today."

"Me? What does he want with me?" asked Aaron as he poured himself another cup of coffee.

"Whatever it is—you can be sure it's something that will benefit him. Although, I suppose, you can't afford to turn down the invitation." Mark buttered a piece of toast and crunched on it thoughtfully before he added, "It's more in the nature of a command performance than just a simple invitation. Hearst is like that, you know."

Aaron leaned back in his chair, picked up his cup and sipped at his coffee, then asked abruptly, "You don't like him, do you?"

"No, I don't. Personally, I think he's a menace. He purposely distorts the news, and he picks and chooses the violent sort of stories to print in his papers to whip up circulation. He's just not a good newspaperman."

Aaron grinned suddenly, his white teeth showing against his tan. "He's a mighty successful one, though. I suppose I'd better go see him."

"I expect it's more about the Yukon. He liked that story that you wrote, didn't you say?"

"So he said. He paid well for it anyhow—a hundred dollars for something that took less than two hours for me to write."

"Well, go see him, then. What about Lewis? Have you had any success in talking some sense into him?" Mark stared at Aaron with a sort of urgency. "Davis and Belle are quite worried about him. Have you been able to sway him about going into the army?"

"No sense talking to him—he's got his mind made up."

"I was afraid it would be that way. Frankly, Aaron, I don't know that anyone could dissuade him."

Aaron finished his breakfast, and then rode into town with his uncle. He got out at the front of the imposing building that housed the *New York Journal*, the flagship for Hearst's newspaper kingdom, and said cheerfully, "Maybe I can catch a ride back with you. I don't think my interview with Hearst will take long. I'm tired of the Yukon, and I don't know much about it anyway."

"All right. Come by my office when you're ready to go," said Mark as he flicked the lines, and the carriage started down the street.

Aaron moved through the large doors and entered into the bustling, noisy world of a big-city newspaper. Wherever he looked, nobody walked. Everyone ran as though they had forgotten *how* to walk. Somehow, Aaron was certain that not all the running was necessary. It was the charged ambience that did something to people. He had read a dime novel or two about the world of newspapers, and would not have been terribly surprised if someone had come rushing in, screaming, "Hold the press!" Nobody did, however, and he made his way to the second floor, where he found the office of William Randolph Hearst. It sat in one corner, occupying the full end of that floor. A small, supercilious man with a hairline mustache looked up disdainfully from a desk as Aaron approached. "I'd like to see Mr. Hearst," Aaron said pleasantly.

"So would a lot of people." The voice was almost a sneer, and with one finger the man caressed his mustache. He did that several times, as if he had to assure himself that it still existed. His eyes looked twice their size through the thick spectacles that perched on his wiry nose.

"I think he's expecting me," Aaron said mildly. The behavior of the clerk amused him. "He sent word to my uncle—Mr. Winslow, Vice President of the Union Pacific."

"Oh, I see." The clerk took one more loving stroke with his finger on the mustache, then said, "If you'll wait here, I'll see if Mr. Hearst can see you." His voice sounded as though he were completely and totally certain that Mr. Hearst would do no such thing. And it was obvious to Aaron that the man enjoyed stopping anyone who dared to interrupt Mr. Hearst's busy schedule. The clerk turned and minced his way through the door after knocking softly.

Aaron walked about the spacious office, noticing that the walls were ornamented with large pictures. They were all paintings of horses jumping over fences. Aaron studied one of them carefully and said aloud, "That fellow doesn't know how to paint horses." Then he heard the door close silently and turned.

"Mr. Hearst will see you." The clerk seemed miffed and sat down and began writing on a sheet of paper.

Aaron passed through the door and found Hearst standing beside a window, staring down at the traffic. He turned at once, his pale eyes revealing nothing, though his lips turned up in a rather formal smile. "Well, Mr. Winslow—you got my message, then?"

"Yes, I did, Mr. Hearst. But if it's about the Klondike—"

"No, no!" Hearst waved his hand airily, dismissing all of the gold rush with one gesture. "That's taken care of. Sit down, won't you?" He waited until Aaron took a seat in a large leather chair and said, "Actually, I have something quite different to talk to you about. I was having lunch with your uncle the other day, along with several other businessmen. Mark Winslow tells me that you have a brother who is going to fight in the war."

"I'm afraid so!" said Aaron, wondering what Hearst wanted from him."

"Afraid so?" Hearst raised his eyebrows and lifted his head. He had a long nose and long face, and now he raised his long fingers and laced them together. "Don't you believe in the war?"

Diplomatically, Aaron said, "I just got back from the Yukon. All we heard there was that the battleship *Maine* got blown up and a lot of Americans were killed."

"Oh, there's more to it than that—much more, I assure you! And we're going to do something about it, too. I've thrown every ounce of power of this newspaper into this business, and it's rolling now like a juggernaut."

"It seems so. Everywhere I go I hear gums flapping just to get the war started."

"Exactly!" Hearst came over, leaned back on the walnut desk, crossed his arms, and stared down at Aaron. "Tell me about your brother," he said abruptly.

Taken aback, Aaron gave a brief history of his family, adding, "Actually, my parents sent me to New York to talk Lewis out of joining the army."

"And what does he say?"

"His mind's made up. He's going and that's that!"

"I'm glad to hear it." Hearst stood up straight, walked over to the window, and stared down for a few moments silently. Finally, he turned back and the grin on his face touched his eyes. "Would you like to go with him?"

"Go with him? Why, I have no idea of doing such a thing, Mr. Hearst!" said Aaron, surprised at the man's sudden offer.

"I can tell you two reasons why you should," said Hearst as he walked back to his desk.

"I'd like to hear them."

Hearst held up one long forefinger and touched it, saying, "First, you can't keep him from going, but if you go with him, at least as an older brother you can try to look out for him."

Aaron stared at Hearst. "Well, I suppose that's true. Although I'm not sure how much help I'd be."

"At least you'd be there. I know how younger brothers are. Your uncle Mark told me that he's quite an idealist. It'd be like him, Mark said, to go charging in with all guns blazing and get himself killed over some romantic idea of his."

"That sounds like Lewis, all right," Aaron admitted. He thought about it for a moment. It was an idea that had not occurred to him, but now that Hearst had mentioned it, somehow it seemed . . . right. "What's the other reason?" he asked quickly.

"The other reason," Hearst smiled, "is that you're a young man who needs a job—and I have an offer to make to you."

"You mean, working for the paper?"

"Exactly!" Hearst grew excited. "I've hired the finest talent in the world! The finest journalists from around the world are going to cover this war. Stephen Crane is going to be there—and Richard Harding Davis has an exclusive contract with my paper to go and report the news. Frederic Remington, the great artist, has accepted an offer to go and do sketches of the war. . . ." Hearst went on, bending back his long fingers as he named the large group he had enlisted to cover the Spanish-American War. As he talked, a smug smile of satisfaction settled on the man, who thoroughly enjoyed the power and influence he had to shape people's lives to benefit his domain.

When Hearst slowed down, Aaron said in a puzzled tone, "Well, you certainly don't need another reporter—which I'm not anyway!"

"Ah, but I want to touch every base! I want to portray every angle," Hearst exclaimed. "Look here, Aaron! Those fellows I mentioned are all professional reporters, standing off somewhere a mile away when the action takes place. What I would like," he said slowly, "is to have the story of the war told by someone right in the throw of it. A private—right where the actual shooting takes place. You see how exciting that could be! Why, everyone would read it!"

"Has it ever been done before?" asked Aaron, feeling drawn into the man's excitement.

"I don't know, but it's going to be done now." Hearst came to stand before Winslow, saying, "You're *perfect* for the job. Your story about the Klondike—it was well written, factual, and very readable. That's the kind of real-life story my readers want to read about."

"I read your version of it—the one that was printed. It was much more exciting than the original," Aaron remarked dryly.

"Oh, that—well, we have to remember that our readers need a bit of excitement. That's what they thrive on. Anyway, what do you think of the idea? Will you accept my offer?"

Aaron straightened himself in his chair slowly and thought for a moment. He wasn't an impetuous young man, but now the impulse to land a job with some adventure was very strong. Finally, he looked up and grinned. "Lewis is supposed to be the romantic one, but we're talking about a salary, I suppose."

"Yes, in addition to what you'll get from your regular army pay. You'll do it, then?"

"All right, I will! But from what I hear, it's hard to get in."

"That's true. There are too many volunteers. Shows the stuff our young Americans are made of! But I think I can help you with that."

"Lewis is dying to join Teddy Roosevelt's Rough Riders. I don't suppose there's a chance we can do that?"

"More than a chance! Teddy loves to be in the spotlight. He'd do anything for publicity. He'd love to have someone right beside him writing up his heroics for the American people. I've already thought of that," Hearst smiled happily. "I'll write him a letter of introduction, and you and your brother can deliver it to him personally. Roosevelt's training his unit of men in San Antonio. Go find your brother and get down there as quickly as you can—I'll see you get tickets on the train."

"Do you really think he'll let us in, Mr. Hearst?"

William Randolph Hearst stared at Aaron. A smile turned the edges of his thin lips upward in a smirk.

"Young man," he proclaimed firmly, "that cowboy will do *anything* to get his picture in the paper!"

CHAPTER TWELVE

AN ARMY IS BORN

★ ★ ★ ★

Its official designation was First Volunteer Cavalry Regiment, but the unit Teddy Roosevelt drew together was known to the public and the men involved as the Rough Riders. San Antonio, Texas, had become the mustering point for the regiment—partly because it was good country to buy horses.

Aaron and Lewis had arrived after a few sleepless nights on a train that had been jammed to capacity. Disembarking at the station, it had been simple enough to find their way to the camp, for everyone they met was talking about Teddy Roosevelt's army. "They're going to put the run on them Spaniards," a scrawny station agent informed the two men when asked for directions. "Don't think you fellows can get in, though. Everybody's trying and nobody's making it."

Aaron, however, reached inside his coat and felt the weight of the letter from Hearst in his inner pocket. Aaron went out to the busy street to employ a carriage while Lewis gathered their bags. Throwing them in, he and Lewis then proceeded to the camp. "Look at that dust!" Lewis said with excitement as they approached the encampment. "Gosh, there must be a thousand horses running around!"

"I guess so," Aaron said. When they'd paid the driver and set their bags on the ground, he stopped a sergeant, asking, "Where can I find Colonel Roosevelt?"

The sergeant, a tall, rawhide individual, studied them, and then answered with a careless, nasal Texas twang. "Right down yonder," he pointed. "You ain't gonna miss 'im. He's likely to be on a horse."

So indeed they found Roosevelt riding a mottled brown-and-white horse. He was wearing a khaki army uniform that was wrinkled beyond recognition, and his brimmed hat was pinned up on one side in the fashion of a white African hunter. Aaron could see his white teeth flashing and hear his shrill voice rising over the sound of horses racing by. "Probably be hard to catch him not busy," he said to Lewis. "Might as well brace up right now."

Aaron marched over, accompanied by Lewis, ignoring the two lieutenants who glared at him. "I have a letter here, Colonel Roosevelt, from Mr. William Randolph Hearst of the New York *Journal*."

Roosevelt settled his glasses more firmly on his nose and stared down at Aaron. "Hearst? Let me see it!" He grabbed the letter, tore open the envelope, and scanned it rapidly. When he glanced up, he looked the two men over carefully. "You know what this letter says?" he demanded.

"Yes, Colonel. I hope you'll find a place for us. We're anxious to serve with you."

Roosevelt crumpled the letter up and closed his mouth for a moment over his prominent teeth. He stared at the two men, his smallish eyes gleaming. "Got no time for excess reporters," he snapped vigorously. "But if you can soldier I can use you. Can you ride?"

"Yes, sir, we both can," Aaron said quickly. He knew Lewis was a poor horseman, but this was no time to bring that up. "We're fit and in good shape, Colonel. And we're good shots, too!" He hoped that Roosevelt would not ask them to prove their marksmanship, for he himself was only mediocre with a gun and Lewis was not much better.

Roosevelt jammed the letter in his pocket and said, "Not a bad idea—getting the reporting from a soldier's point of view. That's what Hearst wants," Roosevelt explained to his two lieutenants.

"Put these men in a good squad where they can be close to the action."

A wave of relief washed over Aaron, and he nodded quickly, "Thank you, sir!"

Roosevelt yanked his horse's head around and rode off in a wild gallop, calling out directions to a group who were assembling a small herd on the perimeter of the camp.

"You two come with me," the officer said. "I'll get you fitted out. I'm Lieutenant Baines and you'll be in my company."

The rest of the day went like a whirlwind. Aaron and Lewis received uniforms, rifles, and were given a chance to prove their horsemanship. Lieutenant Baines was not overly impressed by what he saw.

Lewis was given a mount that had been barely broken in, and he almost got bucked. The officer shook his head in disgust and grunted, "Most of the fighting will wind up being done on foot, anyhow. There is too much of a jungle for cavalry. Go on down to the rifle range and tell Sergeant Hawkins I said to teach you how to shoot."

As they walked away, Lewis said, "I can't believe it!" His eyes were gleaming, and he was practically jumping up and down with excitement. "We're actually Rough Riders, Aaron! Why, there must be twenty million fellows that would give anything to be in our shoes!"

Aaron could not help feeling a little infected by Lewis's excitement. He'd reached this point under duress, but now that it was started, he found himself drawn to it. "Well, we've got one job that's more important than anything else," he said cautiously.

"What's that, Aaron?"

"To come out of this thing alive. Dead is a long time!"

"Oh, we'll be all right," Lewis explained cheerfully. "Let's go down and start shooting."

They took their turns at the firing range, faring better there than they did at riding green broke mounts. When they finished, they walked to the large mess tent that had been set up and ate a supper of tough, poorly cooked beef, along with the inevitable beans. Lieutenant Baines assigned them a small tent on the outer perimeter of the encampment. Lewis went to sleep at once, but Aaron lit a short candle and sat up with his back braced against a pole. By the flickering yellow light, he pulled out a small note-pad and began to write with a stub of a pencil:

> There's never been an army quite like this. I read in the paper that Roosevelt said it's the most typical American reg-iment that's ever marched or fought, that it even includes a score of Indians. But this isn't exactly the way it is. I've never seen such an assortment of men. We've got Ivy League foot-ball players, Indians and Indian fighters, quite a few law-men, including one former Marshall of Dodge City, a na-tional tennis champion, and quite a few professional gamblers have joined the regiment. There's a little bit of everything. A lot of the cowboys are pretty colorful. They've got names like Cherokee Jack, Rattlesnake Roger, and Happy Harrigan. We even have some Texas Rangers in the outfit.

He paused and looked at what he'd written. *I don't have any idea how to write about this*, he thought wearily. *There's never been a war like this.* Weariness caught up with him and he put his writing materials away and lay back on the narrow cot. The sounds of the camp came to him, horses milling in the corral not far away, some-times one of them lifting a shrill whinny over the night. The call of a guard floated to him from far down the line. Hundreds of men all sleeping, waiting to set sail and head into battle. There was something about the quiet and the peace of the air that seemed deceitful. The world was not really like this—quiet and peaceful; it was full of hardships, danger, death, and heartache. A man had to savor these peaceful times when they came—put them in a secret part of his mind so that he could draw on them when things got really tough.

Glancing over at Lewis, Aaron felt a sudden wave of affection for this younger brother of his. *I've got to keep him safe*, he thought almost desperately. *I've just got to!*

★ ★ ★ ★

The response to President McKinley's call for a hundred and twenty-five thousand volunteers had been overwhelming. Over a million men had wanted to enlist. However, two men were sin-gled out and promptly drafted. Fitz Lee, nephew of General

Robert E. Lee, was a portly sixty-three-year-old West Pointer who had not worn a uniform since that day in April 1865 when he'd led the last Confederate charge at Farmville, Virginia. He was chosen because he'd acquired a comprehensive knowledge of the Cuban situation.

But the most unusual choice of all came when President McKinley sent an invitation to a former Confederate. Joseph Wheeler arrived at the White House one day in a fine black Brewster Phaelon buggy, pulled by a large black gelding. He looked like a frail, little old man as he was helped down. He was sixty-one years old, and he drew himself up to his five feet five inches. His hair was neatly trimmed and his beard was snowy white. The dark-suited doorman took his hat and cane and ushered Wheeler in to meet with the President. McKinley came around from the large desk in his office and shook Joe Wheeler's hand, saying, "General, I've sent for you to ask if you want to go—and if you feel able to go."

At once, Joseph Wheeler heard the sound of bugles from his youth. He'd led charges against the Federals with all he had in him, and now said briefly, "Yes, Mr. President. I'm honored that you've considered me. And I will serve this country that I love so much to the best of my ability!"

Later on when one of his former Confederate officers saw Wheeler in his blue Federal uniform, he said, "General Wheeler, Robert E. Lee's going to be mighty surprised seeing you come up to heaven wearing *that* uniform!"

The Commanding General of the army was Nelson A. Miles. He had a distinguished and heroic service in the Civil War, and had been the premier Indian fighter in the Southwest. At fifty-nine, he was a big, athletic man, the ablest of the commanders who would direct this new army—but according to all accounts, he was a hard man to get along with.

As far as the actual assembly of the army, General Rufus Shafter was the most significant factor. Shafter was a huge man, weighing three hundred pounds—or as his enemies liked to put it—almost a sixth of a ton. In Tampa, where he began to pull his army together, the heat, which was well over a hundred degrees, almost brought him to a halt. Two privates had to hoist him onto his horse, but it was still his responsibility to pull this army into a fighting force.

Tampa was not the place for organizing such an army. Tampa and Fort Tampa, where the transport ships swung at anchor, were nine miles apart. The intervening country, for the most part, was very swampy, and no one was satisfied with the site as a training grounds or even a point of departure for the army.

Dr. David Burns arrived at Tampa, accompanied by Gail Summers and Deborah Laurent, and found the city in a general state of upheaval. Every hour, it seemed, volunteers were pouring in from all over the country. The three walked along the tents strung out along the sandy shores, noting that the wooden houses were crumbling, their paint having been removed by sand and the wind off the Gulf. Gail looked around and said, "This is awful! I thought the beach was supposed to be pretty!"

Deborah smiled, saying, "Well, as Jefferson said, 'God made the country and man made the town.' Everywhere you get a lot of people together, they'll manage to uglify their world."

"Uglify?" Burns cocked one eyebrow. "Is that a word?" Without waiting for an answer, he looked around, trying to detect some order in all the confusion. But everywhere soldiers and militia were milling around, while officers shouted out orders above the din. Supplies were stacked everywhere beside the tracks—huge piles of guns and ammunition, tents, cases, and cartons of all sizes. Finally Burns said, "Let's see if we can find someone in authority."

They eventually found their way to the Tampa Bay Hotel. It was filled to capacity with soldiers, including foreign military observers wearing brightly colored, gaudy uniforms. Finally, Burns managed to locate a major named Sievers—a tall, aristocratic man with frosty blue eyes and silvery hair. "Burns? Dr. Burns, you say?" he said, giving a careless look at the three. "And your nurses? Well, we'll see what can be done. Make the best of it till we find a place for you."

This proved to be rather difficult. The three finally managed to find a lowly lieutenant, a good-natured man named Baines, who sympathized with their predicament. He took them to a large barn-shaped building where supplies were being sorted out and said, "Your medical supplies will come here eventually—I hope!"

Burns looked around with discontented eyes. "There doesn't seem to be much order around, does there, Lieutenant?"

"Always that way with a war," Baines grinned. He looked over and said, "You ladies won't find a hotel room, not in Tampa. All the hotels and boardinghouses are already overcrowded with officers and civilian volunteers."

"That's all right, Lieutenant. We'll make out fine in tents."

When the lieutenant had gone, the three of them made their way to a cafe filled with sweaty, loudly talking privates. Gail and Deborah were the object of some careful scrutiny, and several remarks like "Hello, sweetheart!" flew across the crowded room.

Finally, Burns managed to commandeer a table in a corner, and the three ate a meal of sandwiches and apple pie, washed down by tepid water. "I'm not sure about this water," Burns muttered, staring at it warily. "With this many men aboot, sanitation's got to be a problem. I'd better check on it."

"If it's bad here," Deborah said, "think what it's going to be like when we get to Cuba." She looked almost cool in the sweltering heat. It was a quality that she had, a way of making the best of things. Even back at Water Street Mission when things were a challenge, she met them with a calm maturity, letting little trouble her.

Somewhere, Burns thought, *she has learned how to endure difficulties without complaining.*

Deborah looked at Gail and said, "I suppose you and I better learn how to put up that tent. Have you ever done it?"

"No," Gail grinned. "But we'll learn how!"

As it happened, they did not have to know a great deal. As they were attempting to pull the tent into a standing position, the poles fell and the whole thing collapsed. Standing to the side watching was a group of eager volunteers—red-faced young men—all of them cowboys, so it seemed. They were more than willing to help two pretty young nurses put up their tent. By nightfall, Burns and his two assistants had managed to secure a place to sleep, but before they went to bed, he said, "This is not what I thought it would be."

"Things usually aren't," Deborah said quietly. "But we'll do fine."

"I wish I could take it as easily as you do," the physician shrugged. "But we're here to do a job, so let's do our best."

That night, as Deborah and Gail lay in their tent, trying to ignore the sultry humidity and heat, Gail said, "I wish I knew what Jeb was doing. I'm worried about him!"

"Shall we pray, then?" Deborah asked quietly. Without waiting, she began to pray a simple prayer for the boy.

Gail felt her eyes grow dim with tears, and when it was her turn to pray, she began to feel a sense of companionship with Deborah that she'd not felt before. Finally, the two women lay quiet, and it was Gail who said aloud, "I'm glad we came, Deborah."

"So am I," came the answer sleepily. "We'll see what will happen."

★ ★ ★ ★

The Rough Riders were a rowdy, loud bunch, and Lewis reveled in it. Here he was in the most sought-out unit that everyone in the country was trying to get into. He threw himself into the brief and rugged training period with all the enthusiasm of a beginner. By the time he and Aaron left San Antonio on a train bound for Tampa, they'd made great progress—both in riding and shooting.

When the overcrowded train pulled into Tampa, there was a waving and yelling far up the track. Colonel Roosevelt grinned from his position on a flat car; his khaki uniform looked as if it had been slept in—as it always did. He wore a polka dot, blue bandanna, the hallmark of the Rough Riders, except the soldiers all wore red.

When the train stopped they all piled off, and Roosevelt was everywhere, trying to shout orders to his officers. There was no one to meet him and his troops to tell them where to camp, and no one to issue food for the first twenty-four hours. The railroad people simply unloaded them wherever they pleased, or rather wherever the jam of all kinds of trains rendered it possible.

But Roosevelt possessed great administrative ability and sheer resourcefulness. He brought some kind of order out of the chaos of Tampa. Soon rows and rows of tents were pitched, men were appointed to police the camp, and drilling started again in order to keep the troops in top shape. Roosevelt was infuriated when he received the news that the Rough Riders would *not* be a cavalry outfit in Cuba—only the officers' horses would be transported.

Aaron and Lewis worked hard, along with their fellow soldiers, to get settled in. On the second day, however, Lewis said, "Let's go see if we can find Dr. Burns."

"All right." Aaron joined his brother and the two of them began to search for the young Scottish physician. They began asking around, and after a few false leads, they finally ran into a stocky, red-faced corporal who said, "Oh, the Doc? Yeah, he's over by the tracks in a big red barn-looking building, kind of a storehouse."

"Thanks a lot, Corporal," said Lewis, who turned and headed for the tracks.

The two men found the storage depot without too much trouble. They moved inside and at once Lewis called out, "Doctor!" From behind a pile of large wooden crates, Dr. Burns appeared with his hands full of supplies. Lewis rushed forward and shook Burns's hand, demanding at once, "Where are Gail and Deborah?"

Burns turned from Lewis, saying, "Out back sorting supplies." He shook hands with Aaron, exposing a badly sunburned face. He smiled, though, and said, "It's guid to see ye both! When did ye get in?"

"Just two days ago," Aaron said. He glanced at the jumble of supplies and grinned. "It looks like a Kansas tornado passed through here. Can you make any sense out of this?"

Burns's hair was disheveled and he had a harried look. "We'll have to," he said. "We'll need all of these medical supplies when we get to the field. Come along," he said. "The young ladies will be glad to see you."

They followed Burns around some piles of supplies, and he led them through the loose sand to the back of the building, where Lewis called out to Gail and Deborah. The two women looked up, and Aaron took off his hat, remarking, "Look at you two. You're both sunburned."

Gail smiled and shook her head. "There's no way out of it in this place," she said. She touched her nose gingerly, adding, "I'll be lucky if I have any skin left if I stay out in this sun much longer!"

Deborah smiled at Lewis, pleased to see him. "You look fit," she said. "Are you ready for what's coming?"

"Oh yes," Lewis said confidently. He looked over at Aaron and said, "We can whip them, can't we?"

"Sure," Aaron said, shrugging his shoulders. "Let's get out of the sun, though. Maybe we can find something cool to drink."

They stayed only for a brief visit, but Deborah and Lewis went for a short walk. Lewis talked mostly about Alice, unaware that his words brought a twinge of displeasure to his companion. Finally, Deborah said, "I'll be praying that you'll be safe in the battle that's coming." Her voice held a note of urgency, and she took him unexpectedly by the arm, something she'd never done. "It's important that you be careful," she said quietly.

Lewis blinked in surprise and looked at the girl, seeing the seriousness in her face. "Why, I'll be as careful as I can," he said. He halted, then said awkwardly, "Nice of you to care." The two turned and continued their walk and said no more.

As Aaron and Lewis made their way back to their tent, Lewis was very quiet. When they were inside he turned to Aaron and said, "Deborah's worried about us."

"She's a very wise young woman," Aaron replied. He'd faced death in the Klondike, but he knew Lewis was totally unprepared for the ordeal that lay ahead. Carefully Aaron said, "Don't be a hero, Lewis. I've lost Jubal. That's enough."

Lewis cast a quick glance at Aaron, then dropped his eyes. Somehow things were different here, not what he had expected. He went to sleep thinking of Alice—and dreamed of returning to her to lay his triumphs at her feet. But the dream faded as the face of Deborah Laurent drifted into view. He awoke with a start, sat up in bed, and could not make anything of it. Finally he lay down and went back to sleep, wondering what he would do when bullets began to whistle around his head. . . .

PART THREE

SAN JUAN HILL

★ ★ ★ ★

CHAPTER THIRTEEN

A FRAGMENT OF DESTINY

★　★　★　★

The days had crawled by slowly, and no one was more impatient for the invasion to start than Lewis Winslow. It was on June 6 when he finally exploded. Aaron had been sitting on his bunk writing when Lewis stormed in, snatched his hat off, and flung it violently at his bunk. It missed and fell on the floor, whereupon Lewis kicked it, exclaiming, "We're never going to get out of this blasted sandpit!"

Aaron looked up and took in the flushed face of his younger brother. Putting the stub of the pencil in his mouth, he chewed it thoughtfully, then said, "Calm down, Lewis! It's just a matter of time."

"I'd rather be back home watching the wood warp!" Lewis snapped as he snatched up his hat and tossed it under the cot. His face was a light shade of brown, tanned by the southern sun.

Aaron carefully put the pencil in his notebook and wedged it under his bunk. He lay back on the bunk, his fingers laced behind his head, and stared up at the fabric on the tent. A mosquito was snarling busily somewhere around his ear, but he thought wearily, *There's about twenty billion of them in this place—you can't kill them all. Go on—have a bite!* But then, as the mosquito sunk her proboscis into his neck, he slapped the pest and sat up abruptly.

Lewis grinned at him spitefully. "Why don't you let it go

ahead, Aaron? I gave up slapping the pesky things a long time ago." He slumped down on the bunk and put his chin in his hands. There was a doleful look in his eyes as he said, "I'd like to get out of this place. I didn't come down here to be eaten alive by bugs! And they say there have been some cases of yellow fever reported."

"Dr. Burns told you that?"

"Yes, and I don't want to miss the fight by being sick."

The two men sat there idly, the heat sapping their strength, and finally through sheer lack of energy, they lay back until they fell into a fitful sleep.

They rose the next morning at the bugle call and were dressing when Isaiah Wilson, a black trooper attached to their unit as a hostler, opened the flap on their tent and stuck his head inside. His eyes were wide with excitement and he said, "Ain't ya'll heard the news?"

"What is it, Isaiah?" Lewis demanded. He'd become good friends with the wiry, young trooper over the past few days. Reaching out, he pulled him inside the tent, asking, "What's happening?"

"While you two wuz sleepin' yo' life away," Wilson grinned, "the orders done come through." He was at once thrust back and forth between the two as they bombarded him with questions. Shoving them away, he grinned, "Here—don't jostle me around. I done et breakfast. I don't like my food to be all roiled after it's et!"

"Never mind roiling!" Aaron said. "What's going on?" His gray eyes were snapping and he demanded, "When are we getting out of this place?"

"Today, I hear! So you'd better git dis tent pulled down and git your stuff together."

Lewis and Aaron piled out of the tent and found the whole encampment in pandemonium. Officers were yelling and troopers were struggling to take their tents down and pull their gear together. "Come on, Lewis!" Aaron said instantly. "This looks like the real thing. . . !"

An hour later, they found themselves with the rest of the regiment, out of breath and waiting for the train that would take them to the coast. However, after over an hour, they all grew restive.

"It looks like we've been stood up." Aaron shook his head in disgust, then suddenly pointed and said, "Hey—there's the colonel. He looks mad as a hornet!"

Roosevelt came stalking toward the track, accompanied by Major Spotsworth. Aaron was close enough to hear him say, "Major, where's the train?"

"I don't know, sir. It was supposed to be here by now."

Roosevelt stood there, a disreputable-looking figure with his uniform wrinkled as always. Aaron was close enough to see his mouth drawn into a thin line, covering the prominent teeth, and his eyes were pulled almost shut. Suddenly he pointed and blurted out, "What's that train down there?"

"Coal train, sir," the major said nervously. "It hauls the coal in from up north. It's empty now, waiting to go out."

"We're taking that train!" Roosevelt snapped.

"Sir?"

"You heard me, Major. We'll take that train to the coast." Roosevelt lifted his voice and called, "Officers—get your men in that train on the double!"

Lewis laughed suddenly as he began running along with Aaron and the others. "Looks like we're going to begin this war by stealing a train!" he yelped. "Can't think of a better way to do it!"

The men piled into the empty coal cars and were covered immediately by a fine black dust that rose like a cloud. "Well, I sure hope we don't have inspection today," Lewis grinned. The two watched as the engineer was literally forced into the cab, accompanied by Roosevelt and two of his officers. Soon the whistle screamed and the train jerked into motion. As they left Tampa, a wild, ragged cheer went up from the soldiers, and it was Isaiah Wilson, standing next to Lewis, who said, "I sure ain't sorry to say goodbye to this place! Come on, Cuba!"

★   ★   ★   ★

The Rough Riders arrived at the coast and labored all day loading baggage, food, ammunition, and the officers' horses. As night fell, the transport pulled away from the dock and anchored among the other waiting ships. The boat was overloaded, and the men were packed in like sardines—not only below but topside as well. That night it was only possible to walk about by stepping over sleepers. The travel rations that had been issued to the men were not sufficient, and the meat served at the evening meal was very bad. Roosevelt was heard to have called it "nauseous stuff called canned, fresh beef."

"Tastes like embalmed beef to me," Lewis said, spitting out a bite of the stuff and tossing his ration overboard. "I hope we get something besides that to eat before we get to Cuba."

There were no facilities for cooking and, of course, no ice. They discovered the water wasn't good, and there were no vegetables or fresh meat. However, as they were all boxed and ready to go on their way, there was remarkably little complaining. That is, until a telegram came from the Secretary of War in Washington. It read, "Wait until you get further orders before you sail."

They soon discovered that the navy had spotted what seemed to be a Spanish armed cruiser nearby, and through some inexplicable timidity, the navy held up the Spanish-American War until they made certain that there was no Spanish warship. As the troops suffered the heat and crowded conditions for the next two days, Roosevelt jotted down a note to his friend, Cabot Lodge, on June 10:

> The troops are jammed together on this crowded ship. We are in a sewer, a canal which is festering. The steamer that we're on contains nearly a thousand men, and there's room for only five hundred. Several companies are down in the lower hole, which is much like the Black Hole of Calcutta. The officers were embarked last Sunday with the artillery horses, which have begun to die already under these conditions.

Two days later, he fumed and sent off another fiery missive to Lodge:

> I doubt if Cuba is much more unhealthy than is this ship. Five days of this heat and crowded confinement are sapping the strength and health of the troops.

The ship was named the *Yucatan*, and Lewis and Aaron had been pleased to discover that Dr. Burns and his assistants occupied one crowded portion of the first deck. There was no provision of privacy for the nurses, so the two women simply made themselves a compartment by hanging a sheet from the ceiling. They probably had more room than anyone else on the ship.

On the night of June 13, Gail found herself on the fantail in a relatively private situation. She was surprised when a voice called her name, and she turned around to see Aaron step out of the darkness. "Well, Gail," he said, coming to lean on the rail beside her. "How do you like being an army nurse?"

Gail was very much aware of Aaron. She'd spoken to him several times, but always under rather crowded and hectic conditions. Now, as they stood on the deck, a quietness of sorts washed over them.

From across the waters floated the strains of a hymn on the night air. And instead of answering his question, Gail stood there listening to the singing. Evidently, some of the men had found enough talent for a quartet and they sang sweetly, "Amazing grace, how sweet the sound, that saved a wretch like me; I once was lost, but now am found, was blind, but now I see."

Aaron said quietly, "I must have heard that song a thousand times. We sang it every Sunday morning in our church."

Gail turned and studied him thoughtfully. "It must have been nice growing up in a little town like that. Tell me about it."

"I was bored to tears," Aaron said, staring moodily across the water lapping gently against the side of the ship. "To me it was the same thing every day, and church on Sunday. Looking back, I think it was probably the best time of my life—those younger years. I don't have enough sense to know what's good for me. We ought to grab those good times when they come and hang on to them and enjoy them."

"Like this one?" Gail asked quietly.

Aaron turned to look at her with surprise. "I wouldn't call this a good time—mosquitos, heat, bad food."

"No, I mean right now—this moment." Gail's features were caught by the silvery moonlight. There was a smoothness on her cheeks, and her eyes reflected the soft light. "This very minute. All day's been bad—hard, hot, and uncomfortable. When I go below to sleep, it'll be the same. But right now it's fine, isn't it, Aaron?"

Aaron was caught by her observation. He leaned against the

rail, turning to watch her. "That's a good way to look at it," he murmured. "And I believe you're right."

"I always try to think like that," Gail said. "When I was growing up I'd think, 'We've got something to eat in the house today, and we've got a roof over our heads tonight. Tomorrow it may not be so, but we've got to take what we have now and be grateful for it.' Somehow it made things easier."

"You're right about that. I had it easy growing up . . . too easy, I suppose. It made me soft. It was hard for you, but you survived it."

"Yes, I survived. I'm worried about—"

"About Jeb?" Aaron asked quickly. "I've thought about him a lot. If I ever have a son, I hope he's just like Jeb."

Gail, at once, put her hand on his arm. "What a nice thing to say!" she smiled. "I wish he could hear you say it—he'd be so proud! He thinks the world of you, Aaron."

Aaron was embarrassed. He was very conscious of her hand on his arm and said only, "Just because I knocked a couple of pug-uglies on their heels, that's no reason to admire a man."

"It's more than that." Gail was silent for a moment. The sounds of the hymn drifted across the water, clear and beautiful. Overhead, the moon made a large silver circle in the sky, and the stars winked brightly from their places in space. "He's always needed a man to be his friend—and he's never had one. I wish you could spend a lot of time with him. You could make a difference."

"I'd like that. Maybe when this is over we can do something. I could take him fishing and show him how to hunt."

Gail said quickly, "That'd be the best thing that could happen to him!"

"You can come, too!" Aaron said. "I'd like to show you some real mountains and some real cold spring water streams. You'd like it, Gail."

"I'm sure I would. I've never seen anything like that."

She moved her hand and turned her head. The light of the moon touched her honey-colored hair. She'd tied it around her head in a braid, and it looked like molten gold to him. He said suddenly, "You know, I've never felt this much at ease with any woman as I do with you."

"That's because they all wanted something from you."

"What does that mean?" He was a bit taken aback at her bold statement.

"Oh, women are drawn to a man like you, you know," she said, turning her dark blue eyes on him.

"No, I don't know any such thing! But, in any case, why should you be different?"

"You feel relaxed with me because you know I'm not after you."

"Well, that takes me down a peg," Aaron said. "I thought all young women wanted to marry me!"

"Most of them would. You're young, nice looking, have a good family, and that's what a lot of women are looking for."

"But not you?" said Aaron, surprised by her openness.

"I don't think about it. I've got to take care of Jeb and try to help my family."

"Can't you do that and get married?"

The question upset Gail and she said, "I don't think so." She seemed disturbed by the turn in the conversation, and said almost abruptly, "It's getting late and I need to go to bed."

"I think I'll spend the night right here. It's better than down in that hole. Good-night, Gail."

She turned and left, and when she disappeared down the passageway, Aaron turned back and studied the shimmering lines of light that danced across the water. The movement of the ship stirred the waves so that it shattered the lines into millions of fragments that glittered and cast silver lights back to the heavens. He thought about what Gail Summers had said, then shook his head, some thought disturbing him. Then he listened as another song drifted across the water, "On a hill far away stood an old rugged cross. . . ."

As Aaron leaned against the rail on the fantail of the ship, listening to the old hymn, Teddy Roosevelt sat in his small cabin writing diligently in his journal:

> We are off! Invasion of Cuba has begun. Behind us, everything was familiar and routine. Not one of us knows what tomorrow will bring. We have an aspiration to survive, but it was not a condition. The dice is thrown—we are a fragment of destiny.

CHAPTER FOURTEEN

BOUND FOR CUBA

★　★　★

"Well, it's quite a sight, isn't it, Deborah?"

Deborah turned her eyes from the sapphire sea rippled by the ocean breeze as the convoy sailed along under an almost cloudless sky. The gentle wind tossed her auburn hair slightly and brought a glow to her cheeks. "Yes, I've never seen so many ships at one time," she said. Actually, there were forty-eight craft in all, in three columns. The black hulls of the transports set off the gray hulls of the man-of-war ships that trailed behind the one she was on. They had sailed through the night, and from the deck they could hear the band from another vessel playing "The Star-Spangled Banner," and then "The Girl I Left Behind Me."

"This is the biggest thing I've ever done," Lewis said quietly. His face was turned forward, and he seemed to strain to see Cuba over the rounded horizon that lay ahead of the convoy. He turned to Deborah, admiring the gentle curve of her cheek and the fullness of her firm lips. "What about you?"

"It's a big thing," Deborah nodded. "I'm glad to be here!" The ship rose slightly over a large swell, and the two held on to the rail as it plunged back into the rolling waves. The deck was packed with men, the hubbub of their excited voices making a pleasant enough sound in the morning air. "I needed to do something that made my life count," she said. "I hope this is it!"

Lewis was fascinated somehow by this young woman ever since he'd first met her at the mission. He'd never seen a girl so reticent, yet it was that self-measured ability to keep things to herself that intrigued him. Curious to learn more about her, he now said abruptly, "What about yourself, Deborah? Did you come from a large family?"

Lewis's question seemed to take her by surprise, for she turned and stared out across the azure water. It was as if she were in a different place, another time. Quietly, she said, "No, a small family." She said it with a touch of sadness, and yet, there was a finality to her tone that seemed to close the door to more conversation. Turning to him now, she changed the subject, saying, "When do you suppose we'll get to Cuba?"

"We should get there around the twentieth. I'll be ready, won't you?" Lewis said. "It is uncomfortable, but war always is, I suppose." He was restless and said suddenly, "Let's go see if we can talk the cook out of a cup of coffee. I've missed that about as much as I've missed anything."

The two made their way across the crowded deck, then down the stairs that led to the galley.

"How about two cups of coffee, Cookie? I'll make it worth your while." Lewis reached into his pocket and pulled out two bills and waved them in the air. The cook, a large, red-faced man with juglike ears, grinned. "Got some left over. It'll float a horseshoe now, but you can have it if you want."

Lewis procured two cups, and when they were filled with a turgid-looking liquid, the two of them moved across the galley. The messroom was filled with men playing cards on the tables while others were reading. When meals were not being served, it was the only place on the ship where the men could gather for leisure recreation besides the deck. "Well, no privacy it seems," Lewis grinned. They squeezed into a table over to one side close to a porthole and sat there watching the crowd around them.

Deborah looked around the room as she sipped her coffee. Suddenly, she said, "You know, it saddens me to think that on the trip back some of these young men won't be with us."

Lewis put his cup down and turned to face her. He saw the honest concern in her eyes for all the young men about to go into battle. "That's the way war is, Deborah. I try not to think about it."

"Well, I have to think about it. I'm a nurse, and that's why I came. That's what nurses are for—to think about the wounded."

For a while they sat there talking about what each of them thought it would be like when the convoy reached Cuba. Then Lewis saw Dr. Burns, Gail, and Aaron enter the crowded room. He waved at them to come join them. The trio squeezed their way through the crowd and, with some difficulty, managed to wedge themselves into seats beside Deborah and Lewis. As soon as they sat down, Isaiah Wilson, the black trooper that worked with the horses, appeared also. He had a paper sack in his hand and plopped himself down at the table. "Guess what I got in here?" he said with a conspiratorial smile.

"Is it something to eat?" Lewis demanded. "If so, let's have it, Isaiah! Anything would be better than the rations we've been getting."

Isaiah opened the sack, and when Lewis saw what was inside, he whispered, "Doughnuts!" He looked around quickly and said, "Don't let a soul hear about it! Where did you get these, Isaiah?"

"I got me a friend who cooks at night. Dey ain't exactly doughnuts, but dey as close to the real thing as we're likely to come. Here!" He passed the bag around, and all four of his friends extracted a doughnut and began eating them with enjoyment.

"I wish I had some of my wife's peach pie. Now you ain't never et until you taste Lucy's fried pie," Isaiah proclaimed. "If'n we wuz there, I'd show ya'll some cooking that *was* cooking!"

"I'm your friend for life for sharing your doughnuts with me," Lewis said. Since they'd met in the camp, he'd developed a warm feeling for the soldier and asked, "Why'd you come on this trip, Isaiah? A married man doesn't need to be out soldiering."

"Oh, I guess I had to see what it was like on de other side o' de water. I done seen all of Georgia," he said. "Now, I is 'specting to see a bit more of God's good earth. I prayed about it, and it seemed the good Lawd didn't say no, so I figured dat means yes!"

Gail laughed aloud in delight. "That sounds like good theology to me, Isaiah! What would you have done if God had said no?"

The black face beamed, flashing his big white teeth. "Why, I'd do what the Lawd say. Dat's what it means to be a good Christian, ain't it, Miss Gail?"

"I think so," said Gail, smiling at the man's faith.

Dr. Burns studied the cheerful expression on the soldier's face. "What church do you belong to, Isaiah?"

"Why, I'm a totally immersed Baptist, Doctah. And for a while I was a feeler."

"A feeler?" Burns wrinkled his brow. "I don't think I've ever heard of that group."

"Why, when you baptize folks in rivers, Doctah, it can get a leetle dangerous. I means, they's some deep holes in Georgia rivers! So what a feeler does—he gits out and feels around to be sure they ain't none of 'em." Isaiah winked slyly at Lewis, adding, "I'm sho' surprised an educated man like you don't know 'bout feelers."

Burns smiled good-naturedly, understanding that he was being ribbed. "I confess I'm not up on all the branches of theology, Isaiah." He sipped the lukewarm coffee, made a face, then asked, "What's your stand on the question of grace?"

Isaiah's face glowed at the turn the conversation was taking. Soon all the group, except for Aaron, began to talk about church and the Scripture. Aaron kept his face stiff, but he felt as if he'd been walled out. He felt uncomfortable and would have left, except it would have been difficult and rather obvious. Finally, Lewis asked, "What's it like being black, Isaiah?"

Isaiah grinned broadly. "What's it like being white, Mr. Lewis?"

Lewis laughed aloud. "I guess that was a dumb question. But we hear stories of how black people get treated badly, especially in the Deep South."

"Well, you're from Virginia. I guess you had a chance to see how black people was treated there."

"Not well enough," Lewis said, shaking his head. "Does it bother you?"

"Why, I guess it might if I let it. But I don't intend to let it." Isaiah said, "The apostle Paul done said one time, 'I learn in whatever state I am, therewith to be content.' I don't know what state *he* was from, but I'm from the state of Georgia and I'm going to be content in dat state." His eyes clouded slightly, and his good humor seemed strained as he added, " 'Course it do hurt some-times. But heaven's coming and things are gonna be a whole lot better on de other side."

His simple faith impressed Lewis and he said, "You ever think of being a preacher, Isaiah?"

"Me—a preacher! No, suh!"

"Well, you might make a pretty good one," Dr. Burns offered. "You sure know the Bible pretty well."

Isaiah nodded. "I 'spect I don't know it as well as I'd like, but it's good to read about the things of the Lawd, ain't it now?"

Again the conversation went off into a discussion about Jesus Christ, and Aaron shifted in his seat and felt the twinge of dis-comfort nag him again.

Finally, Gail noticed that Aaron had not said anything. She could sense he felt left out, so she began to ask Isaiah more about what he did when he was home.

"I got me a farm and I hunts."

"Do you have a dog?" Lewis asked.

"Do I have a dog! The best bird dog you ever seen!"

"I don't know about that," Aaron said, glad to be included once more. "I've got a dog at home I'd put up against him."

"Why, Mr. Aaron, you don't know nothin' till you sees that dog of mine. Ol' Red, why he'd beat anythin' you ever seen!"

"Is he really good?" Lewis asked.

"Good? He is simply the best they is. Why, one time I went out huntin' with that dog—an ain't got nothin' but my single shot .410. I was huntin' quail, and well—you know how it is when ya got a single shot and a whole covey bust up under your feet and go flyin' off? You only get one of 'em."

"They nearly scare me to death when they do that!" Lewis nodded. "You're right about a single shot—one bird's it."

"Well, it was downright peculiar that day," Isaiah said. He shook his head and scratched his chin thoughtfully. "I come up on a covey and Ol' Red, he was out front and gone to point, so I knows there was a bunch of birds there. Den all of a sudden, one bird fly up and I got 'im! I loaded my shotgun up again and started forward, and you know what? Bless my heart if another bird—just one—he rose up and I got him too!"

"I never heard of that," Lewis said. "Usually the whole covey flies up together."

"Dat's right! But this time, they didn't. I starts again with my gun loaded, and a third time, one single, little ol' quail comes up and I got 'im. Would you believe it! I got six quail what flies up one at a time! Never could have done it iffen dey hadn't come up one at a time, no, suh!"

"I never heard of such a thing," Aaron said doubtfully.

"Well, it ain't common—it ain't common a'tall," Isaiah said. "But finally, I come over the rise and I seen Ol' Red and you know what he was doin'?"

"What was that?" Aaron demanded.

The black trooper closed his eyes and held his hand up. "So help me, Mr. Aaron, that dog, Ol' Red, he'd done found a covey of quail and run 'em all down in a hole! He was coverin' up dat hole with his paw"—Isaiah opened his eyes and looked blandly at Aaron—"and he was lettin' out one at a time to give me time to reload."

A burst of laughter went up from the onlookers, and Aaron colored slightly. Then he laughed heartily with the rest, saying, "You got me that time, Isaiah!"

"Yes, suh, I sho' did—sho' did! But dat's the way it is with these bodacious huntin' stories, ain't it now? The fun's in catchin' someone."

It was the good-hearted humor of Isaiah Wilson that made the long trip fairly pleasant for the two young women. He made it his personal duty to see to their comfort. No matter what they joked about having in the way of small comforts, Isaiah would just flash that big smile of his and walk away. Then he'd scour the ship until he found what the women had only wished for. It meant doing some mighty long bargaining into the wee hours of the night, but the next day he'd reappear at their makeshift room and present them with what he had found. He was so quick at making friends that he even managed to get them better food than the others. When they wanted to wash their clothes, he showed them how to tie their clothes on a rope and throw them over the fantail so the salt water would wash them clean—which worked better than either of them expected.

On June 20, the convoy of ships arrived off the coast of Cuba.

Every soldier that could squeeze on deck was there peering through the mist. And it was Isaiah who said, "Well, here we is in Cuba! I sure hope the good Lawd done take care of us. I been sayin' a special prayer for all you nurses and doctors, and for you too, Mr. Aaron and Mr. Lewis. God give me a special burden for you. I'm praying that not a hair on your head be hurt!"

Lewis moved his eyes away from the sea and looked at this simple friend of his. He put his hand on Isaiah's sturdy shoulder and said, "Thank you, Isaiah, I take that kindly, and may the Lord watch out for you, too!"

"Oh, sure, the Lawd gonna watch out for ol' Isaiah, ain't no question about dat!"

The convoy steamed toward the Cuban coast, whose high, forested mountains rose abruptly on the shore as they rounded the eastern tip and turned west. That night, the Southern Cross shone above the horizon. It seemed strange to see it in the sky with the friendly Dipper. They passed Guantanamo and finally sighted the gray ships of the navy. Beyond the line of breakers, the narrow beach, and the steep bluffs rising above the sea lay Santiago—the goal of all their efforts.

CHAPTER FIFTEEN

ON THE BEACH

★   ★   ★   ★

Stephen Crane lifted his head cautiously, peering at the razor-backed hill that looked innocent enough. He'd climbed over dozens just like it in the past few hours.

The big marine five yards to his left turned a sunburned face toward the journalist. "I don't get paid for doin' your job, Crane," he grinned. "When the lead starts flying, don't come botherin' me with dates and stuff."

"Doesn't look like the enemy's going to show up."

Herbert Norris, the burly first sergeant of C Company, First Marine Battalion, stared at Crane, then turned to spit an amber stream of tobacco juice at a huge beetle lumbering along at his feet. He nodded with satisfaction when the bug was literally baptized with the liquid, then turned his pale blue eyes to the hill that lifted its crest in front of the marines. "They'll hit us, Crane. I got a feelin' about stuff like this."

"We haven't seen anything since we left the coast."

"You don't trust my feelin's?"

Crane, a small man with sharp features, pulled his eyes from the hill and leveled them on Norris. "If you say you've got such a feeling, I guess you have, Herbert."

"You scared, Crane?" asked the sergeant.

"Nothing to be scared of—not yet," said Crane.

"You ever been shot at?"

"No." Crane shrugged his trim shoulder and wiped the sweat that had beaded on his pale forehead. "I'm scared of one thing, Herbert—and that's yellow fever."

"Bad stuff!" shrugged Norris, who turned and spit again.

"I think I'd rather take a wound than get struck with the fever," Crane murmured. "And this is supposed to be the rainy season. We're lucky it's been dry, but it could start raining anytime." He looked up at the hard blue sky, then shook his head. "When it does, it'll turn these roads to mud. Then the artillery and supply wagons won't be able to get through."

"Guess you and the general should've put this thing off, Crane."

The marine was pulling his leg, but Crane shook his head, a doubtful expression in his thoughtful brown eyes. "I'd have waited until October—but that's the height of the hurricane season, and the navy wouldn't hear of it. He glanced at the cloudless skies and thought suddenly, *Hurricanes sometimes hit in the Caribbean as early as June.* . . .

The two men were in the line of six hundred fifty men from the First Marine Division that had landed at Guantanamo Bay, a harbor some forty miles east of Santiago. Crane had been one of the first off the USS *Panther*, and had waited impatiently until the force was shaken into order, then sent inland. The purpose of the expedition was to establish a coaling station for the ships that had set up a blockade around Santiago. Previously they had to make the long voyage all the way back to Key West to recoal.

As the marines had advanced inland cautiously, they'd met no opposition, but there was a sullen look to the countryside—a malevolent air that made the men apprehensive and jumpy. Now as Crane glanced down the line, he saw that the youthful marine on his left had a tic in his right eye. "What's your name, Private?" he asked.

"Jimmy Hope." The private was wearing the soft felt campaign hat, and he straightened up, pulling it from his head. He was no more than eighteen years old, and his hair was soft and blond—much like a baby's first crop, Crane thought.

"Better get down, Hope," Norris growled. He gave the beetle another jolt of tobacco juice, then nodded toward the hill that rose in front of them. "I got a feelin' they's more than cactus up ahead."

Hope was young enough to take this as a personal challenge. "Aw, there' ain't no greasers within a mile of—"

A sharp "pop" broke the still air, and even as Crane watched, a black dot appeared in the exact center of the young marine's forehead. His light blue eyes stared blankly at the hill, a reproachful twist to his mouth as though he'd been somehow terribly disappointed. He leaned to the side, and then slumped stiffly at Crane's feet.

"There they are!" Norris bellowed, and at once the marines began firing. The U.S. Navy Winchester-Lees made an odd flat noise—"Phut!" The Spanish Mausers made a popping noise as sharp and crisp as firecrackers. Crouching behind a hummock with his face pressed against the earth, Crane listened to the Mauser bullets singing overhead. Taking out his notebook and pencil, he scrawled, "The bullets sang as if one string of a most delicate musical instrument had been touched by the wind into a long faint note."

A wiry lieutenant suddenly appeared to wave the marines forward. As Norris leaped ahead, Crane continued to scribble frantically:

> Along the top of our particular hill, mingled with the cactus and chaparral, was a long irregular line of men fighting the first part of the first action of the Spanish war. Toiling, sweating marines; shrill, jumping Cubans; officers shouting out the ranges, 200 Lee rifles crashing—these were the essentials. The razor-backed hill seemed to reel with it all.

Jamming his notebook into his pocket, Crane stood up and moved forward. Dodging from tree to tree, his sharp eyes missed nothing of the action. It was this phenomenal memory that helped him to write the informed dispatches back to the States that appeared in papers across the country—he had already written what many consider the best war novel ever written—*The Red Badge of Courage*.

The assault continued, and soon artillery fire from the USS *Dolphin* began to pound the hills surrounding Santiago. The distant booming of the big guns, the whistling of the shells overhead, and the explosions that tore huge chunks out of the hills continued as the marines moved doggedly forward over the ragged terrain. Crane watched as Sergeant John H. Wick relayed range and bearing instructions to the ship with wigwag flags. The man's courage to stand in the midst of enemy fire prompted Crane to make another entry in his notebook. This was the very stuff that would make headline stories in every paper across the land:

> It was necessary that this man should stand at the very top of the ridge in order that his flag might appear in relief against the sky, and the Spaniards must have concentrated a fire of at least twenty rifles upon him. His society at that moment was sought by none. We gave him a wide berth.

Crane edged forward and saw a black Cuban soldier hit: "He seemed to feel no pain. He made no outcry, but simply toppled over." And he wrote of one marine who lay wounded under a bush: "His expression was of a man weary, weary, weary. . . ."

Time and again the Spanish broke, and Crane watched them scramble back into the thick underbrush. Sometimes the whole squad would vanish, and it was impossible to tell how many of them there were. Marine marksmanship was splendid. The long, grueling hours of practice that the officers had made their men endure were now paying off. Crane jotted down that the rifles were reloaded "like lightning," and that aim was taken with "a rocklike beautiful poise." The Cuban soldiers had less discipline. Crane wrote:

> The entire function of a Cuban lieutenant who commanded the troops was to stand back of the line, frenziedly beat his machete through the air, and with incredible rapidity howl: "Fuego! Fuego! Fuego! Fuego! Fuego!" He could not possibly have taken a breath during the action. His men were meanwhile screaming the most horrible language in a babble.

At last it was over. The marines advanced, forcing the enemy to retreat into the far-off hills. The next day the *Texas, Marblehead*, and *Suwanee* shelled the coastal towns still holding out. The marines established a permanent base on a low hill, naming it Camp McCalla in honor of the commander of the *Marblehead*.

The Stars and Stripes were raised over Guantanamo Bay—and

the first blood of Americans in the Spanish-American War had darkened the soil.

★ ★ ★ ★

General William Rufus Shafter studied the city that seemed to rise from the sea, taking in the long avenues of black and gray buildings topped by smoking chimneys. He glanced back over his shoulder at the blockading warships, the group transports, and water tenders. He calculated the eight hundred and nineteen officers, fifteen thousand enlisted men, thirty clerks, ninety newspaper correspondents, and added to that the two thousand two hundred ninety-five horses and mules that pulled artillery batteries, the wagons, the ambulances, and the single observation balloon. Besides this, there were ten million pounds of rations.

General Shafter looked back at the rugged coastline and studied the wall-like bluff that stood above the beaches to the east of Santiago Bay. He knew that a road ran from a small village called Daiquiri. The information indicated that in order to reach Santiago, he had to land there to use the road from Daiquiri. Finally, he nodded and said firmly, "The landing will take place at Daiquiri. We'll begin at dawn."

All the next day, rain squalls and rough seas soaked the vessels and scattered the transports. The landing was postponed until the following morning. But at daybreak on the twenty-second, the transports all moved in toward Daiquiri.

General Joseph Wheeler, the ex-Confederate Cavalry Commander, put it in his journal:

> With the aid of our glasses we could see the town of Daiquiri, the place selected for our landing. The place has no harbor, but it was a shipping point for iron ore. General Shafter and the naval officers concluded we could safely land the army by the use of small boats belonging to the fleets and transports. A strong iron pier extended out some distance from the shore, but we found it could not be used by us. It extended very high above the water, constructed for the purpose of dumping iron ore from the cars into ships. It was therefore evident that we would be obliged to land on the beach.

The landing turned out to be a complete fiasco. A bombardment began at 9:40, and Aaron and Lewis watched the turrets bursting in the vast bellows of smoke. They could see the shells burst in the jungle, and after thirty minutes, the fleet ceased firing.

"I guess we're going in," Aaron said rather nervously.

"It looks like it," Lewis nodded.

Soon the sea was dotted with rows of white boats filled with men. They each had white blanket rolls and their rifles pointed all angles as they rose and fell in the water. Lewis remarked, "You know, it looks a little bit like a boat race."

"Look at that!" Aaron said quickly. When Lewis turned, Aaron pointed. "Look! They can't get the horses and mules in the boats."

"What are they going to do, then? They've got to have horses and mules to pull the guns!"

Aaron's jaw tensed. "Going to make them swim in, I suppose." They watched as the frightened animals were led to a cargo port and shoved overboard. From where they stood, they could hear the loud braying of the mules. Some of the horses had spooked so that they were kicking in every direction. Officers were whipping them to force them over the side and into the choppy water. The beach was half a mile away, and it was either sink or swim.

"It's not going to work," Aaron muttered grimly. "Some of them are going out to sea."

Lewis stared at the pitiful sight. The water was churning with the kicking and thrashing of hundreds of horses and mules. He hated to see them suffer, and the cries of the terrified animals raked across his nerves. He could not stand to watch those headed out to sea. The ocean soon was dotted with the bodies of drowned horses and mules.

Roosevelt had been marching back and forth on the crowded deck, fuming at the delay. Finally, he obtained a little ship and a pilot, and the disembarkment began. Aaron and Lewis were in the third boat and Isaiah Wilson was with them. "I sure do hate to see dem good horses and mules drowned," Isaiah muttered. He caught the side of the boat as it rose and fell with a whumping sound on the water. "Never did like boats much," he said, his face grayed with the strain of the ordeal.

The boat moved in close, and the men all were wearing their full marching gear. They were weighed down with blanket rolls and cartridge belts around their waists, not to mention their heavy rifles. As they approached the beach, the men prepared to leave the bouncing craft. Aaron bent down and was tying his shoe when he heard Lewis cry, "Look out—!"

Aaron straightened up at once, just in time to see Isaiah fall over the side. At once, he tossed his rifle down, threw his bedroll off his shoulder, and kicked off his boots. The soldiers were shouting at him, but he paid no attention. All he could think of was Isaiah. He went over the side head first, hoping he would not hit anything that would knock his brains out. The water was shockingly cold and he went down deep, moving his arms and feeling for the body of the man. The current was strong and turned him upside down so that he lost his equilibrium for a moment. The pull of the current was frightening. He began to fight his way, his clothes weighted with water dragging him down. Suddenly, he struck his head on a steel object and knew he'd hit the steel hull of the boat. Pain shot through him and he shoved away, forcing himself to the surface. He heard the cries of men and looked around wildly. He saw Lewis, his face pale, and yelled, "I couldn't get him! I'll try again!"

"You can't do it! The current's too swift."

A lieutenant screamed, "Get on board, Winslow! He's gone!"

Aaron hesitated, not wanting to give up. But the current was sucking him under, and there was danger of being crushed against the side of the steel hull. With the minutes that had already dragged by, Aaron knew in his heart that there was no hope in finding Isaiah. Resigned to the loss of his ebony friend, he took several strokes and headed toward land. Soon his feet touched ground, and he waded ashore, falling on the sand, sick and dismayed. He shut his eyes and seemed to see the cheerful face of Isaiah, and the black soldier's words came to him: *Oh, the Lawd's gonna watch out for ol' Isaiah, ain't no question about dat!*

As the boat reached the beach, the landing was chaotic. The troops came stumbling in, and Lewis, stunned at the death of his friend, moved like a man in a dream. It was Aaron who said roughly, "He's gone, Lewis. There's nothing we can do about it." The tragedy of it hit both men hard. Death by an enemy bullet was something they'd thought about—but this was as if a gigantic hand had reached out of the sky and taken a life. They'd grown very fond of the cheerful black man, and to have that familiar voice stilled so suddenly forced them to consider their own mortality. In Lewis's pale face, Aaron saw that his brother recognized at last that this was no charade or mere game that they were involved in, but that good men would die—and the first death had been a well-loved friend. One who had promised them some real good cooking back in Georgia. That would never be, now.

"Come on, let's see what's up there." Aaron had been looking at a Spanish blockhouse that loomed up on the hill against the sky. Roosevelt had watched it too, thinking it might be full of Spanish soldiers ready to open fire on them. To their fortune, the place turned out to be empty. Some of the Rough Riders made their way up the slope with an American flag and fastened it to a pole. When the soldiers on the ship caught sight of the flag unfurled in the wind, drum rolls occurred at once, and the sounds of "The Star-Spangled Banner" reached the soldiers' ears.

That landing at Daiquiri was the beginning of a few days of utter disorganization. It was as if no one was in charge, and every man did that which was right in his own eyes. Six thousand troops, almost half the American expedition, landed on the beaches that day. The following morning, the landing resumed and two regiments of the Second Division made their way down a narrow jungle trail that led to Siboney. Roosevelt spent the time supervising the unloading of the regiment's equipment and soon received orders from General Wheeler to join him at Siboney. Wheeler had already arrived there and met a strong resistance from a large Cuban force. The Cubans had overtaken the retreating Spanish, and needing reinforcements, Wheeler had sent word to bring the Rough Riders.

Roosevelt was electrified at the prospect of entering the fray. He at once called for his officers, and soon bugle calls were rallying the men into marching order. Aaron found himself trudging through a jungle with Lewis right behind him. It was late in the afternoon, and the men were tired, for they already had been aboard a crowded ship for many days. They had suffered patiently the heat of Tampa, and now they were on their way to do what they had come to do. Long after midnight, they tracked through the darkness till they reached Siboney. There they cooked a hasty meal of coffee, pork, and hardtack, while a drenching two-hour thunderstorm poured the heavens down upon them. As they were eating, Roosevelt got orders from Wheeler to attack the following morning.

"I guess we'd better get some sleep," Lewis said. He was huddled in his wet blanket, the water running off his hat. He stared at Aaron, who looked as miserable as he felt.

"I don't see how we're going to get any sleep in this downpour." Exhausted from the trek through the tangled jungle, they stretched out, and the rain drummed into the mud and made a soothing sound.

Finally, Lewis lifted his hat and peered at Aaron, who was sitting upright staring into the darkness blindly. "I sure do miss Isaiah," Lewis whispered. "I thought he'd be with us. He was such a happy fellow—and a good man, too."

"Yes, he was," muttered Aaron, his heart still aching from the death of his friend.

Lewis thought hard for a moment, then lay back, but not before he said, "He knew the Lord, Aaron. He's in heaven now."

Aaron looked over at Lewis and said nothing. The rain continued to beat down on the troops, and the heavens were completely hidden by black thunderclouds. He thought of the cheerful smile of Isaiah Wilson, and a heavy gloom settled upon him. Finally he lay back and shut his eyes, trying not to think what would happen when dawn came.

CHAPTER SIXTEEN

BATTLE CRY

★ ★ ★ ★

William Randolph Hearst had decided to "visit" the Spanish war zone. He had a proprietary attitude toward the war, bearing in his mind the grandiose notion that he had been instrumental in causing it. He had plastered the words "How Do You Like The *Journal*'s War?" on the front-page banners of his newspaper, and stated proudly, "It is a satisfactory thing to be an American and to be here on the soil of Cuba at the threshold of what may prove to be the decisive battle of the war."

Actually, he was not on the *soil* of Cuba, but stood on the deck of the *Sylvia* as he dictated these words to his personal secretary. He'd donated his yacht, the *Buccaneer*, to the navy for conversion into a gunboat, so he had chartered the *Sylvia*, a large steamer belonging to the Baltimore Fruit Company, and fitted it out with offices, a printing press, and even a darkroom fully stocked to develop the action shots he wanted for his feature stories. Firmly convinced that the war was his personal property, he led an army of reporters, artists, and photographers to the front.

He was determined to take advantage of the situation. All America and even the nations of Europe were watching to see the outcome. Hearst was going to make sure this kind of news was in his New York and San Francisco newspapers. He had even brought a staff prepared to distribute a Cuban edition of the *Journal*.

Now as he stood looking out over the rolling sea, he felt pleased with his prodigious efforts. He had come early, in time to interview Admiral Sampson: "A quiet, conservative man with thin features and melancholy eyes." He had been pleased with the impressive appearance of the commander, General Shafter: "A bold, lion-headed hero, and massive as to body—a sort of human fortress in blue coat and flannel shirt." And he had described General Garcia, who had led the rebel troops for years, as: "A splendid old hero in spotless white linen from head to foot."

Not far from Hearst's "press" ship, another civilian vessel swung at anchor. The *State of Texas* had been chartered to carry food, medicine, and other relief supplies to aid the Cuban rebel forces. The Red Cross expedition was led by a woman committed to helping the Cuban people.

Even as Hearst was staring from the deck of the *Sylvia* at the outlines of Santiago, Clara Barton was on her way to the shore. She sat in the stern of the small boat as upright as a soldier, her eyes searching the buildings that lined the beach. As soon as the prow of the skiff nudged into the sand, she rose and stepped ashore. Pulling herself up to her full five-feet height, she took in the soldiers scrambling ashore, the frantic horses and mules that had been shoved overboard, and the disorder along the beach as screaming officers and non-coms tried to get their men into some sort of order. As calmly as if she were strolling along the streets of Boston, she picked her way through the masses of men and animals. For several minutes she walked along the streets of the miserable village, then approached a grizzled sergeant, who stopped shouting at his men long enough to stare at her curiously.

"I'm looking for the medical facilities, Sergeant."

"Ain't any," the sergeant grinned. He nodded impatiently toward his left, adding, "Doc Burns—he come ashore. Down that way, I reckon."

"Thank you, Sergeant."

Five minutes later Miss Barton walked up to a man, asking, "Are you Dr. Burns?"

David was dripping with perspiration, and he took time to wipe his eyes before he answered. "Yes, I'm Burns."

"My name is Clara Barton."

Deborah had been picking up a wooden box filled with medical supplies, but she set it down instantly, her eyes wide with astonishment when she heard the woman's name. Coming to stand beside David, she said, "Miss Barton! I'm Deborah Laurent, one of Dr. Burns's nurses." She gave a half laugh, then added, "I can't believe it's really you!"

A glint of humor appeared in the eyes of Clara Barton. "Most people think I'm dead," she laughed. She was seventy-seven years old, and her hair, which was still brown, had been combed into a bun on the back of her head. Her face was round, with a wide mouth and expressive dark brown eyes. She wore a gray dress with black bands down the front and high on the arms—much like the ones she had worn on the battlefields of the Civil War.

David smiled wearily, but managed to show a touch of chivalry. "I'm an old admirer of yours, Miss Barton," he said. "Your fieldwork during the Civil War was splendid. I'm glad you're here." As Gail emerged from the weatherbeaten building, David turned and introduced her as well. Then he asked Miss Barton, "What are your plans?"

"We landed at Guantanamo," Miss Barton said, "and tried to get some of our supplies overland—but it was very difficult. I thought it best to come here." She looked up at the brooding hills, then added, "I suppose the fighting will be there."

"I think so," Burns nodded. "We'll be following the troops, but I found this empty building and simply started moving our supplies in."

"We've managed to make some sort of order—a place to sleep, anyway," Deborah said quickly. "If you'd like to stay with us, it would be an honor."

"That's most kind of you, Miss Laurent." A thoughtful expression crossed the face of the famous nurse, and she appeared to make an instant decision. "The supplies will be coming ashore soon. I'll have to find room for them. But I'd rather stay ashore than on the ship."

All afternoon the three women and the doctor worked hard to make the building ready to receive the wounded. After a search, they found another empty building for Clara Barton and the Red Cross supplies. The sun was sinking into the copper sea when Gail came to announce that a meal was ready. "It's not much," she warned the others as they came inside and sat around a wobbly table. "But we all need to eat."

"Why, this is fine, Gail!" Burns exclaimed, looking down at the food she had prepared. "I'm hungry enough to eat shoe leather." He waited until the three women were seated, then sat down carefully on a wooden packing crate. He bowed his head and asked a blessing, then smiled at his companions. "No haggis, but I suppose we can't have everything."

"What's *haggis*?" Gail inquired as she spooned stew from a large bowl into her U.S. army-issue tin plate.

"Sheep stomach," David grinned.

Gail halted midair with her spoon, stared at him, then laughed. "I'm glad I didn't find any of *that*! You'll have to be satisfied with stew, potatoes, and army-issue bread."

As they sat on crates, enjoying their simple meal, they speculated about the battle that was to come, and Clara Barton seemed placid. She ate well, asking for a second helping of canned peaches. When a cup of coffee was put before her, she drank it and asked for another. "A fine meal, Miss Summers," she smiled. "I wish I could have fed the troops as well at Bull Run."

Deborah leaned forward, her eyes alive with interest. "I've read about your work, Miss Barton," she said. "But I'd like to hear what it was like."

"It was worse than it will be here, Miss Laurent." Taking a sip of the coffee that she'd laced with canned cream, her deep-set eyes grew thoughtful. She began to speak of her early days, and they could all see that the difficulties she'd encountered were like a barb in her soul that still rankled her otherwise calm demeanor. She related how she'd gathered supplies for the soldiers, but had not been permitted to go to the front.

"Finally I went to Colonel Daniel Rucker, head of the Quartermaster Depot in Washington City," she murmured, and a smile touched her broad lips. "I was so bashful in those days, and when the colonel snapped, 'Well, what do *you* want?' I just burst into tears! He was really a gentle man, but was terribly worried about our wounded. He asked me to take a seat and got me calmed down. Finally I told him I wanted to go to the front. He just stared at me saying, 'The front? Why, that's no place for a lady! Have you got a father or sweetheart there?' I told him I had nobody, but that I had three storehouses full of food and hospital supplies and that I needed a pass and some wagons."

Deborah was delighted with the woman. "What did Colonel Rucker say?" she asked.

"Oh, he was very helpful," Miss Barton nodded. "He gave me the pass and the wagons." A smile creased her lips and she glanced at David. "That was the first time I'd ever broken through the barriers of male military bureaucracy—but not the last!"

"What was it like, Miss Barton?" Burns asked.

"I wore a bonnet, a red bow at the neck, a blouse, and a plain dark skirt," Miss Barton said slowly. "We'd just lost a battle. General Pope had been beaten at Bull Run, and as we pulled into the depot of Culpepper Court House, several hundred wounded men lay bleeding and dying under a blistering sun. There were no medical attendants in sight, and the men were dying for lack of water. I saw filthy bandages and wondered, 'If this is an evacuation area, what will a real battlefield be like?'

"I found a four-horse team and set out to distribute the supplies as fast as I could." She paused and the vivid moment came back to her, casting a shadow over her face. "I'd never seen a field hospital after a battle, of course, and I was stunned. Men with arms and legs blown away, faces mangled, stomachs torn up and intestines hanging out lay on floors in their own filth and blood, crying out for water—some of them begging for death. . . ."

For over an hour the small woman related the details, including what the .58-caliber minié ball could do—shattering, splintering, and splitting human flesh. And the canister was capable of whirling iron balls through the air at great distances that blasted gaping holes in the lines of men, showering the earth with blood, pieces of skin, and decapitated heads.

"And there was no notion of sanitary methods in those days," Miss Barton continued. "Those who survived the battlefield and were taken to a hospital faced what amounted to another serious battle. Nobody knew what caused infection. Surgeons operated in coats stained with pus and blood, their hands unwashed. They dipped their saws, scalpels, and forceps into a bucket of tap water and sewed up wounds with undisinfected silk."

"A man had little chance of surviving under those conditions,"

David murmured. "The death rate must have been monstrous."

"It was! At least ninety percent of those with abdominal wounds died. Any man with a bone-breaking wound in the arm or leg faced amputation." When David pressed her for details of that operation, she said, "The patient was put on the operating table and put to sleep with ether or chloroform. But often there was none, so he got a swig of whiskey or simply a slab of leather placed beneath his teeth. The surgeon would slice through the flesh with a razor-sharp knife, saw through the bone with a sharp-toothed saw, and snip off the jagged ends of bones with pliers. Then he'd place a clamp on the spewing arteries, tie with oiled silk, and dress the bloody stump."

"I don't see how a person could survive such a thing!" Gail shivered, her lips drawn into a tight line from the thought of soon having to face some of the same injuries.

"Many of them didn't. Over one fourth of all who had amputations died."

David shook his head. "We know more about such things now. Surely we can do better."

Clara Barton fixed her dark brown eyes on the young physician. "I trust that is so. But war is terrible, and no amount of science will ever make it less so."

★ ★ ★ ★

Early in the morning, Miss Barton left to visit the sick among the troops. Burns and his two assistants did what they could to get ready for the patients who would soon be brought back from the battle. They had been sobered by the stark details that Miss Barton had related to them, and though they didn't speak of it, they all were apprehensive about the gruesome task awaiting them.

Gail stopped as she was carrying trash out the door and turned to say, "Deborah, what about Isaiah?"

Deborah looked up in surprise. She'd tied a rag around her forehead and was busy scrubbing the floors. "What do you mean, Gail?"

"We've got to have his funeral." Gail's eyes were tragic with grief as she said, "They found his body—it washed up on shore."

"Then we'll have a funeral. He deserves that."

Burns had entered in time to hear the two talking. "I'll see to the arrangements. One of the officers will give us some men to dig a grave."

They worked hard all day, but Burns carried out his word. He persuaded a busy captain to detail two men to dig a grave. Burns, himself, prepared the body. There was no time to build a casket, so the soldier was wrapped in a blanket. They lowered the body into the grave at dusk. Most of the Rough Riders were gone, so only a few gathered around to pay their respects. A few native Cubans came curiously to watch as Burns stood at the head of the grave. The two soldiers who had dug the grave moved back, tossed their shovels down, and waited.

Burns opened his well-worn Bible and read the old words that had comforted thousands: ". . . for this mortality must put on immortality." He spoke of death for a time, then made a few more remarks about the goodness of the man. "Isaiah loved God, he loved his family, and he loved his friends," Burns said. "That's all any man can do that's put on this earth. He was taken from life into death, but God who knows all things knew that it was his time." He spoke quietly, but there was a triumph that overruled the sadness in his voice. Finally he prayed, then with a nod at the two soldiers, turned away.

The sun beat down as Burns walked with Gail and Deborah down to the beach, where they stood looking out over the water. The ocean moaned softly, punctuated by the surf at regular intervals. There was a rhythm and cadence to the sound that fell on them, and they stood silently for a long time. "I wish Lewis and Aaron could have been here. They were his friends," David said finally.

"They were indeed," Deborah said. She hesitated, then said, "I know they loved him. Strange—two Southerners loving a black man. We don't think about something like that where I come from in the North. We think Southerners dislike blacks."

"No, that's not true," Gail said instantly. "Neither Aaron nor Lewis are like that."

They stood for a long time gazing out into the sea, reluctant to leave. But finally David said heavily, "We'd better get some rest. I think there'll be casualties coming soon. We'll probably have to move the hospital closer to the battlefield over by Siboney."

★ ★ ★ ★

Aaron trudged wearily along the winding road—no more than a narrow jungle trail—that led from Siboney toward the main Santiago road. The company had started up the trail at five in the morning, and now they were struggling up a steep coastal bluff. Marching single file, they were led by two Cuban scouts who were accompanied by New York socialite Hamilton Fish, son of one of the wealthiest men in America. Richard Harding Davis and Edward Marshall, two newspapermen, were not far behind Roosevelt, who was marching at the front of the column.

As Aaron looked around, he said with some surprise, "You know, this isn't bad-looking country." He looked down at the glades that spread out below them, then glanced at the line of armed men. "It's like we're on a little hunting expedition." He looked ahead and shook his head. "It'll be a bit different from that, though."

Soon, however, they found themselves lost in a jungle labyrinth. They thrashed around through the jungle, slashing at vines and cursing as bugs attacked them and snakes slithered under their feet. There was no sign of the enemy, but as they turned down the trail, Aaron was startled by a peculiar sound—a sharp crack followed by a hissing noise. His mind said, *That's rifle fire!* and he ducked his head inadvertently. Roosevelt began yelling for the men to move forward faster. They saw no Spaniards, but finally Richard Harding Davis grasped Roosevelt's elbow and pointed across a valley. "There they are, Colonel! Look over there!" Roosevelt turned his own glasses in the direction Davis indicated. "Over there!" he insisted. "You can see their hats."

The men in front, including Aaron and Lewis, looked in that direction and saw the distinctive Spanish hats. Roosevelt at once said, "I want four of the best marksmen in the troop!"

Quickly, the sergeant picked four men, who moved forward and began firing their Krag rifles. At the sound of gunfire, the Spaniards suddenly jumped up and began to retreat. Roosevelt screamed, "Forward, men—after them!" and a running battle through the jungle ensued. Aaron and the others took advantage of the cover, dodging behind the trees.

Once Aaron reached up and yanked Lewis down, shouting, "Get down, you fool!"

Lewis gave him a wild look and grinned faintly, "Right, brother." Even as he spoke, a bullet ripped through a branch overhead, knocking it down on their heads.

For what seemed like hours, they slowly moved forward, unable to do little more than keep their heads down. The Spaniards were impossible to see through the thick vegetation, and their long-range Mausers, fired with great accuracy, found their targets, dropping some of the Rough Riders.

Roosevelt was moving forward when he suddenly stopped. He passed by the pointmen who had fallen during the first seconds of the battle. He stopped, and there lay Hamilton Fish, his dead eyes gazing up at the sky. Roosevelt stared at him and seemed about to speak, then he shook his head and ran on, his sword slapping at his knees.

Stephen Crane, the famous journalist, had arrived in Siboney just in time to make the trip. He had made his way to the battle front just as the Rough Riders moved forward. He wrote in his journal:

> "I know nothing about war, but I have been able from time to time to see brush fighting, and I want to say here that the behavior of these Rough Riders marching through the woods shook me with terror as I have never been shaken."

The battle seemed to end abruptly, as if someone had thrown a switch. An eerie silence fell across the jungle, and Aaron, gasping for breath, looked around. "I reckon it's over," he croaked, his throat dry and his lips parched, but he had no water.

Lewis was lying behind a tree across from him. He held his head up, stared, and said, "I don't see anything. I guess they've cleared out."

It was over—but there were eight dead Rough Riders, and eight more from the ranks of the First and Tenth Regiments. One of the correspondents, Edward Marshall, had suffered a shattered spine, and the field surgeon had told him he was about to die. Stephen Crane stopped and knelt down beside him and tried to cheer him up. "A newspaperman to the last!" he said. "File my dispatches, will you, old boy—if you find it handy."

The wounded were picked up to begin the long trek back to the field hospital that Dr. Burns had set up in the abandoned building. The walking wounded arrived first, and soon Dr. Burns and his assistants had all they could handle. Most of the wounds were clean and some were easily bandaged, but others suffered abdominal wounds and were dying in the small makeshift hospital.

Gail was mopping the brow of a dying boy of no more than eighteen. Knowing he didn't have much time left, she said, "Do you know the Lord?"

The boy looked at her with a frightened look. "No, I don't. I ain't never known the Lord."

"Let me tell you about Him, then." Gail spoke quietly and quoted Scripture to the young man. The whole time she told him of God's love, he held her hand tightly. He was no more than a boy and far from home. He died later that night.

Gail walked over to stand beside a sergeant who'd been watching. The sergeant had his arm in a sling from a bullet he took in the forearm, and he said quietly, "I'm glad you talked to the boy. He needed a woman's touch—a woman of God, at that!"

A look of compassion crept across Gail's face. It was the first of many young men—most only a few years older than Jeb—with whom she would sit holding their hand in their last moments of life. Sighing, she shrugged her shoulders and moved her head from side to side to loosen the tension that had been building up. "Where are the troops now, Sergeant?"

The sergeant ran his hand through his sandy hair. "Up there aways—right down at the foot of those rocky hills."

"What's the name of it?"

"I think they call it San Juan Hill. . . ."

CHAPTER SEVENTEEN

A Matter of Courage

★ ★ ★ ★

Out of the pitch-black darkness, a voice with a New York accent suddenly called out, "Halt! Who's there?" A shot immediately followed, and Aaron sat straight up, recognizing the sound of a .45-caliber Springfield.

Again the cry, "Halt! Who's there?"

"The captain—who are you shooting?"

"Well, I seen a Spaniard—I seen him!" Again the sound of rifle fire pierced the night. Aaron sprang to his feet and groped his way forward. There was a sliver of a moon that lit the floor, and he could see Captain Marvin advance to check it out. "Did you see him?" asked the sentry. "There he is—right there! Look, see down on the ground!" *Bang.* Then farther down the line, another rifle exploded, then a third.

"Stop shooting, blast it!" shouted the captain.

"But—the Spaniards!" said a trigger-happy sentry.

"Those aren't Spaniards! Those are land crabs." The movement the night guard had heard had come from huge creatures—crabs as large as dinner plates. They had two long foreclaws, small eyes, and horny beaklike mandibles—the stuff that makes for bad dreams.

Aaron leaned up against a tree, his knees feeling a little weak.

Lewis's voice came at him with a shaky laugh, "I guess the boys got a little nervous."

"I don't blame them much," Aaron grunted, then tried to rub the sleep out of his eyes. He peered through the murky light and saw that the first rays of dawn were illuminating the San Juan hills.

"All right, you fellows get your gear together!" snapped a sergeant.

"Where we going, Sarge?" asked a private who was standing guard.

"We're going down that road, and we're going to take that hill in front of us!"

That was the simple plan devised by General Shafter. The orders that had come down were that there was to be no attempt of turning or of flanking the enemy—the Rough Riders and the other troops were to march straight ahead. Actually, there was only one obstacle as the men advanced toward San Juan—a small village called El Caney, which was reported to be held by a squadron of Spanish riflemen.

The regiment moved out, led by Roosevelt riding on a large horse. Soon the sound of artillery began to reach their ears, a low, ominous rumble off in the distance. They approached a steep conical hill that was one hundred feet in front of them, and almost at once came the now-hated sound of the Mauser rifles with their sharp cracks followed by "zzzzzz" sounds.

Aaron looked back over his shoulder and blinked. "What's that thing?" he demanded. "Look at that, Lewis!" said Aaron, pointing up.

Lewis was moving forward cautiously down the narrow path, his eyes darting back and forth trying to spot the enemy. When he looked up over his shoulder, he exclaimed, "Why, it's one of those blasted balloons! Just like they used in the Civil War."

"Yeah!" one of the troopers said. "Belongs to a fellow called Maxwell. It's supposed to spot the position of the Spaniards for us."

That had been the idea, but it worked just exactly the opposite. As the balloon slowly floated above the treetops, it did offer the observers a good view of the enemy troops up ahead—but it offered an even better target for the Spanish riflemen. Soon the clicking and buzzing noises of bullets became thicker, and Lieutenant Baines, over to Lewis's left, said, "I wish they'd hit that balloon! They're zeroing in on us!"

They had not gone too far when men began to drop all around them. The Mauser bullets from the Spaniards tore through the jungle almost at random, killing and wounding men.

Roosevelt sat atop his mount, caught up in the thrill of the battle. At one point he acted as if he were riding in a park. He even commented once, "This flora is different from that in the States." He bent over and stared with his nearsighted eyes at an orchid, saying, "Beautiful, isn't it!"

Lewis and Aaron, who were sticking close to the colonel, said, "You've got to give it to him—he's got nerve!"

"I hope he's got sense!" said the colonel. "Our men are getting shot to pieces."

The rifle fire increased, and for a time, it seemed that each bullet was finding its mark, killing or wounding every other man. There was no hiding from the barrage of bullets that ripped through the jungle. The gunfire seemed to come from every side. The smoke from the rifles floated like low-lying clouds amidst the trees, creating a shield for the Spanish. And with the incessant cry of shrapnel and the spit of the Mausers, it was impossible for the Rough Riders to locate them to return fire. The Spaniards had no compunction about killing the men who had come to bear the wounded away; they even killed the wounded men on the litters.

By now, the Americans were pinned down, and Captain William O'Neil stood up and strode back and forth, puffing on a cigarette.

"Get down, Captain!" a sergeant cried. "You'll get hit for sure!"

"Sergeant, there's not a Spanish bullet made to kill me," O'Neil answered. He smiled and resumed his strolling, looking up the trail. Suddenly he turned on his heel and a bullet struck him in the mouth and came out the back of his head. He was dead before he hit the ground.

Finally, they reached a hill and Roosevelt said, "We can't stay here. What's the name of that hill?"

Lieutenant Baines looked at his map. "Kettle Hill, sir."

Roosevelt looked around and realized that his troops could not retreat. He hesitated one moment, then said loudly, "We've got to get up that hill! We'll lose all the men if we stay here."

"But, sir, that's open ground," the lieutenant objected. "We'd be sitting ducks if we tried to cross that."

But Roosevelt would not be deterred; they had to press forward. "Come along, boys!" he called, and urged his horse into a gallop.

Lewis and Aaron were caught up in the charge. They moved across a fairly level spot, and then the ground began to rise rapidly. Roosevelt was galloping ahead, urging his horse up the hill. He stopped when he ran into a wire fence some forty yards from the top, then jumped off his horse, which was called Little Texas. Almost immediately, he found himself in the center of a group of the Rough Riders. "Look up there, boys!" he shouted above the noise of the battle. "Can we do it?"

"We can do it, Colonel!" Lewis cried out. Roosevelt flashed his famous toothy grin and yelled out to his troops, "Bully! Let's go!"

At the top of the hill sat a huge iron kettle used for sugar refining. It became a target for the men, and a cry went up as the Rough Riders surged forward. It was at this point that Lieutenant Baines, who had almost reached the crest of the hill, was struck down by a bullet.

"They got the lieutenant!" a sergeant yelled. "And Massey's down—and Conrad—!"

Lewis saw bullets kicking up dust around the wounded officer. Without a thought for himself, he threw his rifle down and ran forward.

"Lewis, keep down!" Aaron shouted where he lay as a bullet kicked up dust in his eyes.

To Lewis the bullets sounded like a swarm of angry bees buzzing around his head. He made a perfect target, and more than once he felt a bullet tug at his uniform. He reached Lieutenant Baines, who was holding his side, blood running through his fingers. "Get out of here! You can't help me!" Baines gasped.

"Come on, Sarge! We can make it!" Lewis reached down and jerked the officer to his feet. Seeing that Baines could not walk, Lewis threw him over his shoulder. Baines was a slight man, fortunately, and Lewis moved forward in the strength of desperation.

Roosevelt was staring at the pair. "Throw down fire!" he

yelled, and all along the line the Rough Riders began firing all their ammunition, trying to shield the two men in the open as they made for cover.

Lewis reached the huge iron kettle and managed to lay Lieutenant Baines down. He whirled and ran back into the open, yanked another man to his shoulders, and staggered back. He was gasping for breath, but seeing Sergeant Massey squirming in the dust, he ran back and picked up the wounded man. He had just made it to the kettle, when a bullet caught him in the back. He uttered a surprised grunt, and then found that he was lying on the ground. There was no pain, but it seemed as though the world was suddenly hollow. The sounds faded and he tried to say, "It's all right—" But even as he tried to speak, the words died in his throat. The air turned thick, and he seemed to be drawn into a tremendous black whirlpool that sucked him down into a hollow silence. . . .

★   ★   ★   ★

Aaron saw the bullet strike Lewis, and it was as though he himself had been shot. The smell of burning gunpowder scorched his nostrils, and the buzzing of bullets sang all around. Sergeant Bateman was screaming something, but Aaron could not understand what it was he wanted. Bateman's voice seemed thin and weak, like a cry coming from an enormous distance, and Aaron wished he would shut up.

Once while pitching in a baseball game he had been struck in the pit of the stomach by a line drive. He had felt no pain, but the ball had delivered such a blow that he could not move. He had stood there unable to breathe or speak as his teammates had come rushing to him. For one flickering moment the image of that vanished time flashed through his mind—the coach begging him to talk, asking if he was all right. He remembered how he'd tried to say something, but he couldn't utter a word. For that instant he'd become so paralyzed that he was dead to all except the need to breathe—to suck life-giving oxygen into his burning lungs.

Now as the bullets continued to sing a deadly symphony, and the small brown men with straw sombreros moved from tree to tree in a deadly sort of minuet, he was as powerless as he had been on that baseball field a decade ago. He was aware of his hands clutching the Krag rifle tightly, and of the men around him screaming as they fired. Bateman had come over and was clutching his shoulder, shouting in his ear—but he shook his head mutely, unable to frame a single syllable.

And then—despite the scorching heat—a scene of ice and snow flashed across Aaron's mind. A shiver ran through him as the image of the snow-white face of a mountain rampart lifted against an iron gray sky rose before him.

The Chilkoot Pass!

It all came back then, that day in the Yukon when Jubal had died. He could see himself and Jubal fighting the blinding snow, frozen and numb as the icy wind whipped around them. As if he were watching a motion picture, he saw the scene that had risen in his dreams so many times—

A natural break in the pass, a flat saucerlike depression. Four dark figures outlined like specters against the blinding snowbanks that rose ahead. Snow whirled around the climbers, slanting at impossible angles, blinding the eyes and freezing the face.

And then—Aaron saw himself move to the edge of the chasm and stare down. He wanted to shout a warning, but could neither move nor speak. He felt himself carried down until he was the figure peering into the dizzying depths of the pass, and he heard the popping sound—not unlike the explosion of a Mauser rifle.

As he looked up, the walls of the mountain seemed to be moving, and someone was shouting. He stared at the moving mass thinking, *Those are mountains—they can't be moving—it's impossible!*

But it was a wall of snow forty feet high, an avalanche that was racing down the mountainside with the force of a thousand steam locomotives—a relentless juggernaut!

No time to run and no place to hide—! A feeling of absolute helplessness and terror froze him to the spot.

Then Jubal was there, seizing his arm, shouting his name and throwing him aside so that he sprawled on the ice. He struggled to his feet in time to see Jubal lose his balance, caught by the edge of the monstrous slide.

"Jubal—!"

And then abruptly the vision faded and he was back in the steaming jungle of Cuba, crouched on the ground in a fetal position, weeping and crying out Jubal's name.

"Get up, Winslow!"

Aaron snapped his head, rolled over, and saw Lieutenant Miller standing over him, his face contorted with anger. "We've got to get up this hill."

"They killed Lewis!"

"You don't know that," Miller snapped. "If he's alive, he needs a doctor—but we can't go against those guns!"

Aaron had never once thought that Lewis might be alive. He had lived with the pain of Jubal's death cutting into his memory. And when Lewis had gone down, he'd assumed he was dead. Now a sudden gust of hope shot through him. Scrambling to his feet, he lifted his head and saw that the Spanish had thrown up a solid line of riflemen across the crest. Snatching up his rifle, he started forward, but Lieutenant Miller grabbed him and wrestled him back. Miller was a huge man, a regular from Tennessee.

"Keep down, you fool! You can't go out into that fire!"

Aaron struggled wildly, but the officer kept him pinioned, shouting, "You won't help him by getting yourself killed!"

The buzzing sound of Mauser bullets filled the air, and as Aaron stopped fighting to free himself, he knew that Miller was right. The fire was steady, lacing the ground, kicking up mounds of dirt in small geysers. "Okay, Lieutenant," he said, taking deep breaths. "I'm all right."

Miller released his grip and pulled his service revolver from a leather holster. His hazel eyes searched the terrain, and he grunted, "We need artillery—but we're not going to get it."

The thought of Lewis bleeding to death was a torture to Aaron. "We've got to take that hill!" he gasped.

"Sure—but how?"

All up and down the line, the troops were firing steadily at the hidden Spanish riflemen. It was only a matter of time before they'd exhaust their ammunition. Aaron thought frantically, rejecting several plans—then he looked down the line to his left and at once said, "Lieutenant—if we could get to that little ridge—see it? We could filter around behind them."

Miller swiveled around and studied the terrain, then shook his head. "Not enough cover, Winslow. If they spotted a squad, they'd be waiting for them."

"So what we have to do is keep them from looking that way," Aaron said.

"You going to do some kind of song and dance?"

"Look, if we hit them from the right with everything we've got, they won't be worried about that ridge."

Miller studied the situation, balancing the odds. Finally he shook his head dubiously. "It's a long shot—but it might be the only chance we have." He scanned the American line, then turned to Winslow. "No other officers around. You think you could get behind that ridge with a squad if I lead a bunch over there to draw their attention?"

"No, you take the ridge, Lieutenant," Aaron said. "I think I can get our fellows to hit them on the right."

Miller had little confidence in the "thirty-day wonders," as he called the volunteers who had flooded into the regular army. He was a hard-bitten individual who only put his faith in the men who had joined the regular army and been drilled the way a good soldier should be. But men were dying, and the hill had to be taken, so he nodded grimly, weighing Winslow with his hard blue eyes. "All right—we'll try it."

Aaron loaded his Krag as the lieutenant shouted out orders, then moved to his right and said, "When we draw their fire, Lieutenant, don't waste any time—!" The men that Miller had ordered to advance began to filter out from cover, and he nodded, "Come on—we'll get into the coulee over there."

As Aaron led the men into the cupped depression no more than four feet deep, he heard the firing of the Mauser rifles crackle. One man went down with a leg wound, but there was no time to stop. Falling into the ditch, Aaron rolled over and fired at the hidden marksmen, giving all the protection he could to cover the others. When they were all hidden in the gully, he leaned back and loaded his rifle, saying, "Everybody load up."

"What's up, Winslow?" asked a tall, yellow-haired Texan named Sam Jones. He had a pair of pale blue eyes and had been a Texas Ranger at one point. "You tryin' out for a rank?"

"Nope, I just want to take that hill, Sam." Aaron shoved the last shell into the rifle, then stared at the Texan, saying, "Miller's going to sneak around and get behind the enemy. We've got to draw the attention of those guys up there while he does it."

Jones shaded his eyes and peered to his left, then up the hill. "Looks like we're gonna have us a right lively party, don't it, now?"

"Got any ideas?"

"Well, my main idea is to stay alive."

Aaron grinned at the Texan. "So, unless we take this hill pretty soon, none of us will make it out of here alive."

"Yeah—well, if we're gonna bust them greasers up, we better scatter as much as we can." Jones studied the terrain of the hill, then nodded. "When we move out, we dodge around like jack-rabbits. Give them birds less to shoot at. They're worse shots than Mexicans!"

"I figure if we can keep them busy for five minutes, Miller can get his men behind them." Aaron and Jones talked for a few minutes, then he said, "Let's tell the men what to do—then we do it."

After making certain that the men knew what the plan was, Aaron took a deep breath, then said, "All right—here we go—!"

Shoving himself over the lip of the coulee, he looked up at the rim of the hill. Sweat ran into his eyes, but he caught a glimpse of a white garment. Throwing up the Krag, he got off a shot and saw the man go down. A shout ran along the Spanish line and he heard the sound of bullets. Dodging to one side, he saw a geyser of dirt erupt at his feet. The flat retorts of the Krag rifles punctuated the air, and a quick glance revealed that the men were all in the clear—all dodging and firing as they ran up the incline.

Small puffs of dust rose all around the Rough Riders as the Spanish threw a fusillade of angry gunfire down the hill. A slug smashed the head of Al Delgardo to Aaron's left. He felt the stab of grief there'd be for the death of the young man who'd left New York for a bit of adventure. He'd been engaged, but his young fiancee would now have to face life without the curly-haired man she loved. His mother and father would weep, and there would be no grave to stand beside. For the rest of their lives, the word *Cuba* would be a bitter sound, a reminder that the baby boy who had grown up to be a man was no more.

A ricocheting bullet whined like a great bee past Aaron's ear, but he didn't flinch. Climbing the hill had become a chore, and he worked at it like a man building a box. Run forward, throw a slug up at the line of riflemen, dodge violently to the right—then to the left. Aaron stopped once to reload, and as he rose, he noticed that Sam Jones had emptied his rifle and was firing a .44 as he charged upward. The Texan was screaming his version of the Rebel yell, and the shrill, yelping sound grated on Aaron's nerves.

The top seemed to recede as Aaron struggled upward. His breath came in great gusts, his lungs seared from the tropical heat and the effort from climbing over rough terrain. Sweat poured down his face, and his legs trembled as he stumbled forward. The fight picked up tempo and more of the men were left in the dust, some of them bleeding and kicking. Others lay still, bundles that seemed to have fallen from a great height.

Finally the survivors were whirled into an irregular grouping, and without warning they crashed through the first line of the Spaniards. Aaron found himself facing a brown-skinned man wearing a white shirt and pants. He was attempting to load his rifle, and the shell clicked into place as he looked up to see Aaron not five feet away. He had a narrow face and his eyes were filled with fear as he began taking aim.

To Aaron it was like moving in slow motion. His own rifle was empty and he moved forward, watching the muzzle of the Mauser as it rose. His movement was synchronized with the lifting of the rifle, and he knew that either he or the Spaniard would be dead in a few seconds. Strangely enough, an image of a woman's face flashed into his mind—and he knew it was Gail Summers.

Then the muzzle of the Mauser was halfway up, but he lifted his rifle and drove the butt into the face of the small man. As the blow struck, making a sound like a hammer hitting a melon, the Mauser went off and Aaron felt something tug at his side. He felt no pain, and as the force of his blow killed the Spaniard and knocked him to the ground, Aaron looked down and saw that his belt had been split by the bullet.

Nearly got me, Aaron thought, but he had no time to pause. Reloading, he saw that the line of enemy riflemen was falling back. A sudden crackling of rifle fire shattered the air, and Aaron thought, *That's Miller.* Aaron turned toward the rest of the men and yelled, "Come on, we've got them running!"

For twenty minutes the battle raged, but with the arrival of Miller to crumple their flank, the Spaniards were confused. They gave ground, and then Miller yelled to the troops down the hill, "Come on—it's okay!"

Aaron paused only long enough to see that the hill was secured, then threw his weapon down and ran to the iron kettle. Plunging into the shelter, he saw Lieutenant Baines propped up, his back against a bank. His eyes were dull, but he managed a grin. "Glad to see you," he whispered. He turned to Lewis, who was lying on his stomach. "He saved my bacon—I thought I was gone."

Aaron fell on his knees beside his brother. He saw that blood soaked Lewis's back. Carefully, he rolled him over. "Can you hear me, Lewis?" he asked, but he could detect no movement on his brother's pale lips.

"He's lost a lot of blood," Baines whispered. "But he's alive. I don't know about Sergeant Massey—"

Aaron quickly stripped off the shirt, made a bandage of it, and placed thick pads on Lewis's chest and back to try to stop the bleeding. He was cold and afraid, and looked up at Baines. "I'll go get something to take you back to the hospital in, Lieutenant. I don't think the doctors are close." He paused long enough to see that Massey was hit in the side, and a bloody gash had been ripped out of the right side of his head. He shook his head but said, "He's alive—I'll go get some help and be back."

Leaving the shelter at a dead run, Aaron ran back to the trail that the troops had followed up the side of the hill. He spotted an ammunition cart pulled by a mule. "I've got to have this wagon," he stated flatly to the corporal who was holding the harness.

"Why, I can't do that!"

Aaron reached out and ripped the sidearm from the startled soldier. His eyes had a cold glint as he cocked the piece and jammed the muzzle into the stomach of the tall soldier. "I don't have time to argue, corporal. After this is over, you can have me court-martialed—but for now, throw that ammo out and help me load three wounded men. I've got to get them back to the doctor!"

The tall soldier blinked, then grinned. "Why, shoot! You don't have to be so hard-nosed about it! I ain't got no dogs in this fight! Where are these fellers?"

"Up that hill beside the big kettle."

"Well, let's go—but don't point that gun at Rufus here." He

slapped the blue-nosed mule on the shoulder fondly. "If he got stubborn, he'd let you shoot him 'fore he'd do what you wanted. But I can handle him. My name's Ira Pickens. I'm from Arkansas. Now—let's get this here thing done!"

★　★　★　★

Deborah sat bolt upright, startled by a banging on the door. "Wait a minute—" she called out. Pulling on the thin robe hanging over a chair, she groped for a match and lit the oil lamp on the table. Gail was also struggling to get out of bed, her eyes foggy with sleep. "Stay where you are, Gail. I'll see what it is." Picking up the lamp, Deborah walked barefooted to the door, opened it, then walked through the large room they'd filled with rough cots. The door was bolted, and Deborah lifted it, then leaned it against the wall. Pushing it open, she saw the form of a man but could not make out his features. "Yes . . . what is it?"

"Hello, Deborah."

Deborah blinked with surprise, then exclaimed, "Aaron! Come inside!"

"It's Lewis, Deborah. He's been wounded pretty bad and is in very poor shape."

A coldness seemed to fall over Deborah as she stood holding the oil lamp. The yellow beams fell on Aaron's face, highlighting the sharp planes of his features and throwing the hollows of his cheeks and his eye sockets into darkness. He looked old and tired, and there was an angry expression twisting his lips into an ugly shape. "I'll get Dr. Burns," she said. "Can you get him inside?"

"Yes."

Deborah turned at once and went to the hallway. Burns had changed a small side room into his bedroom, and when she knocked on the door, his voice responded, filled with sleep, "What is it?"

"It's Lewis. He's been wounded." She stood there until the door opened, and Burns came out buttoning his shirt. "Aaron brought him in. He says it's bad."

Burns nodded, and the two moved into the ward, where they found Aaron and a tall soldier carrying Lewis's limp body. "Put him right here," Burns ordered. "Light all the lamps, Deborah."

"We've got two more wounded men for you, Burns," Aaron said bleakly.

"Bring them in. Deborah, get my instruments ready."

Aaron and Pickens carried Baines and Massey in, and when they had laid them on the beds, Aaron turned and said, "Thanks, Ira, I couldn't have done it without you."

"Aw, glad I was handy. Want me to hang around?"

"I'll be going back to the fight as soon as I get a word from the doctor. Why don't I see if one of the nurses can rustle up some grub?"

"I'm agreeable. I'll see that Rufus gets a bite of something and some good water. That mule, he's *extra* good, ain't he, though?"

Aaron asked Gail if she would find someone to get them something to eat, then he sat down on a chair in the rough clinic, his eyes cloudy and his lips thin. His thoughts were bleak and he tried not to think of how seriously hurt Lewis was. Finally Gail came to stand beside him, and he looked up at her. She was wearing a white blouse, and there was a softness on her lips as she said quietly, "I'm glad you're all right, Aaron."

Her words seemed to touch some chord inside him, and he remembered the charge up the hill. He leaned his head against the wall and studied her face. "When I was in the thick of it . . . I thought about you."

"Did you?"

"Yes. I don't know why. It's funny the things a man will think of when he's staring death in the eye." He was so exhausted that his speech was slurred, and his whiskers gleamed like spikes as the soft light of the oil lamp caught them. Looking over at Burns as he bent over Lewis, Aaron said bitterly, "Nothing helps. I've lost one friend . . . and now I'm going to lose my brother."

Compassion touched Gail, and she whispered, "Don't say that. Dr. Burns is a very good doctor."

A fatal cloud hung over Aaron Winslow. He seemed beaten down and defeated. He had never gotten over the death of Jubal, and now he shook his head angrily at the sight of his brother lying there. He said nothing, but allowed his chin to drop on his chest. His fists were clenched, and Gail was swept with pity for this strong man who was bearing a burden he had no way of lifting. "We have to trust in God, Aaron," she said quietly. But he gave

213

no response. Finally, she turned and began working on the two wounded men while Burns attended Lewis with Deborah's assistance.

Time crept by—like a slow-moving glacier—for Aaron. He was like one of the wounded himself, though his wound was in the spirit, not in the flesh. When finally one of the nurses set a plate of food in front of him, he was hardly aware of it. He sat there picking at it with a fork but tasting nothing. Finally after many hours had passed, Burns appeared, his thin face grave as he spoke.

"It's a good thing the bullet didn't puncture a lung," he said. "It angled away from it, but I can't tell what other damage it may have done inside."

"Is he going to die?" Aaron asked abruptly.

"I can't say. He's lost so much blood—too much. His life is in God's hands now." He caught the resentful spark reflected in Aaron's eyes and knew he was wasting his words. "We'll do the best we can for him, Aaron. Will you stay here?"

"No. I've got to get back. How are Baines and Massey?"

"Baines is going to be all right. It's too early to say about the sergeant." Burns studied the face of Aaron Winslow, adding, "Baines told me that Lewis saved his life—and Massey's, too. He's very grateful."

Aaron nodded, then said, "Do your best for him." He turned and left the room, leaving Burns with a worried expression.

The doctor went back to check on Lewis and found Gail sitting beside him. "I'm worried about Aaron. He's taking this hard."

"Yes, he is." Gail lifted her face, which was pale and marked with fatigue. "He's bitter over this. If Lewis dies, he'll never be able to forgive."

"The Spanish?" asked Burns, wiping his tired brow.

"No, not them." Gail shook her head. She reached out, brushing back the lock of hair that had fallen over Lewis's brow, her lips broad and maternal. "It's God he blames, David—and he'll never find peace until he discovers that *he's* the one who needs forgiveness, not God!"

CHAPTER EIGHTEEN

DEBORAH'S PATIENT

★ ★ ★ ★

The black mosquito sang a shrill, monotonous chorus, lighting on the smooth cheek of the sleeping young woman. Balancing on her Queen Anne legs, she pierced the skin with surgical precision—but did not live to enjoy the rich red blood of her victim.

"Ouch!" Deborah jerked herself upright and slapped her cheek sharply. Staring at her hand, she saw no blood and nodded with grim satisfaction. "You won't bite anyone else!" Wiping her hand on her blouse, she leaned forward and lifted the mosquito netting she'd rigged to cover the still form lying on the bed.

Lewis's face was flushed and he was hot to her touch. *Fever's down some—but he's still in some sort of coma. . . .* Dipping a cloth in a jar of tepid water, she carefully dampened his face and upper body. The fever had been severe, at times raging like a miniature furnace inside the wounded man. The only thing that seemed to help bring it down was soaking him in water, and so she applied the cloth again and again. When she finished, she paused for one moment and looked down at his still face. Reaching out, she placed her palm on Lewis's stubbled cheek, her touch light and gentle. For a moment she remained motionless, then she bit her lower lip and replaced the netting. Sitting down on the wobbly chair beside the bed, she took up her vigil, but instantly grew sleepy.

"Got to stay awake—!" Arching her back to ease the ache, she blinked her eyes, then picked up the notebook that lay on the wooden packing crate beside the bed. Opening it, she ignored the gritty sensation in her eyes and began to write slowly:

Daiquiri.
　　After two in the morning. Twenty-two more patients brought in today—no room for all of them. Had to take some of them to the other hospital. David worked until midnight, then Gail and I simply forced him to go to bed. He hasn't slept ten hours since the casualties started arriving the other day. We are all exhausted—but how do you sleep when men are dying? Miss Barton has been a great help—not only with supplies, but working with the men. She's a marvel—at her age to be so strong and able—and compassionate!

She broke off when a cry of pain reached her. Putting her journal down, she hastily made her way to a young soldier who was thrashing around on his bunk. "Tommy—you must be still!" Deborah whispered, catching his wrists. "You'll hurt your leg!"

The soldier, a young man no older than eighteen, stared up at her, his eyes filled with fear. He had taken terrible wounds, the Mauser slugs breaking the bones in his upper and lower right leg. His lips were taut with pain as he formed the words, "Please— don't let them cut my leg off, miss—!" Earlier in the day, he had clung to her hand as the ether had taken effect, begging Burns not to amputate his leg. The operation had been successful, though Burns had told her he'd keep the leg, but that it would be stiff the rest of his life.

Deborah placed her hand on his head, soothing his fine blond hair. "Your leg is fine, Tommy. You won't lose it. Doctor Burns was able to save it."

The young man clung to her hand, his feverish eyes searching hers for a lie. "Honest?"

"Honest. Now, you go to sleep. You'll be home soon."

"But it hurts so bad!" moaned the young man.

"I'll give you something for the pain," said Deborah.

Deborah gave him a liberal dose of laudanum, part of the supplies that Clara Barton had generously shared with them. When the soldier swallowed it, she said, "Now, you'll go to sleep."

"My girl likes to dance." Tommy tried to smile, adding, "I'm the best dancer in town. Couldn't dance with one leg, could I, now?"

"You'll take your girl to many a dance, Tommy—now, just lie still." Moving back to her station beside Lewis, Deborah thought of the five cases of yellow fever that had already stricken some patients. *If Tommy gets that, it could kill him as quickly as a bullet in the brain!* Sitting down beside Lewis, she picked up her journal and continued her writing, using a fine script as legible as print:

> Lewis is still in a coma, and his fever is still raging. David thinks some cloth might have been carried by the bullet deep inside the wound, and there's no way to get it out. Aaron thinks he'll die, but I refuse to believe that! I'm clinging to God's promise—and He never fails!

For a moment she hesitated, as if reluctant to put down the thought that had come to her—but she'd decided to spare herself nothing in the journal. Pressing her lips firmly together, she wrote steadily as the yellow light of the lamp threw flickering shadows over the page:

> I never thought I could feel love for a man again—not after Howard. For a long time I've tried to tell myself that what I feel for Lewis is just friendship. He *is* a man I like tremendously. Just being with him is fun. He's witty and so full of life—just what I've always liked in my male friends.
>
> But I've discovered since he was brought in so badly wounded that I care for him in a deeper way. He's been so helpless, and I've robbed some of the other patients to care for him. I'm sure Gail and David have noticed—though I've tried not to be obvious. Night after night as I've sat beside him, I've felt more and more what I can only define as affection. Perhaps it's just a natural maternal instinct. I find myself touching his cheek and whispering little sweet things to him—just as I do with a baby. If he suddenly woke up and found me doing something like that, I'd—well, I must be careful! He's in love with Alice Cates, and I can't change that!

"How is he, Deborah?"

"Oh—Gail! You startled me!" Deborah quickly closed the journal, placed it on the table, then turned to face the young woman standing by her. "He's still got a high fever."

Gail came to stand over Lewis, looking down fondly on his wan face. Lifting the mosquito netting, she felt his forehead, then nodded. "It's down some. That's a good sign." She lowered the netting, then leaned back against the wall. Her eyes were under-shadowed with dark smudges, and lines of fatigue creased her forehead. "I wish we had netting for all the men. Most of them are covered with mosquito bites."

"You can't keep the awful things out," Deborah nodded. They had tried covering the windows, but the shell of a house had thousands of tiny gaps to let in the black swarms of mosquitoes and flies. She slumped in the chair, closing her eyes and throwing her shoulders back to relieve the strain. "Why aren't you sleeping?" she asked.

"I got some rest—but I got to thinking about Aaron." A troubled light appeared in Gail's eyes, and for a time she spoke of the fears she'd harbored about Aaron's rebellion against God. As she spoke quietly, some of the tension that had built up in her seemed to leave. Finally she considered Deborah, and then let her gaze fall on Lewis's face. She had never inquired into Deborah's private life, but the strain of taking care of shattered and dying men had somehow broken down the barriers. "You're fond of Lewis, aren't you, Deborah?"

"Y-yes, I am." Deborah hesitated slightly. She'd grown very close to Gail, and now said what she never would have mentioned before arriving in Cuba. "I have been for some time." She lifted her eyes, which caught the reflection of the amber light shed by the lamp. "I never thought I could feel this way about a man again."

Quickly Gail picked up on the final word. "You were married?"

"No, not married." For a moment it seemed that Deborah would lapse into her guarded manner, but she glanced at the face of the sleeping man, and somehow seemed to find it easy to speak of the past. "I was engaged once."

"You never mentioned it."

"No, it's not something I like to think about." A mosquito

whined in her ear, and she brushed it away with an absent motion, adding, "It seems like something that happened a long time ago."

"Do you want to tell me about it, Deborah?"

"I . . . think so." Deborah clasped her hands together and looked down at them as she began to speak. "It's not really a great tragedy, I suppose. Lots of women have had bad experiences with men. Most of them go on with their lives—but it was my first love. . . ."

Gail listened silently as Deborah related her story. "There was a young man named Howard. We met and fell in love almost instantly. I thought there never had been a love like ours," Deborah said quietly, the old pain rising to form a shadow in her fine eyes. "He wanted me—in every way—and I wanted to wait until we were married. And . . . I gave in to him. . . ."

The simple admission was spoken, but Gail could see how the thing still tormented a sensitive young woman such as Deborah. She felt a warm rush of compassion, and asked, "What happened?"

"He met somebody else."

Something in the blunt statement was like a door closing, and Gail, who saw the need for Deborah to speak of her pain, asked, "Was he poor? Couldn't he afford to marry you?"

Deborah shook her head. "My family has money—and so does his." Gail had known from things Deborah had said that she came from a well-to-do family. Her speech was better than most, and at times Gail had noticed that Deborah had a carelessness about money that people who grew up in the tenements of the lower East Side did not develop.

"I'm sorry, Deborah," Gail said quietly. She moved over and put her hands on the shoulders of the young woman. "It must have been very hard for you."

"It's always hard when a woman is rejected by a man," Deborah answered. Her shoulders shook under Gail's hands, and she caught herself. Reaching up, she put her hand on Gail's. "I've never spoken to anyone about this. Maybe I should have."

"Do you still love him?"

"Oh no!" The idea seemed to shock Deborah, and she rose instantly, turning to face Gail. "It was *never* love, Gail. I was in love with love, I think. But it left a horrible scar on me. I have never been able to trust men after it happened. Even after I gave my heart to the Lord, I was unable to allow a man—any man—to get close to me. She suddenly glanced at Lewis, then whispered, "I . . . I didn't think I'd ever be able to love again!"

Gail put her arms around Deborah, and the two young women clung to each other in the semidarkness of the room filled with wounded men. Deborah began to weep, quietly at first—then terribly. Her whole body shook from the sobs as she let out the pain and rejection she had felt for so long inside. The grief she'd refused to express burst like water over a broken dam, and for a long time she was shaken by a torrent that racked her tired body.

Gail held her tightly, smoothing her hair and whispering gentle words of comfort. Finally, Deborah took a deep breath and stepped back. She found a handkerchief and wiped her face, saying shakily, "I've never broken down like that—"

"I guess it was time for it to come out," Gail smiled. "Do you feel better?"

Surprise touched Deborah's features. "You know, I really do!"

"Sometimes it's good to cry. Now, you go lie down. I'll sit by Lewis."

"Thank you, Gail. I think I will." But she said one more thing before she turned to go. "He's in love with Alice Cates." She struggled with something, then said flatly, "The girl Howard left me for was like her—selfish to the bone."

"Lewis will see what she is really like," Gail said quickly.

"Howard didn't see it. Men can't see what women are sometimes." She turned and left the ward. When she reached her room and lay down, she was shocked at the flood of emotion that had shaken her so deeply. It had been like a violent storm sweeping through her, stirring old and painful memories—but now the storm was over, and she marveled at the peace that had come to her. She closed her eyes and sank into a deep sleep almost immediately.

Gail remained beside Lewis, thinking of Deborah. She had been very fond of the girl for some time, but now that she knew the tragedy that had touched her life, Gail felt a protective urge. She put her hand on Lewis's arm and leaned forward to whisper, "Don't you be a fool, Lewis Winslow. . . !" She thought of Aaron then, and fear flooded her thoughts. He was still out there fight-

220

ing, and when the casualties were brought in she grew tense, dreading to look into their faces—afraid that Aaron would be among them.

"God—take care of him, please!" she prayed, her voice a bare whisper in the quiet ward. Lewis seemed to hear it and stirred restlessly. Placing her hand on his arm, Gail stood there praying for him to get well.

The choir of mosquitoes continued to sing their shrill tiny song, but Gail's thoughts had drifted to the battle—far away in the hills, as rifles cracked at the Americans as they moved forward into the interior of Cuba.

★　★　★　★

The worst sensation was that he was falling from some terrible height, almost unimaginable—and always down, down, down into a black hole. He would tense his muscles, bracing himself for the moment when he would strike the bottom. His ears would always be filled with the roaring of a tornado, but when he would open his mouth to call out, the howling wind would fill his lungs, stifling him like a massive blanket.

Sometimes, though, it would be different. There would be no sound at all, merely an eerie quietness that seemed to have its own tiny echo deep inside. And with the quietness would come a light—soft and gentle—bathing him in a warmth that drove away the bone-cracking chill that racked him.

Sometimes he would dream he was on fire. His body would be parched with a scorching heat that blistered him to the bone, so that his skin crackled like paper. His eyes were almost fried with intense pain.

When the heat would become almost unbearable, he would feel a coolness on his face, a touch so light—like nothing he'd ever known. Then the cool moisture would bathe his burning body, washing away the pain and the fear that surrounded him as if he were in a cocoon.

More than anything else, he had the feeling that he was drowning, trapped under a horrible weight that he could not break free of and escape. He would be far, far beneath the surface, swallowed in darkness with only faint light shimmering far overhead. Sometimes he would move closer to the surface, struggling with all his might. At those times, he could see movement and hear the voices of those who were out of the pit. And he would often cry out, trying to make himself heard.

More than once, he almost broke through, but would always sink back into the stygian darkness. But in that dark abyss, he learned to distinguish between those he could not see. There was more than one person, he knew, but the one voice was gentle as were the hands that went with it. It seemed the voice was calling him out of the pit, and the tender hands were urging him on, but he couldn't understand the words, and sometimes he would cry out in fear as an old nightmare reached up to terrify his mind again.

Somehow, this time it was different. He rose out of the darkness toward the surface. Only this time he broke through. Opening his eyes, Lewis glanced around and saw that he was lying in a semidark room with a lantern over to his left. The amber light of an oil-burning lantern fell across the cots that were all occupied with men, most of them bandaged in white. They looked almost like specters. It was raining outside, he knew, for he could hear the gentle rain hitting the roof, the cadence soft and gentle and incessant. He tried to sit up, and as he did pain raked across his nerves. He lay back gritting his teeth, waiting for the terrible pain to subside. It throbbed at the top of his back, and he looked down to see his chest swathed in bandages. He was covered with a sheet to the waist—and suddenly he was aware that he had no feeling in his legs.

Fear gripped him then, and he moved again, ignoring the pain. He tried to move his feet that lifted the covers in twin canopies.

Nothing!

He tried to draw his legs up, to move his toes—anything—but there was no response. "What's wrong with me?" he cried out.

At once there was movement to his side, and he turned to see Deborah sitting beside him, wearing a white dress with bloodstains on it. Her face was ivory by the lamplight and her eyes were enormous. She came and put her hand on his forehead. It was cool and she whispered, "You're awake."

"Deborah!" Lewis reached up and took her hand and said, "What's wrong? I can't move my legs!"

"You're wounded—just lie still. You've had a bad fever and we thought—"

Lewis was aware of the coolness of her hand, struggling to fight down the fear that coursed through him. "What day is this?"

Deborah said, "You've been here four days, but your fever was so bad that I don't think you even knew it. Some kind of infection—a lot of the men have it. Thank God, you don't have yellow fever!"

"Where's Aaron?"

"He brought you in, but he had to go back to the unit. We'll send word at once that you're all right." Deborah straightened up and took a deep breath. "I'll go get Dr. Burns. He wanted to know as soon as you woke up." She turned to leave, but his voice caught her, and when she turned back, she saw a tension in his hollow cheeks. "You mustn't be disturbed. You're alive and that's what counts!"

"But, my legs—I can't move them!"

Deborah hesitated. Some of the men who had been brought in had had to have their legs amputated, and some had died. Looking at him, she said, "We'll trust in God, Lewis! He's the healer. Now, you lie still while I go and get Dr. Burns."

Lewis lay there, with troubled thoughts swirling through his mind, but he was confused and in pain, and could not sort them out. After a few minutes, he looked up and saw Burns bending over him.

"Well, you've come out of it!"

"My legs—" Lewis began, but the doctor raised his hand and stopped him.

"You got hit by a bullet very close to your spine. We were able to get it out, though," Burns said, "but it was nip and tuck. Another fraction of an inch and you'd be dead. Now, I want to look at the wound. It may hurt when I turn you over."

Lewis knew Burns was trying to be gentle as he turned him, but the pain was still intense. Lewis was past caring about that. He endured the pain stoically, and when Burns rebandaged the wound and turned him back over, Lewis said, "How does it look?"

"The infection is almost all gone and so is the fever. You're going to make it!" Even though Lewis had escaped death, Burns saw the fear in the young man's eyes and said, "I know you're worried about your legs, but we'll hope you get the feeling back. I've seen that happen before."

"But what if I don't?"

"We won't talk about that now. I want you to eat something and get your strength built back up. Nurse Laurent?"

Deborah came at once to his side.

"Bring him something to eat. We've got to get him filled out a little bit." He paused, then said, "I'll send word to your brother. He'll want to come see you."

The doctor turned and left, moving down the rows of cots. Lewis closed his eyes. He felt weak, and the darkness that had engulfed him during his feverish coma tugged at him, beckoning him to return. He thought how wonderful it would be to drift off to sleep and sink back into the comforting sea of unconsciousness, but somehow, his spirit rose within him. He fought against the temptation to give up. He began to pray, seeking God, and for a long time, he lay there silently. Finally, he drifted off into a natural sleep.

★　★　★　★

"How is he, Gail?"

"The fever's gone and the wound is healing cleanly." Gail had been changing the dressing on the foot of a young soldier when Aaron had suddenly appeared beside her. She rose and smiled brightly at her patient, saying, "You'll be all right now, Roger." Then she turned toward Aaron and the two walked out of the ward. Outside, a gentle breeze rustled through the trees, and the falling sun had cast afternoon shadows across the island. "Come along—there's a place where we can sit down and talk. When did you get back?"

"I just got here. I couldn't get away any sooner."

She led him to the quarters that she shared with Deborah and said, "Come inside. There's some cool water in the *olla*. He sat down and she removed the jug, produced two glasses, and poured them full of water. Hanging the olla back up on the peg on the wall, she sat down and said, "I'm glad you're all right." Her eyes were thoughtful and she asked, "Was it bad, Aaron?"

As he sipped the water, she noticed there were hollows in his cheeks. It had only been a few days, but the heat and the strain of the battle had pared him down. "We took the hill," he said. "But we lost a lot of good men."

"I know—the hospital's full of the wounded. And to make matters worse, yellow fever has broken out among some of the men."

Aaron sat there, his sweaty uniform clinging to his shoulders. His beard had grown out to bristles, which were surprisingly of a reddish tint. His eyes were slightly sunken, and he looked tired to the bone. "For all practical purposes, the war is over. It's just a matter of time until they surrender," he said abruptly.

Gail was startled. "You mean, there'll be no more fighting?"

"Oh, there'll be a few skirmishes here and there, but the Spaniards are whipped. It's just a matter of mopping up now."

"I'm so glad!" Gail said, leaning forward, clasping her hands together on the table. "Thank God it's over!" Then she shook her head with a slight gesture. "It isn't over really. This is a terrible country, Aaron. It's a perfect hotbed of malaria, and there is no ground whatever in which to camp. With the lack of sanitation, we're going to have all kinds of sickness spread. It has already started—men are dropping in their tracks almost as if they were hit by bullets. I heard that General Shafter has cabled the States at once, wanting to immediately transport the troops back to the United States. He said if it's not done, the death rate will be appalling."

She looked at Aaron's strained face, then said slowly, "You're worried about Lewis."

"Will he ever be able to walk again?" The question was abrupt, and he shot it at her almost in a harsh fashion.

"I don't know. I don't think anyone can know. With that kind of wound it's almost impossible to tell."

"Has he moved his legs at all?" Aaron asked almost plaintively. He reached out to her as if for assistance. She took his hand and he held on to it. "He's *got* to walk, Gail! He's got to! God wouldn't let it happen—God wouldn't let him be a cripple the rest of his life."

"I'm praying every day. And Deborah and Dr. Burns are too," Gail said quietly. She saw the pain make sharp points in Aaron's eyes, and she wanted badly to say, "And God wants you, too. . . ." but she knew this was not the time. He was holding her hand so tightly that it hurt, but she allowed her hand to remain in his grasp till finally he loosed it. Softly she drew it back and said, "Come on—he'll want to see you."

"I don't think I can take it, Gail."

"Yes, you can. He needs you now, Aaron. He needs all of us." She reached out, took his arm, and pulled him to his feet. When he rose, she said quietly, "We mustn't let him see any doubt or fear."

"That's all right for you," Aaron said. "You have faith in God, but I don't."

"I think you do," Gail answered slowly. "All your life you've known about Jesus. You've told me what wonderful Christians your mother and father are, and you've told me about Jubal, how he believed so strongly in God."

"And he died, didn't he?" The answer was bitter and Aaron shook his head, saying, "And what if Lewis never walks again?"

"Then he won't walk. That's hard, but his fate is in God's hands. He's trusting Jesus Christ." Gail had not meant to say this to try to force her faith upon Aaron, but now she saw a vulnerability in the planes of his face. The battle had not broken him, but the plight of his brother had done something to him. He seemed almost weak as he stood there, and she waited for one moment, then said, "Come—we'll go talk to him."

As if walking in a stupor, Aaron allowed Gail to lead him to the hospital. When they found Lewis, Aaron was surprised to see that he was sitting propped up in a cot.

"Hello, Aaron! I'm glad to see you! Are you all right?"

"Sure—I'm fine!" Aaron said, forcing a cheerful grin. "How are you?"

"Oh, doing well." He looked down at his legs and said, "Still waiting for the feeling to come back in the old legs, but that will come!"

"Sure it will!" Aaron said quickly. "It's just a matter of time." He sat down and talked to Lewis a little about the unit back at San Juan Hill. After half an hour, he rose and said, "I'm going to go try to find a bath."

"Are you going back to the troops?"

"No, the colonel said to get you back home as soon as possible. I'm taking you back to the States on the first ship that leaves here."

"Well, you must have some influence," said Lewis in surprise.

"No, Roosevelt saw you pull the lieutenant out from underneath the firing. He said you'll receive a Congressional Medal of Honor for that, or he'll have somebody scalped." He reached over and put his hand on Lewis's shoulder. "You're a pretty important chap; at least Teddy Roosevelt thinks so."

For one moment, Lewis listened, then he shook his head and said softly, "Well, it'll be good to get home again, won't it?"

"Sure." Aaron smiled, adding, "You won't have a good-looking nurse like Deborah to take care of you, I'd guess. Gail tells me she's pampered you."

"I guess she has at that." The two men talked, then Aaron left, and later that morning when Deborah came by with a basin of water, Lewis sat up. "I can shave myself, Deborah."

"You'd cut your throat," she said, a slight smile turning at the corners of her mouth.

Deborah had appeared early in his confinement with a basin of hot water, a bar of shaving soap, and a straight razor. She'd announced that he looked like a bum under a bridge, and had proceeded to administer a shave. She'd been surprisingly good at it, and now as she sat down and tied a towel around his neck, she said, "Aaron had good news."

"Yes, the war's over—or so he says." He sat quietly as she lathered the brush and applied the rich white lather to his stubbled face. It gave him a luxurious feeling, and he closed his eyes, muttering, "If you ever leave the nursing profession, you can open up a barber shop."

The idea amused Deborah, and she laughed. "Maybe I will. Would you bring all your friends in for a shave and a haircut?" She was a witty girl, and kept him amused as she moved the razor carefully over his skin. "Do your lip tight—" she commanded, and the razor moved swiftly across his upper lip.

Lewis was suddenly aware of the nearness of the young woman. Her hand was resting on his shoulder, and her smooth face was very close. She had bathed, and he could smell the fragrance of the soap on her skin. She was so intent on what she was doing that he could study her without fear of offending. Her skin, he saw, was smooth and clear, tanned a delicate shade of brown. A row of tiny freckles adorned the bridge of her nose; her lips were full and evenly pressed together as she concentrated.

Without thinking, Lewis said, "You know, you're a fine-looking woman, Deborah—ouch!" He lifted his hand, touched his cheek, and then stared at the tiny spot of blood.

"If you wouldn't talk, you wouldn't get cut," Deborah scolded. His compliment had brought a glow to her smooth cheeks, and as she dabbed alcohol on the cut, Lewis saw that she was disturbed.

"I always talk without thinking," he shrugged. "But I just told the truth. You *are* nice looking. I've always thought so."

"You're just trying to get some extra favors from your nurse."

Seeing that she was really embarrassed, Lewis suddenly reached out and took her free hand. "No, I'm not—and I've got to tell you how much I owe you, Deborah."

Deborah was acutely aware of his hand holding hers. She looked at him and smiled. "I'm your nurse. I've just done my job."

"You've done more than that," Lewis murmured. He held her hand and his eyes were serious. "I was in a pretty deep hole, Deborah. Dr. Burns says you saved my life. I don't know how to thank you for that."

"You don't have to—"

"Maybe not—but I *want* to." Lewis grinned, looking suddenly very boyish. "I like owing you my life. When we get home and I get on my feet, I'll find some way of showing how much I appreciate your help." A thought came to him, and he said eagerly, "Maybe you and Alice and I can go out and celebrate together!"

Deborah pulled her hand free, then wiped the soap from his face. "Maybe we will," she said evenly. She rose and took the shaving things away without another word. Lewis sat watching her, a puzzled expression on his face. He thought of what he had said, but nothing in his remarks seemed offensive. He lay down on the bunk, thinking of home and of Alice Cates—and from time to time he thought of how soft Deborah's hands had been on his face.

CHAPTER NINETEEN

AFTER THE BATTLE

★　★　★

"You're going home! Start getting your things ready." Gail and Deborah turned to stare at Dr. Burns, who had just come in almost at a run.

"Are you sure, Dr. Burns?" Deborah asked.

"Yes! I've been talking with one of the officers. If we waited for the wheels of the military to turn, he said all of us could die here. But Roosevelt got tired of waiting around and got the job done!"

"How did he do that? He's just a colonel, isn't he?" Gail inquired.

"The way it came to me, General Shafter couldn't get the government to do anything, so he had Roosevelt write a letter to the President. But he allowed it to leak to the papers back home. When President McKinley read it, so the story goes, he wanted to fire everybody! But the upshot of it all is that we're loading on the transport right away! We ought to be home in ten days."

"Well, I'm ready to go home, and I think everybody else is too," Deborah said. "It seems that all I hear now are the bugles blowing taps over the dead." There was a sadness in her voice as she thought of all the courageous young men who had come to fight an enemy, but were struck dead instead by malaria, yellowjack, or high fever. The new cases of fever among the soldiers—mostly yellowjack—had reached epidemic proportions. In all, more than three thousand men were sick, mostly suffering from the dreaded malaria, but with growing numbers of yellow fever cases showing up.

"I'm going to tell Lewis!" Deborah said at once.

She left the room at a quick pace, and Dr. Burns looked after her thoughtfully. "She's grown very fond of Lewis, hasn't she?"

"Yes, she has. I suppose when you put as much of yourself into saving someone's life as she did in saving his, it happens."

"Well, he's a fine young man, but I'm not too optimistic—from a medical point of view—about his recovery. That bullet wound was pretty serious. He may never walk again." There was a sadness in his blue eyes as he allowed the thought to run across his mind. He was the sort of physician who felt too deeply for his patients. Then he shook his shoulders and said, "I suppose we'll all be glad to get out of this place."

"I thought we might be here much longer," Gail nodded. "But I won't be sorry to be back home."

That was the feeling among everyone, it seemed. When Aaron heard the news, he went at once to the hospital to tell Lewis.

He found Lewis sitting up in bed, propped up against some pillows. He had a notepad on his lap, which he put down when Aaron came in.

"Well, we'll be on our way pretty soon. I'll be glad to get out of Cuba!"

"I was writing to the folks," Lewis said. "But it looks like we might beat the letter home now."

"Go on and write the letter," Aaron said. "You never know how these things will go. We found out once already how it is with this army. Remember, we sat on a crowded ship with lousy food for a week before we left Tampa."

Aaron sat down for a while and talked to Lewis about their imminent departure. He didn't mention Lewis's disability, for he could say nothing positive about it. Lewis had recovered from the fever, and his face had a healthy look about it, despite the weight he had lost. Even though Lewis had survived, Aaron had been depressed over his brother's condition. After a few minutes, he just sat there in silence, not knowing what to talk about. He was glad when Deborah came in with a tray of food, and he rose and said, "Well, I'll be going. Take good care of this fellow, Deborah!"

"I'll do that," Deborah smiled. Aaron left and she said, "Are you ready to eat?"

"Sure!" Lewis said at once. He moved the note pad aside, and she placed the tray on his lap. Then sitting down beside him, she took out a lace handkerchief and began to dab her forehead. "It's warm! But we'll be leaving, so we can endure it for a little while longer, I suppose."

Lewis picked at his food, eating slowly without much appetite. He talked less now than he had before he had been wounded. In the days since he was brought to the hospital, he had grown unusually quiet. It was not that he was saddened, but the paralysis in his legs seemed to have taken away part of the effervescent quality that had bubbled over before. He had lost some of his zest for life, and from some of the things he had said, Deborah sensed more of a soberness about him.

Lewis took a bite of bread, chewed on it thoughtfully, then swallowed it. "Not going to be long before we're home," he said, as though she had not spoken. "I'm glad this war is over and we're leaving this place." He hesitated, then said, "Things turned out a little bit different than what I had expected."

Deborah knew he was referring to his injury and said quietly, "We're trusting God to heal you, Lewis."

A smile turned his lips up and he shook his head. "You never give up, do you?"

"Why, I don't find in the Word that we're supposed to give up. The Bible says to 'run with patience the race that's set before us.' "

"Why do you think these things happen?" asked Lewis.

"Wiser people than I haven't been able to answer that." Without thinking about it, Deborah picked up her handkerchief, reached over, dabbed at a morsel of food on his face, then flushed slightly. "I didn't mean to do that."

"My mother always did it," Lewis said, smiling at her. "I always was a messy eater." He studied her carefully, then continued to speak. "I guess we all wonder why bad things happen to good people. Job wondered about it, didn't he?"

"Yes, he did. He spent a lot of time trying to convince God that He was mistaken. I used to not like that book much; seemed like it was one long argument. But I've been reading it more lately."

"In the end, Job and his friends never did figure out why Job had so many troubles. That was because they could only see one side of the problem. They didn't know that God had allowed the devil to try Job's patience."

"No, that's true, we don't know." She saw a faint look of surprise cause Lewis to lift his eyebrows. "That's part of the problem—we don't know why these things happen—and most of the time I suppose we never will."

"God never did tell Job why He allowed him to lose his family and be sick."

"That's right, and I remember the last part of the book where Job just gave up and said, 'Whatever you say, God, whatever you do, it's all because you're God.'" Deborah leaned forward, her face intense. She had an inquisitive mind and now she said carefully, "I think that's the only theology any of us can have. Once we decide that Jesus Christ is Lord of all this universe, and that He made all the earth and the planets, then we can leave everything in His control. He's aware of it!"

Lewis suddenly said, "You know, I just thought of something! When I was young my mother had a little box, and every time something bad happened or a difficulty would come along, she'd write it down on a piece of paper and put it in that box. I asked her one time why she did that. I never will forget what she said." A smile creased his lips and he ran his hand through his light brown hair. "She said when the devil would come to her and remind her of the problem, she'd just say, 'Why, devil, that's in the Jesus box. You'll have to go talk to Him about it. I gave it all to Him.'"

"I love that," Deborah said. She smiled and her eyes crinkled. They always did when she smiled. The story pleased her, and she sat there thinking of it silently. She had a way of taking a statement, thinking on it, and then letting it sink into her spirit. Lewis knew somehow it would surface sooner or later.

They talked for half an hour, and then Lewis fell silent. "What are you thinking about?" Deborah asked.

"Oh, nothing, really." He sat there, staring down at his lower body, then looked up at her, a shadow in his eyes. "I was thinking about Alice. She won't be expecting me to come home like this."

"She'll be proud of you, just like all of us are," Deborah said evenly. She left the room then with the tray, and there was a frown on her face. Somehow, she knew that Lewis was troubled at what Alice would think of him more than he would admit, but there was nothing she could say to him.

★ ★ ★ ★

Two days later, the troops eagerly boarded the transports and left Cuba. Unlike most military matters, the affair had gone swiftly. Aaron had appeared with a wheelchair and had wheeled Lewis to the steamship *Miami*. He pushed him up the gangplank and found the captain—a bluff, hearty man with a weather-beaten face—waiting for them at the top. "Well," he said, a smile half hidden under his moustache, "you're early!"

Aaron said, "I wouldn't want to miss this boat. My name's Aaron Winslow—this is my brother, Lewis."

The name meant something to the captain. He looked at Lewis and stuck out his hand. "Congratulations! I got a note from Colonel Roosevelt. He said to take very good care of you, that you were an honored guest on my ship."

Lewis flushed and said, "Why, I can't imagine why. I was just one of the troops."

"Mr. Roosevelt doesn't think so! From what I hear, the colonel was impressed by what he saw during the battle at San Juan Hill."

Somehow, Roosevelt had found time from his duties to write a note to the captain of the *Miami*. He had even come by the hospital to visit the sick men, and had spent fifteen minutes talking to Lewis. Roosevelt had met Mark Winslow, and as soon as he found out that Mark was Lewis's uncle, he said, "I'll be seeing you when we get back to New York."

Lewis smiled. "You'll be too busy getting ready to be the new governor, Colonel."

Roosevelt was taken aback at Lewis's statement. "Why, I'm not even a candidate."

Aaron, who knew more about politics than Lewis and had listened to some of the talk between the other correspondents, said, "I'm afraid you're going to be a candidate this time, Colonel. And if I'm a resident long enough, you'll have my vote."

Roosevelt was pleased at the man's vote of confidence, and had left the two men with a warm admiration for their commander.

Now the captain said, "Come along and I'll fix you men up myself."

The ship pulled out the next morning at dawn. Dr. Burns had been unable to move his supplies, but he had given them to the doctor who was staying. That first day they made good time, and on the second night out, Gail and Dr. Burns were taking a leisurely walk around the deck. The *Miami* was not as crowded as the one they had sailed in on, as it was a much larger vessel.

"Almost like a pleasure cruise after the voyage down here, isn't it?" Dr. Burns said. The two paused and leaned against the rail. Dusk had fallen, and there was a hissing sound as the *Miami* cut through the waves.

"It's much nicer," Gail agreed. She was wearing a blue gingham dress, the only nice one she'd brought with her. She'd let her hair down, and it blew in the wind, making an attractive picture.

Dr. Burns seemed to have trouble speaking. He started once to say something, then broke off suddenly. Finally, with something almost like desperation in his manner, he turned to her. Reaching out, he took her arm and pulled her around to face him. "Gail," he said, "there's something I've got to say. It's been on my heart a long time."

Instantly, Gail knew what was in the young physician. She stood there as he held her arm, conscious of the strength of his grip. For some time, she had been aware that David Burns was interested in her as more than just a nurse. She had been so young when they had first met, but since then she had grown into an attractive woman. Now, she saw something in his gentle eyes that he had kept hidden, and she waited as he struggled to find the right words.

"I'm not a man who knows a great deal about women," Burns said quietly. "But for a long time now, I have felt something for you. I didn't want to say anything, for it didn't seem right, but now I've got to speak." He paused for a moment, then said, "I love you, Gail, and that's all there is to it!" Without waiting for her reply, he reached out and pulled her to him. She did not resist, but took his kiss and rested her arms on his shoulders. He was gentle, and this was the quality that she prized most in this man— his gentleness and his strength.

These were the two things that Gail Summers had longed for in a man. She sensed the depth of his love for her in the pressure of his lips and the strength of his hands as he drew her forward.

Surrendering to his arms, she was aware of a stirring inside her own heart. She had felt alone for most of her life, but now, enfolded in his arms, she felt something that she had longed for. She gave herself to him freely, enjoying the sense of belonging and protection she felt in his arms.

The kiss was interrupted by the sound of footsteps, and they moved apart quickly, seeing that Aaron had appeared on the deck. He stopped abruptly, saying, "Oh—sorry!" He turned at once and quickly walked away, the sound of his footsteps echoing on the steel deck.

Gail was embarrassed, and her face showed it, and David no less so. "I'm sorry," he said. "I shouldn't have taken advantage of you like this to speak my heart."

"It's all right, David. I guess we're entitled to one mistake."

"It was no mistake, at least not for me," David said. "Do you think"—he asked deliberately, but with insistence in his fine eyes—"that you could ever learn to care for a man like me?"

"I already care for you, David, but—"

"But you're not sure if it's love?"

"That's right." Gail moved to the rail and stared at the sea restlessly. "I don't know much about love—nothing really! I never had boyfriends like most girls do, so I just don't know." Turning back toward him, she lifted her eyes and smiled. "I do know one thing, though. You're the finest man I've ever known. I admire and respect you more than I thought I could respect a man. If that's love, then I have it."

It was not the answer that Burns wanted to hear, but still hope grew in him. "Well, I'll come courting properly after we get this war settled and all our patients are safely home." A waggish thought came to him. He had a sprightly sense of humor beneath his rather staid exterior. "I think I'll learn to play the guitar, then I can come and sing love songs under your window. Why, I even know one to start with." He began to sing "The Girl I Left Behind Me" in a slightly off-key note.

Gail suddenly giggled and put her hand over his mouth. "Perhaps you'd better just bring flowers," she said. "That'd be better than your singing." Then she said more soberly, "I'm honored that you would think of me in such a way, and I'm also flattered." She hesitated, then smiled up at him. "Thank you, David!" Then she turned and left the deck.

David stood there for a time, thoughts running through his mind. He leaned on the rail and stared into the white water and finally said aloud, "She's a bonny girl—a bonny girl indeed!"

★   ★   ★   ★

The convoy plowed through the waters of the Atlantic, and on the eighth day of the voyage, the word spread around that the ships would dock the next day. Aaron went at once to tell Lewis. The two had spent long hours playing cards and checkers together, and now Aaron said, "We'll be home tomorrow! I'll be glad to get off this ship."

Lewis looked up at him. "So will I." There was an apprehension in him, and Aaron understood that he was thinking of the reception he would get. He had gone out a healthy young man, and he was coming home in a wheelchair, perhaps forever.

"I wish we hadn't come on this trip," Aaron burst out.

"Because of this?" Lewis asked, indicating his legs.

"Yes—because of that!" It was the most that Aaron had ever said, and there was an angry, resentful look in his face.

Lewis said calmly, "God is able to heal me, I know that!" He saw the doubt in his brother's countenance. "You don't believe that now, but someday you will. I've been praying for you, Aaron, and so has Gail. She told me so."

Aaron flushed. He always felt guilty and uncertain when someone mentioned anything about God to him. He stayed for a few more minutes, then left and went up on deck. He had not seen Gail alone since he had encountered her kissing Burns, and he was confused at his own attitude. Now, he saw her as he made his way along the deck. His first inclination was to turn and go the other way, but suddenly a perverse spirit took him. "I can't spend my life running away from her," he said. "It's her business what she and Burns do." He tightened his jaw and walked up to her. "Hello, Gail!" he said.

She turned to face him with an embarrassed smile, and he knew that she was thinking of his interruption.

"How is Lewis today?"

"As well as he ever is."

She could tell by the brevity of his reply that something was troubling him. "He mustn't give up, Aaron! Men wounded worse than that have walked. David has told me about several cases."

"You're telling me that it'll take a miracle," Aaron said. "Well, I don't believe in miracles!"

There was something in his voice that disturbed Gail Summers. She turned to him and saw that there was a glumness about him. She wondered if he had been disturbed by what he had seen between her and Burns. "I'm sorry that you feel that way," she said. "I don't think you will always. It could've been worse. I know that people always say that, but it really could—he could've been killed, Aaron. But there's hope!"

Aaron could think of no answer to that. He stood there quietly for a while, unable to speak. He glanced up ahead, as if seeking to discern the shores, but there was no land in sight. Suddenly, he turned to her and asked directly, "Are you involved with Burns?"

A flush touched Gail's cheeks and she did not answer at once. His eyes were on her, searching her, and she felt an emotion she could not identify. "I can't answer that, Aaron. I don't know much about love. I do know that he's the kindest man I've ever met. Why do you ask?"

Aaron regretted his impulse. "You're right—he is a fine man!" He thought of this young girl's background and what a hard life she had had. *She deserves a man like Burns*, he thought. He turned to her and found a smile. "I just wanted to wish you well," he said. "I've never told you, but I've always admired you. You've had a tough life, and you've come through it better than I would have, I think. Burns is a lucky fellow! Good-night!" He turned and walked away before Gail could answer.

She raised her hand and her lips framed his name—but she said nothing, and when he disappeared, she turned and walked slowly along the deck.

A tendril of wispy fog swept along the surface of the water, and then a cloud suddenly obscured the moon. She glanced up and waited until it passed, and as the silver beams fell on her face, there was a softness in her lips as she thought of the two men that she'd come to know—David and Aaron. She could not think clearly about it for a moment and finally dropped her head and continued along the deck.

PART FOUR

A TIME TO EMBRACE

★　★　★　★

CHAPTER TWENTY

HEROES RETURN

★ ★ ★ ★

William Randolph Hearst greeted the peace as jubilantly as he had welcomed the war. He was prepared to cover it as flamboyantly as he had the struggle on the island of the Caribbean. When he heard that the North Atlantic Squadron was returning, he was delighted. The *Journal* rolled off the presses urging everyone to make "Saturday a full holiday so all the people may see our victorious fleet." New York spared nothing in rolling out the red carpet. The *Journal* arranged to fly an observation balloon over the city, marking the progress of the fleet. Showers of red, white, and blue confetti filled the air as thousands of people gathered in the streets.

On board the *Miami*, Aaron had managed to maneuver Lewis's wheelchair to a favorable observation point along the crowded rail. As the two looked out and spotted the balloon overhead, Lewis looked up and grinned. "Well, at least this one won't bring shells down on us like that one did on the trail to Santiago." He turned again and looked at the shore. The ships moved past Sandy Hook, then steamed into the harbor in a majestic column. Not just the fleet, but a virtual armada of some four hundred vessels—tugboats, ferries, fishing boats, and yachts—moved forward with everyone crowded and screaming at the top of their lungs. A chorus of whistles from scores of boats shrilled welcomes, and guns along the battery thundered volley after volley of salutes that were answered by the guns of the fleet.

"I'll never get over the sight of all this," Aaron said. He pointed to the Statue of Liberty as they steamed by it and started up the Hudson River. The fleet stopped in front of Grant's Tomb, where Hearst's balloon continued to rain patriotic confetti down from the sky.

As soon as the ship docked, a group of high-ranking officers from the army and the navy were waiting near the docks. The captain of the *Miami* came to Aaron, saying, "You and your brother go first. Come along—I'll join you."

Lewis settled back in his chair with an odd look on his face. It was the moment he had long dreamed of—returning from a war as victor. But the moment was overshadowed. He wished the wheelchair had not been in the picture. He sat quietly as Aaron wheeled him along the deck of anxious soldiers waiting to be re-united with family. Then as the gangplank fell into place and they started down, he said, "Look! There's Uncle Mark and the family!"

Aaron looked up, and among the crowd of people waving, he spotted Mark Winslow and Lola, along with Esther. His eyes caught a movement on the wharf and he said, "And there's Alice."

Lewis was startled and turned his head. Apprehension filled him as he wondered how they all would receive him. He stiffened in the chair as Aaron wheeled him onto the wharf, wishing at that moment that he was anywhere else in the world. He hated the helpless feeling that came from having to be pushed in the chair, but there was no avoiding it now.

Suddenly, Alice was there bending over him, throwing her arms around his neck. He felt the touch of her lips on his and heard the thunderous cheer that went up from the crowd. He put his hands up and clung to her for a moment. Then she drew back, and he saw her eyes flashing with the excitement of it all.

"You're going to get a medal, isn't it wonderful!" she exclaimed.

Lewis was embarrassed at what happened next. A band broke out playing "The Star-Spangled Banner" while everyone stood, their heads uncovered and hands over their proud hearts. Then a general stepped forward, and after waiting for the crowd to quiet down, proceeded to make a speech. He came to stand before

Lewis, and Lewis was so overwhelmed by what was happening he hardly heard what the officer said as he spoke. He felt the general's touch and looked down to see a medal dangling from a ribbon. *It's the Congressional Medal of Honor!* he thought in a daze and shook his head. "I don't deserve this," he mumbled, but his voice was drowned by the applause and cheers.

There were so many people gathered at the wharf that it was almost impossible for the soldiers disembarking to go anywhere. The ceremony had as many speakers, and every politician had an important word to say about the glorious victory in Cuba. But finally, Mark and Lola made their way through the crowd and surrounded Aaron and Lewis. Lola bent down and put her arms around Lewis and whispered, "I'm taking you home right now!"

Pushing and shoving their way through the crowd, they finally left the wharf. Lewis was helped into the carriage by Aaron and one of the members of the Rough Riders who had followed. When Lewis looked back, he saw that Alice had not followed. Her face was beaming at the thrill of it all as she stayed to hear more of the speeches.

Catching his glance, Lola said, "Alice will be along later. She's arranging some appearances for you."

Lewis gave her a miserable look. "I don't want any appearances," he said firmly. "All I want to do is get where there's a little peace and quiet."

Lola exchanged a quick look with Aaron, understanding from the look in his face and the slight shake of the head that this was no time to argue. "Come along," she said. "I can't wait to start taking care of you two soldiers!"

★　★　★　★

Burns walked along the hall of Baxter Hospital with Gail and Deborah on either side of him. As soon as they had left the dock, they had caught a cab and come straight to the hospital. The three could hardly wait to give their report to the administrator. He'd been at the celebration on the dock and had greeted them enthusiastically. "Well," he said, "you've done a magnificent job in Cuba, but now I claim you back for Baxter." He'd also given Gail and Deborah a warm welcome, assuring them they could have their same positions. "Both of you need to continue your studies," he said. "You need to become full-fledged nurses."

Now as they walked along the old, familiar hall, Gail felt strange about the appearance of everything. "Everything's so clean," she said with wonder in her voice. "Was it always this clean?"

Deborah turned to smile at her. "When you've been hot and wallowing in mud and filth for a while, I guess you see things a little differently."

"You're right about that! It does look good, doesn't it!" Burns turned into the small room used by the physicians, where they were greeted enthusiastically by their former co-workers. They spent the next hour answering the questions shot at them by the eager physicians. Dr. Burns had had to perform quite a few surgeries on wounded men without all the benefits of a hospital. The other doctors were curious and wanted to hear every detail about the procedures he had to use under less-than-desirable conditions.

Gail finally slipped away, whispering to Deborah, "Tell Dr. Burns that I'll see him tomorrow. I need to go home and see my family."

She left the hospital and at once made her way to Water Street. Strangely enough, after the heat and squalor of Cuba, even the deplorable conditions that she'd grown up in seemed relatively clean. It was not really clean, of course, and she marveled at how her experiences had changed her view of things. She ran up the three flights of stairs and knocked on the door. It opened almost at once, and her mother stood there for a moment; then the two women fell into each other's arms. Martha held her daughter tightly and tears ran down her cheeks. "I'm so glad you're home, Gail," she said. "I've thought of you every day and prayed for you and your friends."

"I could feel your prayers, Ma," Gail said. She looked around quickly and said, "Jeb's not here?" She saw the cloud fall over her mother's face and asked quickly, "Is he still running with that crowd?"

"Worse than ever. I hate to be the one to give you bad news, but I'm worried sick about him. He goes out and stays out all night sometimes. Nothing good is going to come of it."

"Doesn't Pa say anything to him?"

"He's too sick to care much." Martha Lawson glanced at the bedroom and said, "He's much worse, Gail . . . I don't think he'll live much longer."

"Has he had another attack?"

"Yes, two of them since you left. He's practically bedridden now. But come in and see him." She bit her lip and shook her head sadly. "I know he's never been kind to you, Gail, but he's so changed that you can't help but pity him."

Gail went into the small bedroom and was shocked at the change in her stepfather. All of her life she had seen him as a big, burly man with rough strength who was never afraid of anything. Now, however, he looked frail. The color of his skin was pale and his face was gaunt and shrunken. When he saw her, he whispered her name. She went over to his bed and leaned over, kissed him and whispered, "I'm back, Pa! I'm sorry to see that you're not feeling well."

Harry Lawson shook his head and licked his lips. It seemed to be an effort for him to speak, and his voice was raspy as he said, "I've . . . had it!" Fear filled his dull eyes, and he clung to her hand pitifully. Gail stood there talking to him as cheerfully as she could for a while. Finally, she said, "I have to leave now, Pa, but now that I'm back, I'll come and visit you often. I want to tell you all about Cuba."

She turned and went out into the living room. Shaking her head she said, "I'm afraid you're right, Ma. He looks awful!" They sat down at the table and the women began to talk. Gail spent the afternoon with her mother telling her about her time in Cuba. Then she went out to buy some groceries and helped her mother cook the evening meal.

Late in the afternoon, at suppertime, Bart came in accompanied by Riley. After greeting them, Gail said, "Have you seen Jeb?"

Evasively the two looked at each other. "Uh . . . I seen him earlier. He was with Tug Devaney," shrugged Bart.

Tug Devaney was the ringleader of the gang that Jeb had been running with lately. Gail questioned them further and finally Bart mumbled, "I guess he might be down at the pool hall."

At once, Gail rose, saying, "I'll go see if I can find him and bring him back for supper."

She left the building and quickly walked the few blocks to the pool hall—a disreputable-looking hangout for the toughs of the neighborhood. When she walked inside, she was greeted with whistles and rude remarks. Back in the far corner, she saw Jeb. He had a pool cue in his hand and a cigarette in his lips. The sight of him like that wrung Gail's heart. She let none of her dismay show. "Jeb—I just got in! Come home for supper. I want to tell you all about Cuba."

Devaney, a tall, thin individual with black hair and hazel eyes, grinned at her. "Hello, nursie! You want me to come along too?"

Gail ignored him and saw that Jeb was trying to act tough in front of the men he knew in the room. "Oh, you go on, sis. I'll be there as soon as I finish this game."

"All right." Gail was wise enough to know not to make an issue. "Come as soon as you can." She turned and made her way through the clouds of smoke that gathered around the pool tables. She was worried about Jeb and didn't even seem to hear the whistles as she walked past. When she reached the front door, she looked back at Jeb, and a heaviness settled on her. Quickly, she left the pool hall and returned to the small apartment. Pearl had arrived by then and was eager to hear Gail's stories about Cuba.

As soon as the simple meal was set out, they sat down and Gail asked a simple blessing. They had just started eating when the door opened suddenly and Jeb came in looking shamefaced. He slumped in his seat, expecting to be bawled out.

Looking up, Gail only said, "Here—I cooked this especially for you, Jeb. You eat and I'll tell you about Cuba."

The family sat there listening as Gail spoke of her time in Cuba. They all seemed drawn by the story of the war. Bart and Riley, who normally kept their distance, sat quietly as their stepsister spoke of the battle to take San Juan Hill, and the courage of the men she had met and had helped care for. They were full of questions, and Gail was pleased at the interest they seemed to take.

Later on, when it was time for Gail to leave to return to the hospital, she had a word with Jeb alone. She let her arm fall on his shoulder affectionately and said, "I've missed you, Jeb!"

"Well . . . I've missed you, too!"

Gail hesitated, and then said, "Now that I'm home, we'll spend lots of time together. Aaron tells me he's going to take you riding again. Would you like that?"

"I guess so," said Jeb, shrugging his shoulders.

Gail sensed an adamant quality to his voice, and he held his back straight. She had seen this in many of the boys who grew up in the neighborhood. To fit in, they had to make it their aim to be tough. From what she had seen earlier in the pool hall, Jeb had fallen into the same trap. She said no more, but kissed his cheek and said, "I'll see you tomorrow."

Kissing her mother, she left and made her way back to the hospital. All along the way, she fought back the fears that rose within her. *He's turning into one of those tough, hateful boys. God, you've got to do something!* The prayer was on her heart constantly for the next few days, and she knew that it would take God to change her brother's life.

★　★　★　★

Davis and Belle had taken the next train from Virginia as soon as the letter had come from Lola telling them of the arrival of the troops. Now they were seated in the parlor with Mark and Lola, waiting for the arrival of Lewis and Aaron. Davis said finally, "I'm grateful the war is over—but there are a lot of grieving families in this country. I'm wondering if it was worth it all."

Shaking his head, Mark answered quickly, "You can't think about that, Davis. Lots of people who lost their sons and loved ones asked the same thing about the Civil War."

"All wars are the same to parents," Lola spoke up. "No war is worth a son—or a husband or brother."

"I think's that's right, Lola," Belle nodded. She was wearing a pearl gray dress that fit her superbly, and a pair of matched pearls adorned her small ears. "Sometimes I think that if women ran the world, some of these foolish wars would never take place."

Davis grinned at his wife's view, lifting one heavy eyebrow with mock astonishment. "You've managed to run my life for a few years—now you want to run the whole country!"

Belle's dark eyes sparked, and she answered pertly, "I could do better than some of the men who've made such a mess of things."

"Better than William Randolph Hearst?" Davis asked. "With your son working for him, you'd better not let him hear you make such bold claims."

"I think the man's a pompous fool," Belle said sharply. "I hope Aaron has sense enough to see that he's only interested in using people and situations to make money and enhance his own over-blown reputation. He'd do *anything* to sell another newspaper!"

Mark was also somewhat cynical about journalism as a profession. "I don't think Hearst is any worse than Pulitzer or the rest of the lot. Most of them aren't really interested in much except making money."

Lola turned to her husband, saying sweetly, "How nice they aren't as greedy as the railroad barons you work for."

"That's different," Mark sputtered, taken aback a little at his wife's comment. "At least the railroads perform a needed service. They move people and goods from one place to another. What does yellow journalism do for anyone? Hearst's sensationalism just gets people all stirred up."

"If those kinds of stories didn't sell, Hearst would get into an-other line of business," Davis said philosophically. A wicked light touched his mild eyes and he added innocently, "Maybe he'd go into bankrobbing or running a bawdy house in the Bowery."

All three of the others stared at him, then burst out into laugh-ter. "You have a strange mind, Davis," Mark finally stated. "But you've probably put Mr. William Randolph Hearst in the proper perspective—" He broke off as a maid came in right then.

"Mr. Winslow, they're here."

At once the four rose and hurried to the foyer, where Lewis was being wheeled in by a young woman. Suddenly there was a whirl of tears and embraces as everyone greeted one another.

"This is my mother and father, Deborah." Lewis beamed as they embraced him. "They've come all the way from Virginia to see Aaron and me. Dad, Mom—this is Deborah Laurent, the woman who saved my life."

Deborah was not a young woman who was easily embar-rassed, but Lewis's introduction brought color to her cheeks. She'd only come out at Mark and Lola's special invitation and Lewis's insistence to meet his parents. "Oh, Lewis, don't be fool-ish! I was just your nurse for a while."

But Lewis was adamant in his praise of her to his entire family. The last two weeks had put some healthy color back in his cheeks, and he even had gained some of the weight he'd lost. The wound in his back had healed up nicely, so that his upper body was fine, though he still had gotten no feeling back in his legs. "Don't listen to her!" he grinned. "I was in a blue funk and she sat beside me, I don't know how many days, until she pulled me out. She may not look it, as little and as fragile as she is, but she's as stubborn as a blue-nosed mule."

At that, Deborah's cheeks turned a bright crimson and she stared at him. Lewis laughed and went on to tell of how much she had cared for him right after he had been brought to the hospital. Belle Winslow went at once to the young woman and took her hand. "I can't tell you how grateful we are for all that you've done for Lewis," she said warmly. She was impressed by the girl, not with her beauty, but with the serenity that seemed to surround her like a soft cloak. "You've got to tell me all about it. Come along now."

"Wait a minute!" Davis protested. He came over and insisted on shaking Deborah's hand. His smile was kind and he said, "You women can have your little talk, but after that you and I will have a little time, all right, Miss Laurent?"

"Of course, Mr. Winslow," said Deborah, then she turned and followed Belle into the parlor.

All day, Deborah found herself the center of the attention of Lewis's parents. More than once, Belle had come and placed her hand on Deborah's arm and expressed her gratitude for all the young nurse had done to help Lewis. Deborah liked them both tremendously, and finally when she and Belle were alone, she said, "I really didn't do that much for Lewis, but I'm glad he's doing well."

Belle was pouring tea into a bone-white china cup. When it was full, she handed it to the woman, then poured a cup for herself. Holding it, Deborah said, "He's doing fine physically from the waist up, but there's no improvement in the paralysis"—she hesitated momentarily, but then continued—"and it's not only that that's bothering me."

Deborah had been receiving reports of Lewis's condition through Aaron, who made it a point to stop by the hospital from time to time. One thing troubled her, and she finally looked at Belle and asked, "Is Miss Cates visiting him a lot?"

There was a moment's silence and a noticeable hardness came over Belle Winslow's face. Her lips drew together for a moment, then she shook her head and sighed. "She was here every day for the first week—taking Lewis off to some party, but it was a great deal of difficulty. She was always in a hurry to cart him off to introduce him to someone new. It was hard for him, because he couldn't move easily in the chair. I could tell she was annoyed at it at times." Belle hesitated, then went on. "We haven't seen her lately." Her candid words seemed to ring in the air, and Belle lifted her eyes to meet those of Deborah. The two women did not speak, but there was an instant communication between them.

"I'm sorry," Deborah said finally. "He's very much in love with her."

"I doubt that," Belle said, her voice crisp. "I think if anything good has come out of this, it's that he finally has realized that Alice Cates is a superficial young woman." She gave Deborah a straightforward look. "You've always known that, haven't you?"

Deborah met Belle's gaze and nodded slowly. "She's a social butterfly. I think that's fairly easy to see. Is Lewis very much hurt by it?"

"He was—but I think he's slowly getting over it. I pray that he is," Belle said. "He thinks a great deal of you. Please try to encourage him all you can."

Finishing her tea, Deborah thanked Belle, and then went to talk with Lewis. She spent the entire afternoon visiting with him and trying to encourage him. She had a way of seeing the bright things of life that lifted Lewis's spirit. At one point earlier in the day, Davis and Belle, who were watching them from a distance, heard them laughing over something. "That's the first time I've heard him laugh like that," Davis said soberly. "That girl's good for him."

"Yes, she is. Maybe she'll be able to put that frightful Alice out of his mind. I could strangle that girl!" Belle's eyes were alight with anger, and only when Davis put his hand on her arm did she manage to control herself. "We'll have to invite Deborah here often and see that Lewis spends time with her. He needs to get out. It seems she has more influence over him than anyone else. . . ."

★   ★   ★   ★

"Son, how about a walk? I need to stretch my aging legs."

"Sounds good, Dad."

The two men had been sitting in the study speaking of the war, but both of them were glad to step outside into the fresh air. Aaron had been busy spending a few days at the offices of the *Journal*. Since his return from Cuba, Mr. Hearst had kept him extremely busy writing a series of articles about his experiences in the thick of the battle.

The two of them walked slowly down the road that ran in front of Mark and Lola's house. For a time they talked of trivial things, then Davis's voice took a serious tone, and he asked, "What about you, son? Now that the war's over, what's on your mind? Any plans?"

"Right now my only plan is to stay with Lewis. Do you think we should take him home to Virginia?"

"I don't know, Aaron. Your mother and I haven't been able to make up our minds. Not just yet, I think." Davis turned to him and said, "I'm glad you were with him, and I'm glad you're going to stay with him, too." He had a thought and said, "Mark's got a small cabin in the upper part of the state. Nothing fancy, but you and I could take a few days off—just the two of us."

"What about Lewis?"

"Why, he's pretty taken up with that young woman. You and I haven't had much time together lately. It'd do us good to get away. Let's go—even if it's just for a couple of days."

"All right, Dad. I'd like that. Then I'll come back and spend time with Lewis. I don't know what good I'll do him, but I'll do the best I can."

"Lewis says he's going to be healed and that he'll walk again," said Davis.

"I know. But do you think so, Dad?"

"I'm not as sure of it as your mother seems to be," Davis admitted reluctantly. "She thinks so! And so does that young woman—Deborah."

"She's something, isn't she?" Aaron shook his head with admiration. "She never talks about herself much, but I've never seen a woman with so much grit. I don't know about his healing, though. That sort of thing is out of my line."

Davis Winslow looked at his son, admiring the strength in the face so much like his own. "Well, God is still in control, though I must admit things look hard for Lewis. But that's all I have to hang on to for him. It's out of the doctors' hands, I think."

"That's what Dr. Burns says. But he's praying too." Aaron stopped suddenly and looked back toward the house. "It's funny, Dad, the people I know and love the most believe in God. Why can't I be like the rest of you?"

"The Winslow men are pretty stubborn. Most of them come to God the hard way. We talked about that at the reunion, remember? Some of us came kicking and screaming." Suddenly, he laid his hand on Aaron's shoulder and smiled. "You'll come to know the Lord somehow. I don't know what it will take, but I'm believing that Lewis will walk—and you'll find Christ."

Aaron looked at him. He would have thrown off the words at one time, but the war and Lewis's wound had changed him—and the faith of two young nurses had changed him too. He dropped his eyes, studied the ground for a moment, then lifted his head. "That would be good," he said. "Both of those things." The two turned and walked toward the house, and Davis felt the sudden surge of happiness, for it was the first time that Aaron had spoken of becoming a man of faith.

CHAPTER TWENTY-ONE

AT GUNPOINT

★ ★ ★ ★

Gail was changing the bandage on an elderly patient when Dr. Templeton, the administrator, stepped inside the door. "Miss Summers, you have a visitor."

Turning to face him, Gail asked, "A visitor, sir?"

"Yes, he's waiting for you in my office."

"Yes, sir, I'll be right there." Gail finished with the new dressing and pulled the sheet back over the patient, saying, "There—that's better, isn't it?" She left the room and made her way to Dr. Templeton's office. When she entered, she found him speaking with a heavyset man with a bushy mustache. "Miss Summers, this is Lieutenant Darvin of the police department," Dr. Templeton said. He shifted his weight nervously and said, "Why don't you use that small office over there. You can have some privacy."

The policeman turned to Dr. Templeton and said, "That will be fine."

After they entered the room, Gail closed the door and asked at once, "What's the trouble, Officer?" Apprehension suddenly rose in Gail as she waited to hear what this was all about.

Darvin rolled back on his heels and clasped his hands behind him. He had a reddish face and dark blue eyes. "I'm afraid I have some bad news for you, Miss Summers. It's about your brother."

"Jeb? What's wrong? Where is he?" said Gail.

"Well, that's what we'd like to find out. We have a warrant out for his arrest along with some others. One of them is Tug Devaney. Do you know him?"

"Yes, but what's the charge?" she asked nervously.

"Burglary, Miss Summers. They were caught robbing a warehouse. They all got away, but an eyewitness spotted them and identified Devaney and your brother. It happened right there in the neighborhood, so he knew them both."

"I don't think my brother would do anything like that," Gail said defiantly.

"Well, I hope not, but we still have to pick him up. He'll be charged, but since he's a minor that will make a difference."

"What could happen to him if he's found guilty?" Gail asked hesitantly.

"Why, off to reform school, I'm afraid." Darvin's eyes narrowed and he said, "Would you be knowing where he is, Miss Summers? It'd be best if you tell me. There's no trouble that way, but if he goes on the run it could turn out worse for him."

"I haven't heard from him, so I don't know, Lieutenant."

"I see—well, I hate to be the bearer of bad news. Let me know if you hear from him. It'd be best if he turned himself in!" Darvin nodded politely, and then turned and left the room.

At once, Gail sat down in the chair. Her legs were trembling and she tried hard to think. For a few moments she tried to pray. Finally she pulled herself together enough to leave the room. Dr. Templeton was standing outside in the hall, watching the policeman leave. Gail saw him and said at once, "I have some trouble at home, Doctor. I need to leave the hospital."

"Of course, Miss Summers," Dr. Templeton said hastily. "If we can be of any help, please let us know. I'm sorry about this."

"Thank you, Doctor Templeton."

When Gail went to get her things, she encountered David coming out of one of the physician's offices. "What's wrong?" he said at once, noting that her face was pale.

"It's . . . Jeb! He's got himself in some kind of trouble. I've got to go see about him."

A look of genuine concern filled the physician's face. "I can't leave right now, but I'll be there as soon as I can."

"No, you wait here! I'll come back and tell you about it when I know more."

David protested, but Gail was firm, and insisted he wait to hear from her. She left the hospital at once and walked hurriedly to the apartment. She found out that the police had already been there, and her mother could only wring her hands in despair and weep. Gail said defiantly, "I'm going to find out where he is. Somebody has to know where he is."

"You can't go out on the streets asking that!" said her mother, her face in her hands.

"Yes, I can! I've got to try to find him." With that, Gail turned and left.

Gail headed straight for the pool hall and marched inside. She had known several of the young loafers there for years and walked over to one named Dan Sullivan, who was busy playing a game. "Dan," she said, "you've heard about Jeb?"

"Yeah," Sullivan nodded nervously, "and about Devaney, too! It looks like they messed up."

"I've got to find Jeb. Do you know where they are?" demanded Gail.

Defensively, Sullivan shook his head. "I used to run with Devaney, but he was too wild for me. I don't know nothing about it, Gail." Then as if to avoid any further questions, he turned and continued his game.

Within an hour, Gail had exhausted every possibility she could think of. But nobody she talked to either knew or wanted to say anything about Devaney or Jeb. She started home slowly, her heart despondent. When she was a block from the house, she saw her stepbrother, Bart, up ahead walking the same way. "Bart, wait!" She ran to catch up with him. He was fidgety and didn't seem to want to talk, and there was a look of apprehension on his face as they walked side by side.

"Bart, what do you know about this robbery?"

"Me? I don't know nothing—I wasn't there!" he said quickly.

But there was something in his tone and mannerism that alerted Gail. She began to question him, and when he tried to walk off, she grabbed his arm and pulled him back, saying fiercely, "Bart, this isn't a game! You realize that Jeb could go to jail for this? You know where he is, don't you?"

"Let me go!" Bart had lost all of his toughness and looked merely frightened now. He would have walked away, but Gail caught him again and whirled him around. Her eyes were flashing and she said, "You know more than you're saying. Now tell me!" She kept at him until finally his hands began to tremble.

"Listen, I can't tell you. If I did, Devaney—there's no telling what he'd do to me."

"You're going to tell me or I'll go to the police and tell them you were in on it."

"You wouldn't do that!"

"If you don't tell me, I'll do whatever I have to do to help Jeb get out of this mess. Now, do you know where they are?"

Bart was thoroughly afraid of Devaney. He knew the gang leader had no scruples and could be very dangerous. Everyone knew that Devaney had used a knife twice on those who had crossed him. Fearing what could happen, Bart said. "Gail, he'd kill me if I told where he was!"

"He won't know. Where is he?"

"You've got to promise me that you won't tell a word about how you found out!" said Bart as his eyes darted up and down the street, afraid somehow that someone was watching them.

"All right, I promise. Now, out with it!" insisted Gail.

"I ain't for sure, but there's a hideout that Tug uses sometimes. It's a room up over the old furniture factory. The factory's closed down now and it's just an empty building. But there's a way to get in through the back. We used to go there and have our meetings. I don't think anybody knows about it except the gang. But, you can't—"

As Gail loosed his arm and turned and ran down the street, he cried, "Hey! Remember—you promised not to say a word about me!" He bit his lip as Gail disappeared around the corner. He pulled his shoulders together and said, "Ain't none of my affair. I ain't got nothing to do with it."

★ ★ ★ ★

Aaron stepped down from the cab, paid his fare, and stood staring at Baxter Hospital for a moment. Then he climbed the stairs and entered the hospital. He went at once to the head nurse,

Agnes Smith, who was busy trying to give instructions to one of her nurses. "Excuse me, I'm looking for Miss Summers, Miss Smith," said Aaron when she had finished.

"You wait here and I'll get her. She's down the hall."

Aaron nodded and as the nurse disappeared, he took a note out of his pocket and stared at it. "I must see you at once, Aaron." It was simply signed, "Gail." A special messenger had brought it, and he had come to town hurriedly. He was mystified, for it was not like Gail to do such a thing. He was still wondering about it as she appeared around the corner down the hall. He looked at her and saw that her face was pale and her lips were pulled together in a thin line. "What's wrong?" he asked sharply.

"Come down here where we can talk." She led him into a side room where supplies were kept, and at once turned and said, "It's Jeb—he's in terrible trouble. We've got to help him."

Aaron listened, his eyes narrowing as Gail quickly explained in detail what Lieutenant Darvin had told her about Jeb. As soon as she finished, he said, "Where is he? Do you know?"

"Yes. I can't tell you how I know. Aaron, we've got to get him away."

"But he needs to turn himself in," said Aaron.

"Aaron, I want you to help, but you have to promise me something."

"What is it?"

"If we get him away from there, I . . . I don't want him to think we're like policemen. I don't want to force him to do anything. It has to be his choice whether he gives himself up. You have to promise me that."

Aaron paused and saw the lines of strain on her face. He thought hard for a moment, shrugged, then said, "It'd be better if he did, but, okay—I promise. Now, where is he? I think it would be better if I went alone."

"No, I'm going with you." She listened as Aaron argued against it, but said defiantly, "You can't go unless I tell you where it is, and I'm not telling unless I go with you."

Seeing the stubborn set of her face, Aaron said abruptly, "All right! I've got to have a few minutes, though—I have an errand to run. I'll meet you outside in an hour." He turned, and as soon as he left, he walked quickly to a seedy section of town that contained a series of pawn shops. He entered one, and when the owner came to ask what he needed, Aaron looked at the glass case in front and said, "I'll take that .44. Do you have any shells for it?"

The owner gave him a quick look and said, "I'll have to have your name and some identification, sir."

"That's fine," Aaron said briefly. "Let's see the gun."

Ten minutes later, he was out of the pawn shop, walking back toward the hospital. Inside his coat pocket was tucked the gun. His mind was working rapidly, and by the time Gail came out of the hospital, he said at once, "There may be trouble, Gail. I'd rather you didn't go—you might get hurt."

Gail looked up at him and her lips were firm. "I'm going and that's all there is to it. Do you promise you won't make Jeb turn himself in?"

When he nodded, she said, "Let's go then."

★ ★ ★ ★

Tug Devaney was sound asleep and did not even hear the sound of footsteps coming up the stairs. Jeb, however, was awake. He had not slept much since the two had fled and the gang had scattered. He, himself, had not been actively involved. Tug had not even told him where they were going, but he had begged so hard that Tug had finally said, "Okay, you can tag along, but that's all." When they had made their way to the dark street, they had come to a corner and Tug had simply said, "You stay here. If you see any cops, come running down the street yelling."

That had been all Jeb had known until suddenly Tug and the three others had come rushing down the street, feet pounding. They had passed Jeb without speaking, and when he saw the pursuer, he turned and fled with them. They had taken a circuitous route until they finally ended up at this hideout, but the other three had left almost at once.

As the hours ticked by, Jeb had asked himself a thousand times why he'd gone and done such a foolish thing. But he had no answer, and sat in the darkness shaking his head, afraid at what could happen now. As he heard the footsteps approaching stealthily, he thought, *It's the police—I'm going to jail!* He got up and turned to face the door. He thought of waking Tug, but he knew that Tug kept a gun and was afraid that he would use it. All he wanted was to get out of here, even if it meant getting arrested. Tug had refused to let him go, saying, "No, you'd spill the beans, boy. You stay with me till this blows over."

The doorknob turned and the door slowly opened. Jeb could make out two figures standing there, and then—he saw that one of them was Gail. When he spoke her name, Tug instantly came awake. Seeing the two strange figures in the door, he made a wild grab for his gun that lay on the table next to him.

"Hold it right there or you're dead!" Aaron had entered the room and laid the muzzle of the pistol on Devaney, his finger tightening on the trigger, for the man's hand was almost touching the revolver on the table.

"I ain't shooting!" Devaney cried out sharply, throwing his hands up. "Who are you, anyway?" Then he saw Gail and let loose a relieved sigh. "Oh, it's you, Gail! How'd you find us?"

Gail did not even answer. She looked at Jeb and said, "Come on, Jeb, we're leaving." At once, Jeb turned to her, and as soon as he reached her, tears formed in his eyes. "I . . . I'm sorry, sis."

Aaron did not turn, but kept his gun leveled at Devaney. He walked over to the table, picked up the pistol, and slowly slipped it into his pocket. "Don't follow us," he warned. "Or it will be unpleasant for you." He backed out of the room, thinking the man might have another gun. When Aaron stepped outside and shut the door, he said, "Let's get out of here."

They left the building at once and turned and walked quickly down the dark street. As soon as they were two blocks away, Aaron said, "Here—we've got to get you out of sight, Jeb." He turned to the boy and said, "It would be best if you give yourself up."

Fear swept through the boy. "No, I ain't gonna do that. Let's just run away."

Aaron knew it would go better for the boy if he went immediately to the police station, but he saw the fear in Jeb's eyes and remembered his promise to Gail. "All right, we'll go somewhere and talk about it."

"Where can we go?" Gail said. "They'll be looking everywhere for him."

Aaron had already thought about this. "I know a place," he said. "Uncle Mark has a hunting camp right in the middle of nowhere. It's in the upper part of the state in the middle of the woods. Dad and I spent a couple of days there. It's a good place to hide."

"We can't just disappear. Our people would be worried sick," said Gail.

Aaron nodded. "Right! We'll have to send them word. Write a note to your folks, and I'll do the same for mine."

"But . . . what will we say?"

"Just say we're all right but that we have to be gone for a few days. When we get there, we can write if we need to. Be sure you write Deborah a note. And be *sure* you tell them not to tell a soul about the notes."

"I . . . I wish we didn't have to do this, Aaron!"

"So do I—but right now we've got to think of Jeb." A strange look crossed his features, and he added, "I didn't know how much I'd come to think of Jeb—not until now!"

Gail reached up and touched his cheek, whispering, "You're so sweet, Aaron! No other man would do this!"

For a moment they stood there in the shadows, and Aaron was conscious of the pressure of her hand. He took it, held it, and smiled as he said, "I'm not all that sweet, I guess. Come on, we've got to hurry!"

CHAPTER TWENTY-TWO

"LOVE IS MORE THAN A KISS!"

★ ★ ★ ★

"We'd better get settled in," said Aaron as he set down the bags he was carrying. Glancing around the murky interior, he said, "I'll try to rig up something to make a bedroom for you, Gail. Why don't you see if you can throw some kind of supper together. Jeb, go find some wood and start a fire in that cookstove, then you can bring the rest of the stuff in."

The cabin had only the one large room, and though it was fairly spacious, there was no privacy. Aaron went outside into a toolshed that leaned in a precarious fashion and began to rummage around. Finding some wire and an old canvas tarp that was torn in several places, he grunted with satisfaction. After scrounging around, he came up with some nails, a rusty hammer, and a pair of pliers he found in a wooden box. Picking up his findings, he went back inside the cabin. Jeb was blowing on a pile of small sticks inside the stove, and Gail was emptying sacks and cans, stacking them in boxes that had been nailed to the wall for shelves.

Measuring the cabin with his eye, Aaron moved to the end away from the stove and table. He drove a nail firmly into one of the weathered uprights, then did the same on another across the room. He looped one end of the rusty wire over the nail, bent the nail so that it held fast—then stretched the wire across the room and fastened it, pulling the wire as tightly as possible before cinching it. He clipped six-inch pieces of the wire from the roll, then shoved them through one side of the canvas about a foot apart. When he'd finished this, he held one end of the canvas up, looped the ties over the taut wire, and twisted the two ends. When the entire canvas was hanging limply from the wire, he grunted with satisfaction and turned to find Gail smiling at him.

"You're quite resourceful." She came to look behind the hanging, and then said, "Thank you, Aaron. This is better than anything we had in Cuba."

"For a fact." Picking up the tools, he carried them back outside to the toolshed. He saw that some wood had been cut and hauled, but was not split. He'd spotted a double-bitted ax in the shed, and soon he was splitting the logs. Darkness was falling fast, and when Jeb stepped outside, Aaron said, "Take some of these chunks inside, will you, Jeb?"

"You sure do know how to split wood." Jeb was watching with admiration, and he asked, "Can I try it, Mr. Winslow?"

"Why not?" Aaron gave the boy a few pointers, then stood by as Jeb took a few swings at the wood. He was awkward at first, but Aaron said, "You've got a good swing. All you need is a little practice." He watched the boy for a while, then the smell of cooking meat came to him. "That'll be enough. Let's wash up."

The two entered the cabin, and Aaron saw three tin plates set out on the table, along with cups and forks. "I was just about to call you," Gail said. "It's nothing fancy, just bacon and eggs tonight."

"Smells mighty good to me," said Aaron as he sat down and Jeb settled himself across the table. Gail walked over from the cookstove and set a platter of scrambled eggs and another one of crisp bacon on the table, then poured three cups of coffee. When she seated herself, she glanced at Aaron, asking, "Shall I ask the blessing?" When he nodded shortly, she spoke a few words of thanks, then looked up and said, "I'm starved!"

"Me too!" Jeb began to eat hungrily, and twice refilled his plate.

"The way you're shoveling that down," Aaron grinned, "we'll either have to start raising chickens and hogs or go to the store every day."

"Tomorrow I'll make biscuits," Gail promised. She was eating with enjoyment, and when they were through, she said, "I'm not usually so hungry. I ate like a starving wolf!"

"It's the outdoors," Aaron commented. Leaning back in his chair, he teetered dangerously, then added, "Don't know why, but being out in the fresh air gives you an appetite. When I was growing up and Dad took Lewis and me hunting, I had to take so much grub along that he got disgusted with me." He got up and started to take his plate.

"I'll do that," Gail said quickly. "You and Jeb can chop the wood, and I'll do the cooking and dishwashing."

"Sounds fair enough to me," grinned Aaron. He waited until she'd washed the dishes and cleaned up, then said, "Let's walk supper off. There's a nice little pond about a quarter of a mile from here."

The three of them left the cabin and strolled along under the bright light of the full moon. "Harvest moon," Aaron commented, admiring the fullness of the silver disk. "Best time of the year for hunting, too." He led the way down the narrow path that was worn smooth, followed by Gail and Jeb. Enormous trees rose on each side, forming thick walls, and the path made a serpentine track through the woods. Finally he stopped and stepped aside. "There it is."

Gail stepped to the bank and took a deep breath. "It's so beautiful!" she whispered. The pond was not large, no more than three acres or so, but it was spring fed. The moon was reflected in the waters, and a small breeze ruffled the surface so that the gleaming image quivered like quicksilver.

"There's a path around it," Aaron said. "Made by Indians a long time ago, I guess. Come along."

Gail and Jeb walked along the bank, struck silent by the beauty of the pond. Suddenly, a shadow passed over them and Gail gave a small cry of alarm. Looking up she saw a large bird outlined against the sky. As she watched, it wheeled and floated over the pond, disappearing into the night.

"What was *that*?" Jeb whispered.

"Great horned owl. A big one."

"Are they dangerous?" Gail asked timidly.

"Only to mice and small game."

"I've never seen a bird that big!" exclaimed Jeb.

"Last time I was here," Aaron remarked, "I saw quite a few bald eagles. Now those fellows are something to see! You haven't lived until you see one of them swoop down out of the sky and catch up a fish with their talons." He caught the look of amazement on the boy's face and asked quietly, "You've never been in the woods, Jeb?"

"No, not ever."

"Well, you'll see some fine things. I always enjoy the woods."

They moved around the small pond, finally coming back to the path. As they stood for one last look, Gail said, "It's so quiet, Aaron! It's so quiet it . . . it hurts my ears!" Even as she spoke, a large fish broke the surface of the water with a tremendous splash, almost at their feet. Both Gail and Jeb started, but Aaron laughed.

"That was a bass. A big one."

"Can we catch him, Mr. Winslow?"

"Not now. We'll try and get him early in the morning. And you can call me Aaron. *Mister* sounds kind of formal out here in the woods."

They turned back on the path through the woods and returned to the cabin. Gail bustled around with the blankets for a time making a bed of sorts. Aaron heated up the coffee, speaking idly with Jeb—who was bursting with a thousand questions about fishing and hunting. Finally Gail came and sat down with them. She held a black book in her hand and gave Aaron a shy look. "Will it be all right if I read some of the Bible out loud before I go to bed?"

"I ain't sleepy!" Jeb protested, but when Gail had read two chapters from Psalms, she saw that his head was drooping. Closing the Bible, she said firmly, "All right, into bed with you."

"Aw, sis—!"

"No arguments."

Jeb protested, but after a stern look from Gail, he slipped into the blankets. "Can we go fishing in the morning, Aaron?"

"If you can get up at dawn," said Aaron as he sipped his coffee.

"I'll get up! If I don't, just jerk me out of this bunk!"

Gail made one more surveillance of the stock of groceries they'd brought along, then turned to say, "I'm tired. Good-night, Aaron."

"Good-night."

For a long time after Gail moved behind the canvas, Aaron sat at the table thinking. One of the psalms Gail had read was the twenty-second psalm—his mother's favorite. As he sat leaning on the table, an old memory stirred, a fragment of his childhood. His mother had read the psalm to him and Lewis, and he'd seen tears in her eyes. "Why are you crying, Ma?" he'd asked her. In the quietness of the cabin, he seemed to hear her reply: "Because this is about the time my Savior died for my sins," she'd whispered.

"A long time ago . . ." Aaron whispered. He sat there quietly, thinking of that time, wondering where a man's youth went— where was the young boy that had been? Finally he rose, took off his boots, then fell into the cot and dropped instantly into a deep sleep.

★   ★   ★   ★

"Aw, Aaron, you promised we'd go fishing!" Jeb rubbed his eyes and rose up to give the man a reproachful look. His hair was wild, and he shoved his fingers through it as he came out of the bunk.

"Thought we'd go hunting instead," Aaron said. He'd slept until dawn, but when he awoke and saw the boy still deep in sleep, he decided that the fishing could wait. He was sitting at the table regarding the boy, and said, "Come on now, let's eat and get out of here."

An hour later the two were walking through the woods. Aaron carried the single-shot rifle he'd managed to buy at the last stop. He'd given Jeb the shells to stick in his pockets, and now as they moved along, he asked, "Ever shoot a shotgun, Jeb?"

"Never shot no kind of gun at all."

"Well, maybe you'd better have a little practice." Aaron handed the boy the gun, saying, "Whatever else you do, don't shoot me—or yourself." He looked around and saw a pine tree fifty feet away with a bald spot about the size of a dinner plate. "See how many shot you can put into that bald spot."

Jeb lifted the rifle, took careful aim, and nervously pulled the trigger. The sharp explosion split the still air, and when he lowered the gun, Jeb yelled, "I hit it, I think!"

"Let's go see," Aaron said, grinning at the boy's excitement.

The two of them made their way to the tree, and sure enough, three of the pellets had made definite holes in the wood. "Good shot," Aaron remarked. "If that was a bear, you'd have slowed him down a mite."

Jeb shot a startled glance at Aaron. "Are there *bears* around here?"

"Maybe," Aaron grinned. "Lots of rabbits and squirrels, for sure. We'd better start with a cottontail. Load up, and we'll see."

With Aaron's instruction, Jeb broke the shotgun down, withdrew the spent shell, and inserted a fresh one. "Do we save the old one, Aaron?" he inquired.

"Nope. Now, you go in front. There's a small field up ahead, an open spot. It was full of rabbits when I was here before. Just remember, don't shoot at the rabbit—shoot at where he's *going to be*."

Jeb's thin face was tense with thought. He nodded and turned to walk down the path. Aaron followed close behind. He saw two rabbits that Jeb missed, but said nothing. Then when they reached the field, he said "Heads up, Jeb—!"

Jeb had seen the rabbit dart out from behind a bush and quickly lifted the gun. He tried to follow the twisting dashes of the frantic rabbit, but when he fired he saw the dirt fly two feet behind the young cottontail.

"Good shot!" Aaron said. "Load up."

"But—I *missed* him!" said Jeb as he watched the frightened rabbit scamper away.

"You won't miss the next one," Aaron promised. "Now you see what I mean about shooting where the rabbit will be? Your shot was good—you just didn't lead him enough."

Jeb's lips tightened with determination, and he moved ahead, his back straight and his eyes searching the ground. Five minutes later, a rabbit leaped up almost under his feet. Jeb raised the gun, but this time he let the rabbit turn, then aiming ahead of the bobbing jack, pulled the trigger. The jolt of the shotgun kicked his shoulder back, but he saw the rabbit knocked down.

"I got 'im, Aaron!"

"Sure did! Give me the gun, and you go get him."

Aaron watched as the boy literally flew across the open ground, stooped and lifted the limp body with a shrill cry. When he got back, Aaron admired the kill. "Nice big, plump jack," he nodded. "Make a good stew—or maybe we'll roast him over an open fire."

"Gosh, Aaron—!" Jeb's eyes were wide as saucers, and he was so excited that he could hardly speak. He stroked the soft fur of the rabbit, and then looked up to say, "I ain't never had such a good time!"

Aaron felt a wave of pity for the boy. *I killed hundred of rabbits when I was his age—and never was grateful for the chance.* Aloud he said, "It's a thing every boy ought to do, Jeb. I'm glad we're here."

The words caused Jeb to look up, and there was adulation in his blue eyes. For the moment the fear of the future was gone, and Aaron knew suddenly that when he was an old man, he'd be able to call back the memory of this fair-haired boy with awe and pleasure in his eyes holding his first kill. . . .

★   ★   ★   ★

Gail awakened from a sound sleep with a start. "Jeb—?" she called, then when no answer came, she rose and pulled her dress on. Stepping from behind the canvas covering, she saw that Jeb and Aaron were gone. *I must have slept like a log,* she thought, then was glad that the two had gone together.

She got busy stirring the fire and made a good breakfast. When it was ready, she took it outside to sit on the steps and eat. The sun was bright, shining through the canopy of the tall trees, but she had no idea of the time. She ate slowly, enjoying the food. She went back for another cup of coffee, bringing her Bible outside, then spent the next half hour reading.

Finally, she went inside and began making biscuits. She mixed up her dough, then using a cup, pressed out the fat circles. Greasing a pan and placing the dough inside, she put them in the oven. For some time she cleaned the cabin, but then after checking the biscuits she decided to go for a walk. When she reached the pond, she saw a small bird with a huge head fly by and wondered what it was.

"Aaron will know," she said aloud. She watched the pond, noting the silvery minnows schooling at her feet in the shallows, then saw a fish rise and thrash the surface. After a few minutes, she walked back to the cabin, checked the biscuits, and sat down to read some more.

When the biscuits were finally done, she put them on top of the stove and let the fire die down. Ten minutes later, she heard her name being called, and ran to the door. Jeb came running up, crying, "I shot three rabbits, Gail—look!"

Gail looked up at Aaron, who was smiling, then admired the limp bodies as Jeb laid them out. "Aaron says they're good to eat—and he's going to let me clean them, Gail. Can we have them for dinner?"

"Fried rabbit and fresh biscuits sound good to you two?" Gail asked. When they both nodded, she said, "Good. You clean these and I'll build up the fire."

Aaron took Jeb to a stump and skinned and dressed one of the rabbits slowly, explaining every step. Then he grinned and said, "Now, you do the other two, then bring them inside when you're finished." He left the boy hacking away with more enthusiasm than skill. Stepping inside he found Gail waiting for him, her eyes filled with pleasure.

"I've never seen him so excited," she said. "Did he really shoot them?"

"Sure did. He's a good shot. I hope he doesn't cut his finger off cleaning them, though." He sniffed the air and said, "I smell fresh-baked bread. Let's have some of those biscuits."

"You'll spoil your appetite!"

"I could eat a cow and not spoil my appetite." He walked over to the stove, pulled the cloth from the golden biscuits, and plucked one out. Taking a bite, he closed his eyes and chewed slowly. "Well, you can cook. I guess I won't have to hire somebody."

Gail laughed and shoved him away from the stove. "That's all you get! Now, tell me about it. . . ."

An hour later the three of them were sitting down to fried rabbit, gravy, and biscuits. Gail asked the blessing, and as soon as she said the amen, Jeb snatched up a piece of rabbit and bit into it. It was hot, and he sputtered, but finally nodded, "It's *good*!"

"Well, I've got a partner to shoot game, and a fine cook to get it ready," Aaron grinned. "Guess I can retire and be waited on."

As soon as Gail cleaned the table off and washed up the dishes, she went to get her Bible. Aaron listened to her read as he cleaned the shotgun, and the words seemed to strike him with a cadence he'd never known. He'd heard the Scripture read all his life, but somehow in this rough cabin buried in the deep woods it meant more. He felt strange stirrings and wondered what they meant.

* * * *

The next three days were halcyon days for Jeb. He hunted and fished and ran through the woods, calling out to Aaron to name everything he was curious about. He wanted to learn the names of all the plants growing around, and the types of birds that flew overhead. He caught his first fish—only a one-pound bass—but insisted on cleaning and eating it himself. He learned the rudiments of woodcraft, a little about tracking, and each night fell into his bunk and slept like a little baby without a care.

Only once did he mention to Aaron the shadow that lay over him. They were fishing for catfish late one night, and he'd broken the silence by saying, "Aaron—"

"Yep?"

"Let's just stay here always."

Instantly, Aaron knew that the boy was thinking of the threat that awaited him back in New York. He said slowly, "I don't think that would work, Jeb—though I'd kind of like it myself."

A long silence followed, and then Jeb whispered, "I *can't* go back! Why can't we just hide out here?"

Carefully Aaron said, keeping his voice soft and even, "Well, I guess because God didn't make us to hide. A man's got something to do in this world—and a woman, too."

"Maybe God made us to live here." A flicker of hope was in the youthful voice, and he added quickly, "You . . . you and Gail could get married."

"Why, I don't think that's the way it works, Jeb."

"Don't you like her?"

"I like her fine—but she has to like me."

"She does! More than she likes anybody!"

Aaron felt he was getting out of his depth and said quickly, "She's interested in Dr. Burns, Jeb." When the boy didn't answer, he added, "A person can't pick a wife or husband for another."

All of a sudden, the cork in front of Jeb suddenly began skimming across the pond. Then his pole seemed to take a dive of its own as it bent low in a huge arc. A few minutes later, to Jeb's surprise, he landed a two-pound fish. "That's a blue channel cat," Aaron nodded. "Best kind of catfish there is to eat." He removed the fish from the hook, dropped it into a sack, then sat back on the bank.

Jeb sat there in silence for a long time—and Aaron thought, *I was doing so well with him, but now I've scared him off.* But he said nothing, and finally Jeb turned to face him, saying, "I'm . . . I'm scared to go back. What I did was a bad thing—I'll go to jail."

"Jeb, sometimes a fellow does wrong. When that happens, most of us want to run away from what we've done. But there's no end to the running. If you run from something small, you'll run from something else." He let his hand fall on the boy's thin shoulder, realizing that somehow a love for this youth had found its place in his heart. "We have to face up to bad things, Jeb. All of us."

The two sat there for some time soaking up the silence. Finally Aaron stood, picked up the poles and their catch and said it was time to get back. As they walked up the path toward the cabin, Jeb hardly said a word. When they entered the cabin, Jeb went straight to bed. Gail caught Aaron's eye, motioning toward the door. When they were outside, she asked, "Can we walk for a little?"

"Sure."

They took the path back to the pond, and neither of them spoke until they reached the shore. Turning to him, Gail asked, "What's wrong with Jeb? He's not himself tonight."

Aaron stood silently, then said, "He's worried about going back to New York."

"Did you bring it up?"

"No, he did."

"He hasn't said a word to me," Gail said. "It's as if he's blocked all of that out of his mind." She looked up into his face, searching his features, then asked, "What did you tell him?"

"That all of us have to face up to hard things—mistakes we've made." His voice dropped as he said this, and he gave her an odd look. "Gail, I felt like the world's worst hypocrite telling him that."

"Why should you feel like a hypocrite? It's true enough."

He seemed to find it difficult to answer. She could see by the bright moonlight that he was tense. He was a strong man, she knew, and she was curious about his words.

Finally he said, "Because I'm telling Jeb to face up to his problems—his bad time—and I've not been able to do that myself."

"I think you could face anything, Aaron!"

"Do you? Well, you're mistaken." He moved away from her and sat down on the same log that he and Jeb had sat on earlier while fishing. She came to sit beside him, saying nothing. Finally he turned to her and said unexpectedly, "A strange thing—the Bible."

"The Bible, Aaron?" she echoed, bewildered at his words. "What's strange about it? You've been reading it all your life."

"No, I haven't," he shook his head sharply. "I've had it read *to* me—by preachers and my parents. And ever since I left home, I've been careful to stay away from churches and preachers." He shook his head in wonder, and turning to face her, he said, "Somehow it gets to me when you read the Scripture. You read the same things I've heard my parents read—but it's different."

Gail was startled, and her voice was quiet as she asked, "Different in what way?"

"I can't really say," Aaron muttered. He shook his head and tried to put into words what he was feeling about the Bible. "When you read, it's like the words have some kind of echo inside me. I remember when my parents read them twenty years ago. And when I go to bed, they come to me."

Gail understood at once that God was speaking to Aaron. She said, "The Word of God is very powerful, Aaron."

He seemed to try her words, then turned and stared out over the still pond. For a long time the only sounds were the frogs croaking and the faint splash of some night-feeding fish. Finally he rose, and when she stood with him, he took her by the arms. "I've never been able to face up to Jubal's death," he said with an effort. "I've blamed myself all this time—and blamed God. And tonight when I was talking to Jeb, telling him he had to face up to things, a scripture you read once came to me. The one that says not to tell a man he's got a speck of dust in his eye while you've got the whole plank in yours!"

Gail reached up and touched his cheek. It was an involuntary gesture, one she might have used with Jeb. But as she touched him, he put his arms around her and pulled her close. She opened her eyes with shock and could not speak.

"You're so beautiful, Gail!" Aaron said softly. "I don't know how to run my life—but I know you're the most desirable woman I've ever seen. . . ." He was aware of the fragrance of her hair and the touch of her hand on his cheek. He kissed her, savoring the softness of her lips. As he kissed her, he was aware that she was not pulling away. Her lips had their own pressure, and she put her hand on his neck, holding him firmly.

As for Gail, a flood of emotions rushed through her. One part of her demanded that she break away—yet something stronger came to her, so that she clung to Aaron. She welcomed his strong embrace, finding in his arms an unexpected source of joy and protection. His hands pulled her closer, and she surrendered to him, thinking, *Nothing I've ever experienced has been like this!* She met him and held his kiss—and then finally broke away and looked up at him, her lips parted with surprise at the power he had to stir her.

Aaron said, "Do you kiss Dr. Burns like this?"

Shame ran through Gail, and she half turned, unable to speak. She walked toward the path, but he caught her. Turning her around, he held her fast. "Answer me, Gail," he said, an edge on his words. He had been moved by her kiss and had to know her feelings for the doctor. "Are his kisses what you want?"

Gail looked up at him, confused by the strong emotions that were still rushing through her. She shook her head, unable to explain—for she did not understand what was happening to her. Finally she whispered, "Aaron—love is more than a kiss. . . ."

Then she whirled and ran back to the cabin, leaving him alone on the shore of the pond. He stood there trying to sort out the surge of emotions he felt. Her closeness had stirred him. As he moved down the path, the great horned owl glided over the trees, silent and grim. Aaron looked up and followed the flight of the great bird, then he turned and moved to the cabin, his spirit troubled. When he entered the cabin, Gail was standing beside the canvas—and it seemed to him that that piece of canvas was a barrier of steel which he would never be able to pass through.

CHAPTER TWENTY-THREE

A NIGHT TO BE REMEMBERED

★   ★   ★   ★

Gail looked up quickly at Aaron when the door opened, and he entered the cabin—very much aware of the wall that had come between them since the kiss by the pond. Neither of them had spoken of it in the last few days, but the ease they'd felt between each other on first coming to the woods was now gone. Aaron had kept himself busy outside, chopping more wood or going off in the woods with Jeb. Even at mealtimes, he hardly said anything. *I wish I could tell him why I kissed him—but I don't know myself,* she thought almost desperately.

"We can't stay out here forever, Gail." Aaron's face was heavy with strain, and he avoided her gaze by going to stare out the window. "We've got to get word to your family—and mine."

"I know." Gail turned to watch him, and when he moved away from the window, she said, "I think you should go back, Aaron."

"What about you and Jeb?"

"I . . . I can't make him go back . . . not yet anyway."

"You can't hide here for long." Aaron looked almost angry. He shook his head slowly, adding, "Sooner or later someone is going to come here. I'm surprised they haven't already."

Gail had been expecting this, and had made up her mind. She held her head high, saying, "You've done so much for Jeb and me . . . but you can't help anymore. Go back home, Aaron."

Aaron could sense the wall between them, and now her words troubled him. He'd been confused over the effect the Bible was having on him, and then Gail's embrace the other night by the pond had stirred something deep inside him. His mind was racing with troubled thoughts. He felt restless, and doubt seemed to fill him. "I can't do that," he said flatly. He turned and walked out of the cabin.

Gail stood there, watching him through the window as he walked down the path and into the woods. She felt an impulse to give in to fear. *What if he leaves us?* she thought. *But he'll have to sooner or later. . . .*

All morning Aaron kept to himself, but late that afternoon, when Aaron came into the cabin with some more wood, Jeb reminded him, "You said you'd take me out on the hills tonight, Aaron. Can we go soon?"

"I guess so." Aaron had no desire to go, yet he wanted to escape from the confines of the cabin—and from Gail. Yet he now knew that he loved her—he had come to admit that to himself—but the knowledge that she was drawn to Dr. David Burns soured him. He said gruffly to Gail, "We may stay out all night."

"All right."

The brevity of her ready acquiescence angered him. He realized he was being a fool, that he was in one of those moods when nothing would satisfy him. As he left the cabin with Jeb by his side, he thought, *I'll leave in the morning. No other way—and she'll have to come with me, and Jeb, too.*

★   ★   ★   ★

Stars lit up the sky overhead, and sparks from the campfire rose, fiery and temporal, dying even as Aaron and Jeb watched. They had come some five miles through the woods, then set up camp in a clearing beside a small stream.

Jeb had talked much at first, but sensing the tense mood of the man, he had lapsed into silence. They had eaten the food they had brought, and now sat silently staring into the campfire. Aaron stole a glance at the boy's face, and saw that the happiness that had been there as they left the cabin was gone. A stab of pity came to Aaron as his eyes traced the thin face, and he wondered, *How did I get so fond of this boy? I've never been much for kids.* He had no answer, but suddenly it came to him: *Why, he reminds me of Jubal!*

Startled, he shook his head in denial, for it was not a thought he welcomed. He'd buried Jubal far away in the Klondike and needed no reminders of that bitter loss. *I'm imagining things!* he told himself. *He doesn't look anything like Jubal.* He studied the boy's face to assure himself, yet discovered that though the features were different, there was *something*! He suddenly realized that Jeb reminded him of Jubal because of what he *was*—young, vulnerable, and hungry for love.

A stick broke and fell into the fire with a hissing, and Aaron was brought back to the present moment. He knew that Jeb was sick with fear and worry, and though he had no answers for the troubled boy, he had to try to help Jeb.

"You know, Jeb, I've been afraid of some things in my life."

"When you were going up San Juan Hill?"

"No, not so much then. Some things are worse than getting hurt physically."

Jeb moved closer to Aaron, coming close enough to touch him. It was an unconscious gesture, but one that told Aaron of the boy's need for a man to lean on. "I don't see why that would be," Jeb said finally. "What could be worse than dying?"

"I can think of one or two things," Aaron said quietly. "Having a long, painful sickness, that would be worse. Losing your family—or living in fear all the time—just to name a few."

Jeb huddled in front of the fire, staring at the flames as they danced. The wind was sharp and he'd worn only a light shirt despite Aaron's warning. He looked forlorn as he clutched his legs and shivered slightly. "I guess so." He was silent for a time, then said in such a low tone that Aaron had to strain to catch his words, "I'm afraid, Aaron. I . . . I'm so scared of being sent to reform school I feel sick to my stomach."

A few times in his life Aaron Winslow had been faced with a difficult decision—and had known without a shadow of doubt what to do. And as he sat in the dark hills beside the trembling boy, he suddenly had that same inner knowing of what he must do. He moved closer to Jeb and put his arm around the thin shoulders. Jeb was taken by surprise and looked up startled, but Aaron only increased the pressure of his embrace. He began to speak quietly and almost without emotion. So certain was he of what he had to do, he moved to it as man would approach a job that must be done—with distaste and not a little fear.

"I had a cousin named Jubal. . . ."

Jeb was very much aware of the pressure of Aaron's arm on his shoulder. He had never been embraced by anyone except his mother and sister. He didn't remember his own father, and the only touch he had experienced from his stepfather had been when Harry Lawson had boxed his ears or given him a brutal beating with his belt. Now as he watched Aaron's face, he was astonished at the pain he saw in the man's face. As Aaron's story unfolded, Jeb saw that it was hurting Aaron to speak. His face grew stiff and strained, and when he got to the part where his cousin died, his voice grew thin and broke.

As for Aaron, he had tried to bury the details of Jubal's tragic death. Now he searched his memory for all the particulars of what happened at Chilkoot Pass. Instantly, they came flooding back into his mind and burned like fire as he spoke them aloud. He had to stop when he told of the final words of Jubal—but cleared his throat and forced himself to speak of the dead youth—of his courage, his wit, his love of God and man.

"He was all a man should be, Jeb—the finest I've ever known," Aaron said as he stared into the crackling fire.

When Aaron stopped short, Jeb asked almost timidly, "Aaron—why are you telling me all this? It hurts you to talk about him—I can see that."

"I had to tell you, Jeb, because it's what I've been running from. I haven't been able to face up to what happened. It was *my* fault he died—and I can't bear the thought of it—!"

Jeb was shocked to see the tears run down the face of the man who held him. He stared at them and felt the choking sobs that stirred the strong chest he leaned against. "I didn't . . . think you ever cried, Aaron," Jeb said quietly. He dropped his head and looked away, whispering, "I cry sometimes—when it's dark and nobody's looking."

Aaron said, "It's okay to cry, Jeb. All of us have something to cry about."

Jeb started at the words. Aaron felt the small form stiffen—then begin to shake convulsively. Putting his other arm around the boy, he held him as the sobs began to come more quickly. There was something almost frantic in the heart-wrenching sobs that choked out of Jeb—as though the tears had been bottled up for years, and now that they were loose, they couldn't seem to come quickly enough.

Overhead the glittering points of light blinked and did their old dance. Aaron had heard that some of them were giants, a million times larger than earth—but he thought as he held the shaking boy, *Not all of them together are worth this boy I hold!*

Finally the sobs ceased, and then with an embarrassed motion Jeb pulled away. But he stopped and looked up at Aaron, and his tear-stained face grew strangely content. He took a deep breath, and held on to Aaron's arm as he said, "I'm glad it's all right to cry. . . ."

Aaron felt cleaned out, somehow. Telling what had happened on a cold mountain pass far away in the Yukon, and shedding the tears over Jubal's death had finally released something inside of him that had kept him chained in anger and bitterness for months. "Me too, Jeb," he said, smiling slightly. "Some things are harder than going up San Juan Hill—and I guess for us men, telling what's eating us on the inside is one of the worst!"

Jeb's voice was shaky, but his eyes were steady as he said quietly, "I got to go back to New York, Aaron."

"I guess you do, Jeb."

"I'm plenty scared—but I know now that I've got to do it!"

Aaron stood up and looked up at the skies, standing still for a moment as though he heard something that the boy could not hear. Then he looked at Jeb, his face filled with love. "Let's put the fire out—then we'll go tell Gail. . . ."

As they walked back up through the woods toward the cabin, Aaron thought about what had just happened. The trip back seemed short to Aaron. After having opened his heart to the boy about Jubal, he was amazed at the peace that had settled on him. He'd heard his mother say once that the only way to get rid of a guilt is to speak it out to somebody—and now he knew she had spoken the truth.

I should have done this a long time ago, he thought as they were finally approaching the cabin. A soft light burned in one of the windows when they broke into the clearing, and he said, "Looks like she's still up, Jeb." Aaron opened the door, and as he stepped inside, followed by Jeb, he saw Gail rise from the table. She'd let her hair down and it hung to her waist. Her eyes were enormous and her lips formed his name.

"Jeb's got something to tell you, Gail," Aaron said. He paused, then added, "I'll leave you two alone. I've got some thinking to do." Before she could say anything, he turned and left the cabin, plunging at once onto the path that led back down to the pond. He had not intended to do anything like this—but an insistence rose in him, and his heart began to beat faster. He was afraid— yet there was a powerful stirring of emotion beginning to swell inside him that he could not quench.

He walked as fast as he could for two miles, skirting the pond, until he came to a clearing illuminated by the moonlight. Finally, he stopped and looked up into the starlit sky, his heart beating hard. Then he moved to the huge trunk of a fallen tree, where he slumped to the ground, leaning his back against it. For five minutes he sat there in silence, then he whispered, "God—I've got to have you—!" That honest plea from the depths of his tortured soul broke something deep inside him. It was like the ear-splitting crack that starts to break up an ice floe on a frozen river—a river of hurt and bitterness and anger that had brought so much pain and despair to his life. Soon a torrent of heartfelt praying for help and forgiveness poured from out of Aaron's heart. He prayed as if his very life hung in the balance—aloud and with a wild intensity that he'd never thought lay within him. Then suddenly it happened, just like Jubal had said it would that night they had all sat around a fire listening to him. He knew that God had made him His own, and a deep sense of love and forgiveness flooded him.

★　★　★　★

Gail had not slept all night. She'd listened to Jeb tell how he and Aaron had wept together, and tears had run down her cheeks as he spoke. Then when he'd said, "I'm scared, sis—but we got to go back!" she knew a wild surge of joy such as she'd never experienced. She'd hugged Jeb, and the two of them had clung to each other.

Jeb had finally gone to bed, but Gail had gone to sit on the front porch, and now as the sun was rising, she wondered about

Aaron. *He wouldn't leave without saying something!* No, she knew he would be back, and even as the red orb of the sun fired the tops of the distant pines, she saw him emerge from the woods and come striding quickly toward the cabin. She rose at once and went to meet him.

"Aaron—what is it?" she whispered, for there was a strange smile on his face. He came and reached out his hands, and she took them, confused but not afraid. "Tell me!" she said, her eyes fixed on his beaming face.

Aaron squeezed her hands tightly, and he seemed very tired. There were lines of strain about the corners of his lips, but his voice was clear. "I've found God," he said quietly, and then he smiled. "Gail—I've given my life to Jesus!"

"Oh, Aaron!" Tears filled Gail's eyes and his face was blurred. She could not speak, so tight was her throat, and she suddenly fell against him, burying her face against his chest.

Aaron looked down at her, holding her lightly. He was stunned by what had taken place in his heart. He had to tell someone, and pulling her from his chest, he said, "Come and sit down—I want to tell you about it. . . !"

Gail listened as he told how God had seemed to call him out to a private place, then how he'd wrestled with his sins for a long time. "I knew *how* to be saved," he said finally. "I've heard the Gospel all my life, but it was how to turn loose of myself that was hard."

"For a man like you, it must have been," Gail answered. "I was saved when I was only ten years old. It was simple for me."

"I guess we collect a lot of baggage as we get older," Aaron nodded. He leaned back and thought of what had transpired. "I spent a lot of time arguing with God. Finally, though, I had to give up." He smiled at her, saying wryly, "I ran out of arguments, and God seemed to say, 'Well, now that that's out of the way—what about *you*? Will you serve me all your life?'"

"You're different—I can see it," Gail nodded. "There's a peace about you. I always thought you were like . . . like a watch that was wound too tight."

"Not a bad description," Aaron said, smiling at her. "Now I'm all out of springs. Got no energy at all! But God's inside me—I know that! I always wondered what Mother meant when she said she knew Jesus was *in* her. Well, now I know!"

"Your parents will be so happy for you, Aaron! And so will Lewis and Deborah."

They spoke quietly for some time, and finally Aaron asked, "What did Jeb say to you?" He listened as she recounted the story, then nodded, "He's a fine boy, Gail! He's got some toughness in him. He's scared—but he's going back anyway."

Gail looked around the clearing wistfully, saying, "I'll never forget this place!"

"Nor will I," Aaron said. He hesitated, then added, "When we get everything cleared up, I'd like to come back."

"That would be wonderful, Aaron!" A moment of doubt clouded her face, and she asked, "Do you think it will go well—about Jeb?"

Aaron stood to his feet and pulled her up. "What was that scripture you read last night? 'With God all things are possible.' Well, I'm going to hang on to that with both hands!"

After a last breakfast and loading the wagon, they left the cabin at ten. They left most of the food, and Aaron said as he turned to give the place a last look, "We'll come back to this place—the three of us."

"Can we really, Aaron?" Jeb was sobered by the thought of what awaited him when he got back to New York, and his hands were clenched tightly together.

Aaron pulled the horses to a halt, then turned to put his arm around the boy. "Jeb, I think God is going to save you out of your trouble. I believe that—but I want you to remember this—" He squeezed the boy's shoulder, and his voice was warm and strong and steady as he said, "No matter what happens, I'm your friend. If things go well, we'll get to do a lot of things right away. If they don't, I'll still be your friend. If you have to go to reform school for a time, the first person you'll see every visiting day will be me. And the first person you'll see when you walk out the gate will be me!"

Gail was watching her brother's face as Aaron spoke. She saw that his words were like balm to his troubled heart. Jeb stared at Aaron for a long time, then his face relaxed and he smiled with an expression of love and complete trust.

"All right, Aaron, I'm ready now."

Aaron looked at Gail with victory in his fine eyes, and then he said, "Git going hosses—we've got things to do. . . !"

CHAPTER TWENTY-FOUR

A COUPLE OF MIRACLES

★　★　★　★

By the time Aaron reached the outskirts of New York, he was tired of driving the wagon. When he pulled up in front of the livery stable, he was glad to turn the rig over to the stable hand. As the three of them climbed into a carriage, he murmured, "We better go by your place first."

Jeb had been very quiet on the last leg of the journey, and as the carriage rolled down the busy street, he looked out the window at all the people. "Sure is different from the woods," he said. There was a poignancy in his face that spoke of the anxiety that stirred inside him.

Gail put her arm around him, saying, "It'll be all right, Jeb. God won't let us down. He never does."

Aaron said little for some time, but just before they pulled up in front of the tenement, he said thoughtfully, "I guess most of the time we've got to struggle with something we can't really handle. If it's something we *can* take care of, we just fly at it and do the best we can." He was caught up in a new way of looking at things that had come to him since he'd made his commitment to God. Already he'd discovered that old ways would not do—and now he mentioned it. "The big question in the Bible, it seems to me, is, how much do I let God do for me—and how much do I just do for myself?"

Gail studied Aaron's face carefully, fascinated by how much he had changed in such a brief time. He'd always been so quick to throw himself into things, but now he was very conscious of the fact that as a Christian he was not free to do as he chose. "I think all Christians struggle with that problem, Aaron," she said finally. "But some things we don't have to wonder about."

"What kind of things?"

"Oh, the Bible says that he who fails to provide for his own is worse than an infidel—so we don't have to struggle with the question, 'Shall I work and make a living for my family or not?' We're not to sit around waiting for manna to fall, but do whatever we can to earn an honest living to take care of those we love."

"That's plain enough—but most things aren't that simple," Aaron nodded. "I *know* I've got to work—but work at *what*? I can find ten jobs, I guess—but which one of them is the one God wants me to have?"

"Sometimes God speaks to us pretty plainly—in our spirits, I mean." Gail searched her memory and smiled as an example came to mind. "When I was offered a job at the hospital, I felt God whispering, 'Take it!' But since that was the only job I could get, that's not what you mean."

The carriage pulled up in front of the tenement, and they stepped down to the pavement. Aaron paid the fare, and they entered the rundown building and climbed the steps. When they opened the door, Martha Lawson took one look at them and instantly threw her arms around Jeb. Aaron and Gail stood quietly watching, and it was Jeb who told his mother, "I've got to go to the police, Ma." His face was pale, but he didn't waver in the least.

Finally after Gail explained the situation to her mother, the older woman nodded. "It's got to be—but I'm afraid for him. . . ."

"Aw, Ma, I'll be all right," Jeb piped up. He looked up at Aaron and found confidence in what he saw. "Aaron's gonna do what he can—and even if I do have to go to reform school, he's promised to come to visit me as much as he can."

Their visit was brief, for both Aaron and Gail were aware that there was a possibility of Jeb being picked up by the police. "It's better if he goes in voluntarily," Aaron assured Mrs. Lawson. "I'm going to get him a good lawyer, and with God's help, I'm believing he can get off without going to reform school."

They left the building and made their way to Mark Winslow's office. When they gave their names to the secretary in his outer office, the man stepped inside the door behind his desk, but it was only a few seconds before Mark appeared, relief on his face. "Come in," he said, pulling them inside. As soon as the door was shut, he demanded, "Where have you been, Aaron? Lola and I have been worried sick! Not to mention how upset your parents have been."

Aaron glanced at Jeb, then said, "I've been helping a friend, Uncle Mark. This is Jeb Summers, Gail's brother—and he's in trouble. I thought you might be able to help us."

Mark shot a glance at Gail—noting the pale face and the marks of strain—then stepped forward and shook hands with Jeb. "Well, now, suppose we sit down and see what this is all about." He listened as Aaron explained the problem, then said at once, "I know a man who we need to get on our side—a lawyer named Simon Carwell." A slight smile crossed his lips, and he added, "He's a pretty tough bird, Carwell, but he hates to lose more than any man I ever saw!" He put his hand on Jeb's shoulder gently, saying, "I'm sorry about the trouble you're in—but we'll do what we can—and we'll believe God to do what we can't."

"Why, that's what Gail and I were talking about on our way here, Uncle Mark!" said Aaron.

Getting up to go to the telephone, Mark nodded. "Been a rule of mine for a long time—and God hasn't failed me yet." He rang for an operator, who connected Mark to the lawyer. He spoke briefly to Carwell, setting a time for a meeting, then hung up the telephone receiver. "Come on, we've got to get you home," he announced.

"But—aren't we going to the police?" Aaron asked.

"Not until we've seen Carwell. And I've got to take you home. Lewis and Lola would have my hide if I didn't do that!" He looked at Jeb and asked, "Have you ridden on a train much, Jeb?"

"Ain't never ridden on even one."

Mark winked at him confidentially, saying, "How'd you like to ride in the engine—maybe even drive it for a little bit? I think I could arrange it."

Jeb could not have been more amazed if the tall man had asked him to go to the moon. "Aw, you couldn't do that, could you?"

"Think I can."

"Gee, you must be a pretty important man!"

Mark Winslow came over and slapped Jeb on the shoulder, smiling at the boy. "We're all important, Jeb," he said. "I know you're worried, but years ago I was sitting in a Mexican jail about to go to prison for a long time. I tell you, I was a pretty sick young man! Scared, too."

Jeb's eyes were large and he asked, "Did you go to prison?"

"Nope."

"How'd you get out of it?"

Mark winked at Aaron and Gail, then looked down at Jeb before saying thoughtfully, "Why, God sent an angel to get me out."

Jeb stared at him incredulously. "Aw, Mr. Winslow, you're jokin' me!"

"Not a bit, Jeb." Mark thought of that time and said slowly, "The angel's name was Lola—and as soon as we get home, I'll introduce you to her. I married her, you see—but I always had a suspicion that she was sent from God to get me out of jail."

"I wish He'd send an angel to get me out of this jam," Jeb sighed. Then he asked, "Can I really ride in the engine?"

"What's the use of being a big shot railroad executive if I can't get my friend behind a throttle?" Mark said. "Come on, we'll catch the two twenty. . . ."

Jeb only half believed that Winslow was serious, but when they got to the station, Mark led them straight to where the train was pulled up to take on passengers. "These folks are guests of the Union Pacific, Charlie," he told the conductor. "Take good care of them."

"Yes, sir, Mr. Winslow!"

"Have a good ride," Mark said to Gail and Aaron. "Jeb and I will take care of the engine." He moved down toward the engine and spoke to a big man in overalls and a billed cap who was oiling one of the large wheels. "Got room for a couple of passengers, Ted?"

The engineer grinned broadly and nodded at once. "Sure, Mr. Winslow. Who's this with you?"

"A very special friend of mine. Jeb, this is the best engineer on the Union, Ted Rounds. And this is Jeb Summers."

"Well, Jeb, you must have been named after General Jeb Stuart."

"Yes, sir. My grandfather was in his army."

"So was mine, Jeb," Rounds grinned. "Now, you come along with me, and we'll get this train on the way. We've got a schedule to keep." Mark winked, and the engineer knew that Winslow wanted the boy to have a memorable time, so when they were inside, he spent some time pointing out the controls and gauges. Finally he said, "See that cord? That blows the whistle. Got to do quite a bit of that on this run—lots of crossings." He winked at Mark Winslow over Jeb's head, adding, "Tell you what, Jeb—I stay pretty busy with other things, so you're in charge of that whistle on this run."

"Gosh, I don't know—"

"Oh, just reach up and yank that cord when I holler at you," Rounds assured him. Pulling out a thick watch, he cocked one eyebrow and said, "Time to pull out—give that cord a good hard yank, will you, Jeb?"

Jeb glanced at Winslow, who gave him a nod. Reaching up he grasped the cord and pulled it firmly. The shrill blast of the whistle rent the air, and Rounds laughed and slapped Jeb on the shoulder. "You're going to do just fine! Now, let's get this old train moving. . . ."

Aaron and Gail found seats, and soon the train had pulled clear of the city. As the open country seemed to fly by, Gail said, "Your uncle is so kind, Aaron. He makes me feel . . . well . . . *safe* is the word that comes to me."

Aaron took his eyes from the small farms that spread out over the rolling landscape and gave her his attention. "He's a fine man. Dad thinks the world of him."

"Do you think this lawyer friend of his can help Jeb?"

"I guess I'm thinking of what Uncle Mark said about it. How did he put it? Do all you can, then leave it with God to do all He can." Right then the thought of Lewis, helpless and tied to a wheelchair, filled his mind. "I think we need a couple of miracles, Gail—one for Jeb and one for Lewis."

"You've never really believed that Lewis would be healed, have you, Aaron?"

"No, I haven't." The conductor passed by, taking tickets and punching them. He smiled down at the pair, then passed on. Aaron looked down at his hands that were clasped together. "I guess I've always thought that the miracles in the Bibles were for that time—not for people today. My parents don't believe that. They always said that God is the same yesterday and today and forever."

"It's hard to believe something when your eyes are telling you it's not so," Gail murmured. "Do you know the story of Abraham and Isaac? I've thought about that so much lately."

"Read it to me."

"You mean—now?" Gail said, surprised at his request.

"Why not?"

Gail laughed shortly, but pulled the Bible from her bag. She opened it and, finding the scripture, read the story of the patriarch. She began in the fifteenth chapter, reading the promise of God: "Fear not, Abram; I am thy shield, and thy exceeding great reward." Then she read of Abram's plea to God for a child, and looking up at Aaron, she said with awe, "And Abram was eighty-five years old when he asked God for a son!"

"What did God say?"

Gail looked down and read slowly: ". . . he that shall come forth out of thine own loins shall be thine heir. And he brought him forth abroad, and said, Look toward heaven, and tell the stars, if thou be able to number them: and he said unto him, So shall thy seed be." She paused, then nodded as she read the next verse: "And he believed in the Lord; and he counted it to him for righteousness."

"Now that's real faith!" Aaron nodded. "Not much a man can do in a case like that except believe God—but most of us wouldn't."

"No, and nothing happened for fifteen years." Gail's eyes were filled with wonder as she looked at him. "Can you imagine what that must have been like? God didn't give him a thing for all those years, and finally he was ninety-nine years old, but he still believed God's promise!"

"Didn't some angels come to Abram and Sarah about that time?"

"Yes, and when Sarah heard one of them say that she would have a child, she laughed."

285

"I can understand that!"

"I suppose I can, too. But the angel rebuked her. And I've written what he said in the front of my Bible. I read it every morning— and I've been whispering it in my heart ever since Jeb got into trouble."

"Let me see—" Mark looked down at the words written in Gail's plain script, reading them aloud, "Is there any thing too hard for God?" He sat back and smiled slightly. "That's a good thought—that nothing that comes to us is too hard for God. And Abraham did have that son, didn't he?"

"Yes, he did." Gail found a verse and read, "And Abraham was an hundred years old, when his son Isaac was born unto him."

They sat there feeling the rhythm of the steel wheels as the train sped along the rails. From time to time the whistle loosed a shrill clarion blast, and the landscape seemed to blur as it flew by the window. Finally Aaron said, "Well, then, I'll claim that verse with you for the two miracles we need."

A warmth flowed through Gail, and without thinking she reached over and took Aaron's hand, whispering, "All right— that'll be our verse." His hand was strong as he returned the handclasp, and she was aware that God had *already* done a mighty miracle in the heart of Aaron Winslow!

★   ★   ★   ★

"You'll make a fine railroad man, Jeb," Ted Rounds grinned as he shook hands with the boy. "You make Mr. Winslow here give you a job firing up this engine for me, you hear?"

"I'd like that, Mr. Rounds!" said Jeb, his face aglow with a huge smile.

Mark winked at Rounds, saying, "You have all the fun with this railroad—and I have all the headaches! Thanks for the ride, Ted." He turned and said, "Come along, Jeb. I want you to meet the angel that changed my life." He collected Aaron and Gail from the passenger car, and soon the four of them were speeding along in a carriage at a fast clip behind a fine team. He kept up a running conversation, and when he pulled the horses up in front of the house, he said, "Always glad to get home! Everybody out—look, there's Lola."

Jeb was shy, but when Winslow introduced his wife, he saw there was a kind expression in her eyes. "Come in, Jeb," she smiled. Then she looked at the couple standing back, saying, "You two gave us a scare. I want to hear all about it."

They entered the house, and Aaron was immediately embraced by his parents. "Mother—Dad—I'm sorry I worried you so much."

"How are you, son? Are you all right? Where have you been these past few days?" his father said, voicing his concerns.

Aaron looked at Gail, then smiled. "I've been out in the woods—getting converted," he said. He laughed aloud as both his parents stared at him. "Well, you've been praying for that for years. Can't you believe God's finally answered your prayers?"

Then there was a time of weeping and laughing, and Gail was smothered by Belle and Davis when Aaron told them how much God had used her to bring him to faith. Finally Belle wiped her eyes with her handkerchief and said in a tremulous voice, "Thank God! I'll never give up on a prayer as long as I live!"

Davis's eyes were also damp, but he pulled himself together. "Come along—you've got to tell Lewis all about this!"

Belle and Lola were smiling, and Mark turned to them, a strange excitement in his eyes. "Come along, Aaron. Lewis will be glad to see you."

"I wanted to get word to him, but there didn't seem to be any way to work it," Aaron said. "How is he?"

"I'll let him give you his own report." Davis opened the door and walked into the bedroom, calling out, "Well, here's the prodigal at last—"

Aaron entered with Gail beside him, and they saw Deborah standing beside Lewis, who was lying in a bed. He was wearing a pair of dark blue pajamas, and his face lit up as he cried, "Aaron—where have you been? I've been worried sick!"

"Sorry about that," Aaron mumbled. He moved to shake Lewis's hand, then looked at the young woman who was watching him. "How's the patient, Deborah?" he asked.

Deborah's serene countenance bore more than one evidence of excitement. She looked down at Lewis and said quietly, "I'll let him tell you that, Aaron."

Something in her tone surprised Aaron. He exchanged a puzzled glance with Gail, who'd gone to stand beside Deborah, then swung his gaze back to his brother. "What's going on, Lewis?"

Lewis reached up and took Deborah's hand, which caused her to show some embarrassment. "This is the stubbornest woman in the whole world," he said roughly. "She's been in here for days making me work!"

"Making you work?" Aaron asked in a puzzled tone. "What kind of work?"

"Why, she came in one morning and I never saw such a mean look on a woman's face!" Lewis exclaimed. "She ripped the covers off me and she said, 'All right—let's get to work! Move those legs!' " Lewis laughed at the look of astonishment on Aaron's face and went on, never releasing Deborah's hand. "She drove me worse than that sergeant we had in the Rough Riders, I promise you! I got so sick of her that more than once I just about cried and told her to leave me alone."

"I think he would have whipped her if he could," Belle added. "But she never gave him a minute's rest." Her eyes were fond as she looked at Deborah, adding, "She never gave up on him—and she never stopped quoting scriptures about how God is able to do anything."

Aaron stared at Lewis, and suddenly a glimmer of hope came to him like a fresh breeze. "What's happened, Lewis?" he demanded.

"Look at this!" Lewis stared down at his legs, and Aaron followed his gaze. He saw the right foot suddenly move spasmodically—and then it came up from the bed! Lewis gasped with the effort, but cried out, "Now the other one!" The left foot moved, and then Lewis drew his legs up, his face contorted with the effort. He looked at Aaron and whispered, "I can *feel* them, Aaron! I can actually *feel* my legs and feet!"

Tears sprang to Aaron's eyes, and he was not ashamed. He leaned forward and the two brothers embraced. Gail was weeping openly, and she turned to Deborah, who reached out and held her as she too wept with joy.

Jeb was watching with startled eyes, and when Aaron finally straightened up and turned to him, he saw the tears and thought, *He said it was all right to cry!*

What followed was a wild time, with Lewis and Deborah telling the story of Lewis's slow recovery, both of them insisting it was a miracle from God. Then Aaron had to recount the story of how he'd gotten saved—and Aaron kept his hand on Jeb's shoulder the whole time he was talking.

Finally, when Gail and Aaron had a moment alone, she said, "Well, Aaron, we needed a pair of miracles. We've got the first one."

Aaron nodded, his eyes bright with hope. "Yes—and now we'll trust God for the second one!"

★　★　★　★

Simon Carwell was not a man who believed in miracles all that much. He was a man with a calculating look, one who had a driving energy to accomplish what he set out to do. He'd come to the Winslow home early in the morning the day after Aaron and Gail had arrived to meet his newest and youngest client. Mark had called the two of them into the library, and they hurriedly located Jeb, who was helping out in the stables. "Come along, Jeb," Aaron said. "It's time to meet your lawyer."

When they entered the high-ceilinged room lined with books, Jeb looked nervously at the short man almost concealed behind a cloud of smoke that rose from a cigar he was smoking. "This is Mr. Carwell, Jeb," Mark said quickly. Mark introduced the three to the lawyer, who rose and nodded with a jerky motion.

"Sit down, Jeb," he said in a deep voice that seemed to rise from his chest. "I want to hear about the robbery."

"Y-yes, sir." Jeb's face was pale as he told his story. He didn't spare himself, but confessed that he'd known that Tug Devaney was a tough one.

"Did you know there was going to be a robbery?" Carwell inquired. He had a pair of intense brown eyes—deep-set and bright—that seemed to stare straight through the young boy.

"I . . . heard one of the guys say they were going to make a haul."

"But did he say they were going to rob the warehouse?"

"No, sir—but I guess I knew—"

"Don't say that!" Carwell spoke sharply, his eyes unblinking.

"You were never *told* by anyone that there was going to be a robbery. Is that true?"

"Yes, sir."

Carwell went over the story three times, probing and asking questions. Finally he leaned back and puffed on his cigar. "I guess that's all I need from you right now, young man." He studied Jeb carefully, then said, "You and I are going into town. When we get there we'll go to the police and you'll be questioned."

"Will I have to . . . go to jail?" asked Jeb nervously.

"I expect not. Do you know what 'bail' is?" asked the short man as he took another puff of his cigar.

"No, sir."

"Bail is money that somebody puts up to be sure you don't run away."

"I don't have any money," said Jeb, worry creasing his brow.

"I'll take care of that, Jeb," Mark Winslow broke in. "Don't worry about it."

"Can Gail go with me?" Jeb asked.

Carwell shook his head. "I think it would be better if just you and I go in—and Mr. Winslow." Carwell saw the anxiety on the face of Gail Summers and said gently, "I'll take care of the boy. It may take a while, but I'm sure he'll be released on bail. There's nothing you can do at the station."

"You'll bring him to us as soon as possible?" It was Aaron who spoke up, and both Gail and Jeb warmed at his use of the word *us*. Gail felt his hand on her arm, and when Carwell agreed, she thought, *What would I do if it weren't for Aaron?*

"I want a word with you, Mr. Winslow," Carwell said, and when the room had cleared, he said at once, "I think you ought to know something, Mark. Didn't want to bring it up in front of the boy."

Mark was good at interpreting faces, and saw that Carwell was troubled. "What's wrong, Simon?"

Carwell stared at his cigar for a moment, then put his eyes on Winslow. "The case against the boy is weak—but I'm more worried about who the judge is."

"Why is that?"

"Well, it'll be Judge Cross handling the case—Albert Cross."

"I never heard of him," said Mark, waiting for Carwell to state his concerns.

"He handles mostly juvenile cases—and they call him 'The Hanging Judge.' "

"I see." Mark studied the lawyer for moment, his mind working. "Is he a bad judge, Simon?"

"I don't say that," Carwell said slowly. "He's got a hard job. Lots of tough ones come out of the city, some of them killers at the age of sixteen or even younger. He's seen some go free to rob and kill who should have been locked up. That's made Cross a little harder than most." Carwell puffed nervously on his cigar, sending clouds of purple smoke spiraling into the air. He gave Mark Winslow a hard look, adding, "I'd feel a lot better if it were any other judge than this one, Mark."

"Let's have it all, Simon."

"Well, Jeb's been positively identified at the scene of the crime. Devaney's been caught, and two others. They've all confessed— made a deal with the D.A. To Judge Cross, it will be plain that Jeb was there—and he'll have only the boy's word that he didn't know there was going to be a robbery. I think he'll sentence him to reform school. About all we can shoot for is a short sentence."

Winslow thought hard, then shook his head. "I don't like it, Simon. I want you to fight for the boy."

"I can't guarantee anything—"

"Do your best." Mark's face was set, then he looked at Carwell solemnly and said, "We'll do all that men can do—and then we'll trust God to do what He can do."

Carwell lifted one heavy eyebrow, studying the face of the man before him. "I expect He'll have to do most of it, Mark," he said finally as he turned to stub out his cigar.

★ ★ ★ ★

Gail held to Jeb all the way out to the carriage, and when she kissed him, she whispered, "I love you—and so does Aaron."

Jeb nodded, his lips drawn tightly together. He looked up at Aaron, who suddenly bent and hugged him. "I'll be right with you, Jeb," he whispered.

Carwell got into the carriage, and Jeb kept his eyes on Aaron and Gail until they were on their way. He looked at the lawyer, who was deep in thought, and fear rose in Jeb. Then he remembered the time by the campfire when Aaron had held him. The words came to him, *I'll be the first one you see on visiting day—the first one you'll see when you come out the gate.*

Jeb swallowed hard and clenched his fists tightly together as the carriage made its way toward the station. And as he sat in the train later, he was still hearing the sound of Aaron's voice. . . .

★ ★ ★ ★

Lewis caught at Deborah's hand, held it fast, then said, "I have to talk to you."

The house was quiet, for it was late. Everyone had already gone to bed, but Lewis had insisted that Deborah stay with him. She had formed the habit of reading to him, and he had insisted that she read from *Bleak House*, one of Dickens' novels. He had claimed that he was too excited to sleep, and she had, in fact, been pleased to spend some more time with him.

But as she closed the book, saying, "I must go—it's late," he had seized her hand and pulled her back. Now her eyes opened wide as he put his arm around her and pulled down. Overbalanced, she toppled forward, but he caught her and pulled her onto his lap. "What . . . what in the world—!"

"I want to talk to you," Lewis said. He held on, smelling the lilac scent she used, and grinned as she struggled to stand up. "Don't try to get away. It would be a scandal. Wouldn't Mr. Hearst love to have a story like that? It would make front-page news— 'War Hero Kisses Nurse in His Bedroom!' "

Deborah tried to move, but he held her fast. She turned to him indignantly and said, "I'm surprised at you, Lewis. I thought you were a gentleman!"

"You were wrong," he shrugged. "Whatever made you think that?"

"Why—you've never tried to—force yourself on me," Deborah faltered. "Please, Lewis—let me go!"

"I will—after about forty or fifty years."

Deborah was struggling hard to pull away—but his words caught at her. She turned to face him, and there was a tension in her. "Why would you say a thing like that?"

Lewis loosened his grip, reached up, and touched her soft hair. "You have lovely hair, Deborah," he said quietly. "I've always been partial to it." He saw that her lips were half-parted in astonishment, and he pulled her head forward. Her lips were soft, yet he felt the tension that flowed from her. There was a surrender in her—but not a complete one. When he lifted his head, he said simply, "I love you, Deborah. I want to marry you and live with you the rest of my life."

Deborah seemed to freeze, to turn to stone. The shock of his words rolled over her, and she said, "You don't know—what I've been, Lewis."

"Before we met? Doesn't count!"

"Yes, it *does*! Let me up." He released her, and she turned her back on him, struggling to find words to put to her turbulent thoughts. Finally she straightened and turned to him. "I loved a man once, or thought I did. . . ."

Lewis listened as Deborah spoke, and when she was finished, he reached out and took her hand, saying gently, "I love you, Deborah. I haven't led a perfect life—but we have to take each other where we are. We must walk in God's love and His forgiveness. I've always admired your courage—and now the past is over. The one question is—do you love me?"

Deborah felt a surge of joy, of full release. "Yes! I love you!"

At her words, Lewis seized her and pulled her back on his lap, kissing her thoroughly. Finally they began to laugh. "I'm pretty unromantic—but you just wait! I'll carry you over the threshold!" Holding her tight, he whispered, "I'll always love you!"

Deborah could not keep the tears back as she held him tightly. To her it was like coming home, and she knew that she was at last secure—secure in the arms of a man who would not leave her, but would remain at her side for the rest of her life. Lifting her face, she studied his features, then smiled, "We'll always have each other, Lewis. Nothing matters but that!"

CHAPTER TWENTY-FIVE

AN ODD SORT OF TRIAL!

★ ★ ★ ★

Aaron looked at the new suit that Jeb was wearing for the trial and nodded. "You look fine, Jeb. Clothes make the man."

The three of them were sitting in a small side room reserved for those to be tried, just outside the courtroom. They'd come early and were anxiously waiting for the hearing to begin. Gail was sitting close to Jeb and tried to smile. "You look real nice— almost grown up."

"I'll be glad when it's over," Jeb said as he shifted nervously. The judge had set the hearing for late afternoon, and time had crawled by for the boy. He felt awkward in the stiff new trousers and coat and twisted uncomfortably as he sat on the hard bench. The past three days of waiting had been difficult for him. Aaron had taken him to a baseball game—the first he'd ever seen—and to Coney Island, but the threat of what lay before him hung over him like an ominous dark cloud.

Suddenly the door opened and a clerk came out to say, "Hearing for Jeb Summers. Come inside, please."

Jeb swallowed as he rose, determined to hide the fear that was clawing inside him. When he entered the courtroom, he saw that it was half-empty. One quick glance and he saw Mark Winslow and his wife, Lola, sitting near the front of the room. Lewis was sitting in his wheelchair in the aisle, and next to him was the pretty nurse, Miss Laurent. Sitting close to Lewis were Davis and Beth. Across the courtroom he saw his mother sitting with Dr. Burns, and at once Gail and Aaron went to sit beside them.

"Sit down here with me, Jeb." Simon Carwell was standing, holding out his hand, and Jeb went behind the table to sit in the chair that the lawyer pulled out.

Just as he sat down, a door opened and a tall, thin man dressed in a long black robe came out and took his seat as the bailiff spoke loudly, "Juvenile court of the City of New York is now in session—His Honor Judge Albert Cross presiding. Be seated!"

Judge Albert Cross looked down at some papers before him, then put his eyes on Jeb. "The State of New York versus Jeb Summers." Leaning forward and locking his hands before him, Cross demanded, "This is the defendant?"

"Yes, Your Honor. My name is Simon Carwell. I am representing the young man."

Cross stared at the attorney silently. "You usually have more affluent clients, Mr. Carwell. I'm surprised to see you here."

"I have special ties to Jeb Summers, Your Honor."

The judge weighed the man's words, then shrugged his shoulders. Looking down at the papers in front of him, he studied them momentarily, then looked up, saying, "This is not a trial, Jeb. There will be no jury. Do you understand that?"

"Yes, sir!" said Jeb.

"Very well. I have the statement here from an eyewitness who has testified that you were seen at the scene of the crime on the night of September fifteenth. Were you in the vicinity of Cooper Warehouse at eleven o'clock that evening?"

Jeb felt Carwell's arm nudging him and he spoke up, "Yes, sir. I was."

"And were you in the company of the men who robbed the warehouse?"

Swallowing hard, Jeb nodded.

"Speak up, young man!" said the judge.

Jeb swallowed hard and said, "Yes, sir."

For what seemed forever, the questioning went on relentlessly, and Aaron whispered nervously, "That judge has a mean streak! He's already got his mind made up." He watched the face of Carwell, but could not make anything of the blank expression he wore.

For thirty minutes Judge Cross fired questions at Jeb, hoping to catch him off guard, but Carwell had trained the boy well. In the short time he had spent with Jeb, he had made the boy tell the story over and over, saying, "If you tell the truth, you don't have to *remember* what you said. The judge will try to confuse you. Don't lose your temper. Be polite and answer his questions as clearly as you can."

The sound advice of the experienced lawyer stood Jeb in good stead, for Carwell could see that Judge Cross was not able to rattle the boy. *He's got a chance if he just doesn't give in,* the attorney thought. He hated to lose any case, and yet he had been almost certain that there was no way to keep Jeb out of reform school. Because the odds were against him and there seemed to be no chance to win, Carwell had pressured himself more than he would have ordinarily. Besides, in these few short days he'd learned to like the boy.

Judge Cross called the witness who'd seen Jeb at the scene of the crime, and the man was sworn in. Taking the witness stand, he answered the judge's questions, then identified Jeb, leaving no doubt that he was absolutely certain Jeb was there. The judge then addressed Carwell, "Do you want to question this witness, Mr. Carwell?"

"No questions, Your Honor."

"You are dismissed, Mr. Delaughter." The judge waited until the witness stepped down, then leaned back in his chair. "Mr. Carwell, you may speak on behalf of the boy."

Carwell rose and a silence fell over the courtroom. Some men have whatever it is that draws the attention of others—and Simon Carwell had that quality to command center stage when he spoke. The minute he entered a room, every eye turned toward him. It was not that he was impressive, for he was of middle height and not at all handsome. But there was something in his eyes that drew men, and now as he stood and began to speak in a deep baritone, most of those in the courtroom leaned forward to listen intently.

Carwell began in an easy tone, "Your Honor, Jeb Summers was born on Water Street. He has spent his entire life there, and I would like to briefly sketch that life. . . ."

Carwell painted a graphic picture of the Lower East Side of Manhattan. He knew it well, and was a master at commanding the English language to his advantage. He spoke of the abject poverty, dirt, and despairing hopelessness that those who lived in that area suffered under every day of their lives. With accuracy he dramatized the dark dens of temptation that no dweller on Water Street—young or old—could hope to avoid. And how so many boys and girls had become entrapped, destined to live as denizens of a world filled with abuse and moral degradation.

"It is a whirlpool, a maelstrom that draws even the best of young and old into the sordid depths of crime. To try to rise above such horrible circumstances is like trying to swim *up* Niagara Falls! In that world, brute strength is worshiped, and those who are not strong are quickly crushed. The wealthy landlords who own the tenements are even more brutal than the men-beasts who roam the streets! They may eat from silver plates—"

"Mr. Carwell, you may spare the court your political views," Judge Cross interrupted. "As it happens, you are correct, but corruption in high places is not the issue of this hearing."

"With all due respect, Your Honor," Carwell shot back, "I am convinced that it *is* the system that is on trial!"

"It was not the system that robbed Cooper Warehouse. I must warn you, Mr. Carwell, I will not stand for this line of approach," admonished Judge Cross as he leaned forward.

"Thank you, Your Honor. I will be more careful." Carwell smiled and began to speak of his young client. He gave a quick summary of Jeb's life, then said, "He is twelve years old, Your Honor, and has spent his life in the midst of crime and vice—" Carwell paused dramatically, then said forcefully, "In all that time, Your Honor, he has not been in serious trouble—not even once."

The judge wrinkled his brow and put his eyes on Jeb. He listened as Carwell spoke of how the boy was a hard worker and a regular attendant at the Water Street Mission. "He even turns his meager earnings over to help his family, who need it desperately."

"Are the parents in this court?" the judge asked.

"Mr. Lawson, the boy's stepfather . . . is ill, Your Honor. The boy's mother is here. Would you stand, Mrs. Lawson?" He let Mrs. Lawson remain standing, for the strain of suffering on her pale face could not be ignored. Finally he said gently, "You may sit down, Mrs. Lawson." He turned to the judge, saying, "The young lady with Mrs. Lawson is her daughter, Jeb's sister. Her name is Miss Gail Summers." Again the dramatic pause—"Miss Summers is in training to become a nurse. She's just returned from nursing our gallant young men who are fighting in Cuba—"

A mutter went around the room, and the judge politely nodded toward Gail. Instantly Carwell said, "I would like to call Private Lewis Winslow as a character witness for my client."

"Very well," said Judge Cross, motioning for the bailiff to swear in the new witness.

Again the pause—"Private Aaron Winslow—will you bring your brother forward?"

Every eye in the room was on the two men as Aaron wheeled the chair down to the front. Judge Cross leaned forward, his deepset eyes fixed on the young man. "You were wounded in Cuba, sir?"

"At San Juan Hill, Your Honor." Lewis was looking fit, his eyes clear as he smiled at the judge.

"You were close to Colonel Roosevelt?"

"Why, we were all as close as we could get to the colonel! He was leading us up that hill! He's a fine commander! He came by to see me when I was in the hospital." Lewis smiled more broadly. "I'm going to vote for him when he runs for governor of this state!"

Cross smiled for the first time. "So am I," he said quietly. "How were you wounded, Private?"

"Oh, just got in the wrong place at the right time, sir!"

"I must correct Private Winslow, Your Honor." Seeing his opportunity, Carwell spoke clearly, and there was a gleam in his eye. "Private Winslow exposed himself to enemy fire by courageously charging across an open field to save his lieutenant and two of his fallen comrades. He carried them off the field on his back and was wounded just as he was saving the life of the third."

A mutter of exclaim ran around over the courtroom, and then Carwell said dramatically, "Private Winslow was awarded the Congressional Medal of Honor for his heroic deeds that day under Colonel Roosevelt."

The effect of his words was tremendous. People murmured

loudly, and some stood to get a better look at Lewis. "Order in the court," Judge Cross said, but his voice was mild. He turned to Lewis and studied him for a long moment. Then he said, "The court honors you, sir, and I must add that it is good to see one so young ready to serve with such devotion."

Lewis flushed. "Thank you, Your Honor—but the real heroes are still there—those who died for their country."

"Well said, Private." Cross hesitated, then gave a rather bitter look at Carwell, thinking, *You've boxed me in, haven't you, you weasel?* He turned to Lewis and asked, "You are acquainted with the defendant, Jeb Summers?"

"Yes, sir, I am."

"Let the court hear of your relationship."

Lewis spoke briefly, making the most of his rather limited experience with Jeb. He'd seen the boy often enough at the mission, and focused on that, but almost at once said, "My brother, Aaron, knows the boy much better."

"Very well. You may take your brother back, Mr. Aaron Winslow, then approach the bench." When Aaron had done so and been sworn in, the judge asked, "You were at the battle of San Juan Hill with your brother?"

"Yes, sir."

"Were you wounded?"

"No, Your Honor."

"Well, then, please tell the court what you can about this boy."

Aaron made an exemplary witness. He was a handsome man, and the aura of his war experience clung to him like a medal. He spoke not of himself, but of his time with Jeb. "He's had a hard life, sir, and I wanted to make it a little easier."

"He's accused of robbing a warehouse, Mr. Winslow. You can't admire that!"

Aaron said carefully, "I don't admire robbery, Judge. But I'm convinced that Jeb isn't a hardcore thief. He was hanging out with the wrong crowd and did a foolish thing, but he's got good stuff in him."

Judge Cross stared at the tall man, who looked him straight in the eye. "What about your family?" he asked curiously.

"My father is president of a Christian college in Virginia, Your Honor."

"You and your brother are to be commended. Thank you for your time, sir."

Aaron returned to his seat, and Gail squeezed his hand. "You did fine!" she whispered.

"Do you have other witnesses, Mr. Carwell?" Judge Cross asked.

"Just one, Your Honor."

"You may call him, sir."

"I call Robert Devaney to the stand!" said Carwell in a rather loud voice.

Jeb turned pale and stared at the face of the attorney. Then when the outer doors opened and two armed guards entered with Devaney between them, he shot an agonizing glance at Aaron. Then he turned to listen as the judge said, "You are incarcerated, Mr. Devaney?"

"Yep, I'm in the clink, Judge."

"You were convicted of robbing the Cooper Warehouse?"

"Sure. Sentence was only five years." Devaney stood sneering at the judge. "I can do that standing on my head!"

"Mr. Carwell, would you explain the purpose of this witness? Let me warn you. I am not likely to be swayed by the words of a convicted felon."

"I think you should hear what he has to say, Your Honor. What he has to say is relevant to my client."

"Very well—but make it brief."

Carwell turned to face the felon and asked, "I will ask you, was Jeb Summers one of your gang?"

"Him?" Devaney snorted in derision. "He's nothin' but a pest, that's wot he is!"

"Was he involved with the robbery of the Cooper Warehouse?"

A silence fell on the room, and Carwell grew tense—though he didn't allow it to show on his face. He'd spoken in private with Devaney, and had gotten nothing but curses at first. But when Devaney learned that Carwell had influence with the parole board, he changed his tune. However, he was a volatile individual, and on impulse would dare anything. Carwell held his breath, seeing the desire in the man to get attention. *He might implicate Jeb just for the sake of seeing the boy squirm!* Carwell thought.

Then Devaney laughed loudly, saying carelessly, "He was always around, looking to get in—but he's nothin'! Doesn't have what it takes." He grinned at Jeb, adding, "He wuz around that night, but the dumb cluck didn't even know there was a robbery goin' on. I let him tag along, but when we got there, I told him to stand on the corner and holler if he saw a cop. He didn't know beans—and he still don't!"

"Thank you. Do you have any questions for this witness, Your Honor?" Carwell asked smoothly, anxious to get the young criminal out of the courtroom as quickly as possible. He saw the judge's brow arc as he took in Devaney's words. For one moment Carwell thought Cross meant to question Devaney—but the moment passed. "Take him back to his cell," Cross ordered.

When Devaney had been ushered out of the courtroom by the guards, Simon Carwell knew the moment had come. In every trial or hearing, there is that single moment when the whole process hangs on the razor's edge. Carwell was the finest lawyer in the state because he had an innate ability for recognizing those moments. *I've got a weak case—and nothing we can do is going to wipe out the fact that Jeb was present at the scene of the crime. It's now or never—!*

"Your Honor, I submit that Jeb Summers is not a criminal. He made a bad choice, and if he'd kept on, he might have continued in that direction. But he's learned his lesson. We all know that reform school doesn't 'reform' as many young boys as it corrupts. Unfortunate, but true. . . ."

Carwell made an impassioned plea for the court to be lenient with Jeb. The whole time, Aaron and Gail sat there on the edge of their seats trying to read the face of Judge Cross. Nothing showed in his chiseled features, however, and neither of them had any experience in court matters. As Carwell wound down, both of them sat there tense and praying silently.

" . . . and so, Your Honor, I ask you to return this boy to his home. To send him to reform school would serve no purpose. The defense rests its case, Your Honor."

Cross sat like a man of stone, his face stiff and unyielding. The silence that fell on the room was almost palpable. Finally he said, "I recognize that our reformatories are institutions that are not what they should be—no one knows that better than I. And I am aware that this young man seems to be a cut above many of the youth I see in this court." He hesitated for one moment, then shook his head slightly. "But I am aware that only a technicality kept Jeb Summers from being an active participant in the robbery. Punishment must be given as a deterrent to others. I therefore propose to give the minimum sentence in such cases."

"Your Honor, isn't there some way this can be avoided?" Carwell pleaded.

Judge Cross hesitated. "I have before me the record of the defendant's stepfather. It is not a good record, and I could not release the boy into such a home with any hope. If there were a good home environment to place the boy in, I might be persuaded to permit that."

"Your Honor!" Every eye turned toward Gail, who had leaped to her feet and walked toward the high bench. She stopped and went to Jeb, putting her arm around him protectively. She had heard the doom in the judge's voice, and had not been able to bear it. Turning her eyes to the judge, she said, "Let me take him, Your Honor! I have a good job, and he's my brother!"

"Why, Miss Summers!" Judge Cross was jolted out of his calm by the girl's suggestion. Shaking his head sadly, he said in a voice that was not unkind, "You are a single woman, are you not?"

"Yes, but—"

"The boy needs a father. Part of his problem comes from not having one, I think."

"I can take care of him, Your Honor. Please—let me have him!"

"If you were married, I'd agree to your offer, but it's not possible. The law is against it."

Aaron had been transfixed by Gail's sudden action—and filled with admiration. He thought suddenly of Burns and turned to give him a sharp jab in the ribs, whispering, "Burns—tell the judge you're marrying Gail!"

"I wish I could," Burns shot back, "but she won't have me!"

Aaron was aware that Gail was still pleading with the judge. He was shocked at Burns's statement, and turned to stare at him. "Are you serious? You're not in love with her?"

Pain touched Burns's fine eyes. "Nothing I have to say about that—but she's not in love with me." Anger touched his voice, and he said, "It's you she loves, you fool!"

Aaron stared at Burns, and then he turned his eyes back to the front of the room and was aware that the judge was beginning to pronounce Jeb's sentence. "I therefore sentence you, Jeb Summers . . ."

"Your Honor—!" Aaron's stentorian yell made everyone in the courtroom jump in their seats. Leaping to his feet, he cried, "Gail, I love you. I've loved you for a long time. Do you love me?"

Every eye turned to Gail, who had turned from the bench and was staring with her mouth open at Aaron. This was high drama indeed! Carwell, a veteran of hundreds of court battles, felt his jaw drop—and didn't care!

Judge Cross practically fell over the bench as he leaned forward to see the girl's face more plainly.

Gail stood there, her eyes enormous. Her face was pale, but she held her head high. "Yes, I love you, Aaron Winslow," she said quietly.

Suddenly, a shrill yelping cry rent the air, and Lewis began beating on the sides of his wheelchair. "What a brother I've got! What a brother!"

Aaron smiled then, turned to the judge, and asked, "Can you marry us, Judge? I want to be the father of that boy and the husband of Gail Summers."

Judge Cross stared at the tall young man, then let his eyes fall on the young woman, whose eyes were now filled with tears. "You two, I'll speak with you in my chambers. Court dismissed!"

Carwell bent down and snatched Jeb up in a bear hug. "We made it, Jeb! We made it!"

Jeb struggled to free himself, and when he had broken free of the man's embrace, he ran to meet Aaron. He threw his arms around the man and held him with all his might. Aaron put one arm around the boy, and the other he rested on the lad's fine brown hair. Leaning down, he whispered, "How'd you like to live on a farm in Virginia, son?"

Jeb lifted his head and his lips trembled. "That'd be great—Dad!" he said. He released Aaron and went to stand beside Lewis and Deborah. "I guess I can call you Uncle Lewis now, can't I?"

"You can call me anything, Jeb!" Lewis turned to his father and mother, saying, "I hope you two are ready for a rash of grandchildren! Looks like the place is going to be cluttered up with wives and kids!"

Belle smiled and pressed Davis's hand. "We're ready, Lewis."

Aaron then was standing before Gail. She was tall and strong—everything he wanted in a woman. Putting his strong arms around her, he whispered, "Will you have me for your lawful wedded husband?"

"I will—for ever and ever!"

The judge waited at the door, a smile on his thin lips, and as Aaron kissed Gail, a cheer went up, even the sour-faced bailiff joining in!

When Aaron lifted his lips from hers, he smiled at her. She was weeping openly, and he said, "We'll cry together, Gail—but we'll laugh, too."

"Yes! Come on, Aaron—we can't keep the judge waiting! We've got too much to do. . . !"